PENGUIN  CLASSICS

BÜCHNER: COMPLETE PLAYS, *LENZ* AND OTHER WRITINGS

GEORG BÜCHNER was only twenty-three when he died in Zurich in 1837 (the victim of a typhus epidemic), but he crammed an astonishing amount into his brief life. Politically he had attracted the keen attentions of the Hesse police through his revolutionary activism, particularly his central involvement in the clandestine pamphlet *The Hessian Messenger*, and he only just escaped arrest in 1835 by fleeing to Strasbourg. He threw himself with characteristic energy into the biological sciences, and already had the beginnings of a considerable scholarly reputation by the time he went to Zurich in late 1836 to teach comparative anatomy at the new university, where he also intended to give courses in philosophy. Although little known as a writer at the time of his death and throughout most of the rest of the nineteenth century, he has long since become recognized as one of the most remarkable voices of German literature, not least because in both mood and technique he so often uncannily anticipated the twentieth century.

His poetic output is small, but startling in its variety as well as its power. *Danton's Death* is arguably the finest drama of violent revolution in any language; the story *Lenz* (the first description of schizophrenia) is widely held to be the starting-point of modern German prose-writing; *Leonce and Lena* is only now coming into its own as a chiaroscuro comedy of great depth and subtlety; and the *Woyzeck* fragments, both in their focus on an extreme underclass hero and in their rapid succession of gauntly expressive scenes, constitute one of the most original masterpieces of modern theatre.

JOHN REDDICK was born in 1940 and was educated at King's School, Worcester, and St Peter's College, Oxford. After teaching-posts at the universities of Edinburgh, Cambridge and Sydney, he took up his present position as Professor of German at the University of Liverpool. Although over the years he has published widely on German prose-writers (Grass, Hoffmann, Stifter), his energies have increasingly become focused on Georg Büchner, not least as a result of his involvement in stage productions of Büchner's plays, variously in German and English. This present volume is complemented by a full critical study of Büchner by John Reddick, *Georg Büchner: The Shattered Whole* (Oxford, 1994).

GEORG BÜCHNER

Complete Plays, *Lenz* and Other Writings

Translated with an Introduction and Notes by
JOHN REDDICK

PENGUIN BOOKS

PENGUIN BOOKS

Published by the Penguin Group
Penguin Books Ltd, 27 Wrights Lane, London w8 5tz, England
Penguin Putnam Inc., 375 Hudson Street, New York, New York 10014, USA
Penguin Books Australia Ltd, Ringwood, Victoria, Australia
Penguin Books Canada Ltd, 10 Alcorn Avenue, Toronto, Ontario, Canada m4v 3b2
Penguin Books (NZ) Ltd, 182–190 Wairau Road, Auckland 10, New Zealand

Penguin Books Ltd, Registered Offices: Harmondsworth, Middlesex, England

First published 1993
5 7 9 10 8 6 4

Copyright © John Reddick, 1993
All rights reserved

All inquiries regarding performing rights in these
translations should be made to the translator,
c/o Penguin Books Ltd, 27 Wrights Lane, London w8 5tz, England

Filmset in 10 / 12 pt Monophoto Baskerville
Typeset by Datix International Limited, Bungay, Suffolk
Printed in England by Clays Ltd, St Ives plc

CONTENTS

Preface   ix
Introduction   xi
Chronology   xxii

DANTON'S DEATH   1

LEONCE AND LENA   75

WOYZECK   109

LENZ   139

THE HESSIAN MESSENGER   165

ON CRANIAL NERVES   181

SELECTED LETTERS   187

Notes and Background to Texts
    Danton's Death   209
    Leonce and Lena   238
    Woyzeck   247
    Lenz   265
    The Hessian Messenger   273
    On Cranial Nerves   284
    Selected Letters   291
Select Bibliography   303

PREFACE

This new edition of Georg Büchner's work arose from the coincidence of two related but separate compulsions: the practical and the scholarly. As a literary critic I have been haunted by Büchner for a long time, and in recent years have increasingly tried to lay the ghost with scholarly research. On the practical side: having become variously involved in stage work on Büchner's plays, I began making English versions for particular productions – and became haunted all over again, this time by the challenge of capturing as much as possible of the richness of meaning and mood in Büchner's original, while also retaining its spectacular verve and crispness. Both compulsions have continued undiminished, and I hope that in this edition they have yielded a happy combination of solid background supporting vivid texts – and in the case of the plays, texts that actors find easy to *speak*.

Many friends and colleagues have been generous with their help, and warm thanks are due especially to Mike Butler, Brian Crow, Gerry McCarthy (Birmingham); Tim Blanning, John Guthrie, Jill Mann, Barry Nisbet (Cambridge); Jim Simpson (Liverpool); and Martin Swales (London).

Special thanks are also due to the Oxford University Press for allowing me to base the Introduction to this edition on the opening chapters of my monograph *Georg Büchner: The Shattered Whole*.

John Reddick
February 1992

INTRODUCTION

Georg Büchner is perhaps the most extraordinary phenomenon of
modern German literature. He impinged scarcely at all on the
consciousness of his own century. When he died in 1837 at the
age of twenty-three (the victim of a typhus epidemic), he was
practically unheard of beyond his own circles – no wonder,
considering that only a single work had been published under his
name (a bowdlerized version of *Danton's Death*). After another
half-century he was scarcely better known: although most of his
writing had meanwhile appeared in one form or another, it had
made little impact; he rated a mention in most literary handbooks
and encyclopedias, but only as an obscure, peripheral, often
dubious bit of history. Then, towards the end of the century,
perceptions changed. Other writers, in particular, began to re-
spond to his voice and to recognize his astonishing modernity.
One by one his plays reached the stage: *Leonce and Lena* in 1895;
Danton's Death in 1902; *Woyzeck* in 1913 (and Alban Berg's opera
Wozzeck in 1925). Edition began to follow edition. An initial
trickle of monographs and theses soon turned into a stream, then
a flood. All of a sudden Georg Büchner was a classic. But more
important he was – and is – a living presence. No other German
writer before Brecht so vividly catches the modern imagination –
or is more frequently performed on the stage both in Germany
and abroad. No other writer is more enthusiastically hailed by his
present-day successors: Heinrich Böll has spoken of his 'remarkable relevance', Günter Grass of his 'incendiary' force; for Christa
Wolf, 'German prose begins with Büchner's *Lenz*' – which constitutes her 'absolute ideal', her 'primal experience' in German
literature; Wolf Biermann has gone so far as to describe him
simply as Germany's 'greatest writer' ('unser größter Dichter').

But whilst there is universal agreement about the power
and immediacy of Büchner's voice, there have been bitter disputes about what that voice is actually saying. This is scarcely

surprising, for a number of factors make him a natural focus of controversy.

Most obviously, there is the smallness of scale and 'interrupted-ness' of his output. If he had lived into his seventies (like his father and four of his siblings, the youngest of whom lived on into the twentieth century), his early writings would not only have been definitively finalized and published, they would also very probably have been contextualized as part of a much larger oeuvre. As it was, they survived – if at all – only in scrawled, incomplete, often illegible manuscripts, or else in printed versions that were variously mutilated, truncated, bowdlerized or garbled, as well as being almost entirely posthumous and unauthorized. It seems scarcely credible, but even today, more than a century and a half after his death, there is still no definitive historical-critical edition of his work.

Then of course there is the provocative nature of his themes and concerns. Sex, for a start: from the very first lines of *Danton's Death*, with their image of the two-timing 'pretty lady' who offers her heart to her husband and her cunt to her lovers, Büchner's 'obscenities' ensured him the status of *enfant terrible*, and in the process served to betray the blinkers and blindspots of countless critics. Religion, too, is a persistent irritant. Again and again, gods, God and spirits are invoked by his characters, to be scorned, denied, defied, entreated – and thus to serve as a constant challenge to believer, agnostic and atheist alike. Most explosive of all, perhaps, is the question of his politics. Here is a man who was arguably the most radical left-wing thinker of his age in the German lands, a dedicated revolutionary who – though he entered the fray as a militant propagandist and activist for only a brief period of time – remained clearly committed throughout the rest of his life to the violent overthrow of what he saw as a parasitical, illegitimate and effete ruling class, and to the resurgence and emancipation of the viciously exploited popular mass. Given the paucity and unreliability of direct evidence, such as Büchner's letters (most of which survive – if at all – only in carefully excerpted and perhaps sanitized form), and likewise of indirect evidence, such as reminiscences of friends and acquaint-ances, police files, court records, etc., there is considerable scope for argument even about his precise activities and stance within the political macro- and micro-realities of the time. But there has been particularly fierce controversy about the politics to be inferred from his writing (almost all of which came *after* the grim fiasco of *The Hessian Messenger*, which profoundly affected the course of his life – not least by forcing him into exile abroad). Interpretations in this crucial area have differed quite radically, from those at one extreme who see undaunted militant revolutionism in every phase of his writing, to those at the opposite extreme who claim that his bitter experience propelled him into 'absolute nihilism', and in the process depoliticized him entirely. (Both extremes are now largely discredited.)

Quite apart from the scant and uncertain status of the texts, and the inflammatory nature of the issues they contain, there is another, much more fundamental element in Büchner's work that encourages controversy, and that is the very manner of his writing – the language, modes and structures that he uses to express his concerns. For the flickering image that his writing projects is profoundly un- and anti-classical, and consciously remote from the prevailing conventions and expectations of his age. Whether in language, mood, plot or character, he offers no steady development, no sense of anything rounded, resolved or unified. Instead of unfolding in clearly measured rhythm, his works progress through a succession of kaleidoscopic convulsions, enacting what has been called a 'law of discontinuity'. Wholeness – when it appears – is always false: a pretence, an illusion, at best a transitory state. It is always *particles* that loom large, discrete elements that he highlights in startling isolation, or in disparate clusters and combinations that create a constant sense of multivalence, mystery and paradox. This is a chief mark of his spectacular modernity: what he is already doing in the 1830s will seem shockingly new when practised by the most avant-garde painters, composers and writers of the early twentieth century. But it also makes him especially difficult to interpret. In particular, it entails the problem of perspective: being so disparate and discrete, the elements in his work change their aspect and apparent importance quite radically when viewed from different vantage points.

Needless to say, Büchner's systematic discontinuity is not an accident – and certainly not, as has sometimes been suggested, a mark of immaturity – but a central, even defining characteristic of his work. If we look at an exemplar of German classicism such as Schiller's *Mary Stuart*, we see magnificent complexity – but a complexity like that of a Baroque fugue with its rich but measured elaboration of lucidly stated themes. Georg Büchner's undertaking is fundamentally different. He is never concerned to deliver conclusions or solutions. Instead, his writing is a kind of happening, a constant search, a dynamic enactment of the very process of argument and conflict, of the collision and interaction of contrary possibilities. His works begin, but never at a beginning; they come to an end, but never to a conclusion. This can easily leave us exhilarated but perplexed – and make us all too prone to seize on some particular discrete element and regard it as a summation of the whole, or as the definitive fixing of a position. Many critics have fallen prey to this temptation, hence the persistent misrepresentation of Büchner as being variously a programmatic pessimist and nihilist, a programmatic fatalist, a programmatic Christian, a programmatic Jacobin revolutionary. There *is* an underlying consistency and unity in Büchner, but it may be found only within and through the multiplicities of his work – not despite them.

It helps if we recognize what is surely the paradox of paradoxes in Georg Büchner: his disjunctive mode with its relentless insistence on fragments and particles is always the expression of a radiant vision of *wholeness*. Again and again, in every area of his existence – his politics, his science, his aesthetics, his poetic writing – we find an ardent sense of wholeness, but almost always a wholeness that is poignantly elusive: it *was* but is no longer; or *will* be but isn't yet; or – most poignant of all – it *is* in the present, but can be possessed only partially or transiently. Büchner is thus forced to be a maker of mosaics. But the more jagged the fragments in these mosaics, the more strident they are in their invocation of the whole – a pattern spelt out in the earliest pages of his work when he has a character in *Danton's Death* use just such terms to define the protagonist's quest amongst the tarts of the Palais Royal: 'He's trying to re-create the Medici Venus piece by piece ... "Making a mosaic", he calls it ... What a crying

shame that nature has smashed beauty into pieces . . . and buried
it in fragments in different bodies.' Minutes later the theme is
echoed and intensified in Danton's yearning response to Marion
with its double stress on 'totality' and its unattainability: 'Why
can't I draw your beauty completely into my being, enfold it
completely within my arms?' At the beginning of *Lenz* we find the
same essential image as the 'mad' protagonist journeys through
the Vosges: 'he thought he should draw the storm right into
himself, embrace all things within his being, he spread and lay
over the entire earth, he burrowed his way into the All'. In *Leonce
and Lena* it is the totality of love that is fragmented, burst asunder
into the separate notes of the musical scale, the separate colours
of the rainbow. But here, as always, the emphasis on fragments
implies a belief in wholeness. And so it is precisely Leonce's
experience of a love-inspired totality of being that is celebrated in
the intense but fleeting climax of the play: 'All my being is in this
single moment . . . More is impossible.'

The centrality of Büchner's vision of wholeness becomes clearer
still when we realize that it also lies at the heart of his work as a
scientist-philosopher. When he died in February 1837 he had just
embarked on an exceptionally promising career at the new University of Zurich. His Strasbourg thesis on the anatomy of the
barbel, *Mémoire sur le système nerveux du barbeau*, had earned him
not only a doctorate from Zurich, but also the offer of a teaching
post as a *Privatdozent*, and on 5 November 1836 he duly delivered
his 'Trial Lecture' (a standard requirement for the confirmation
of such posts). Already in the closing lines of his *Mémoire* he had
intimated his view of the natural world as a grand harmonious
whole in which even the most complex entities derive from a 'type
primitif'; in which 'les formes les plus élevées et les plus pures' are
fashioned by nature according to 'le plan le plus simple'. In the
prefatory paragraphs of the 'Trial Lecture' he expands on this
theme. Summarizing the recent history of comparative anatomy,
he remarks that 'everything was striving towards a certain unity,
towards the tracing of all forms back to the simplest primordial
type' (and this was the essence of his own attempt, in the lecture and
the *Mémoire*, to prove the hypothesis that skull, brain and cranial
nerves, for all their supreme complexity, developed originally

from the relatively simple structures of the vertebra). The final sentence of the *Mémoire* is specifically echoed in the Lecture when Büchner speaks of 'the highest and purest forms' being produced from 'the simplest outlines and patterns'; but whereas he was content in the *Mémoire* to cite Nature as the agent of this process, he is now much more explicit. At the heart of nature, he declares, there has to be a 'fundamental law', a 'primordial law' giving shape and form to the 'entire organic world'. This is startling enough in itself; more startling still is Büchner's proposition that the assumed 'primordial law' is none other than a 'law of beauty', which moreover necessarily produces 'harmony' amongst all its manifestations. It is perhaps only against this kind of background that we truly appreciate the yearning for beauty ascribed to Danton as he contemplates Marion; or Leonce's climactic words (immediately after his 'More is impossible'): 'Out of chaos comes creation, bursting forth towards me, so alive and new, so radiant with beauty'; or – above all – the words given to Lenz in the course of Büchner's most famous statement of an aesthetic position: 'The most beautiful images, the most resonant harmonies, coalesce, dissolve. Only one thing abides: an infinite beauty that passes from form to form, eternally changed and revealed afresh.'

Büchner's postulation in the 'Trial Lecture' of an all-encompassing order of rich simplicity, instinct with beauty and harmonious in its workings, can seem thoroughly bewildering, coming as it does from the man who for many decades was almost universally represented as a supreme pessimist or nihilist, as the purveyor of 'an extreme form of pessimism' that is 'deeper and darker than any to be found in the previous history of German thought, with the possible exception of Schopenhauer' (M.B. Benn). Even if we disregard this traditional view (which has meanwhile fallen into disfavour), we are still faced with a strident paradox within the texts themselves: on one hand the beauteous order and harmony so calmly posited in the 'Trial Lecture', and on the other the desperate visions so often and so eloquently projected in the poetic works – the terrifying isolation of the un-hero at the end of *Lenz* or of the child in the 'anti-fairytale' in *Woyzeck*; the famous cry of Danton that 'The world is chaos, nothingness its due messiah'; Leonce's fears that all our images of self and world may be mere delusions masking a reality of blank vacuity. Examples could be multiplied. But the paradox is just that – a paradox; it is not a contradiction. The raucous anguish so common in Büchner's writing does not negate or belie his faith in fundamental beauty and order: it derives entirely from it.

In this crucial respect he is quite unexpectedly old-fashioned: whereas *Lenz* and the three plays are magnificently modernist in their articulation, the faith and vision underlying them are grounded largely in a *Zeitgeist* that was already outdated when Büchner embraced it. Like so many other writers before him in the febrile period from the *Sturm und Drang* through Weimar Classicism to German Romanticism, he was blessed and cursed with an idealist vision of essential wholeness and harmony – but at a time when the prevailing reality was by contrast ever more janglingly discordant. We find precisely this bitter contrast voiced in one of Büchner's most poignant letters to his beloved fiancée, Minna Jaeglé, written in March 1834 as he was just emerging from a period of severe illness – and severe personal crisis. He has 'just come in from outside', he tells Minna, where 'A single resonant tone from a thousand larks bursts through the brooding summer air, a heavy bank of cloud wanders over the earth, the booming wind rings out like its melodious tread.' Such is his vibrant, sweet-sounding present. But, he continues, until the spring air served to free him and give him life again, he had long been transfixed by a kind of *rigor*, by a sense of being already dead, while all around him seemed like corpses with glassy eyes and waxen cheeks. The 'corpses' speak and move, and with his description Büchner launches into one of his characteristically thrilling cadenzas of despair:

then, when the whole machinery began to grind away with jerking limbs and grating voice, and I heard the same old barrel-organ tune go tralala and saw the tiny prongs and cylinders bob and whirr in the organ-box – I cursed the concert, the box, the melody – oh, poor screaming musicians that we are – could it be that our cries of agony on the rack only exist to ring out through cracks between the clouds and, echoing on and on, die like a melodious breath in heavenly ears?

– an unnerving antiphon: in nature, the wind and the larks and their liberating melody; among men, a deathly mechanical rasping, and tortured screams extracted perhaps by some distant deity for its private titillation. And it is this same drastic antiphon that Büchner uses nine months later to initiate the grand-opera climax of *Danton's Death*:

PHILIPPEAU: My friends, we don't have to stand very far above the earth to lose all sight of its fitful, flickering confusion, and feast our eyes on the grand simplicity of God's design. There is an ear for which the riotous cacophony that deafens us is but a stream of harmonies.

DANTON: But we are the poor musicians, and our bodies the instruments. The ugly sounds scratched out on them: are they just there to rise up higher and higher and gently fade and die like some voluptuous breath in heavenly ears?

But then the question arises: *why* have we become such 'poor musicians', so remote from the 'stream of harmonies', from that 'necessary harmony' supposedly inscribed in nature by the primordial law of beauty? The image of sadistic gods forcing discordance on us for their own delight is more a rhetorical flourish than a serious proposition. Büchner seems to see the real reasons as lying in humankind itself – and most particularly in the undue influence of Mind and the artificial systems and constructs it so readily devises.

It is yet another paradox that this man who was an heir of the Enlightenment, a dedicated scientific inquirer, a voracious intellectual, an aspiring academic who wanted above all to lecture at Zurich University on philosophy, was none the less deeply suspicious and scornful of human reason, and especially of its manifestations in rationalist philosophy. Both the scorn and, more importantly, the grounds for it are made very clear in the preamble to the 'Trial Lecture'. Büchner claims that it has never yet proved possible 'to bridge the gulf between the [dogmatism of rationalist philosophers] and natural life as we directly apprehend it', and he continues: 'A priori philosophy still dwells in a bleak and arid desert; a very great distance separates it from green, fresh life, and it is highly questionable whether it will ever close the gap.'

This sense of an absolute gulf between rationalism and Life in all its directly apprehensible vigour and exuberance is exactly what animates Büchner's fundamental criticism of Descartes and his *cogito ergo sum*. In a crucial passage in his lengthy and complex commentary on Descartes's philosophy he distinguishes categorically between 'being' and 'thinking'. What matters is our Being; thought is no more than a 'secondary activity'. The defining characteristic of Being is its immediacy: it affords us 'immediate' (or 'unmediated') truths and knowledge, and a quite spontaneous, natural 'awareness that the self exists'. This primary realm of Being is not only independent of rationalistic thought processes, it is – in Büchner's radical view – wholly inaccessible to it. Given the primacy of this unmediated, authentic Being and its inaccessibility to ratiocination, the entire edifice of Cartesian rationalism appears suddenly false, its claims to truth merely a set of fictions arbitrarily constructed by, and in, the logical mind, remote from directly intuited, living reality. More damningly still, Büchner suggests that rationalist logic cannot even deal adequately with the specifically philosophical abysses over which it turns out to be wholly constructed. This applies with particular force to the supposed proofs of God. Thus the God of Descartes is to Büchner a purely expedient mechanism, a device specifically contrived to 'fill the abyss' between thinking and knowing, to be a 'bridge' between self and world, a 'ladder' for escaping from the 'grave of philosophy', a 'rope' for clambering out of the 'abyss of doubt'. At another point he argues that while the logic of Descartes's proof of God may be compelling in its own terms, nothing compels us to accept that logic in the first place; indeed it is contradicted by the primary experience of both our mind and our emotions: 'Once one enters upon the definition of God, one has to admit the existence of God. But what justifies us in making this definition? / Our *mind*? / It knows imperfectness. / Our *emotions*? / They know pain.'

But why should any of this matter? Why can't rationalism be left to its own devices in its desert of abstractions? Here lies a crucial problem for Büchner: however remote Cartesian systematizing may be from 'fresh, green life' as we directly apprehend it, its false constructs – and others of similar kind – are threatening to prevail, they are threatening to condition our understanding and handling of the world at large. This is particularly clear within Büchner's own field of biology. Under the deadening hand of Descartes, the living body is reduced to a mere machine held together with nuts and bolts. He remarks that in *De homine*, Descartes's treatise on physiology, the human being becomes 'l'homme machine', an 'artificial' assemblage of 'screws, prongs and cylinders', of mechanical 'apparatuses'; and in his 'Trial Lecture' he uses exactly the same kind of vocabulary to attack the cold and reductive functionalism of what he calls the 'teleological' school in physiology and anatomy. He was fighting a losing battle: the 'teleologists' were perfectly in tune with an age increasingly driven by functionalism of one kind or another. This becomes graphically clear when we realize that their view of the living organism as 'a complex machine provided with functional devices enabling it to survive over a certain span of time' is remarkably close to that most revolutionary and influential biological theory of the nineteenth century: Charles Darwin's *Origin of Species* with its proposition that it is the creatures that happen to be the best adapted, the best equipped, that survive in the 'struggle for life' – a far cry indeed from Büchner's *Naturphilosophie*-inspired belief in a primordial law of beauty producing perfect, sublime, noble, beauteous, enspirited, harmonious richness from a matrix of essential simplicity. None the less, he sticks firmly to his unfashionable faith – and particularly to his sense of the absolute value of the *individual*. It is perhaps his most crucial criticism of the 'teleologists' that, in accordance with their one-and-only principle of 'the *greatest possible fitness for purpose*', they regard the individual 'only as something that is meant to achieve a purpose beyond itself'. For Büchner by contrast – and this is arguably the single most powerful ontological statement anywhere in his work – 'Everything that exists, exists for its own sake.'

This, then, is the credo at the heart of the 'Trial Lecture'; but I suggest that it is also the credo at the heart of Büchner's entire output. In his poetic writing as much as in his scientific philosophy he holds sacred the fullness of natural, unmediated Life and its rich manifestation in the being of every least individual. The trouble is that he can celebrate it positively for its glorious presence only on rare and fleeting occasions; for the most part he must celebrate it negatively for its absence – by railing rhapsodically or sardonically at its loss, denial, suppression. In particular he relentlessly pillories any attempt to subordinate life to *systems* – especially intellectual systems. Hence the mocking of rationalism in the figure of King Peter (*Leonce and Lena*); of arrant scientism in the maniacal Doctor-Professor (*Woyzeck*); of moralism in the Officer (*Woyzeck*); of Jacobin ambitions to refashion humanity (*Danton's Death*); of appalling reductivism in the contemporary arts (*Danton's Death*). At the same time he also repeatedly fixes on protagonists – all of them male almost by definition – whose *minds* are too active, who are paralysed or galvanized by the fact that they know and see far more than is good for them.

But all such reflections are at worst misleading, at best merely part of the story. Georg Büchner is one of the most elusive and challenging of writers. His vitality and multiplicity can only be truly appreciated *within* his works – and the purpose of this edition is to let them speak for themselves in all their astonishing vigour and depth.

CHRONOLOGY

1813   18 October: Karl Georg Büchner born in Goddelau, Hesse, the first child of Ernst Karl Büchner and his wife, Caroline. (Continuing a family tradition of many generations, Ernst Büchner was a doctor; he later entered grand-ducal service and ultimately achieved the rank of *Obermedizinalrat*. The couple had five further children; all except one – the older of the two girls – achieved distinction in their various fields, particularly Ludwig, the second youngest, who became far more famous than Georg in the nineteenth century thanks to his book *Kraft und Stoff*, which popularized materialist philosophy.)

1816   The family moves to Darmstadt, capital of the Grand Duchy of Hessen-Darmstadt.

1825   After primary schooling from his mother and then at a local private school, Büchner begins secondary schooling at the Ludwig-Georg-Gymnasium in Darmstadt.

1831   October: having left school in March, Büchner becomes a student in the medical faculty of Strasbourg University. He takes lodgings with a widowed protestant pastor, Johann Jakob Jaeglé, and in due course becomes secretly engaged to his daughter Minna (Louise Wilhelmine, 1810–80).

1833   Government regulations require Büchner to continue his studies within the Grand Duchy, and in October he becomes a student at the University of Giessen in the province of Upper Hesse. (His teachers probably included both the great chemist Justus von Liebig and J.B. Wilbrand, one of the foremost exponents of *Naturphilosophie*.) Late November: he suffers an attack of meningitis.

1834 Late February–early March: he suffers a serious bout of illness that affects his equilibrium both physically and mentally. Mid-March (or perhaps earlier): the 'hideous fatalism' letter to Minna. Late March: he writes his version of what later becomes *The Hessian Messenger*, and founds the Giessen section of his Society of Human Rights, a radical revolutionary cell with working-class as well as middle-class members; in April he founds a second section in Darmstadt. August: Carl Minnigerode is arrested with a large batch of freshly printed copies of *The Hessian Messenger*; Büchner avoids arrest by the skin of his teeth. September: he leaves Giessen for good and returns to the relative safety of the family home in Darmstadt.

1835 Late January–late February: Büchner completes *Danton's Death* 'in five weeks at most'; in this period he was probably also called in for interrogation. Early March: he flees to Strasbourg (followed not long afterwards by a 'Wanted' notice). July: *Danton's Death* published in bowdlerized form. October: *Lenz* probably completed.

1836 31 May: after hectic months of work, Büchner completes his *Mémoire sur le système nerveux du barbeau*, having read a draft of it at sessions of the Strasbourg Société d'histoire naturelle in April and early May. June–October: another astonishingly hectic period of activity in which Büchner works by turns on *Leonce and Lena*, *Woyzeck*, a projected series of philosophy lectures and the Zurich 'Trial Lecture'; he may also have planned/drafted/completed a further play, *Pietro Aretino*. September: Büchner is awarded a doctorate by the new University of Zurich on the basis of the *Mémoire*. 19 October: following his twenty-third birthday the previous day, Büchner travels to Zurich with a view to becoming a *Privatdozent* in the university's Faculty of Philosophy (which includes Comparative Anatomy). 5 November: he delivers his 'Trial Lecture', and is formally confirmed in his post; in the following weeks he teaches his first course, 'Comparative anatomy of fish and amphibians'; he also does further work on *Woyzeck*.

1837   2 February: he falls ill; typhus is diagnosed. On 17 February Minna Jaeglé arrives from Strasbourg. Büchner dies on 19 February.

DANTON'S DEATH

A Drama

CHARACTERS

Georges Danton
Legendre
Camille Desmoulins
Hérault-Séchelles
Lacroix } *Deputies*[1]
Philippeau
Fabre d'Eglantine
Mercier
Thomas Payne

Robespierre
Saint-Just
Barrère } *members of the Committee of Public Safety*
Collot d'Herbois
Billaud Varennes

Amar } *members of the Committee of General Security*[2]
Vouland
Chaumette   *Procurator of the Paris Commune*
Dillon   *a General*
Fouquier Tinville   *Public Prosecutor*

Herrmann } *presidents of the Revolutionary Tribunal*
Dumas

Paris   *a friend of Danton's*
Simon   *a theatre prompter*
Laflotte
Julie   *Danton's wife*

Lucile   *Camille Desmoulins's wife*
Rosalie
Adelaide } *prostitutes*
Marion

Men and women of the people, prostitutes, deputies, executioners, etc.

ACT I

Scene 1

HERAULT-SECHELLES *and* SUNDRY WOMEN *around a gaming table. Some distance away*: DANTON *on a stool at the feet of* JULIE.[3]

DANTON: Look at the pretty lady: handles her cards like a real little angel! She certainly knows how to play her suits: shows her heart to her husband, so they say – and her 'diamond' to her lovers. You women, you could make a man fall in love with lies.

JULIE: Do you believe in me?

DANTON: How should I know? We know damn all about each other. Thick-skinned elephants, that's what we are; we stretch out our hands to each other, but it's a waste of time, hide grating on hide, that's all – we're on our own, completely on our own.

JULIE: You know me, Danton!

DANTON: Yes, what they call 'knowing'. You've dark eyes and curly hair and a delicate complexion and you never stop saying 'dear Georges!' But [*he points at her eyes and forehead*] there, there: what lies behind *there*? Let's face it, our senses are pretty crude. Know one another? We'd have to smash our skulls open and tear the thoughts from the very fibres of each other's brain.[4]

A WOMAN: What the hell are you up to with your fingers?

HERAULT: Nothing!

WOMAN: Don't stick your thumb in like that, it's disgusting.

HERAULT: Just look at it though, the thing has a character all of its own.

DANTON: No, Julie, I love you like the grave.

JULIE [*turning away*]: Oh!

DANTON: No, listen! People say there's peace in the grave, and that peace and the grave are the selfsame thing. If that's the case, then I'm dead and buried here in your lap. You sweet grave, your lips are passing-bells, your voice my death knell, your breast my burial mound, your heart my coffin.

WOMAN: Blast, I've lost!

HERAULT: Real love saga, that was. Costs money, like they all do.

WOMAN: You must have declared your love with your fingers then, like the deaf and dumb.

HERAULT: And why not? People even say *they're* the easiest to understand. I contrived an affair with one of the queens, my fingers were princes turned into spiders, you, dear lady, were the Good Fairy, but it turned out badly, the queen was constantly in labour, and kept on producing knaves. I'd never allow my daughter to play such games, the kings and queens tumble on top of each other in such disgusting fashion, and the knaves soon follow after.

CAMILLE DESMOULINS *and* PHILIPPEAU *enter.*

HERAULT: Philippeau, what a gloomy face! Have you ripped a hole in your red bonnet?[5] Has St Jacob[6] given you a dirty look? Did it rain during the guillotining? Or did you get a lousy seat and miss the fun?

CAMILLE: You're parodying Socrates. Do you know what the great old man asked Alcibiades one day when he found him all gloomy and depressed? 'Have you lost your shield on the field of battle? Have you been trounced in a race or a swordfight? Has someone outdone you in singing or playing the zither?' Such classical republicans![7] But then look at our guillotine romanticism!

PHILIPPEAU: Yet another twenty victims have been slaughtered today. We were wrong, the Hébertistes[8] were only sent to the scaffold because they weren't systematic enough in their butchery – perhaps, too, because the Decemvirate[9] reckoned they themselves were done for if even for a week there were men around more feared than they were.

HERAULT: They want to take us back to the ark. Saint-Just wouldn't mind if we started crawling around on all fours again, so that the lawyer from Arras[10] could stick us in leading-reins, stuff us in a schoolroom and reinvent religion in the mechanical image of the Genevan clockmaker.[11]

PHILIPPEAU: And they wouldn't think twice about adding a few more noughts to Marat's estimate of the number of people that need to be killed.[12] How long are we to go on being filthy and bloody like newborn babes, with coffins for cradles and heads for playthings? We've got to move forward. The Clemency Committee's got to be pushed through,[13] the deputies they've thrown out have got to be reinstated.

HERAULT: The revolution has reached the stage where it *must* be reorganized.[14] The revolution must end and the Republic must begin. The basic principles of the state must change: instead of duties – rights; instead of virtue – well-being; instead of punishment – protection. Everyone must be able to come fully into their own and assert their own nature. No matter whether they're reasonable or unreasonable, educated or uneducated, good or bad: that's no business of the state's. We're all idiots, and no one has the right to inflict his own particular idiocy on anyone else. Everyone must be able to enjoy life in his own way, but not at other people's expense or by getting in the way of *their* enjoyment.

CAMILLE: The state must be a diaphanous cloak that snugly envelops the body of the people. It must yield to each throb of the arteries, each flexing of the muscles, each thrill of the sinews. No matter whether the body is beautiful or ugly, it has the absolute right to be as it is, and we've no right to stick it in whatever little coat happens to suit our fancy. We'll rap the fingers of those who seek to throw a nun's veil over the naked shoulders of France, this sweetest of sinners. We want naked gods and priestesses and Olympian athletes and, oh, from melodious lips the sounds of wicked, limb-melting love. We don't want to stop the Romans squatting in their corner and boiling their turnips, but we want no more of their gory gladiators. Divine Epicurus[15] and sweet-arsed Venus[16] must replace Saints Marat and Chalier[17] as guardians of the Republic.[18] Danton, you'll launch the attack in the National Convention.

DANTON: I will – you will – he will. If we live to see the day, as the old women say. In one hour, sixty minutes will have passed. Am I right, Camille?

CAMILLE: What's that supposed to mean? It goes without saying.

DANTON: Oh, everything goes without saying. So who's going to bring about all these wonderful things?

PHILIPPEAU: Us and the honest folk of France.

DANTON: Your 'and' is a very long word, it keeps us just a little bit apart; there's a long way to go, and honesty will be exhausted before we ever get together. And even if we did – these 'honest folk' of yours: you can lend them money, stand godfather to their kids, get your daughters married off to them – but that's all!

CAMILLE: If you're so sure of that, why start the fight in the first place?

DANTON: Those pompous puritans were more than I could take. The very sight of such people was always enough to make me give them a kick up the arse. It's just the way I'm made. [*He gets up.*]

JULIE: Are you going?

DANTON: I have to get out of here or they'll drive me mad with their politics. [*As he exits*] Just by the bye, I give you a prophecy: the statue of freedom is not yet cast, the furnace is roaring, all of us can still burn our fingers. [*Exit.*]

CAMILLE: Let him go. Do you imagine he could keep his fingers to himself once the action starts?

HERAULT: Maybe, but only for the sake of killing time, like a game of chess.

Scene 2: A street

SIMON *the prompter,*[19] *his* WIFE.

SIMON [*beating his wife*]: You miserable pimp, you poxy old bag, you stinking heap of corruption you!

WIFE: Help! Help!

VARIOUS PEOPLE [*come running*]: Pull them apart! Pull them apart!

SIMON: Friends, Romans, unhand me, that I may tear this carcass limb from limb! A real Vestal Virgin you are!

WIFE: Me a Vestal Virgin? That'll be the day!

SIMON:
> From thy shoulders shall I rip thy raiment
> And let thy naked carcass wither in the sun.

You bed of whores, there's lechery lurking in every wrinkle of your body. [*They are separated.*]

1st CITIZEN: What's going on?

SIMON: Tell me, where's my child? No, that's no good. My little girl? Nor that neither. Miss? Madam? No good, no good! There's just one name that fits, and it sticks in my gullet, I can't get it past my lips.

2nd CITIZEN: Just as well or it'd stink of booze.

SIMON: Virginius,[20] cover your ancient head: raven shame is perched there pecking at your eyes. Friends, Romans, hand me a knife! [*He sinks to the ground.*]

WIFE: He's a decent bloke normally, he just can't hold his liquor, a couple of drinks and he's got no legs left.

2nd CITIZEN: Then he goes on all three legs.

WIFE: No, he falls down.

2nd CITIZEN: Quite right, first he goes on all three legs, then he falls on his third one, till that one falls as well.

SIMON: You vampire, you're sucking the blood from my very heart!

WIFE: Just leave 'im be. He's always sentimental at this time of day, it don't last long.

1st CITIZEN: What's up then?

WIFE: Well, I was just sitting there in the sunshine warming m'self, see, cos we've got no firewood, see –

2nd CITIZEN: Why not use your old man's nose?

WIFE: – and me daughter was doing her stuff round the corner, she's a good girl, takes good care of her parents.

SIMON: There, she admits it!

WIFE: You Judas! Would you have a single pair of trousers to put on if 'er young gentlemen didn't take theirs off? You old brandy barrel, do you want to die of thirst if her little trickle runs dry? Do you? We work with all the rest of our body, why not with that bit as well? I used mine when she was born, and it was painful too, can't she use hers for me, eh'? And does it cause her any pain? You stupid old fool!

SIMON: Oh Lucretia![21] A knife, dear friends, a knife! Oh Appius Claudius![22]

1st CITIZEN: Yes, a knife, but not for the poor tart. What has *she* done? Nothing! It's her hunger what whores and begs. A knife for the people that buy the flesh of our wives and daughters! Death to them that whore with the daughters of the people! You suffer hunger, and they suffer indigestion; you have ragged jackets, and they have warm overcoats; your fists are calloused, and their hands are velvet. Ergo, you work and they do nothing; ergo, you earned it and they have stolen it; ergo, if you want to get back a few pence of your stolen property, you have to go whoring and begging; ergo, they're rats and must be destroyed.

3rd CITIZEN: The only blood in their veins is what they've sucked out of us. They told us: 'Kill the aristocrats, they're a pack of wolves!' So we strung them up on every streetlamp. They told us: 'The King with his veto[23] is scoffing your bread!' So we killed the King. They told us: 'The Girondists are starving you to death!' So we guillotined the Girondists.[24] But *they* stripped all the clothes off the corpses, and *we're* still freezing with nothing to wear. Let's tear the skin from their thighs and turn it into trousers, let's melt the fat of their bellies to lard our soup with. Come on! Death to all them with no holes in their coats!

1st CITIZEN: Death to all them that can read and write!

2nd CITIZEN: Death to all them that walk with a swagger!

ALL [*screaming*]: Kill them, kill them, kill the lot of them!

A YOUNG MAN *is dragged in.*

VARIOUS VOICES: Look, he's got a snotrag! Fucking aristocrat! String him up, string him up!

2nd CITIZEN: What, he doesn't blow his nose with his fingers? String him up! [*A streetlamp is lowered.*]

YOUNG MAN: Oh sirs, dear sirs!

2nd CITIZEN: There are no sirs here, lad! String him up!

VARIOUS VOICES [*singing*]:
> Who'd be buried six feet under
> Ready for the worms to plunder?
> Better to dangle from a rope
> Than rot beneath a grassy slope.

YOUNG MAN: Mercy!

3rd CITIZEN: Just a bit of fun with a twist of hemp around your neck! It's all over in the twinkling of an eye: we're more merciful than you lot. We're murdered by work for the whole of our lives, for sixty years we twist and squirm on the end of a rope, but we're going to cut ourselves free.

On to the lamp with him!

YOUNG MAN: All right, go on, but you won't see any better for me being dead!

CROWD: Good one! Well said!

VARIOUS VOICES: Let him go! [*He runs off.*]

Enter ROBESPIERRE, *accompanied by* WOMEN *and* SANS-CULOTTES.

ROBESPIERRE: What's going on here, citizens?

3rd CITIZEN: It's about time something *was* going on! The few drops of blood spilt in August and September[25] didn't put enough colour in the people's cheeks. The guillotine's too slow. We want blood by the bucketful.

1st CITIZEN: Our wives and kids are screaming for bread, we want to feed them on the flesh of aristocrats. Death to all them with no holes in their coats!

ALL: Kill them, kill them!

ROBESPIERRE: In the name of the law!

1st CITIZEN: What is the law?

ROBESPIERRE: The will of the people.

1st CITIZEN: We *are* the people and we want no law, ergo our will is law, ergo in the name of the law there is no law, ergo kill the lot of them!

VARIOUS VOICES: Listen to Aristides![26] Listen to the Incorruptible!

WOMAN: Listen to the Messiah whose mission it is to seek and destroy. He shall smite the wicked with the might of the sword. His eyes are the eyes that seek them out, his hands are the hands that wreak judgement upon them!

ROBESPIERRE: My poor, virtuous people! You do your duty, you sacrifice your enemies. Greatness is yours, dear people of France. Your might bursts forth with the crash of thunder and the dazzle of lightning. But your blows must not injure your own body: in your rage you are doing yourself to death. Nothing can bring you down but your own strength. Your enemies know that. But your leaders are watchful, they shall guide your hand: their eyes are infallible, your hand inescapable. Come with me to the Jacobin Club. Your brothers will greet you with open arms; we shall bring bloody justice upon the heads of our enemies.

MANY VOICES: To the Jacobins! Long live Robespierre!

Exit everyone except SIMON *and his* WIFE.

SIMON: Poor me! They've gone and left me! [*He tries to get up.*]

WIFE: There you are then. [*She helps him.*]

SIMON: Ah, dear Baucis,[27] you are heaping coals upon my head.

WIFE: Up you get!

SIMON: You turn away? Porcia,[28] can you ever forgive me? Did I truly hit you? 'Twas not my hand, 'twas not my arm, my madness did it.

His madness is poor Hamlet's enemy,
Hamlet does it not, Hamlet denies it.

Where's our daughter, where's my little Susanna?

WIFE: She's just round the corner.

SIMON: Let's find her; come, dear spouse so rich in virtue. [*Both depart.*]

Scene 3: The Jacobin Club

MESSENGER FROM LYON:[29] Our brothers in Lyon have sent us to pour out all their bitter discontent. We don't know whether the tumbril that took Ronsin[30] to the guillotine was also carrying the corpse of freedom, but we *do* know that the murderers of Chalier have been strutting around ever since as though they alone were safe from death. Have you forgotten that Lyon is a blot on the face of France that must be buried beneath the bones of its traitors? Have you forgotten that the disease-ridden body of this whore of kings can only be cleansed in the waters of the Rhône? Have you forgotten that this revolutionary river must make Pitt's fleet in the Mediterranean run aground on the corpses of aristocrats? Your mercy is murdering the revolution. The heartbeat of an aristocrat is the death rattle of liberty. Only a coward dies for the revolution, a Jacobin kills for her. I tell you this: if you don't have the vigour of the men of August 10th, of September, of May 31st,[31] then we too, like the patriot Gaillard,[32] will have nothing to turn to but the dagger of Cato.[33] [*Applause and confused shouts.*]

A JACOBIN: We'll drink the cup of Socrates with you.

LEGENDRE [*climbs onto the podium*]: We don't need to look as far as Lyon. Those people here in Paris who wear clothes of silk, swan about in carriages, enjoy boxes at the theatre and talk like the Dictionary of the Academy have turned all cocky these last few days: they think their necks are safe at last. They're full of wit: Marat and Chalier should be honoured with a double martyrdom, they say – their statues should be guillotined. [*Violent commotion throughout the assembly.*]

VARIOUS VOICES: They're as good as dead. Their tongues are their guillotine.

LEGENDRE: May the blood of these saints be upon them! I ask those members of the Committee of Public Safety here present: since when have you been so deaf –

COLLOT D'HERBOIS [*interrupts him*]: And I ask *you*, Legendre, whose voice it is that speaks through you and dares to spawn such thoughts? It's time to tear these people's masks away. Would you believe it: the cause is blaming its effect, the shout its echo, the reason its consequence! I tell you, Legendre, the Committee of Public Safety has a better grasp of logic! Don't you worry: the statues of our saints shall not be defiled, like Medusa they shall turn their betrayers to stone.

ROBESPIERRE: I demand to speak.

THE JACOBINS: Quiet! Quiet! The Incorruptible!

ROBESPIERRE:[34] If we have kept silent up to now, it is only because we have been waiting for this cry of outrage that now rings out on every side. Our eyes were open. We watched the enemy gird himself and rise up, but we did not give the alarm: we let the people be their own sentinel – and they have not slept, it is they that have given the call to arms. We let the enemy burst from his hiding-place and come out into the open – now he stands exposed and naked in the clear light of day, he is utterly defenceless, you have only to fasten your eyes upon him – and he is dead.

I have told you before: the internal enemies of the Republic are divided into two factions, like separate armies. Under different banners and by the most diverse routes, they rush to achieve the self-same goal. One of these factions[35] is no more. By painting our most valiant patriots as played-out weaklings, these prancing lunatics tried to cast them aside, and thus rob the Republic of its mightiest defenders. By declaring war on religion and property, they created a diversion on behalf of the kings. They undermined the glorious drama of the revolution by parodying it with grotesque and deliberate excesses. If Hébert had triumphed, the Republic would have collapsed into chaos and the despots would have smirked all over their faces. The sword of the law has struck the traitor down. But why should that bother the enemy without, if other criminals of a different hue are ready and waiting to attain the same goal? So long as another faction[36] remains to be destroyed, we have achieved nothing. This other faction is the very opposite of the first. They urge us to be weak, their battlecry is 'Mercy!' They want to rob the people of their weapons and their strength, and deliver them cowed and naked to foreign monarchs.

The weapon of the Republic is terror, the strength of the Republic is virtue. Virtue, because without it terror is destructive; terror, because without it virtue is impotent. Terror is an emanation of virtue, it is justice in its purest form: swift, stern, unswerving. Some say that terror is the weapon of tyrants, and that in consequence our regime resembles tyranny. Of course it does – but only as the sword of a fighter for freedom resembles the sabre of a tyrant's henchman. The despot that dominates and degrades his subjects through terror is fully within his rights *as a despot*; you as founders of the Republic are no less within your rights if through terror you smash the enemies of freedom. Revolutionary government is the despotism of freedom against tyranny.

'Have mercy on the royalists!' certain people cry. Mercy for men of evil? Never! Mercy for the innocent, mercy for the weak, mercy for the unfortunate, mercy for mankind. Only peaceful citizens have a right to society's protection. In a republic, the only citizens are republicans: royalists and foreigners are enemies. To punish the oppressors of mankind is merciful, to pardon them is barbarism. All these displays of false compassion seem to me like sighs of sympathy for our enemies in England and Austria.

But not content with depriving the people of their weapons, these creatures seek through *vice* to poison the most sacred wellsprings of their strength. Of all assaults on liberty, this is the most devious, most dangerous, most foul. Vice is the mark of Cain stamped upon the brow of aristocrats and their imitators. In a republic it is not simply a moral crime, it is a political crime: the man of vice is the enemy of freedom – and the greater the services he *seems* to have rendered to freedom, the greater the danger he represents. The most dangerous citizen of all is the sort that more readily wears out a dozen red bonnets than performs a single decent act.

You will grasp my meaning easily enough if you think of people who once lived in garrets, but now boast a carriage and indulge their lust with former contessas and marchionesses. When we see these tribunes of the people flaunting the depravity and luxury of the courtiers of old, when we see these counts and barons of the revolution gamble, keep servants, give opulent banquets, marry rich women, wear sumptuous clothes – then we might well ask: have they plundered the people, and kissed the golden hand of kings? Well may we stand amazed at their pose of elegance, their veneer of wit, their façade of culture. There was recently a shameless parody of Tacitus;[37] I could answer with Sallust and give a travesty of the Catiline conspiracy.[38] But I think there's no need for me to sketch-in more detail: my portraits are finished.

No treaty, no truce with men who were solely bent on plundering the people and hoped to accomplish their aim with impunity, men for whom the revolution was nothing but a workaday job, the Republic nothing but a speculator's paradise. Terrified by the raging tide of justice, they are secretly trying to stem its force. If they had their way, we should all decide that 'We don't have enough virtue to inflict such terror!' 'Be philosophical!', I hear them say, 'Take pity on our weakness! I haven't the courage to admit that I'm bad, so I beg you instead not to be cruel!'

Rest assured, you people of virtue! Rest assured, you valiant patriots! Tell your brothers in Lyon that the sword of justice does not sleep in the hands of those to whom you entrusted it. —We shall offer the Republic a great example . . .

MANY VOICES [*amidst general applause*]: Long live the Republic! Long live Robespierre!

PRESIDENT: The session is closed.

Scene 4: A street

LACROIX, LEGENDRE.

LACROIX: What on earth have you done, Legendre? You realize whose heads you've knocked off with your 'statues'?

LEGENDRE: A few fops and fancy women, that's all.

LACROIX: Committing suicide, that's what you're doing; an image in the mirror that murders its original — and therefore itself.

LEGENDRE: I don't know what you mean.

LACROIX: I should have thought Collot made it clear enough.

LEGENDRE: So what, he was drunk again.

LACROIX: Who do they say speaks the truth? — Idiots, children — and drunks. Who the hell do you think Robespierre meant by Catiline?

LEGENDRE: Well?

LACROIX: It couldn't be more simple. They've sent the atheists and the ultras to the scaffold, but the people are no better off than they were before, they still go barefoot around the streets and want to make shoes from the hide of aristocrats. The guillotine must be kept well stoked: if its temperature drops any further, the Committee of Public Safety can look forward to a very long sleep in the Place de la Révolution.

LEGENDRE: What have my statues got to do with it?

LACROIX: Don't you see? You've turned the counter-revolution into a public issue, you've driven the Decemvirate to *do* something, you've forced their hand. The people are a minotaur: if that lot want to avoid being gobbled up themselves, they *have* to keep feeding the beast its diet of corpses.

LEGENDRE: Where's Danton?

LACROIX: God knows! He's trying to re-create the Medici Venus piece by piece from amongst all the tarts of the Palais-Royal.[39] 'Making a mosaic', he calls it. God knows what bit of the anatomy he's working on right now. What a crying shame that nature has smashed beauty into pieces like Medea her brother,[40] and buried it in fragments in different bodies. —Come on, let's go to the Palais-Royal.

Scene 5: A room

DANTON, MARION.[41]

MARION: No, leave me be! Down here at your feet. I want to tell you a story.

DANTON: You could put your lips to better use.

MARION: No, just leave me be. My mother was a clever woman. She kept telling me what a beautiful virtue chastity is. Whenever folk came to the house and started to talk about certain matters, she told me to leave the room. If I asked her what the people had meant, she told me I ought to be ashamed of myself. If she gave me a book to read, there were always some pages I had to miss out. But I could read the Bible as much as I liked, everything there was holy writ. But there were bits in it

I didn't understand, there was no one I cared to ask, I brooded on my own. Then spring arrived. Things happened all around me from which I was separate. The strangest atmosphere suddenly enfolded me: I could scarcely breathe; I looked at my body, it seemed to me sometimes as though I were double, then melted again into one. About this time a young man came to visit us, he was very good-looking and said funny things. I'd no idea what he wanted, but he made me laugh. My mother told him he could come just as often as he liked, that was fine by us. After a while we thought we might as well lie side by side between a pair of sheets as sit side by side on a pair of chairs. I enjoyed that more than his conversation, and saw no reason why, of the two pleasures, I should be allowed the lesser but denied the greater. We did it in secret. And so it went on. But I became like an ocean that devours everything and bores its way deeper and deeper. For me all men became indistinguishable, they melted into a single body. It's simply my nature – can anyone escape it? In the end, he noticed. He came one morning and kissed me as though he was trying to choke me, he tightened his arms around my neck, I was terribly afraid. Then he let me go, and laughed, and said he'd nearly done something stupid, but he didn't want to spoil my fun too soon, I should keep my body and use it, it was all I had, it would wear out all on its own in the end. Then he left. Again, I didn't know what he wanted. That evening I sat by the window letting the waves of evening light engulf me: I am all sensation, I connect with the world around me through feeling alone. Then a crowd of people came down the street, at its head the children, the women gaping from their windows. I looked down, they were carrying him by in a basket, his forehead shone pale in the moonlight, his hair was wet, he'd drowned himself. I couldn't help crying. That's the only disruption my being has known. Other people have Sundays and weekdays, they work six days and pray on the seventh, they have a spasm of emotion once a year on their birthday, a flicker of thought for their New Year's resolutions. All that for me is beyond comprehension. I know no pause, no change. I am ever the same. A ceaseless yearning and holding, an ardent fire, a swirling stream. My mother died of grief, people point their fingers. How stupid. It makes no difference in the end what gives people pleasure, whether it's flowers or toys, naked bodies or pictures of Christ, it's all the same feeling, those that pray the most are those that enjoy the most.

DANTON: Why can't I draw your beauty completely into my being, enfold it completely within my arms?

MARION: Danton, your lips have eyes.

DANTON: I wish I were part of the air so I could bathe you in my flood and my waves could break on every ripple of your beautiful body.

Enter LACROIX, ADELAIDE, ROSALIE.

LACROIX [*standing in the doorway*]: I've got to laugh, I've really got to laugh!

DANTON [*crossly*]: What's the matter?

LACROIX: I was just thinking about the street.

DANTON: Well?

LACROIX: There were these dogs in the street, a great bull mastiff and a tiny pekinese, they were giving each other such a terrible time.

DANTON: What the hell are you talking about?

LACROIX: I was just thinking about it and couldn't help laughing. An edifying spectacle, that's for sure! The girls were all standing in their windows gawping. People should be more careful and not even let them sit out in the sunshine or the gnats will start doing it on the back of their hands – it'll give them ideas.

Legendre and I have done the rounds of nearly all the cells in this holy establishment, the Little Sisters of the Revelation of the Flesh clung to our coat-tails and begged for our blessing. Legendre is inflicting a penance on one of them right now, but it means he'll go hungry for a month. I've brought two of them with me, these votaries of the body.

MARION: Good day, Miss Adelaide, good day, Miss Rosalie.

ROSALIE: It's *such* a long time since we had the pleasure.

MARION: *So* sorry not to have seen you.

ADELAIDE: My God, we're so busy, both night and day.

DANTON [*to Rosalie*]: Hey, my little one, how smooth and supple your hips have become!

ROSALIE: Ah yes, we grow ever more perfect.

LACROIX: What's the difference between the Adonis of old and the Adonis of today?[42]

DANTON: And how demurely intriguing Adelaide has become! What a piquant change! Her face is like a fig-leaf that she holds before the whole of her body. Such a shady fig-tree on such a well-travelled road: how very refreshing!

ADELAIDE: So they walk all over me, do they? –

DANTON: All right, dear lady, don't get cross!

LACROIX: Listen to this, a modern Adonis gets torn to pieces not by a wild boar but by rutting sows, they go for his balls and not for his leg, it's not roses that spring from his blood but crystals of mercury.[43]

DANTON: Miss Rosalie is a classical statue that's been restored, but only her hips and her feet are the genuine article. She is a magnetized needle, what her North Pole repels, her South Pole attracts, in the middle is her Equator: cross the line, and you're ducked in mercury.

LACROIX: They're two Sisters of Mercy, each hard at work in the hospice of her body.

ROSALIE: Shame on you for making us blush!

ADELAIDE: You ought to have more manners! [*Exit* ADELAIDE *and* ROSALIE.]

DANTON: Good night, you pretty little things!

LACROIX: Good night, you mines of mercury!

DANTON: Poor things, we've stopped them from earning their supper.

LACROIX: Listen, Danton, I've just come from the Jacobins.

DANTON: Is that all?

LACROIX: The people from Lyon have delivered an ultimatum: they said that unless things changed, they'd have no choice but suicide. Everyone had an expression on his face as if he was about to stab himself and tell his neighbour to follow his example. Legendre ranted on about people trying to smash the statues of Marat and Chalier; I think he's trying to daub his face with blood again, he'd turned his back so completely on the Terror that even the kids in the street point their fingers at him.

DANTON: And Robespierre?

LACROIX: Stabbed the air with his finger and said that virtue must rule through terror. The very words hurt my neck.

DANTON: They're carving planks for the guillotine.

LACROIX: And Collot screamed like a madman that it was time to tear people's masks off.

DANTON: Their heads'll get torn off in the process.

PARIS *enters.*

LACROIX: Any news, Fabricius?[44]

PARIS: I went straight from the Jacobins to see Robespierre. I demanded an explanation. He put on a face as though he were Brutus nobly sacrificing his own sons.[45] He droned on about his 'duty', said he'd stop at nothing for the sake of liberty, he'd sacrifice everyone – himself, his brother, his friends.

DANTON: That's clear enough, just invert the order and *he's* the one ushering his friends to the scaffold. Legendre deserves our thanks, he's forced them to speak out.

LACROIX: The ultras are still a threat, the people live in wretched poverty: things are cruelly in the balance. If the scale-pan of blood is allowed to rise it will take the Committee of Public Safety with it – on the end of a rope. They need ballast, they need a nice weighty head.

DANTON: I know, I know – the revolution is like Saturn, it devours its own children.[46] [*Ponders for a few moments.*] But come on, they won't dare.[47]

LACROIX: Danton, you were once a true saint of the revolution, but the revolution is no respecter of relics, they chucked the bones of all the kings in the gutter, and all the statues from the churches. Do you think they'd leave you standing there as a monument?

DANTON: My name! The people!

LACROIX: Your name! You're a moderate, so am I, so are Camille, Philippeau, Hérault. To the people, moderation means weakness. They destroy anyone who can't stick the pace. The tailors of the Red Bonnet Section will feel the whole of Roman history quivering in their needles once it dawns on them that the great hero of September[48] is a moderate.

DANTON: Very true, and besides – the people are like children, they have to smash things to pieces to see what's inside them.

LACROIX: What's more, Danton, we're 'full of vice', as Robespierre puts it, in other words we enjoy life, and the people are 'virtuous', in other words they *don't* enjoy life, because the grind of work has blunted their senses, they don't get drunk, because they've got no money, they don't visit the whore-house because their breath stinks of herring and cheese and the girls can't stand it.

DANTON: They hate people who enjoy life like a eunuch hates men.

LACROIX: They call us scoundrels and, [*leaning towards Danton's ear*] just between ourselves, there's more than a grain of truth in it. Robespierre and the people will be virtuous, Saint-Just will put together a pack of lies, Barrère will wallow in triumph and wrap the Convention in a cloak of blood – I can see it all.

DANTON: You're dreaming. They never had courage without me – they won't have courage against me. The revolution isn't finished yet, they might still need me, they'll keep me in reserve.

LACROIX: We have to *act*.

DANTON: All in good time.

LACROIX: All in good time! We'll have had it by then!

MARION [*to Danton*]: Your lips have gone cold. Your words have stifled your kisses.

DANTON [*to Marion*]: Have we lost so much time? What a waste of energy! [*To Lacroix*] Tomorrow I'll go and see Robespierre, I'll get him in a rage and he'll blurt it all out. That's it then: tomorrow! Good night, my friends, good night, and thank you!

LACROIX: Come on, let's get out of here! Good night, Danton! Mademoiselle's thighs are your guillotine, her mons Veneris your Tarpeian Rock![49] [*Exit* LACROIX *and* PARIS.]

Scene 6: A room[50]

ROBESPIERRE, DANTON, PARIS.

ROBESPIERRE: I'm telling you, anyone who grabs my arm when I'm drawing my sword is my enemy, whatever his intentions may be. Stop me from defending myself, and you kill me as surely as if you attacked me directly.

DANTON: Where self-defence ends, murder begins. I see no reason why we have to go on killing people.

ROBESPIERRE: The social revolution is not yet finished, and to try to end a revolution in the middle is to dig your own grave. The world of the idle rich is not yet dead, the healthy vigour of the people must replace this utterly effete and played-out class. Vice must be punished, virtue must rule through terror.

DANTON: I don't understand the word 'punishment'.

You and your virtue, Robespierre! You've taken no bribes, made no debts, slept with no women, kept your nose quite clean and never got drunk. Robespierre, you are disgustingly decent. It would fill me with shame if I'd pranced about the world for thirty years with the same self-righteous expression on my face just for the pleasure of finding others worse than myself.

Is there never a voice within you silently, secretly telling you, 'You're lying! You're lying!'?

ROBESPIERRE: My conscience is clear.

DANTON: Our conscience is a mirror! – only idiots are bothered by what they see there. People tart themselves up just as well as they can, and it's pleasure they're after, each in his own special way. Scarcely an issue worth fighting about! Everyone's entitled to defend themselves if others spoil their fun. But do you have the right to turn the guillotine into a wash-tub for other people's dirty linen and use their severed heads as scrubbing brushes for their soiled clothes, just because *you* always wear a nice clean coat? If they tear your coat or spit on it, then go ahead, defend yourself – but is it any of your business so long as they leave you in peace? If *they* don't mind going around in such a state, does that give you the right to send them to their graves? Are you heaven's policeman? Your precious God Almighty looks kindly enough on all these things: if *you* can't do the same, just hide your eyes!

ROBESPIERRE: Do you deny virtue?

DANTON: Yes, and vice! We are all Epicureans, some blatant, some subtle – Christ was the subtlest of all. That's the only difference I can see between human beings. Everyone behaves according to his nature: we do what we do because it's what does us good.[51]

Well, Incorruptible, aren't I cruel to kick your stilts from under you?

ROBESPIERRE: There are times, Danton, when vice is high treason.

DANTON: Don't go and proscribe it, for Christ's sake, what an ungrateful act, you owe it too much: where would your virtue be without vice?

And by the way, just to put things in your sort of language: when we strike our blows they must serve the Republic, we mustn't kill the innocent along with the guilty.

ROBESPIERRE: What makes you think that any have been innocent?

DANTON: Hear that, Fabricius? Not a single innocent has died! [*To Paris, on the way out*] There's no time to lose, we have to show ourselves at once. [*Exit* DANTON and PARIS.]

ROBESPIERRE [*alone*]: Go on, go! He thinks he can make the mighty horses of the revolution stop at the brothel, like a coachman reining his docile hacks; they'll have strength enough to drag him to the Place de la Révolution.

Kick my stilts from under me! Put things in my sort of language! But wait, wait! Is *that* the real reason? They'll say his giant figure cast its shadow across my path and that's why I bundled him out of the sun.

And what if they're right?

Is it so very necessary? Yes it is, it is! The Republic! He has to go! Anyone who stands still in a moving mass offers the same resistance as if he were opposing it from outside: he gets trampled underfoot.

We shall not allow the ship of the revolution to run aground on the filthy mudflats and shallow calculations of these people, we must hack off the hand that dares to impede it, no matter how desperately they care to try.

To hell with a society that has stolen the clothes of the dead aristocracy and inherited all their foul diseases! No virtue! Virtue simply the stilts I strut on! My sort of language! How it keeps coming back!

Why can't I drive the thought from my mind? With bloody finger it points and points. I swathe it in layer upon layer of rags, but always the blood comes bursting through. [*After a pause*] I don't know which bit of me is lying to the rest. [*He goes to the window.*] The night snores above the earth, tossing and turning in terrible dreams. Thoughts and wishes, scarcely sensed, confused and formless, that dared not face the light of day, now take on shape and substance, and steal into the silent house of dreams. They open doors and stare from windows, become half flesh in the murmur of lips, the sudden stir of sleeping limbs. – And even our waking life, is it not but a dream in brighter light? Don't we always sleepwalk? Are our actions not like those in a dream, just a little more distinct, more precise, more complete? Who would blame us for that? The mind enacts more deeds in a single hour than our lumbering bodies can achieve in the space of years. The sin is in the thought. Whether thoughts become deeds, acted out by the body, is a matter of chance.[52]

SAINT-JUST *enters*.

ROBESPIERRE: Who's that? In the darkness there? A light, bring a light!

SAINT-JUST: Don't you recognize my voice?

ROBESPIERRE: Ah, it's you, Saint-Just! [*A* SERVANT GIRL *brings a light.*]

SAINT-JUST: Were you alone?

ROBESPIERRE: Danton just left.

SAINT-JUST: I saw him in the Palais-Royal. He had that revolutionary glint in his eye and talked in epigrams; he was all pally with the sans-culottes, the tarts were fawning on him like dogs, and people hung about in the street tittle-tattling his every word. – We'll lose the initiative. Are you going to vacillate for ever? We'll act without you. We've made up our minds.

ROBESPIERRE: So what's your plan?

SAINT-JUST: We'll call a formal session of all the committees – Legislative, General Security, Public Safety.

ROBESPIERRE: Overdoing it, aren't you?

SAINT-JUST: We must bury the great corpse with honour, like priests, not murderers. And we must bury it whole, with *all* its appendages.

ROBESPIERRE: What do you mean?

SAINT-JUST: We must lay him to rest with all his armour, and slaughter his slaves and horses on his burial mound: Lacroix –

ROBESPIERRE: A rogue if ever there was one! – yesterday a lawyers' clerk, today a general in the armies of France. Go on.

SAINT-JUST: Hérault-Séchelles.

ROBESPIERRE: Such a handsome head!

SAINT-JUST: He was the gilded preamble to the Act of Constitution, we don't need such embellishments any more, we'll rub him out. Philippeau. Camille –

ROBESPIERRE: Him too?

SAINT-JUST [*hands him a piece of paper*]: Just as I thought. Read that!

ROBESPIERRE: Ah, his pathetic rag,[53] is that all? It's just childish fun at your expense.

SAINT-JUST: Read it, here, here! [*Points to a particular place.*]

ROBESPIERRE [*reads*]: 'Robespierre the bloody Messiah, flanked by those thieves Couthon[54] and Collot,[55] up there on his Calvary, not sacrificed himself but sacrificing others. The holy sisters of the guillotine stand below him like Mary and Magdalene. Saint-Just is at his bosom like St John the Evangelist, conveying the apocalyptic revelations of the Master to the National Convention; he carries his head like the holy sacrament.'

SAINT-JUST: I'll make him carry his like Saint Denys[56] – under his arm.

ROBESPIERRE [*continues reading*]: 'Are we to believe that the spotless coat of the Messiah is the winding sheet of France? That his spindly fingers chopping the air at the rostrum are guillotine blades? And you, Barrère, who said that riches would be coined in the Place de la Révolution! – But no, why bother with the miserable wretch. He's a widow that's buried several husbands already.[57] There's nothing we can do. It's his talent, he sees people's deaths in their faces six months in advance. And no one likes the stench of rotting corpses.'

You too, Camille?

Death to the lot of them! Now! Only the dead can never return. Is the indictment ready?

SAINT-JUST: It's easily done. You prepared the ground at the Jacobin Club.

ROBESPIERRE: I wanted to frighten them.

SAINT-JUST: Act on it: that's all I need to do. We'll have forgers for hors d'oeuvre and foreigners for dessert[58] – they'll choke to death on the meal, I promise you.

ROBESPIERRE: Quick then, tomorrow. No protracted death agonies. I've been so on edge these last few days. Let's get it over with. [Exit SAINT-JUST.]

ROBESPIERRE [alone]: Yes, indeed: 'bloody Messiah, not sacrificed himself but sacrificing others'. – He redeemed them with his blood, I redeem them with their own. He made them sin, I take sin upon myself. He had the ecstasy of pain, I have the agony of the executioner. Who denied himself the more – him or me? –

Though there's madness in the thought –

Why do we always look to this one man? Verily the son of man is crucified in all of us; we writhe in blood and sweat in the Garden of Gethsemane, but none of us redeems the others with his wounds. – Camille, dear Camille! – They're all going from me – all around is emptiness and desolation – I'm utterly alone.

ACT II

Scene 1: A room

DANTON, LACROIX, PARIS, CAMILLE DESMOULINS.

CAMILLE: Hurry, Danton, we've no time to lose.

DANTON [*getting dressed*]: But time is losing us.

How boring life is: day after day we put on our shirts and pull up our trousers, crawl into bed in the evening and out again in the morning, place one foot relentlessly in front of the other, with nothing to suggest things will ever be different. It's terribly sad. And that millions before us have done just the same and millions in the future will do so again; on top of all that, we consist of two halves that ape one another, so everything happens twice over. It's terribly sad.

CAMILLE: You're talking childish nonsense.

DANTON: Dying men are often childish.

LACROIX: By not *doing* anything you're destroying yourself *and* all your friends! Tell the fence-sitters it's time they rallied round you, call on radicals and moderates alike. Cry out against the tyranny of the Decemvirate, speak of daggers, go on about Brutus: that way you'll jolt the rank and file, you'll even win over what's left of the Hébertistes. Let your anger rage! For Christ's sake don't let's die disarmed and humiliated like the wretched Hébert.

DANTON: You've a bad memory, you said my days as a saint were over. You were even more right than you thought. I've been out among the Sections, they were respectful enough, but like mourners at a funeral. You were right, I'm a relic, and relics get thrown in the gutter.

LACROIX: But why did you let it come to this?

DANTON: To this? The truth is, in the end I found it all so boring. Traipsing around for ever in the self-same coat with the self-same creases. It's pathetic. To be such a dismal instrument yielding a single note on a single string.

It's unbearable. I wanted an easy life. I'm getting one too: the revolution's pensioning me off, though not quite in the way I'd imagined.

And anyway, what support do we have? Our whores might stand a chance against the hags around the guillotine, but that's about all. You can tick it all off on the fingers of one hand: the Jacobins have made virtue the order of the day; the Cordeliers call me Hébert's executioner; the Commune is busy doing penance;[59] the Convention – that might be a way, but it would be just like the 31st of May:[60] they'd never give in willingly. Robespierre is the dogma of the revolution – something no one can touch. And anyway it wouldn't work. We didn't make the revolution, the revolution made us.

And even if it did work – I would rather be guillotined than guillotine others.[61] I've had enough, what's the point of us humans fighting each other? We should sit down together and be thoroughly at peace. A mistake crept in when we were made, there's something missing, I don't know what it is, we'll never discover it by groping around in each other's guts, so why smash open each other's bodies to try to find it? Let's face it, we're lousy alchemists.

CAMILLE: To put it more grandly: 'How long is mankind in his eternal hunger to continue devouring his own limbs?' Or: 'How long are we shipwrecked sailors in our unquenchable thirst to continue sucking each other's blood?' Or: 'How long are we mathematicians of the flesh in our hunt for the ever elusive x to continue to write our equations with the bleeding fragments of human limbs?'

DANTON: You're a mighty echo!

CAMILLE: There we are, you see: a pistol can sound as loud as a thunderbolt! All the better for you, you should keep me near you all the time.

PHILIPPEAU: So France is to be left to her executioners?

DANTON: What difference does it make? People are very well off the way things are. They're in the depths of misfortune: what a perfect opportunity to be noble or witty, sentimental or virtuous – above all, to avoid being bored!

What difference does it make whether they die because of

the guillotine, or from disease or old age? It's better to skip into the wings with sprightly limbs and a cheery wave and the applause of the audience ringing in your ears. How killingly jolly, how perfectly apt: we prance on the stage throughout our lives – even if, in the end, we are killed for real.

What an excellent thing to have our lives a little shortened: the coat was too long, our bodies never did fill all the space. Life is becoming an epigram, and why not? – who ever had the breath and the spirit to endure an epic of fifty or sixty interminable cantos? It's time to drink the paltry essence from minuscule glasses, not great big tubs – that way you get a decent mouthful, otherwise you're lucky if you gather a few stray drops in the bottom of the barrel.

And anyway – I'd have to scream, it's all too much bother, life isn't worth all the effort it costs just to keep it going.

PARIS: Then flee, Danton, get away from here!

DANTON: Can you take your country with you on the soles of your shoes?

And anyway – and that's the main thing – they won't dare. [*To Camille*] Come on, lad, I tell you they just won't dare. Goodbye! Goodbye! [*Exit* DANTON *and* CAMILLE.]

PHILIPPEAU: So there he goes.

LACROIX: And believes not a single word of anything he says. Sheer bloody laziness. He'd sooner be guillotined than make a speech.

PARIS: What can we do?

LACROIX: Go home, pretend to be Lucretia, and start rehearsing a graceful death.

Scene 2: A promenade

Sundry PROMENADERS.

A CITIZEN: My dear Jacqueline – I meant Cor . . ., er, Cor . . .

SIMON: Cornelia, citizen, Cornelia.[62]

CITIZEN: My dear Cornelia has blessed me with a baby boy.

SIMON: Correction: has borne the Republic a son.

CITIZEN: 'The Republic', that sounds a bit too general to me, you might as well . . .

SIMON: Exactly: the individual must give way to the general . . .

CITIZEN: Ah yes, that's just what my wife says.

STREET SINGER:
>   Tell me, tell me, if you can
>   What is true bliss for every man?

CITIZEN: Names are the problem, I just can't decide.

SIMON: Call him 'Pike, Marat'.

STREET SINGER:
>   From dawn to dusk he loves to slave
>   Nursing his sorrows from cradle to grave.

CITIZEN: Three names is what I'd really like, three's sort of special; something useful, and something proper; I've got it − 'Plough, Robespierre'.

SIMON: 'Pike'.

CITIZEN: Oh, thank you, neighbour! Yes! 'Pike, Plough, Robespierre', what lovely names, they're truly beautiful.

SIMON: I'm telling you, your Cornelia's breast will be like the udder of the Roman she-wolf − no, that's no good, Romulus was a tyrant, that's no good at all. [*They walk on.*]

A BEGGAR [*singing*]:
>   A clutch of earth
>   A scrap of moss . . .

Kind sirs, pretty ladies!

1st GENTLEMAN: Do some work, man! You look positively well-fed.

2nd GENTLEMAN: Here! [*Gives him money.*] He's got hands like velvet. What confounded cheek!

BEGGAR: How did you come by your coat, sir?

2nd CITIZEN: Work, man, work! You could have one too, I'll give you work, come and see me, I live at −

BEGGAR: Why did you work, sir?

2nd CITIZEN: To buy the coat, you fool.

BEGGAR: You gave yourself hell for the sake of a luxury, 'cos a coat like that's a luxury all right, any old rag does just as well.

2nd CITIZEN: Of course I did, there's no other way.

BEGGAR: A right idiot I'd be! A lovely coat but a worn-out

31

body: it don't make sense. The sun shines warm out here in the street, and life's so easy. [*Sings*]

A clutch of earth

A scrap of moss . . .

ROSALIE [*to Adelaide*]: Soldiers! Come on! We've not had nothing hot in our bodies since yesterday!

BEGGAR [*sings*]:

Is all that's left

When life is lost!

Kind sirs! Dear ladies!

SOLDIER: Whoa! What's the hurry, my little chickens? [*To Rosalie*] How old might you be?

ROSALIE: As old as my little finger.

SOLDIER: Sharp as nails, you are!

ROSALIE: Blunt as a doorknob, you are!

SOLDIER: Then you can help me to get a real nice point on. [*Sings*]

Tell me, do, my sweet little whore,

Does the shafting make you

Sore, sore, sore?

ROSALIE [*sings*]:

Oh no no no, my dear kind sir,

I beg you, give me

More, more, more!

Enter DANTON *and* CAMILLE.

DANTON: Oh what fun they're having!

It's in the air, I can smell it, as if the heat of the sun were hatching lechery.

Doesn't it make you want to leap in amongst them, tear your trousers from your body, and fuck them from behind like dogs in the street?[63] [*They walk on.*]

YOUNG GENTLEMAN: Ah Madame, the peal of a bell, the evening sunlight dappling the trees, the delicate twinkle of a star –

LADY: – the scent of flowers, these natural pleasures, this pure delight of nature! [*To her daughter*] Look, Eugénie, virtue alone has eyes to see it.

EUGENIE [*kisses her mother's hand*]: Ah, dear Mama, I see but you!

LADY: Such a *good* little girl!

YOUNG GENTLEMAN [*whispers in Eugénie's ear*]: Look, see the pretty woman with that old fart over there?

EUGENIE: Yes, I know her.

YOUNG GENTLEMAN: They tell me her baker's left a bun in her oven.

EUGENIE [*laughs*]: What naughty things you say!

YOUNG GENTLEMAN: The old bloke happens by, sees how the little bud is sprouting, takes it walking in the sunshine, and thinks *he's* the downpour that made it grow!

EUGENIE: How very indecent, I quite want to blush!

YOUNG GENTLEMAN: I'd go white as a sheet if you did!

DANTON [*to Camille*]: Just don't expect me to be serious. I can't see why people don't stop in the street and laugh and laugh in each other's faces, they should laugh from their windows and laugh from their graves, the heavens should burst and the earth convulse with helpless laughter.

1st GENTLEMAN: I do assure you, an extraordinary discovery! It puts a whole new face on modern technology. Mankind is speeding with giant strides towards its noble destiny.

2nd GENTLEMAN: Have you seen the new play? A veritable tower of Babel! A labyrinth of vaults and stairs and passage-ways, and all so lightly, so boldly flung in the air. It makes you giddy just to watch – What a strange imagination! [*He stands still, embarrassed.*]

1st GENTLEMAN: What on earth's the matter?

2nd GENTLEMAN: Oh nothing! Your hand, sir! That puddle! There we are! I thank you! I only just managed, that might have been dangerous!

1st GENTLEMAN: You were *afraid*?!

2nd GENTLEMAN: Indeed I was. The crust of the earth is exceedingly thin: when I see such a hole I'm always afraid I might fall right through. We must tread very carefully, it could give way beneath us. – But go to the theatre, I can really recommend it.

Scene 3: A room

DANTON, CAMILLE, LUCILE.

CAMILLE: I tell you, unless they get everything in stilted imitations, a little bit here and a little bit there in concerts, theatres, art exhibitions, they have neither eyes to see nor ears to hear. Cobble up a puppet with conspicuous strings and make it jerk round the stage on iambic feet: 'What stunning psychology! How neat and logical!' Take a jaded maxim, a half-baked emotion, a commonplace idea, stuff it into coat and trousers, paint on a face, stick on hands and feet, make it wheeze and puff its way through three acts till it gets itself married or shoots itself dead: 'An idyllic ideal!' Scratch out an opera that expresses the ebb and flow of emotion as a cracked tin-whistle conveys the song of the nightingale: 'Ah! the power of art!'

Put these people out of the theatre and into the street: 'Ugh! miserable reality!' They forget their Maker for his incompetent copyists. They hear and see nothing of the glow, the hum, the radiance of creation regenerating itself in and around them each second of the day. They visit the theatre, read poems and novels, ape their ridiculous contortions, and dismiss God's creatures as 'Oh so ordinary!'

The Greeks knew what they were talking about when they said that Pygmalion's statue indeed came to life but never bore children.

DANTON: And artists in general treat nature like David,[64] who cold-bloodedly drew the dead of the September massacre as their bodies were flung from their gaol into the street, and claimed he was 'catching the final spasms of life in these evil rogues'. [DANTON *is called from the room.*]

CAMILLE: What do you say, Lucile?

LUCILE: Nothing; I love to watch you talk, that's all.

CAMILLE: And do you hear what I say?

LUCILE: Of course I do!

CAMILLE: Am I right? Do you actually know what I said?

LUCILE: No, I honestly don't.

DANTON *returns.*

CAMILLE: What's wrong?

DANTON: The Committee of Public Safety has ordered my arrest. Someone's warned me; they've offered me a place to hide. So they want my head: that's fine by me. I'm fed up with this botching and bungling. Let them take it. What difference does it make? I'll die with courage, it's easier than living.

CAMILLE: Danton, there's still time.

DANTON: It's impossible. I never would've thought . . .

CAMILLE: You and your damned lethargy!

DANTON: I'm not lethargic, I'm tired. I need to get out of here.

CAMILLE: Where are you going?

DANTON: If only we knew!

CAMILLE: But seriously, where?

DANTON: For a walk, my lad, for a walk! [*Exit.*]

LUCILE: Oh Camille!

CAMILLE: Sweet child, don't worry!

LUCILE: This precious head – to think that they could. . . Dear Camille! It's nonsense, tell me it's nonsense, tell me I'm out of my mind!

CAMILLE: Don't worry yourself: I'm not Danton's shadow!

LUCILE: The world's so big with so much in it: why pick on this one thing? Who'd take it from me? Who'd be so cruel? And what good would it do them even if they had it?

CAMILLE: I keep telling you, there's no need to worry. Only yesterday I was talking to Robespierre, he was very friendly. Things are a bit strained, it's true, a difference of opinion, that's all.

LUCILE: Why not go and see him?

CAMILLE: We shared a desk at school.[65] He was always a lonely, gloomy sort. I was the only one to seek him out and make him laugh now and then. He's shown me so often how much I mean to him. Alright, I'll go.

LUCILE: So soon, Camille? Go on then! No, stay! Just this [*she kisses him*] and this! Go on now, go! [*Exit* CAMILLE.]

   These are evil times. It's the way things are. What can anyone do? Be brave and accept it. [*Sings*]

Who had the heart
To make lovers part
And part and part and part?

Why *that*, of all things? For that to come into my head on its own: it's bad.

As he went away, I had this feeling he could never turn back and would have to go further and further away from me – further and further.

How empty the room is; the windows agape as though a corpse had lain here. I can't bear it. [*Exit.*]

Scene 4: Open country

DANTON: No further. No more sullying the silence with the panting of my breath and the muttering of my feet. [*He sits down, pauses.*]

Someone told me once about an illness that makes you lose your memory. Death's supposed to be a bit like that. I sometimes hope that death might do even more and blot out *everything*. If only it would!

In that case I'm running like mad to save my own enemy – my memory! The hiding-place is safe enough, they said. Yes, for my memory, but not for me. The grave will give me greater safety, at least it will let me *forget*! It will annihilate my memory. Carry on, and my memory will survive and destroy me. It, or me? The answer is easy. [*He gets up and turns back.*]

I'm flirting with death; it's very agreeable, making eyes at him through a spyglass like this, from a nice safe distance.

But come on, I can't help laughing about the whole damn business. There's this feeling inside me: nothing's going to change, tomorrow will be just like today, and so will the next day and all the days that follow. It's sheer bravado; they're trying to frighten me; they'd never dare.

Scene 5: A room, at night

DANTON [*by the window*]: Is it never going to stop? Will the glare never pale, the roar never die? Will it never be dark and still, so we're no longer forced to see and hear our horrible sins? – September! – [66]

JULIE [*from within*]: Danton! Danton!

DANTON: What's the matter?

JULIE [*enters*]: Why are you shouting?

DANTON: Shouting? Was I shouting?

JULIE: You called out something about 'horrible sins', and then you moaned 'September'!

DANTON: Me, me? It wasn't me that spoke, scarcely me that even thought such secret, silent thoughts.

JULIE: You're shaking, Danton.

DANTON: Aren't I right to shake, when even the walls begin to talk? When my body's so broken that my thoughts escape and scatter and speak through brick and stone? It's all so strange.

JULIE: Georges, dear Georges.

DANTON: Yes Julie, it's so very strange. I don't want to think at all any more if it's going to mean these voices. Julie, there are thoughts that no ear should hear. It's a terrible thing if they holler and scream like babies the moment they're born, a terrible thing.

JULIE: God keep you sane, Georges. Georges, do you recognize me?

DANTON: Of course I do: you're a human being, you're a woman, you're my wife, and the earth has five continents, Europe, Asia, Africa, America, Australia, and two times two is four – there you are, you see, I'm perfectly sane. The scream was 'September': isn't that what you said?

JULIE: Yes, Danton, it rang through every room.

DANTON: When I got to the window – [*he looks out*] the city's quiet, the lights all out . . .

JULIE: There's a child crying somewhere near.

DANTON: When I got to the window, a single word howled and screamed through all the streets: 'September!'

JULIE: Be strong, Danton: you were dreaming, that's all.

DANTON: Dreaming? Yes, I was dreaming, but it was something else, I'll tell you right now, my poor frail head, right now, there, that's it, I've got it! Beneath me the earth's whole sphere, roaring and snorting in headlong flight, with me astride it like on a wild stallion, clutching its mane and gripping its flanks with giant limbs, my head bent low, my hair streaming out above the infinite abyss. And so I was swept along. I screamed in terror, and woke. I went to the window – and that's when I heard it, Julie, that word.

What does it want, for God's sake? Why that of all words? What's it got to do with me? Why does it stretch its bloody hands towards me? I never hurt it.

Oh help me, Julie, my mind's gone numb. September, Julie: isn't that when it happened?

JULIE: The foreign kings were only forty hours from Paris.

DANTON: The outposts had fallen, the aristocrats were in the city.

JULIE: The Republic was doomed.

DANTON: Yes, doomed. We couldn't leave an enemy at our backs, we'd have been fools; two enemies on a plank, it's us or them, whichever is the stronger chucks the other one off, that's fair, isn't it?

JULIE: Yes, yes!

DANTON: We fought them and won, that wasn't murder, it was – war with the enemy within.

JULIE: You saved your country.

DANTON: I did, I did! It was self-defence, we had to do it. The man on the cross, how easily it tripped off his tongue: 'It must needs be that offences come, but woe unto him through whom they come.'

'It *must* needs be': it's this 'must' that did it. Who'd ever curse the hand on whom the curse of 'must' has fallen? Who spoke the curse, who? What is it in us that whores, lies, steals, murders?[67]

Puppets, that's all we are, made to dance on strings by unknown forces; ourselves we are nothing, nothing – mere swords in the hands of warring spirits, the hands themselves cannot be seen, that's all, like in some child's fairy-tale.

That's it, I'm happy now.

JULIE: Truly happy, my darling?

DANTON: Yes, Julie; come on, let's go to bed!

Scene 6: Street in front of Danton's house

SIMON, CITIZENS-IN-ARMS.

SIMON: How far into the night are we?

1st CITIZEN: How *what?*

SIMON: How far's the night?

1st CITIZEN: About as far as from dusk to dawn, I reckon.

SIMON: Bugger you, what's the time?

1st CITIZEN: Try looking at your watch. It's the time when all those stiff little pendulums stop swinging beneath the bedsheets.

SIMON: Let's go and get him![68] Come on, you lot! Dead or alive, or it's curtains for us. Strong as a giant, he is. I'll lead the way. Mind your backs, here's freedom coming! Take care of my wife! She'll prick up her ears all right when she hears what I've done!

1st CITIZEN: Prick up her ears? She won't go short of pricks, don't you worry!

SIMON: Forward, citizens! You will render great service to your country!

2nd CITIZEN: I wish the country'd render some service to us! For all the 'oles we've made in other people's bodies, not a single 'ole has gone from our own trousers!

1st CITIZEN: Do you want your flies sewing up then? [*Laughter.*]

SIMON: Come on then, let's go! [*They force their way into Danton's house.*]

Scene 7: The National Convention

A group of DEPUTIES.

LEGENDRE: Is this slaughter of the deputies never going to end? Who's safe if Danton falls?

A DEPUTY: But what can we do?

ANOTHER DEPUTY: He must be tried here, in the National Convention. It's bound to work: how could they match the power of his voice?

ANOTHER DEPUTY: It's impossible, there's a decree that'll stop us.

LEGENDRE: It must either be set aside, or an exception made. I'll propose the motion. I'm banking on your support.

PRESIDENT: I declare the session open.

LEGENDRE [*mounts the rostrum*]: Last night, four members of the National Convention were arrested. I know Danton is one of them, I don't know the names of the others. But whoever they may be, I demand that they be heard at the bar of this assembly. I tell you, citizens, as one who is surely beyond reproach, that in my view Danton is as pure and innocent as I am myself. I mean to attack no particular member of the committees of Public Safety or General Security – but I fear on the soundest evidence that private hatred and personal vendetta may rob the cause of freedom of men that have done her the greatest service. The man whose sheer energy made him France's saviour in 1792[69] deserves to be heard; if he's to be charged with high treason he *must* be allowed to have his say.[70] [*Violent commotion.*]

VARIOUS VOICES: We support Legendre's motion!

A DEPUTY: The people put us here, without their say-so no one can tear us from our seats.

ANOTHER DEPUTY: Your words reek of corpses, you snatched them from the mouths of Girondists! Do you want special privileges?[71] The sword of the law is equally poised over the heads of all.

ANOTHER: We *make* the law! We cannot permit our committees to drive us from the sanctuary of the law to the steps of the guillotine!

ANOTHER: Crime has no sanctuary! Only criminals with crowns find sanctuary – on their thrones!

ANOTHER: Only the guilty plead the right of sanctuary.

ANOTHER: Only murderers refuse to recognize it.

ROBESPIERRE:[72] Such uproar has not been seen in this Assembly for a very long time, and it shows how grave are the matters before us. Today will decide whether a handful of individuals win a massive victory over this great country. How could you so utterly flout your own principles that you would grant to a few individuals today what yesterday you refused to Chabot, Delaunay and Fabre?[73] Why this sudden change for the sake of a few? What do I care about the praises that certain people heap on themselves and their friends? We've seen all too often what *that* is worth. We do not ask whether a man has accomplished this or that patriotic deed, we look to his entire political career.

Legendre appears not to know the names of those arrested – but the entire Convention knows who they are. His friend Lacroix is amongst them. Why does Legendre appear not to know that? Because he knows full well that none but the most brazen could defend Lacroix. He named only Danton because he believes that privilege attaches to his name. But no: we want no privilege, we want no idols! [*Applause.*]

What makes Danton so different from Lafayette,[74] Dumouriez,[75] Brissot,[76] Fabre, Chabot, Hébert? What can be said in *his* favour that could not be said in theirs? But did you spare *them*? What has *he* done to deserve preferential treatment? Or is it perhaps because a few deluded individuals, and others who weren't so deluded, gathered around him to sweep to power and fortune on his coat-tails? The more he deceived those patriots who trusted him, the more he must suffer the wrath of the guardians of freedom.

They want to make you afraid of 'abusing' a power that you have already exercised. They rant about the 'despotism' of the committees, as if the trust that the people have placed in you, and which you have transferred to the committees,[77] were not a sure guarantee of their patriotism. They profess to be trembling. But I tell you, all who tremble at this moment are guilty, for innocence never trembles in the face of public vigilance. [*General applause.*]

They tried to frighten me as well. I was given to understand that I too might be vulnerable to any danger besetting Danton. Letters were sent to me claiming that Danton's friends had me trapped: they thought my loyalty to an old friendship, and blind acceptance of pretended virtues, would lead me to moderate my zeal and my passion for freedom.

I therefore most solemnly declare that nothing will stop me, even if Danton's danger should become my own. A certain courage and greatness of spirit is needed in all of us. Only criminals and feeble spirits are afraid to see others of their company fall at their side – fall, because they are no longer hidden in a crowd of accomplices, but stand exposed to the glare of truth. But if in this assembly there be such feeble spirits, there are also heroic ones. The tally of criminals is not that great. We need only strike at very few heads and our country is saved. [*Applause.*]

I demand that Legenure's motion be rejected. [*The deputies rise en masse in a show of universal approval.*]

SAINT-JUST: There appear to be some sensitive ears in this assembly that cannot bear to hear the word 'blood'. A few general reflections may serve to convince them that we are no more cruel than nature, or the age we live in. Nature follows her own laws, calmly, irresistibly; man is destroyed wherever he comes into conflict with them. A change in the composition of the air, a burst of subterranean fire, a shift in the equilibrium of a mass of water – and an epidemic, a volcanic eruption, a flood kills thousands. And what is the outcome? An insignificant, scarcely perceptible ripple on the surface of the physical world that would almost have disappeared without trace were it not for the jetsam of corpses. I ask you now: should *moral* nature be any more considerate in her cataclysmic revolutions than *physical* nature? Does an *idea* not have just as much right as a law of physics to destroy whatever stands in its way? An event that transforms the whole of moral nature, in other words mankind: does it not have the right to come about through blood? The world-spirit acts through us in the realm of ideas just as, in the physical realm, he acts through floods or volcanoes. What difference does it make whether people die of an epidemic or the revolution? –

The progress of mankind is slow, and can only be reckoned in centuries; behind each forward step loom the graves of generations. To arrive at the simplest discoveries and principles cost the lives of millions who died along the way. Is it not therefore straightforward that, in an age when the pace of history is faster, rather more people should run out of breath?

In conclusion, a quick and simple point: having all been created under the same conditions, we are therefore all equal, apart from the distinctions made by nature herself. In consequence, everyone may have merits but no one may have privileges, neither an individual, nor any class of individuals whether large or small. Putting this proposition into practice meant that each of its clauses exacted its toll of human lives. Its punctuation marks were the 14th of July,[78] the 10th of August, the 31st of May. Turning it into reality would normally have taken a century and been punctuated by whole generations: we did it in four years. Is it so surprising that at each new turn the raging torrent of the revolution disgorges its quantum of corpses?

Sundry conclusions still need to be added to our basic proposition: are a few hundred corpses to stand in our way?

Before establishing his new state, Moses led his people through the Red Sea and into the wilderness until the old, corrupt generation was utterly consumed. We have neither the Red Sea nor the wilderness; but we have war and the guillotine.

The revolution is like the daughters of Pelias:[79] it rejuvenates humanity by hacking it to pieces. Humanity will rise up from the bloodbath as the earth arose from the waters of the Flood: with pristine vigour in all its limbs, as though created for the very first time. [*Sustained applause. Various deputies leap to their feet in their enthusiasm.*]

All you secret enemies of tyranny, all you in Europe and throughout the world that have the dagger of Brutus concealed beneath your coat: we call on you to share with us this moment of supreme sublimity! [*The entire assembly strikes up the 'Marseillaise'.*]

ACT III

Scene 1: The Luxembourg: a room with prisoners[80]

CHAUMETTE, PAYNE, MERCIER, HERAULT-SECHELLES *and* OTHER PRISONERS.[81]

CHAUMETTE [*tugs Payne's sleeve*]: Listen, Payne, things *could* be that way after all, it suddenly came over me just then. My head's aching today, can't you help me a little with your logic? – There's this horrible feeling inside me.

PAYNE: All right, Anaxagoras[82] my philosophical friend, here is your catechism. There *is no God*. For God either did create the world, or else he did not. If he did *not* create it, then the world is grounded in itself, and there is no God, since God can be God only by containing within him the ground of all being. – But God *can't* have created the world, for either creation is eternal like God, or it had a beginning. If it had a beginning, then God must have created the world at a particular point in time, which means that after being at rest for an eternity God must suddenly have become active, and thereby suffered a change within himself, making him subject to the concept of *time*. But 'time' and 'change' are both inconsistent with the timeless and immutable being of God. Therefore God cannot have created the world. However, since we know for certain that the world or at least our own self exists, and that – as I have just shown – it must be grounded either in itself or in something else that is not God, therefore *there can be no God*. QED: *Quod erat demonstrandum!*

CHAUMETTE: I see the light again now, I really do: oh thank you, thank you!

MERCIER: But hold on, Payne, what if creation is eternal?

PAYNE: In that case it isn't creation any more, it's one with God, or, as Spinoza puts it, one of his attributes; in that case God is in everything, in you, my worthy friend, in our philosopher Anaxagoras, in me. There'd be nothing wrong with that

44

– but you have to admit there's not much to be said for divine majesty if the dear Lord can have toothache in all of us, get a dose of the clap, and be buried alive, or at least suffer horrible nightmares about it.

MERCIER: But there must be a first cause.

PAYNE: No one's denying it. But why identify this first cause with what we think of as 'God', in other words perfectness. Do you think the world is perfect?

MERCIER: No, I don't.

PAYNE: Then why on earth infer a perfect cause from an imperfect effect? – Voltaire did it, but only because he was just as scared of alienating God as he was of alienating kings. People with nothing but brains, but without the nous or the courage even to use them properly, are miserable bunglers.

MERCIER: On the other hand I ask you: can a perfect cause ever have a perfect effect? Can perfectness create perfectness? Isn't that impossible, since anything created can never be grounded in itself – and that, as you say, is the condition of perfectness?

CHAUMETTE: That's enough, that's enough!

PAYNE: Don't fret yourself, philosopher! You're quite right; but supposing God *does* have to create, then he should leave well alone if all he can create is something imperfect. Isn't it typically human that we can only think of God as busily creating things? Just because *we* have to constantly hustle and bustle to prove to ourselves that we really exist, do we have to impute this pathetic compulsion to God as well? When we enter in mind and spirit into the presence of a perfect bliss that is timeless, harmonious, rounded, replete, do we *have* to suppose that it will suddenly stir itself to action and start making manikins like an impatient dinner-guest fiddling with his bread? Out of an overwhelming yearning for love, as we assure one another in cryptic whispers? Do we have to do all that, just to turn ourselves into the progeny of gods? I'll make do with a lesser father, then at least I won't be able to accuse him of bringing me up below his own station – in a pigsty or a slave-galley.

Get rid of unperfectness: only then can you prove the existence of God. Spinoza tried it. Evil you can deny, but not pain. Only the intellect can prove the notion of God, all the emotions

45

rebel against it. Mark this, Anaxagoras: why do I suffer? That is the rock of atheism. The tiniest spasm of pain, be it in a single atom, and divine creation is utterly torn asunder.[83]

MERCIER: And what about morality?

PAYNE: First you prove God on the basis of morality, and then morality on the basis of God. What do you want with your morality? I've no idea whether Good and Bad exist as absolutes, but that makes no difference to the way I behave. I behave according to my nature: whatever is appropriate to my nature is good for me, and I do it; whatever is opposed to my nature is bad for me, if it crosses my path I ward it off. You can remain true to so-called virtue and hostile to so-called vice without necessarily despising those of a different persuasion – a pathetic attitude if ever there was one.

CHAUMETTE: True, very true!

HERAULT: Then again, dear Philosopher Anaxagoras, one could also say that for God to be everything, he must also be his own opposite: perfect and unperfect, good and bad, full of happiness and full of suffering – but the outcome would be zero, each would cancel out the other, we'd be left with nothing. Cheer up, you've passed the test, you can happily worship your luscious friend Madame Momoro[84] as nature's masterpiece, at least she's left you with a groinful of rosaries.[85]

CHAUMETTE: Thank you, gentlemen, I'm most obliged. [Exit.]

PAYNE: He's still not sure. Before he's done he'll take Extreme Unction, point his feet towards Mecca and have himself circumcized – just to be on the safe side.

DANTON, LACROIX, CAMILLE, PHILIPPEAU are led in.

HERAULT [rushes up to Danton and embraces him]: It should be 'Good morning', but I'd better say good night. I can't ask you how you've slept: how will you sleep?

DANTON: Very well. Go to bed laughing, that's the trick.

MERCIER [to Payne]: Look at him: this dove-winged mastiff![86] He's the evil genius of the revolution. He tried to rape his own mother, but she was even stronger than he is.

PAYNE: His life and his death are equal catastrophes.

46

LACROIX [*to Danton*]: I didn't think they'd come so quickly.

DANTON: I knew they would, someone warned me.

LACROIX: And you said nothing?

DANTON: Why bother? The best kind of death is a sudden stroke. Or do you prefer the slow, lingering sort? And anyway – I never thought they'd dare. [*To Hérault*] Better to take it easy *under* the earth than dash around on top getting corns. I'd rather use it as a pillow than a footstool.

HERAULT: At least we shan't have calloused fingers when we fondle the lovely cheeks of old Lady Decay.

CAMILLE [*to Danton*]: Just don't strain yourself. You can stick your tongue out as far as you like, you still won't be able to lick the cold sweat of death from your forehead. Oh Lucile, it breaks my heart.

The prisoners crowd round the new arrivals.

DANTON [*to Payne*]: What you did for the good of your country, I tried to do for mine. I wasn't so lucky, they're sending me to the scaffold. Let them: I shan't stumble.

MERCIER [*to Danton*]: You're drowning in the blood of the twenty-two Girondists.[87]

A PRISONER [*to Hérault*]: Remember what you said? – 'The might of the people and the might of reason are one and the same.'[88]

ANOTHER [*to Camille*]: Well, Procurator-General of the Street-lamp, your improvements to the lighting haven't brightened the prospects for France.[89]

ANOTHER: Leave him alone. His are the lips that spoke the word 'mercy'. [*He embraces Camille; several prisoners follow his example.*]

PHILIPPEAU: We are priests that prayed with the dying: we caught their disease, and now we die of it.

VARIOUS VOICES: The death blow aimed at you will kill us all.

CAMILLE: Gentlemen, I'm only sorry that our efforts proved so fruitless. Why am I going to the scaffold? Because I was moved by the fate of a few poor bastards!

Scene 2: A room

FOUQUIER TINVILLE, HERRMANN.

FOUQUIER: Everything ready?

HERRMANN: It's going to be tricky. It would all be so easy if Danton weren't one of them.

FOUQUIER: It *has* to be Danton that leads the dance.

HERRMANN: He'll frighten the jury. He's the bogeyman of the revolution.

FOUQUIER: The jury had better just do their stuff!

HERRMANN: There *might* be a way, but it's not strictly legal.

FOUQUIER: Well, go on.

HERRMANN: We don't draw lots, we pick and choose the people we can trust.

FOUQUIER: Not bad, not bad! That should see off the whole bunch, no trouble. There are nineteen altogether. A nice mixed bag, I've seen to that. The four forgers, a few bankers and foreigners. A tasty dish. The people need such things. Right, some reliable jurors! Any suggestions?

HERRMANN: Leroi,[90] he's stone-deaf and never hears a word the prisoners say. Danton can shout himself hoarse where he's concerned.

FOUQUIER: Excellent! Who else?

HERRMANN: Vilatte and Lumière: one's always drunk, the other fast asleep; the only time they open their mouths is to say the word 'Guilty!' Girard: his attitude's quite simple – come before the court, and you deserve the chop. Then there's Renaudin . . .

FOUQUIER: Him too? He helped some priests to get off once.

HERRMANN: Don't worry! He came to see me a few days ago: he wanted all the condemned to be bled just before their execution to take the stuffing out of them – he's fed up that so many show defiance.

FOUQUIER: Just the job! Right then, I'm relying on you.

HERRMANN: Just leave it to me.

Scene 3: The Luxembourg: a corridor

LACROIX, DANTON, MERCIER *and sundry* PRISONERS *milling about.*

LACROIX [*to a prisoner*]: Are there really so many poor bastards, and in such a terrible state?

PRISONER: Did the tumbrils never tell you: Paris is a slaughter-house.

MERCIER: How did it go, Lacroix? – 'All are subject to the sword of Equality!' 'The lava of the revolution is in fiery spate!' 'The guillotine is the crucible of the Republic!' The spectators cheer, the Romans rub their hands with glee, but none of them realize that every word is the blood-choked scream of another victim. Just follow your slogans through to the point where they turn into flesh and blood. Look around you: what you see is what you've said – a precise translation of all your words. These miserable wretches, their executioners, the guillotine: they are your speeches come to life. Like Bayezid with his pyramids,[91] you've built your grandiose schemes out of human heads.

DANTON: You're quite right. These days everything is fashioned out of human flesh. It's the curse of our age. And now my body's to be used as well.

It's a year since I set up the Revolutionary Tribunal. I beg forgiveness from God and man. I wanted to avoid more September massacres, I hoped to save the innocent – but this slow murder with all its formalities is even more hideous, and just as inexorable. Gentlemen, I had hoped to get you out of this place.

MERCIER: Oh, we'll get out of it all right!

DANTON: We're in it together now. Heaven knows how it's all going to end.

Scene 4: The Revolutionary Tribunal

HERRMANN [*to Danton*]: Your name, citizen?

DANTON: The whole revolution speaks my name, which will live for ever in the pantheon of history. My place of abode? – will soon be the void.

HERRMANN: Danton, you stand accused by the National Convention of conspiring with Mirabeau,[92] Dumouriez, Orléans,[93] the Girondists, the foreigners and the faction of Louis the Seventeenth.

DANTON: My voice, that has so often rung out on behalf of the people, will easily confound these calumnies. The miserable wretches that dare to accuse me: let them show themselves here, and I shall cover them with shame. Summon the Committees: I shall answer only before them. I need them as my accusers and my witnesses. Make them appear!

Anyway, why should I bother with you and your verdict? I have already told you: the void will soon be my refuge. My life is a burden: go ahead, snatch it from me, I can't wait to get rid of it.

HERRMANN: Danton, defiance is the badge of criminals: the innocent show nothing but composure.

DANTON: Private defiance is no doubt reprehensible. But the national defiance that I have so often displayed is the noblest of virtues. Such is the defiance with which I have so often battled for freedom, such is the defiance I now invoke on behalf of the Republic and against my pitiful accusers. How should I keep my composure in the face of such infamous calumnies? I am a true revolutionary: expect no cool and calm defence from the likes of me. Men of my stamp are the stuff of revolutions, the spirit of freedom shines from our brow. [*Signs of applause from the courtroom public.*]

They accuse *me* of conspiring with Mirabeau, Dumouriez, Orléans! *Me* of crawling at the feet of wretched despots! It's *me* that is summoned to answer to implacable, inexorable justice! – Saint-Just, you miserable cur, you'll answer to posterity for this vile slander!

HERRMANN: I demand that you control your tongue! Remember Marat:[94] he showed his judges due respect.

DANTON: They have laid hands on my very existence, so let it rise up and do battle: I shall bury the lot of them beneath the weight of my deeds. I feel no pride: fate guides our arm – though only the mighty can be its instrument.

It was I that declared war on the monarchy at the Champ de Mars;[95] I that defeated it on the 10th of August; I that destroyed it on the 21st of January[96] and threw down the head of a king as a gauntlet to challenge the rest of the monarchs. [*Repeated signs of applause. He picks up the indictment.*] I look at this scurrilous screed and shudder to the innermost core of my being. Who *are* these people that had to 'force' Danton to make his appearance on that glorious day, the 10th of August? Who *are* these privileged creatures who were supposedly the fount of his strength and energy? Let my accusers appear! I demand it – and I know very well what I'm doing. I shall tear the masks from these abject villains and hurl them back into the blackness from which they should never have crawled.

HERRMANN [*rings his bell*]: Don't you hear the bell?

DANTON: The voice of a man defending his honour and his life must drown your puny bell!

It was I in September that fed the tender brood of the revolution on the shattered bodies of aristocrats. It was my voice that forged weapons for the people from the gold of the rich and the nobility. My voice was the hurricane that buried the lackeys of despotism beneath waves of bayonets. [*Loud applause.*][97]

HERRMANN: Danton, you're straining your voice, you're over-excited. You can finish your defence at the next session. You need some rest. – The court is suspended.

DANTON: Now you know your Danton! A few hours more, and he will sleep for ever in the arms of fame.

Scene 5: The Luxembourg: a dungeon

DILLON, LAFLOTTE, *a* GAOLER.

DILLON: Hey, keep your nose to yourself: it's so full of moonshine it's dazzling my eyes! [*Laughs.*]

LAFLOTTE: Ugh, shut your mouth as well: your breath's so thick it's obscuring your moon! [*Laughs.*]

GAOLER [*laughs*]: Do you reckon it's bright enough to read by, sir? [*Points to a piece of paper he is holding in his hand.*]

DILLON: Come on, hand it over!

GAOLER: Well, sir, my moonshine has brought me to a very low ebb.

LAFLOTTE: More like a flood, to judge by your trousers.

GAOLER: No, sir, they get wet all on their own. [*To Dillon*] It's like this, sir: you're such a bright star that my moon's gone dim; a little contribution is all what's needed to give it some fire – if you want to be able to read by its light.

DILLON: Damn you, now bugger off! [*He gives him money; exit the* GAOLER.]

[*Dillon reads*] Danton's put the wind up the tribunal, the jury's wavering, rumblings in the public gallery, a fantastic jostle of people, the Palais de Justice besieged by crowds reaching right to the river. – Oh for some money to bribe my way out of here! Hell and damnation! [*He paces up and down, occasionally pouring himself a drink.*] If only I could just get a foot in the street! They won't take *me* like a sheep to the slaughter! *One* foot in the street, that's all!

LAFLOTTE: Street – tumbril: what's the difference?

DILLON: There's a difference all right – big enough to fit all the Decemvirate's corpses into. It's time for right-thinking people to stand and fight with their heads held high.

LAFLOTTE [*aside*]: The higher the better: it's easier to remove them. Keep at it, you old fart: I'll float to freedom on your torrent of booze.

DILLON [*pacing up and down*]: These criminals, these idiots! They're so fanatical they'd cut their own heads off!

LAFLOTTE [*aside*]: You could grow to love life all over again, like your own child, if you'd fathered it yourself. You don't often get the chance to commit incest with coincidence and become your own father. Father and child all rolled into one! Oedipus the cosy way!

DILLON: You can't feed the people on corpses – it's cash they need. The wives of Danton and Camille must shower them with money.

LAFLOTTE: I won't tear my eyes out afterwards: I might need them to weep for our worthy General here.

DILLON: *Danton* in the firing line! Now nobody's safe! They'll join together out of sheer fright.

LAFLOTTE: He's had it anyway. What does it matter if I step on a corpse to climb from the grave?

DILLON: All I need is a foot in the street! I'll find allies enough – ex-soldiers, Girondists, erstwhile aristocrats. We'll smash the gaols and get the prisoners to join us.

LAFLOTTE: It stinks a bit of treachery, there's no denying it. But so what? Let's give it a try: I've been far too honest up to now. My conscience will bother me, but anything for a change; no one really minds their own foul smell.

The prospect of the guillotine has become a real bore, I've faced it too long. I've been through it in my mind a thousand times, and it's lost its fascination, it's become plain sordid.

DILLON: We have to get a message to Danton's wife.

LAFLOTTE: And then – it's not death I'm afraid of, but pain. It might hurt, who can prove that it won't? They say it only lasts a moment, but pain has the subtlest sense of time: a fraction of a second can last an eternity. No, pain is the only sin, and suffering the only vice – I'll stick to virtue.

DILLON: Hey, Laflotte, where's that bloody man gone? I've got money. It's bound to work. Strike while the iron's hot, that's the thing! My plan's all ready.

LAFLOTTE: Alright, alright, I'm coming. I know the turnkey, I'll talk to him. You can count on me, General, we'll get out of this hole. [*To himself as he goes off*] *I* shall swap it for the big wide world, *he* will swap it for a tight little grave.

Scene 6: The Committee of Public Safety

SAINT-JUST, BARRERE, COLLOT D'HERBOIS, BILLAUD VARENNES.

BARRERE: What's the message from Fouquier?

SAINT-JUST: They've had the second hearing. The prisoners are demanding that several members of the Convention and of this Committee be called before the court. They're appealing directly to the people, saying that witnesses are being denied them. They've stirred things up to a fantastic pitch. Danton parodied Jupiter, roaring away and tossing his mane.

COLLOT: All the easier for the executioner to grab hold of him.

BARRERE: We'd better keep out of the way: the fishwives and rag-pickers might find us less impressive.

BILLAUD: The masses enjoy being humiliated, even when it's just by haughty looks. They relish the sneering insolence of it. Such faces are worse than a noble coat of arms: blazoned all over them is contempt for humanity, the subtlest form of aristocracy. They should be smashed to pieces, with everyone joining in who hates a supercilious stare.

BARRERE: He's charmed, like Siegfried: the blood of September has made him invulnerable.

What does Robespierre say?

SAINT-JUST: Nothing: he just sits on the fence pretending to get off.

The jury must say they've heard all they need, and stop the arguing once and for all.

BARRERE: Impossible, it can't be done.

SAINT-JUST: They *have* to go, whatever the cost – even if we have to strangle them with our bare hands. Dare to do it! Dare! Danton taught us the word – let's show him we learnt it! Kill them, and the revolution won't stumble on their corpses. Leave Danton alive, and he'll grab the revolution by the scruff of its neck; just take a look at him: the rape of freedom is well within his powers. [SAINT-JUST *is called outside.*]

Enter a GAOLER.

GAOLER: Prisoners are dying in Sainte-Pélagie,[98] they're asking for a doctor.

BILLAUD: Quite unnecessary: less trouble for the executioner.

GAOLER: There are pregnant women among them.

BILLAUD: So much the better, their brats won't need a coffin.

BARRERE: Every aristocrat with consumption saves a session of the Revolutionary Tribunal. Medicine would be counter-revolutionary.

COLLOT [*takes a piece of paper*]: A petition! In a woman's name!

BARRERE: No doubt one of those who'd like to have to choose between the boards of the guillotine and the bed of a Jacobin. Once dishonoured, they die like Lucretia, but somewhat later than she did – not from a dagger, but from childbirth, cancer or even old age. It can't be so very disagreeable to drive a Tarquin[99] from the virtuous terrain of a virgin's body.

COLLOT: She's too old for that. Madam begs to die, she's very articulate: gaol, she says, presses upon her like the lid of a coffin. Four weeks, that's all she's done. The answer is easy. [*He writes, then reads it out*] 'Citizen, you've craved for death nowhere near long enough.' [*Exit the* GAOLER.]

BARRERE: Well said! All the same, Collot, it isn't good for the guillotine to start laughing, or people will stop being afraid of it. We shouldn't be so familiar.

SAINT-JUST *returns.*

SAINT-JUST: A denunciation has just arrived. There's a conspiracy in the prisons. A young man called Laflotte has squealed. He and Dillon were sharing a cell. Dillon got drunk and blabbed it all out.

BARRERE: He's not the first man to do it: cut his throat with his own bottle.

SAINT-JUST: The wives of Danton and Camille are to hand out money to the people, Dillon's meant to escape, they're going to storm the gaols, then attack the Convention.

BARRERE: But that's fairy-tale stuff!

SAINT-JUST: Maybe it is, but it'll do very nicely to send them to sleep. The denunciation's in the bag. On top of that there's the insolence of the accused, the rumblings amongst the people, the disarray in the jury. I'll write a report.

BARRERE: Go on, Saint-Just, concoct your paragraphs: every comma the stroke of a sword, every full stop a severed head.

SAINT-JUST: The Convention must issue a decree instructing the Tribunal to continue the trial without interruption, and to exclude from the proceedings any of the accused who fails to show respect to the court, or provokes the least disturbance.

BARRERE: You've the true instincts of a revolutionary. It all sounds perfectly balanced and moderate, yet achieves exactly the purpose we want. They cannot stay silent. Danton has to roar, it's his only chance.

SAINT-JUST: I'm counting on your support. There are those in the Convention who share the same disease as Danton – and fear the same remedy. They've grown bold again, they'll yammer on about 'violations of procedure' –

BARRERE [interrupts him]: Then I shall point out that the consul who uncovered the Catiline conspiracy in Rome and despatched the criminals there and then was also accused of 'violating procedures'. And who were his accusers?

COLLOT [with declamatory fervour]: Go, Saint-Just. The lava of the revolution is in full spate. Freedom with her hot embrace will stifle those puny weaklings who sought to penetrate her mighty womb. Like Jupiter with Semele,[100] the majesty of the people will appear before them in thunder and lightning and turn them to ashes. Go, Saint-Just, together we shall hurl down our thunderbolts upon the heads of these cowards. [Exit SAINT-JUST.]

BARRERE: Did you hear that word 'remedy'? They'll end up turning the guillotine into a panacea for the pox. They're not fighting the moderates, they're fighting vice.

BILLAUD: We've shared the same goals – so far.

BARRERE: Robespierre wants to turn the revolution into a school for morality, with the guillotine as his lectern.

BILLAUD: Or his prayer-stool.

COLLOT: On which he will put not his knees but his head.

BARRERE: That shouldn't be difficult. The world would have to be completely upside down for the so-called bad lot to start getting chopped by the so-called good lot![101]

COLLOT [to Barrère]: When are you coming for some more fun at Clichy?[102]

BARRERE: When the doctor's finished having his fun with me.

COLLOT: Yes, there's a fiery star over that place, the *stella syphilitica*, your spinal cord is shrivelling in its scorching radiance!

BILLAUD: Before long the pretty little fingers of his delightful mistress Demahy[103] will yank it from its casing and dangle it down his back like a pigtail.

BARRERE [*shrugs his shoulders*]: Ssh! Our lilywhite friend mustn't hear of these things.

BILLAUD: He's an impotent Mohammed [, a fanatic without balls]![104] [*Exit* BILLAUD *and* COLLOT.][105]

BARRERE [*alone*]: What monsters! 'You've craved for death nowhere near long enough'! Such words should have shrivelled the tongue that spoke them.

And what about me?

In the September massacres, when they burst into the gaols, one of the prisoners grabbed his pocket-knife, slipped in amongst the assassins, stabbed a priest through the heart – and saved his own skin! Who could blame him? What difference does it make whether I slipped into a gang of assassins, or joined the Committee of Public Safety? Whether I resorted to the blade of a knife or the blade of the guillotine? It's basically the same in both cases, it's just that one is a little more subtle.

But then: if he was justified in killing *one* man, would he have been justified in killing two? Or three? Or even more? Where does it all end? It's like the grains of barley: how many does it take to make a heap? – is it two, is it three, is it four? How many? Come, my conscience, come, little chicken, chk chk chk. Hush now: here's fodder.

Wait though: was *I* a prisoner, trapped in gaol? I was under suspicion, and that comes to the same – I was doomed for sure.[106]

Scene 7: The Conciergerie[107]

LACROIX, DANTON, PHILIPPEAU, CAMILLE.

LACROIX: How mightily you roared, Danton! Things would be very different if you'd started your battle for survival a little bit earlier. It's quite something, eh, when death comes leering up to us like this with his stinking breath, and paws at us more and more cheekily?

CAMILLE: If at least he'd rape us and tear his prey from our limbs in the heat of a frenzied struggle! But to die like this with all these formalities, as though we were marrying some ancient crone: the contract's drawn up, the witnesses summoned, the ceremony gone through – then there's a tug at the bedcovers and in she crawls, slowly seizing us in her cold embrace.

DANTON: Yes, if only there was a real fight, tooth and nail, no holds barred. But I feel as though I've fallen into a huge machine whose cold, unfeeling power is slowly, systematically tearing me limb from limb. How appalling: to be killed so mechanically!

CAMILLE: To lie there cold, stiff, alone, in the rank miasma of decay. Perhaps death only slowly squeezes the life from our being, perhaps we're still conscious while our bodies rot away.

PHILIPPEAU: Don't worry, my friends. Like autumn crocuses, we only bear seed when winter is through. Like flowers in the spring, we're being transplanted, the difference being that we'll stink a little in the process. Is that really so bad?

DANTON: What an edifying prospect! From one dung-heap to the other! So that's divine progression, is it? From first form to second form, from second form to third form, etcetera, etcetera? I'm sick of school benches, I've sat on them so long my backside's as bald as a baboon's.

PHILIPPEAU: So what do you want?

DANTON: Peace.

PHILIPPEAU: Peace is in God.

DANTON: In nothingness. What offers more peace, more oblivion, than nothingness? And if ultimate peace is God, then doesn't that mean that God is nothingness? But I'm an atheist![108] How I curse the dictum that 'something can't become nothing'![109] And I *am* something, that's the misery of it!

Creation's so rank and rampant that no void is left, there's a seething and swarming wherever you turn.

Nothingness has killed itself, creation is its wound, we are the drops of its blood, the world the grave in which it slowly rots.

It sounds mad. But there's truth in it.

CAMILLE: The world is the Wandering Jew,[110] and nothingness is death – but such death is impossible. If only the song were true: 'Never, never shall I die'!

DANTON: We're all buried alive and encased like kings in fourfold coffins: our shirts, our coats, our houses, the sky. For fifty years we scratch at the coffin-lid.

Yes, if only one could believe in total annihilation, what a relief it would be! But there's no hope in death: death is putrefaction plain and simple, in life we putrefy with more sophistication, more subtlety, that's the only difference!

But this is the putrefaction I'm used to, the devil only knows how I'll make out with another kind.

O Julie! If I had to go on my own! If she left me all alone!

Even if I utterly dissolved, utterly disintegrated, became but a handful of tortured dust — every last atom could only find peace with her.

I cannot die, no, I cannot die. We must rage and roar, they'll have to squeeze the life from my body drop by drop.

Scene 8: A room

FOUQUIER, AMAR, VOULAND.

FOUQUIER: I just don't know what else to say: now they're demanding a Special Commission!

AMAR: Don't worry, we've got the bastards! Here, this is what you wanted. [*He hands Fouquier a piece of paper.*]

VOULAND: That should make you happy.

FOUQUIER: It certainly does. Just what we needed!

AMAR: Get on with it then! Let's get it over — for us *and* for them.

Scene 9: The Revolutionary Tribunal

DANTON: The Republic's in danger, and the President of this court pleads a 'lack of instructions'! We appeal to the people! My voice is still strong enough to bury the Decemvirate. I repeat, we demand a Special Commission, we have vital disclosures to make. I shall take refuge in the fortress of reason, I shall burst forth with the mighty cannon of truth, and I shall blow my enemies utterly to pieces. [*Signs of applause.*]

Enter FOUQUIER, AMAR, VOULAND.

FOUQUIER: Silence in the name of the Republic! Give ear to the law!

The National Convention has issued the following decree: 'In consideration that evidence of mutiny has come to light in the prisons; in consideration that a conspiracy is afoot whereby the wives of Danton and Camille are to bribe the people, and General Dillon is to break out of gaol and free the accused with a band of rebels; in consideration moreover that the latter are making every attempt to provoke disturbances, and have repeatedly sought to insult the court: in consideration of these things, the Tribunal is hereby empowered to continue its proceedings without interruption, and to exclude from the court any prisoner who fails to pay the full respect that is due to the law.'

DANTON: I ask all those present: have we mocked or maligned the court, the people or the National Convention?

MANY VOICES: No! No!

CAMILLE: The miserable swine! They're murdering my Lucile!

DANTON: One day the truth will be recognized. I see terrible misfortune descending upon France. I speak of dictatorship: it has cast aside its veil and struts about with head held high, trampling our corpses underfoot. [*Pointing at Amar and Vouland*] Just look at those murdering cowards, those carrion crows of the Committee of Public Safety![111]

I accuse Robespierre, Saint-Just and their fellow butchers of high treason. They want to drown the Republic in blood. The tracks of the tumbril are highways intended to lead the foreigners' armies to the heart of France!

How long must the march of freedom be marked by graves?

You cry for bread, and they throw you heads! You thirst, and they have you lick blood from the steps of the guillotine! [*Tumult in the public gallery, hubbub of approval.*]

MANY VOICES: Long live Danton! Down with the Decemvirate! [*The prisoners are forcibly removed.*]

Scene 10: Square in front of the Palais de Justice

A MOB.

VARIOUS VOICES: Down with the Decemvirate! Long live Danton!

1st CITIZEN: Yes it's true: heads instead of bread, blood instead of wine.

VARIOUS WOMEN: The guillotine's a lousy flour-mill, the executioner's a lousy baker-boy: we want bread, bread!

2nd CITIZEN: It's Danton that gobbled your bread: cut off his head and there'll be bread a-plenty.

1st CITIZEN: Danton was with us on the 10th of August, Danton was with us in September. Where were his accusers?

2nd CITIZEN: Lafayette was with you in Versailles, but he was still a traitor.[112]

1st CITIZEN: Who says Danton's a traitor?

2nd CITIZEN: Robespierre.

1st CITIZEN: Robespierre's a traitor.

2nd CITIZEN: Who says so?

1st CITIZEN: Danton.

2nd CITIZEN: Danton has fine clothes, Danton has a fine house, Danton has a fine wife, Danton bathes in burgundy, eats venison off silver dishes, and sleeps with your wives and daughters when he's drunk. Danton was poor, like you. Where did all his riches come from?

From the King, so he'd save his crown.

From the Duke of Orléans, so he'd *steal* him the crown.

From the foreigners, so he'd betray you all.

What riches does Robespierre have, our virtuous Robespierre? You all know what he's like!

ALL: Long live Robespierre! Down with Danton! Down with the traitor!

ACT IV

Scene 1

JULIE, *a* BOY.

JULIE: It's all over. He's frightened them. They're killing him out of fear. I'll never see him again – go and tell him I couldn't bear to see him like that. [*She gives him a lock of hair.*] There, give him that and tell him he won't go alone. He'll know what I mean. Then hurry back: I want to read his look in your eyes.

Scene 2: A street

DUMAS, *a* CITIZEN.

CITIZEN: To condemn so many poor bastards to death after a trial like that!

DUMAS: Quite extraordinary, it's true, but revolutionaries have an instinct that other men lack, an instinct that never deceives them.

CITIZEN: The instincts of a tiger,[113] – what's this about your wife?

DUMAS: I shan't have a wife for very much longer.

CITIZEN: So it's true!

DUMAS: The Revolutionary Tribunal will pronounce our divorce, the guillotine will cut her out of my life.[114]

CITIZEN: What a monster you are!

DUMAS: What an idiot *you* are! Do you admire Brutus?

CITIZEN: With all my heart.

DUMAS: To sacrifice all that you love to your country, you surely don't *have* to be a Roman consul, with a toga for hiding your tears? I shall dry my eyes with the sleeve of my red jacket – that's the only difference.

CITIZEN: It's horrible.

DUMAS: You don't understand these things. [*Exit both.*]

Scene 3: The Conciergerie

LACROIX, HERAULT *on one bed,* DANTON, CAMILLE *on another.*

LACROIX: One's hair and nails grow so much – I feel quite ashamed.

HERAULT: Hey, a bit more careful when you sneeze, I got a face full of sand!

LACROIX: And don't you tread on my toes like that, I've got corns.

HERAULT: You've got lice as well.

LACROIX: Bugger the lice, it's the worms that bother me.

HERAULT: Anyway, sleep well, we just have to cope with one another as best we can, there's not much room.

And keep your nails to yourself while you sleep! There! Stop tugging at our shroud, it's cold down there.

DANTON: Yes, Camille, tomorrow we'll be a pair of worn-out shoes, flung into the lap of beggar earth.

CAMILLE: The hide from which the angels cut their slippers, according to Plato, then used them to potter about the earth in. Just what you might expect. My poor Lucile!

DANTON: Take it easy, lad –

CAMILLE: How can I, Danton, how can I? They can't touch her, they mustn't. The radiant beauty that streams from her body so sweet can never be quenched. It's impossible. The earth would not dare to devour her, it would rise up vault-like all around her, the sepulchral dank would sparkle like dew upon her lashes, crystals would sprout like flowers around her limbs, pellucid springs would whisper her to sleep.

DANTON: Sleep yourself, lad, sleep.

CAMILLE: Listen, Danton, just between ourselves: dying like this is such a miserable business. And it serves no purpose. The face of life is so full of beauty: right to the last I shall gaze into its eyes with my own eyes wide open.

DANTON: They'll stay open anyway: no one at the guillotine bothers to shut them. Sleep is more merciful. Come on, lad, sleep.

CAMILLE: Lucile, your kisses dance on my lips, each kiss a dream, captured in my sleepy eye.

DANTON: Will the clock never rest? With every tick it pushes the walls around me that bit closer, like a coffin. I read a story like that as a child: my hair stood on end. Yes, 'as a child'! What a waste of time it was feeding me up and keeping me warm, just to make work for the gravediggers!

I feel as if I'm already beginning to stink. Dear body of mine, I'll hold my nose and pretend you're a woman, sweating and reeking from the dance, and murmur sweet nothings in your ear. After all, we've already killed a lot of time together.

Tomorrow you're a broken fiddle, its tune played out. Tomorrow you're an empty bottle, its wine all drunk – yet I go sober to bed, stone cold sober. They're lucky, the people who can still get drunk. Tomorrow you're a pair of worn-out trousers, they'll chuck you in a cupboard and the moths will devour you, stink as you will.

It's no good: it doesn't help. He's right: dying's a miserable business. Death is a parody of birth: we die helpless and naked, like newborn infants. We even get swaddled – but in a shroud. Anyway, it makes no difference. We'd cry in the grave as we cried in the cradle.

Camille! He's asleep. [*Leaning over him*] A dream is playing in his eyes. I'll leave him be, bathed in the golden dew of sleep.

[*He gets up and goes to the window.*] Julie, thank you! I won't go alone. And yet I would have liked to die an easier death – to melt away, like a falling star; like a fading chord, kissing itself to death with its own lips; like a beam of light burying itself in crystal waters –

The night is sprinkled with stars like shining tears: what terrible grief there must be in the eyes that wept them.

CAMILLE: Oh! [*He has sat up and is groping at the ceiling.*]

DANTON: Camille, what's wrong?

CAMILLE: Oh, oh!

DANTON [*shakes him*]: What are you trying to do, bring the ceiling down?

CAMILLE: Danton, oh my God, hold me, speak to me, please!

DANTON: You're trembling all over, you're dripping with sweat!

CAMILLE: You're you, this is me, that's my hand! Yes, now I know where I am. Oh Danton, that was horrible.

DANTON: What, for Christ's sake?

CAMILLE: I was half dreaming, half awake. Then the ceiling disappeared and the moon came down, right down, my arm took hold of it. The roof of heaven had sunk right down with all its lights, I banged against it, I touched the stars, I flailed like a drowning man beneath the ice. Danton, it was horrible.

DANTON: The circle of lamplight on the ceiling, that's all you saw.

CAMILLE: Could be. It doesn't take much to make us lose what little reason we possess. Madness had me in its claws. [*He gets up.*] I don't want to sleep any more, I don't want to go out of my mind. [*He picks up a book.*]

DANTON: What's that?

CAMILLE: *Life, Death and Immortality.*[115]

DANTON: Do you want to die twice over? It's *La Pucelle* for me![116] I want to slip out of life as though from a brothel, not from a church: life is a whore that fucks and fornicates with the entire world.

Scene 4: Square in front of the Conciergerie

A GAOLER, *two* CARTERS *with tumbrils*, WOMEN.

GAOLER: Who told you to come 'ere?

1st CARTER: I'm not going to *come* 'ere! You've got a nerve!

GAOLER: Very funny. Who charged you with the job then?

1st CARTER: Charged me? *I* charge *them*: ten sous a nob.

2nd CARTER: Trying to take the bread from me mouth, the bastard!

1st CARTER: What d'you call bread? [*Points to the prisoners' window.*] Food for the worms, that lot are.

2nd CARTER: My kids are little worms too, they want their share. Dear oh dear, what a lousy trade we're in – and we're the finest carters in the whole bloody world.

1st CARTER: 'Ow's that then?

2nd CARTER: Who d'you reckon is the best sort of carter?

1st CARTER: Him what delivers furthest quickest.

2nd CARTER: Well, you blockhead, who delivers further than to the next world? And who does it faster than a quarter of an hour? That's what it takes from 'ere to the Place de la Révolution: exactly a quarter of an hour.

GAOLER: Come on, you lazy sods! Nearer the gate! Out of the road, you women!

1st CARTER: Stay right where you are! Never go round a woman, go straight up the middle!

2nd CARTER: You've said it! Straight up the slot with 'orse, cart an' all, just follow the tracks! Once you're out, though, it's quarantine for you![117]

They drive up to the prison gate.

2nd CARTER [*to the women*]: What are you lot gawping at?

A WOMAN: Waiting for old customers, we are.

2nd CARTER: What d'you take my cart for, a brothel? Very respectable cart, this is. Took the king and all the nobs of Paris to their last supper!

LUCILE *enters, and sits on a stone below the prison window.*

LUCILE: Camille, Camille! [*Camille appears at the window.*] Listen, Camille, how funny you look with your long coat of stone and your mask of iron! Can't you bend down? Where have your arms gone? Come on down, little bird, shall I sing you a song? [*She sings*]

> Two little stars up there in the sky
> Twinkle more brightly than even the moon
> Both shine down on my true love's chamber
> One on her window and one on her door.

Come, my dearest, come! Quietly up the stairs, they're all asleep. The moon has helped me to wait and wait. But dressed like that in stone and iron, you won't even manage to pass through the gateway. Come on, that's enough, you're spoiling the game! – You're not stirring at all! But why won't you

66

speak? You're making me frightened. Listen, the people, they're saying you have to die, saying it too with such long faces.

'Die'! Them and their long faces! I just have to laugh. 'Die'! What does *that* mean? Tell me, Camille! 'Die'! I want to think about that. There, there it is! I'll run after it. Come, my darling, help me catch it. Come on, come on! [*She runs off.*]

CAMILLE [*shouts*]: Lucile! *Lucile!*

Scene 5: The Conciergerie

DANTON *at a window giving on to the next room.* CAMILLE, PHILIPPEAU, LACROIX, HERAULT.

DANTON: You've grown very quiet, Fabre.

VOICE [*from within*]: It's the privilege of the dying.

DANTON: Do you know what we're going to be doing from now on?

VOICE: What?

DANTON: Just what *you've* done all your life: *nous ferons des vers!*[118]

CAMILLE [*aside*]: Lucile! Madness lurked in her eyes. Many people have gone mad, it's the way of the world. What can we do about it? Wash our hands and carry on regardless, that's the only way.

DANTON: What a terrible mess I'm leaving behind me. No one but me has a clue how to govern. Things might just be alright if I left my whores to Robespierre and my legs to Couthon.[119]

LACROIX: And they're trying to say we made a whore out of freedom!

DANTON: What difference would it make? Whores and freedom: they're the most cosmopolitan things under the sun. Freedom will now prostitute herself with every semblance of propriety in the marital bed of the lawyer from Arras. But I fancy she'll prove to be his Clytemnestra.[120] I don't even give him six months. I'll drag him down after me.

CAMILLE [*aside*]: God grant her the comfort of a cosy delusion. The ordinary delusions that people call 'sanity' are all so unbearably boring. The luckiest man of them all was the one that imagined he was God the father, God the son and God the Holy Ghost.

LACROIX: The idiots – as we go by they'll bellow: 'Long live the Republic!'

DANTON: So what if they do? The great torrent of the revolution can dump our corpses wherever it likes: even our fossilized bones will serve to smash the skulls of kings.

HERAULT: Yes, provided some latter-day Samson turns up to brandish our jawbones.[121]

DANTON: Fratricidal bastards!

LACROIX: Nothing more clearly proves that Robespierre is a Nero than the fact that he was never more friendly to Camille than he was two days before his arrest. Isn't that true, Camille?

CAMILLE: If you say so. I couldn't give a damn.

This madness she's given birth to: what a sweet child it is! Why do I now have to leave? Together we'd have kissed it and cuddled it and had such fun with it.

DANTON: When history comes to open its tombs, the scent of our bodies will still be enough to make despots perish.

HERAULT: We stank enough while still alive.

Come on, they're platitudes for posterity, aren't they, Danton. They've nothing at all to do with us.

CAMILLE: He's putting on a face as if he expected it to turn into stone and be dug up by posterity as a precious relic.

It's a waste of effort to pout and prink and talk all posh. It's time we removed our masks: we'd think ourselves in a hall of mirrors – wherever we looked we'd see only the same ass's head, no more, no less: primeval, infinite, indestructible. The differences between us are not that great. We're all of us angels and villains, idiots and geniuses, all at the same time: there's plenty of room in a single body for all four things, they're none of them so big as we might imagine. We all of us do the selfsame things: we eat, we sleep, we fuck. The rest: mere variations on a theme. There's no point putting on airs or pretending to be bigger than we are, no point being embarrassed in front of each other. We've all eaten ourselves sick at the same table, we're racked by the same pain: why hide your face behind your napkin? – Just sob and scream to your heart's content. Above all, I beg you:

no tortured pretence of wit or virtue, courage or genius. We know each other too well for that, so spare yourselves the trouble.

HERAULT: Yes, Camille, let's sit down with each other and scream and yell. When in pain there's nothing more stupid than tight-shut lips. The Greeks and the gods always screamed out loud, heroical postures were for Romans and Stoics.

DANTON: Epicureans the lot of them! They all built their own little nest of self-satisfaction. It's quite a feeling to wrap yourself in a flowing toga and glance back to check how impressive your shadow is. Why bother to tie ourselves in knots? What does it matter whether we hide our prick behind garlands of roses, vine or laurel – or leave the filthy thing for dogs to lick and all to see?

PHILIPPEAU: My friends, we don't have to stand very far above the earth to lose all sight of its fitful, flickering confusion, and feast our eyes on the grand simplicity of God's design. There is an ear for which the riotous cacophony that deafens us is but a stream of harmonies.

DANTON: But we are the poor musicians, and our bodies the instruments. The ugly sounds scratched out on them: are they just there to rise up higher and higher and gently fade and die like some voluptuous breath in heavenly ears?[122]

HERAULT: Are we sucking-pigs, whipped to death with rods to make their meat more tasty for a princely feast?

DANTON: Are we children, roasted in the fiery arms of a Moloch world, tickled to death with tongues of flame so the gods can delight in our laughter?

CAMILLE: Are the heavens with their winking eyes of gold a bowl of golden carp that stands on the table of the blessed gods, and the blessed gods laugh for ever and the fish die for ever and the gods delight for ever in the dancing colours of their dying agony?

DANTON: The world is chaos, nothingness its due messiah.

The GAOLER *enters.*

GAOLER: Gentlemen, you may leave, the carts are waiting at the door.

PHILIPPEAU: Good night, my friends, let's go calmly to bed and draw that cover over our head beneath which all hearts stop and all eyes close. [*They embrace each other.*]

HERAULT [*takes Camille's arm*]: Be glad, Camille, it's a beautiful night we'll be getting. See how the clouds hang in the silent, deepening sky. Like the twilight of Olympus; its gods grow deathly pale, then disappear. [*Exit all.*]

Scene 6: A room

JULIE: Everyone was hurrying through the streets, now all is still. I won't keep him waiting even for a moment. [*She takes out a phial.*] Come, my dearest priest and minister, whose 'Amen' gives us perfect rest. [*She goes to the window.*]

How lovely it is to say goodbye. All I need do is to close the door behind me. [*She drinks.*]

Oh, to stand like this for ever!

The sun's gone down. The earth had such strong features while it shone, but now her face is grave and still, like someone on the edge of death. How beautifully the twilight plays around her cheeks, her brow.

Paler and paler she grows. She's like a corpse, drifting slowly downward in the mighty flood of air. Is there no arm to seize her by her golden hair and pull her from the stream to give her burial?

Ssh, I'll go to her. No sighs, no kisses: the merest breath might wake her.

Sleep, my darling, sleep. [*She dies.*][123]

Scene 7: The Place de la Révolution

The tumbrils arrive and stop in front of the guillotine. MEN *and* WOMEN *sing and dance the 'Carmagnole',*[124] *the* PRISONERS *strike up the 'Marseillaise'.*

A WOMAN WITH CHILDREN: Let me through, let me through!

The kids are so 'ungry they're screaming their 'eads off. Get
'em watching and it'll shut 'em up. Let me through!

A WOMAN: Hey Danton, you can fuck the worms now!

ANOTHER WOMAN: Hérault, that gorgeous 'air of yours: make
me a lovely wig!

HERAULT: A bald old cunt like you needs more thatch than I've
got.

CAMILLE: Bloody witches! Go on, quote the Bible: 'Fall upon us,
ye mountains'!

A WOMAN: The mountain already 'as fallen on yer, or else
you've fallen down the mountainside![125]

DANTON [to Camille]: Calm down, lad, you've yelled yourself
hoarse.

CAMILLE [gives the Carter money]: There you are, Charon,[126]
your cart makes a good serving-dish. Gentlemen, let me be the
hors d'oeuvre. A truly Roman banquet: we lie down to eat,
and by way of libation we spill some blood. Goodbye, Danton.
[He ascends the scaffold, the other prisoners following one after the
other. Danton is the last.]

LACROIX [to the people]: You're killing us on the day you lost
your reason. The day you get it back again – you'll kill
them.

SUNDRY VOICES: We've 'eard that one before! 'Ow boring![127]

LACROIX: The tyrants will trip on our graves and break their
necks.

HERAULT [to Danton]: He reckons his corpse'll be the hot-bed of
freedom!

PHILIPPEAU [on the scaffold]: I forgive you all. May your hour
of death be no bitterer than mine.

HERAULT: I knew it! Trust him to bare his heart just to prove to
that lot his underwear's clean!

FABRE: Goodbye, Danton. I'm dying twice over.

DANTON: Goodbye, my friend, there's no better doctor than the
guillotine.

HERAULT [tries to embrace Danton]: Damn it, Danton, I can't
even manage a joke any more. It's time. [An executioner pushes
him back.]

DANTON [to the executioner]: Do you want to be crueller than death itself? Can you prevent our heads from kissing each other in the basket?

Scene 8: A street

LUCILE: There's something in it after all, something serious. I do want to think about it. I'm beginning to understand such things. Words like 'die', 'die' –

Everything else is allowed to go on living, this tiny insect here, that bird. Why not him? The stream of life should stop aghast if even a single drop is spilt. The earth should show a gaping wound from such a blow.

Everything's astir: clocks tick, bells ring, folk pass, water flows, everything continues just as before, for ever and for ever. – But no! It mustn't happen, no! I shall sit on the ground and scream, so everything stops, shocked into stillness, not a flicker of movement. [*She sits down, covers her eyes, and screams. After a pause, she stands up.*]

It makes no difference. Things are just as they were. The houses, the street. The wind blows, the clouds drift. – Perhaps we just have to bear it.

A group of WOMEN *come along the street.*

1st WOMAN: Good-looking man, that Hérault.
2nd WOMAN: When I saw 'im standing there by the triumphal arch at the Festival of the Constitution,[128] I said to meself, 'Well 'e'll look good on the guillotine,' honest I did. Talk about seeing the future!
3rd WOMAN: You've got to see these people in all possible circumstances: what a good thing dying's so public these days. [*They disappear again.*]
LUCILE: Dear Camille! Where do I look for you now!

72

Scene 9: The Place de la Révolution

Two EXECUTIONERS *busy about the guillotine.*

1st EXECUTIONER [*standing on the guillotine, singing*]:
    When home I go
    The moon's a-glow
    Shining on me grandpa's door
2nd EXECUTIONER: Hey, aren't you finished yet?
1st EXECUTIONER: Give us a minute!
    'You sod' he cries
    With blazing eyes
    'Doing it so long with a bloody whore!'
Right, that's it. Chuck us me jacket! [*They exit, singing.*]
    When home I go
    The moon's aglow
    Shining on me grandpa's door.
LUCILE [*enters and sits on the steps of the guillotine*]: Silent angel of death, I sit on your lap. [*She sings*]
    There is a reaper, Death by name,
    Whose power from God Almighty came.
Dear cradle, you lulled my Camille to sleep, you smothered him with roses red.
You darling passing-bell, you sang him to his grave with voice so sweet. [*She sings*]
    Countless are the myriad lives
    That fall beneath his sweeping scythe.

A PATROL *enters.*

A CITIZEN: Who goes there?
LUCILE: Long live the King![129]
CITIZEN: In the name of the Republic!

She is surrounded by the guards and led away.

LEONCE AND LENA

A Comedy

Preface[1]

Alfieri: 'E la fama?'
Gozzi: 'E la fame?'

CHARACTERS

King Peter *of the Kingdom of Bum*
Prince Leonce *his son, betrothed to*
Princess Lena *of the Kingdom of Piddle*
Valerio
The Governess
The Court Tutor
The Master of Ceremonies
The President of the Privy Council
The Court Chaplain
The Local Prefect
The Schoolmaster
Rosetta

Servants, privy councillors, peasants, etc.

ACT I

'Oh that I were a fool!
I am ambitious for a motley coat.'
As You Like It

Scene 1: A garden[2]

LEONCE *half lying on a bench. The* TUTOR.

LEONCE: Well, sir, what do you want of me? Prepare me for my job in life – is that it? I'm up to my eyes in work, I'm so busy I don't know which way to turn. First of all, d'you see, I have to spit on this stone here 365 times in a row. Haven't you ever tried it? *Do* try it, it's most extraordinarily diverting. And then – do you see this handful of sand? [*He picks sand up, throws it in the air, and catches it again on the back of his hand.*] – Up it goes! Let's have a bet, shall we? How many grains do I have on the back of my hand? Odds or evens? – What?! You don't want to bet? Do you believe in God? Or are you a heathen? I bet against myself as a rule, I can do it for days at a time. If you can drum up someone who'd fancy a bet with me, I'd be most profoundly obliged. And then of course I must ponder the problem of how I might contrive to see the top of my head. Oh what bliss if we could catch but a glimpse of the top of our head! It's one of my ideals. It would help me enormously. And then – and then an infinitude of tasks of a similar nature. – Am I an idler? Am I without occupation? – Ah yes, it is sad . . .

TUTOR: Very sad, your Highness.

LEONCE: . . . sad that the clouds have gone on drifting from west to east for three whole weeks. It fills me with melancholy.

TUTOR: Quite right, your Highness, such justified melancholy.

LEONCE: For God's sake, man, why don't you contradict me? You have urgent business to attend to, do you not? *So* sorry to have kept you. [*The* TUTOR *withdraws with a deep bow.*] Congratulations, dear sir, on performing such an exquisitely bow-legged bow!

LEONCE [*alone, stretches out on the bench*]: How lethargic the bees are, lolling on their flowers, how sluggish the sunlight sprawled across the ground. A terrible idleness teems on every hand. – Idleness is the fount of all the vices. – The things people do out of sheer boredom! They study out of boredom; they pray out of boredom; they fall in love, get married and reproduce out of boredom; in the end they die out of boredom. What's more – and that's the joke of it all – they do it with the most earnest of faces, without realizing why, and thinking God-knows-what in the process. All these fearless heroes, these idiots and geniuses, these saints and sinners, these fecund fathers – in the end they're nothing but well-disguised loafers. But why does it have to be *me* that knows it? Why can't I take myself seriously like everyone else and stuff this poor puppet of a body into a nice smart coat, stick an umbrella in its hand, and turn it into something thoroughly decent, thoroughly useful and thoroughly moral? That fellow that left me just now, I envied him so, I could have beaten him black and blue out of pure envy. What bliss to be someone else for once! If only for a single minute! – My God, how the fellow runs! If only I knew of a single thing in the world that could still make me run.

Enter VALERIO, *somewhat drunk.*

VALERIO [*places himself directly in front of the Prince, puts his finger on his nose, and stares at him fixedly*]: Yes!

LEONCE [*follows suit*]: Quite right!

VALERIO: You grasp my meaning?

LEONCE: Absolutely.

VALERIO: Right, then let's change the subject. [*He lies down in the grass.*] In the meantime I shall deposit myself in the grass and let my nose sprout forth amidst the blades of green and inhale romantic sensations whilst the bees and butterflies rock themselves on it as though on a rose.

LEONCE: Easy, old chap, you're snorting at the flowers like a giant taking snuff: the bees and butterflies will starve to death.

VALERIO: Ah sir, I have such a feeling for nature! The grass is such a splendid sight I'd like to be an ox to gobble it up, then a man once again to gobble the ox that gobbled the grass.

LEONCE: Poor wretch: you too, it seems, are afflicted by ideals.

VALERIO: It fair makes you weep. You can't jump off a church tower without breaking your neck. You can't eat four pounds of cherries, stones and all, without getting the runs. I tell you, sir, I could squat in a corner from dusk till dawn singing, 'Heigh ho there's a fly on the wall, a fly on the wall, a fly on the wall!' – just like that, over and over, till the day I die.

LEONCE: Enough, enough! That song of yours – it's enough to drive a man mad.

VALERIO: At least then you'd *be* something. A madman! A madman! Who'll trade me his madness for my sanity? Hey presto: I'm Alexander the Great! See how my uniform sparkles, how a crown of sunlight glints in my hair! Generalissimo Grasshopper, sound the advance! Finance Minister Frog, I need some cash! Dear Lady Dragonfly, how fares my beloved Queen Beanpole? Oh, Dr Cantharides, I'm desperate for an heir![3] And on top of these delectable delusions you get good soup, good meat, good bread, a good bed and your hair cut for nothing – in the madhouse, that is. But as for me with my impeccable sanity: I'd be lucky if it earned me a job in a cherry tree helping the fruit to get ripe by – by – well come on then: help me!

LEONCE: By making the cherries go red with embarrassment at the holes in your trousers! But tell me, most nobly noble sir: your work, your trade, your profession, your station, your craft?

VALERIO [*with dignity*]: Sir, my consuming occupation is to be thoroughly idle, I am uncommonly skilled at doing nothing, I have colossal endurance in the realm of laziness. Not a single callus defiles my hands, the earth has drunk not a drop from my brow, I'm an absolute virgin where work is concerned, and if it wasn't just too much trouble I should gladly take the trouble to explain these virtues at greater length.

LEONCE [*with comic enthusiasm*]: Come to my breast! Are you one of those spirits divine that glide without effort and unbesmirched through the dust and sweat of the teeming highway of life, then enter Olympus like blessed gods with shining feet and pristine bodies? Come to me! Come!

VALERIO [*singing*]: Heigh ho there's a fly on the wall, a fly on the wall, a fly on the wall! [*Exit both, arm in arm.*]

Scene 2: A room

KING PETER *is being dressed by two* VALETS.

PETER[4] [*while he is being dressed*]: Man must think, and I must think for my subjects, for they never think at all, they never think at all. – The essence is the in-itself, and that is me. [*He runs around the room almost naked.*] Have you got that? The in-itself is the in-itself, do you understand? Now it's the turn of my attributes, accidents, properties and modifications: where is my shirt, where are my trousers? – Stop, how disgusting, free will is a wide-open issue down there. Where is morality: where are my shirt-cuffs? My categories are in the most scandalous confusion: two buttons too many have been done up, my snuffbox is sitting in the right-hand pocket. My entire system is ruined. – Aha! What does this knot in my handkerchief mean? Well, man, what is the meaning of this knot, of what did I desire to remind myself?

FIRST VALET: When it pleased your Royal Majesty to tie this knot in your royal handkerchief, your Royal Majesty desired to . . .

PETER: Well?

FIRST VALET: To remind yourself of something.

PETER: What a convoluted answer! – Well now, what do *you* think?

SECOND VALET: Your Royal Majesty desired to remind yourself of something when it pleased your Royal Majesty to tie this knot in your royal handkerchief.

PETER [*running back and forth*]: What? What? These people are making me all muddled, I am in the most appalling confusion. I don't know which way to turn.

Enter a SERVANT.

SERVANT: Your Majesty, the Privy Council is assembled.

PETER [*joyfully*]: Yes, that's it, that's it – I wanted to remind myself of my people. Come, gentlemen! Walk symmetrically. Isn't it very hot? You too, now: take your handkerchiefs and wipe your faces. I get so flustered when I have to speak in public. [*Exit all.*]

KING PETER, *the* PRIVY COUNCIL.

PETER: My dear and faithful subjects, I wanted herewith to declare and announce, to declare and announce ... – for my son shall either marry, or not marry, [*places his finger against his nose*] either, or – you understand me surely. There is no third alternative. Man must think. [*Stands for a while thinking.*] Whenever I speak out loud like that, I never know who it really is, me or someone else, it frightens me. [*After long reflection*] I am me. – President, what is your opinion on the matter?

PRESIDENT [*slowly and gravely*]: Your Majesty, it may be the case, but then again it may not be the case.

THE ENTIRE PRIVY COUNCIL [*in chorus*]: Yes, it may be the case, but then again it may not be the case.

PETER [*with emotion*]: Oh how wise you are! – But what were we talking about? What was it I wanted to say? President, why do you have such a very short memory on such a solemn occasion? I hereby declare this session closed. [*He makes a solemn departure, followed by the entire Privy Council.*]

Scene 3: A richly appointed room. Candles burning

LEONCE *with various* SERVANTS.

LEONCE: Are the shutters all shut? Light the candles! Do away with the day! I want night, deep ambrosian night. Set the lamps beneath crystal domes amongst the oleanders so they glint between the leaves like the flickering eyes of sleeping, dreaming girls. Move the roses closer, so the wine can bathe their blooms like drops of dew. Music! Where are the violins? Where is Rosetta? Away with you! All of you away!

Exit the SERVANTS. LEONCE *stretches out on a couch. Enter* ROSETTA, *delicately dressed. Distant music.*

ROSETTA [*approaches with tender flattery*]: Leonce!
LEONCE: Rosetta!
ROSETTA: Leonce!
LEONCE: Rosetta!
ROSETTA: Your lips are tired. From kissing?
LEONCE: From yawning!
ROSETTA: Oh!
LEONCE: Alas, Rosetta, I have the appalling task . . .
ROSETTA: Go on!
LEONCE: Of doing nothing . . .
ROSETTA: Except loving?
LEONCE: Hard labour, that is!
ROSETTA [*hurt*]: Leonce!
LEONCE: Or it's my kind of pastime?
ROSETTA: Or your kind of laziness?
LEONCE: You're right, as always. What a clever girl you are, I do so appreciate your penetrating insights.
ROSETTA: So you love me out of boredom?
LEONCE: No, I'm bored because I love you. But I love my boredom as much as you. You're one and the same. Oh *dolce far niente*, I look into your eyes and dream as though gazing into wondrous deep and secret streams, your lips caress me to sleep like murmuring waves. [*He puts his arms around her.*] Come, dear boredom, your kisses are a lascivious yawn, your every step a delicate emptiness.
ROSETTA: Do you love me, Leonce?
LEONCE: Why not, after all?
ROSETTA: And for ever?
LEONCE: It's a long word, 'for ever'! If I love you for another five thousand years and seven months, will that be long enough? It's admittedly much less than for ever, but it's quite a good while all the same, and we can take our time with our loving.
ROSETTA: Or time can take our love away.
LEONCE: Or love can take our time away. Dance, Rosetta, dance, so that time goes by to the rhythmic beat of your pretty little feet.

ROSETTA: My feet would sooner go out of time. [*She dances and sings*]

> My poor, tired feet, you have to dance
>> In shoes so gay,
> And yet you'd sooner rest deep, deep
>> Beneath the clay.
>
> My poor, hot cheeks, you have to flare
>> With passion's might
> For all the pallor you would sooner wear
>> Of roses white.
>
> My poor, poor eyes, you have to sparkle
>> In the candles' light,
> And yet to flee your pain you'd sooner sleep
>> In darkest night.

LEONCE [*meanwhile talking dreamily to himself*]: Oh, a dying love is far more beautiful than one that's growing. A Roman, that's what I am: to bring the glorious banquet to a fitting close the golden fish disport themselves in all the colours of their dying agony.[5] See how the red of her cheeks dies away, how quietly the fire in her eye goes out, how gently the lilt of her limbs first quickens, then fades! *Addio, addio*, my love, I'll cherish your corpse. [ROSETTA *approaches once more.*] Tears, Rosetta? What subtle epicureans[6] are they that can cry! Go stand in the sun to make these precious droplets turn to crystal, what fantastic diamonds it would yield. You can make a necklace out of them.

ROSETTA: Diamonds, yes: I can feel them cutting into my eyes. Oh Leonce! [*Tries to embrace him.*]

LEONCE: Be careful! My head! I've buried the corpse of our love in there. Look through the windows of my eyes. Do you see how beautifully dead the poor thing is? See the two white roses on her cheeks, the red ones on her breast? Don't touch me, one of her tiny arms might break off – such a pity if it did. I shall have to carry my head quite straight on my shoulders, like a weeper bearing the coffin of a child.

ROSETTA [*playfully*]: You're mad!

LEONCE: Rosetta! [*Rosetta makes a face at him.*] Thank God! [*Covers his eyes.*]

ROSETTA [*frightened*]: Leonce, look at me.

LEONCE: Not for anything!

ROSETTA: Just once!

LEONCE: Not even once! Are you crying? It wouldn't take much for my darling love to be reborn. I'm glad I've buried her. I'll cherish the memory.

ROSETTA [*moves away slowly and sadly, singing as she leaves*]:

Such a poor waif am I
   So frightened on my own
Oh dear grief I beg you –
   Won't you take me home?

LEONCE [*alone*]: What a strange thing love is. You lie abed for an entire year in a kind of dream, then one fine morning you wake up, drink a glass of water, put on your clothes, pass your hand across your forehead, and you come to your senses – you just come to your senses. – My God, how many women does a man need to sing his way right up and down the scale of love? Any one woman covers scarce but a single tone. Why is the haze above our earth a prism that splits the white-hot stream of love into all the different colours of the rainbow? – [*He drinks.*] So where's the wine I'm to get drunk on today? Or won't I manage even that? I sit as though in a vacuum-jar. The air's so sharp and thin I feel as cold as if I were skating in winter in cotton trousers. – Gentlemen, gentlemen, do you know what Nero and Caligula were? *I* know.[7] – Come on, Leonce, give me a monologue, I'm willing to listen to every word. My life gapes at me like a great white sheet of paper that I'm supposed to fill with writing, but I can't manage even a single letter. My head is an empty dance hall, on its floor a few wilted roses and crumpled ribbons, in a corner the remnants of broken violins, the last few dancers have removed their masks and gaze at one another with dead-tired eyes. I turn myself inside-out twenty-four times a day, like a glove. Oh yes, I know myself. I know what I'll be dreaming and thinking in a quarter of an hour, a week, a year. God, what ever have I done that you make me recite my lesson so often, like a naughty schoolboy? –

Bravo, Leonce! Bravo! [*He claps.*] It gives me a real kick to call out to myself like that. Hey! Leonce! Leonce!

VALERIO [*appears from under a table*]: Seems to me your Highness is well on the way to becoming a fully fledged lunatic.

LEONCE: Yes, all things considered, that's just how it seems to me as well.

VALERIO: Hold on, we'll discuss the matter at greater length in a moment. I've just got one more hunk of meat to scoff that I pinched from the kitchens, and a bit of wine I stole from your table. It won't take long.

LEONCE: How he smacks his chops! What idyllic sensations the fellow arouses in me; I could start again with the simplest of things: eat cheese, drink beer, smoke tobacco. Get on with it, but less of that grunting and snorting, and do stop gnashing those fangs of yours!

VALERIO: Most worthy Adonis,[8] do you fear for your legs? Don't worry, I'm neither broom-maker nor schoolmaster: such thin little sticks are no use to me.

LEONCE: You certainly give as good as you get!

VALERIO: I wish I could say the same for my master.

LEONCE: You mean, so you never miss out on the beatings you need? Are you really so worried about your education?

VALERIO: God knows, it's a damned sight easier to father a brat than further its education. It's terribly sad how a Happy Event can eventuate in unhappiness! What labours I've been through since my mother was in labour! No good that I can conceive of ever came from my conception.

LEONCE: Concerning your conceits I am quite unconcerned. Express yourself better, or I shall impress upon you my irrepressible displeasure.

VALERIO: When my expectant mother finally made it round the Cape of Good Hope . . .[9]

LEONCE: And your father came to grief on Cape Horn . . .

VALERIO: Quite right, he was a night-watchman after all. Even so, he didn't put his horn to his lips as often as the fathers of princes get horns on their heads.[10]

LEONCE: Your barefaced cheek, sir, is out of this world. I feel a decided need to get in contact with it. I have this passionate desire to beat you black and blue.

VALERIO: What pugnacious logic, what a striking reply.

LEONCE [makes to attack him]: You'll be struck for sure: I'll give you a thrashing for answering me back.

VALERIO [runs out of the way, Leonce stumbles and falls]: And you are an argument that remains to be proved, considering the tangle your legs are in; in fact your legs themselves will take some proving: your calves are incredible, your thighs problematical.

Enter the PRIVY COUNCIL. LEONCE *remains sitting on the floor.* VALERIO.

PRESIDENT: Your Highness, forgive me –

LEONCE: I do, I do, just as I forgive myself for my extravagant generosity in listening to you speak. Gentlemen, won't you take a seat? – What a terrible face these people make when they hear the word 'seat'! Just squat on the ground, and don't be embarrassed – after all, sooner or later it'll be the last position you ever fill, though there's nothing in it except for the gravedigger.

PRESIDENT [snapping his fingers in embarrassment]: If it please your Highness –

LEONCE: Stop snapping your fingers like that, or you'll drive me to murder.

PRESIDENT [snapping his fingers ever harder]: If you would be so kind, so extremely kind, in view of the fact –

LEONCE: For God's sake stick your hands in your pocket, or sit on them! He's gone completely to pieces. Pull yourself together.

VALERIO: Never interrupt a child in the middle of a piss: it can never get going again.

LEONCE: Get a grip, man! Spare a thought for your family and the nation. Lose your power of speech and you could suffer a stroke.

PRESIDENT [draws a paper from his pocket]: If your Highness will allow me –

LEONCE: Good heavens, you can read!? Right then, let's have it . . .

PRESIDENT: What his Royal Majesty is pleased to convey to

your Highness is the news that the keenly awaited arrival of your Highness's bride, her Most Serene Highness Princess Lena of Piddle, may be expected tomorrow.

LEONCE: If my bride is awaiting me, then I shall do her the favour of letting her wait. I saw her last night in a dream, her eyes were so huge that Rosetta's dancing-shoes would have done her for eyebrows, and instead of dimples in her cheeks she had cesspits each side to devour her laughter. I have a lot of faith in dreams. How about you, President, do you dream sometimes? Do you have premonitions?

VALERIO: Of course he does. Like clockwork, the night before the royal roast gets burnt, a capon kicks the bucket, or his Royal Majesty gets gut-rot.

LEONCE: By the way, isn't there something else you wanted to say? Spit it all out.

PRESIDENT: It is the supreme royal will that on the day of your wedding all the instruments of the most supreme royal will shall pass into your Highness's hands.

LEONCE: Kindly inform his supreme Willynillyness that I shall attend to everything save that which I shall ignore, which however will be decidedly less than if it were twice as much. – Gentlemen, you will excuse me if I do not escort you to the door, but I have a passion at present for remaining seated. Nevertheless, my graciousness is so great that even my legs are inadequate to measure it. [*He spreads his legs apart.*] President, I beg you, measure the distance, so you can remind me of it later. Valerio, show the gentlemen out.

VALERIO: Shoo them out? What, like a herd of cattle? Perhaps I should fasten a bell on the President?

LEONCE: Good heavens, man, you're nothing but a walking pun, and a bad one to boot. You're the fruit of libidinous vowels, not ordinary mortals.

VALERIO: And you, dear Prince, are a book without letters, full of nothing but dashes. – Come now, gentlemen. There's something very sad about the word 'come': if it's income you want, you have to steal; to come up in the world you have to be hanged; the ultimate outcome is when you are buried; but when it comes down to it you can rely on your wits when

you've run out of words, like me right now, or you even *before*
you have opened your mouth. There, gentlemen, you've had
your come-uppance, so seek – I beseech you – a comely
departure. [*Exit* PRIVY COUNCIL *and* VALERIO.]

LEONCE [*alone*]: How mean I am to lord it so over those poor
devils! But there's no denying it, there's a certain pleasure to
be had from a certain meanness. – Hm! Marriage! You might
as well try to drink a well dry. Oh Shandy, dear Shandy, if only
someone would give me your clock![11] – [VALERIO *returns*.] My
God, Valerio, did you hear what he said?

VALERIO: So you're to be king: what a laugh that'll be! You'll
be able to swan around the countryside all day in your carriage
ruining folks' hats with the constant doffing; you'll be able to
reduce proper people into proper little soldiers as if that was
the most natural thing in the world; you'll be able to convert
black frock-coats and white neckties into public servants; and
then when you die all the mirror-bright buttons will go blue in
the face and the bells will be tolled so much their ropes will
part like rotten string. Won't that be fun?!

LEONCE: Valerio! Valerio! We need to do something completely
different. What's your advice?!

VALERIO: There's the world of learning, how about that? Let's
become philosophers! A priori? Or a posteriori?

LEONCE: A priori – that's something my venerable father could
teach us. A posteriori – that's how everything begins, like an
olden-day fairy-tale: Once upon a time . . .

VALERIO: Then let's become heroes. [*He marches up and down
making drum and bugle noises*.] Brrr-oom! Pah-pah!

LEONCE: But heroism wears so terribly thin, gets stricken with
the fever, and can't survive without new recruits and rash
lieutenants. You and your Alexander-the-Great and Napoleon
romanticism!

VALERIO: Then let's become literary geniuses.

LEONCE: The nightingale of poetry is around us all day with its
beautiful song, but the best of it has gone to the devil by the
time we've torn out the feathers and dipped them in paint or
ink.

VALERIO: Then let's become useful members of human society.

LEONCE: I'd sooner resign from the human race.

VALERIO: Then let's go to the devil.

LEONCE: Alas the devil's only there for the sake of the contrast, to make us appreciate that there really is something in heaven after all. [*Jumps to his feet.*] Valerio, Valerio! I've got it! Can't you feel the wafting spirit of the South? Can't you feel the rhythmic pulsing of its ardent, azure air? The light glinting on the golden, sun-splashed earth, the sacred sea, the ancient marble columns and bodies? Pan the great god sleeps, and in the shade above the distant roar of waves the mighty figures dream of Virgil and his ancient magic, of tarantellas and tambourines, of torrid, teeming nights alive with masks, guitars and flickering torches. Lazzaroni, Valerio, let's be lazzaroni![12] It's Italy we'll go to![13]

Scene 4: A garden[14]

PRINCESS LENA *in bridal array, the* GOVERNESS.

LENA: Yes, it's here. It's now. I never bothered my head at all. Time slipped slowly by. And all of a sudden the 'special day' is full upon me. A wreath of flowers adorns my hair – and the bells, the bells! [*She leans back and shuts her eyes.*] See, if only the grass would grow up all around me and the bees go humming above my head. See now, I'm fully robed, with sprigs of rosemary in my hair.[15] Isn't there an old song:

In the churchyard bury me deep

Let me like a baby sleep –

GOVERNESS: Poor child, how pale you are beneath your sparkling jewels.

LENA: Oh God, I could fall in love, of course I could. We're so alone, after all, and grope in the dark for a hand to clasp until we die and our hands are loosed and laid out each on our separate chests. But why drive a nail through hands that never sought each other? What has my poor hand done to deserve it? [*She takes a ring off her finger.*] This ring is like a viper's sting.

GOVERNESS: Yes, but – they say he's a real Don Carlos.[16]

LENA: Yes, but – he's a man . . .

GOVERNESS: Go on –

LENA: . . . a man for whom I feel no love. [*She gets up.*] O fie, what shame I feel! – Tomorrow all my bloom and fragrance will be gone. Am I like the poor, helpless stream that must needs mirror in its silent depths whatever images appear above it? Even the flowers open and shut as they wish to the morning sun and the evening breeze. Is the daughter of a king then less than a flower?

GOVERNESS [*weeping*]: Poor angel: you're such a little lamb, and they're taking you to slaughter.

LENA: Yes – and the priest has the knife already poised in his hand. – My God, my God, is it really true that redemption comes only through our own pain? Is it really true that the earth is a crucified Christ, the sun his crown of thorns, and the stars the nails in his feet, the spears in his side?

GOVERNESS: My child, my child! I can't bear to see you like this. It can't go on like this – it's killing you. Perhaps, who knows! I have an idea. We'll have to see. Come! [*She leads the Princess away.*]

ACT II

A wondrous voice has sounded
Deep within me,
And silenced at a single stroke
My strident memory![17]
Adalbert von Chamisso

Scene 1: Open country. An inn in the background

Enter LEONCE *and* VALERIO, *the latter carrying a bundle.*

VALERIO [*panting*]: Some mansion this world is, Prince, I'm telling you: space, space, then more space!

LEONCE: No, not at all. To me it's like a narrow hall of mirrors: I scarcely dare stretch out my hands, for fear of banging into it on every side and finding the beautiful pictures lying in pieces at my feet, and there before my eyes the bare, blank wall.[18]

VALERIO: I'm lost.

LEONCE: That's nobody's loss but his that finds you.

VALERIO: I'll take a rest quite soon in my shadow's shadow.

LEONCE: You're evaporating clean away in the sun! See that beautiful cloud up there? It contains at least a quarter of you. It's gazing down in perfect contentment upon your grosser material self.

VALERIO: It wouldn't harm your own head if they shaved it bare and made the cloud fall on it drip by drip in the best Chinese fashion. – What an appealing idea! We've already passed through a dozen principalities, half-a-dozen grand-duchies and a couple of kingdoms, at breakneck speed in half a day,[19] and why? Because you're to be king and marry a beautiful princess. What a *ghastly* prospect – and you carry on living?! Your resignation is quite beyond me. It's beyond me why you haven't swallowed arsenic, climbed onto the parapet of a high church tower, and put a bullet through your brain, just to make sure.

LEONCE: Ideals, Valerio, ideals! I have this ideal of a woman within me and must go and seek it. She is infinitely beautiful and infinitely mindless. Her beauty is as helpless and touching as a newborn child. Such an exquisite contrast: these eyes of heavenly stupidity, this mouth of godlike inanity, this profile of asinine sublimity, this deadness of mind in this spiritual body.[20]

VALERIO: Can you beat it, we're back at the border! This country's like an onion: skin within skin within skin. Or like Chinese boxes: in the bigger boxes smaller boxes, in the smallest box – nothing. [*He throws his bundle on the ground.*] Is this bundle to be my gravestone? There you are, Prince, I am becoming philosophical: a perfect image of human life. I hump this bundle with bleeding feet through freezing snow and scorching sun, just because I like a clean shirt of an evening. And when at last the evening comes, I have sunken eyes, a furrowed brow and hollow cheeks, and just enough time to pull on my shirt – to serve as my shroud. Wouldn't I have been wiser to take the bundle from its stick, flog it at the next best inn, get drunk on the proceeds, then sleep in the shade until evening came? – That way I'd have avoided the pouring sweat and the painful corns. And now, Prince, it's time to apply our new theory in practice. Out of sheer modesty we shall now proceed to clothe the inner man in jacket and trousers. [*Both start towards the inn.*] Well, dear bundle, what about that! – Such delectable smells, such sweet aromas of roast and wine! And you, dear trousers, you're taking root, you're sprouting, you're bursting with fruit, great clusters of grapes are dangling in my mouth, the press is at work and the juice is bubbling. [*Exit both.*]

PRINCESS LENA, *the* GOVERNESS.

GOVERNESS: The day is bewitched, I'm sure: the sun's not going down, and it's such an eternity since we made our escape.

LENA: Not at all, dear heart, the goodbye flowers I picked as we left the garden have scarcely wilted.

GOVERNESS: And where shall we sleep? We've come across nothing at all so far. Wherever I look: no cloister, no hermit, not even a shepherd.

LENA: Our dreams were very different, I suppose, as we read our books behind the walls of our garden amidst myrtle and oleander.

GOVERNESS: Oh how disgusting the world is! And not the slightest chance of a wandering prince.

LENA: Oh how beautiful the world is, and oh so wide, so infinitely wide. I'd like to carry on like this for ever, night and day. Nothing stirs. The red of the cuckoo-flowers glows and dances over the meadow, and the distant mountains rest on the earth like slumbering clouds.

GOVERNESS: Oh dear Jesus, what *will* people say? And yet it's all so delicate and feminine! It's self-denial, that's what it is. It's like the sacred flight of St Ottilia.[21] But we *must* find shelter – it's getting late.

LENA: Yes, the plants are closing their tiny leaves for sleep, the rays of sunlight nod on the slender blades of grass like tired dragonflies.

Scene 2: Inn in elevated position by a river, with views into the far distance. The garden of the inn

VALERIO, LEONCE.

VALERIO: Well, Prince, don't your trousers make for a delicious drink? Don't your boots slip down your throat with the greatest of ease?

LEONCE: See the ancient trees, the hedges, the flowers? They all have their stories to tell, their own precious little secret stories. See the ancient friendly faces amongst the vines by the door? Look how they sit there clasping their hands, afraid because they're so old and the world so young. Oh Valerio, I'm so young and the world so old. I get frightened for myself at times and could sit in a corner and weep hot tears out of sheer self-pity.

VALERIO [gives him a glass]: Take this bell, this diver's bell, and sink into a sea of wine so it froths and sparkles above your head. See, above the delicate bloom of the wine, the hovering elves with shoes of gold and tinkling cymbals.

LEONCE [jumping up]: Come on, Valerio, we must do something, we must do something! Let's busy ourselves with profound thoughts. Let's consider the serious question of why a chair stays standing on three legs but not on two, and why we wipe our noses with our fingers and not with our feet, like the flies. Come, let's anatomize ants and count the filaments of flowers – I shall yet contrive to embrace some princely pastime or other! I shall yet discover some infantile bauble that only drops from my fingers when I turn up my toes. I still have a sizeable dose of enthusiasm to use up – but once I've got it all nicely warmed, it takes me an eternity to find a suitable spoon, and in the meantime it's all gone cold again.

VALERIO: Ergo bibamus![22] This bottle is neither demanding

lover nor mere idea, causes no birth-pains, never gets boring and never unfaithful, is consistently the same from first drop to last. Break its seal, and all the slumbering dreams within it burst forth to greet you.

LEONCE: O God! I'll give half my life to prayer if you grant me but a single straw to clutch at and ride like a mighty stallion until the day I'm laid on straw myself. – What a strange, uncanny evening. Down below, a perfect stillness; up above, the fleeting, shifting clouds, the sun appearing, disappearing. See those strange figures up there all chasing one another, those long white shadows with terrifying matchstick legs and batlike wings – and all such swirling turmoil, while down below nothing stirs, not a leaf, not a single blade of grass. The earth has curled into a ball of fear, like a stricken child, and above its cradle the ghosts go marching.

VALERIO: I don't know what you're on about, I'm in a lovely mood, perfectly lovely. The sun looks like an inn sign, the fiery clouds above it are its legend: 'The Golden Sun'. The earth and river down there are like a wine-splashed table, and we're lying upon it like playing-cards that God and the Devil are having a game with out of pure boredom. You're the King, I'm the Knave, all we need is a Queen, a beautiful Queen with a great big heart adorning her chest and a very long nose sentimentally buried in a mighty tulip [*enter the* GOVERNESS *and the* PRINCESS] and – by God, there she is! But it's not really a tulip, it's a pinch of snuff, and it's not really a nose, it's a giant proboscis. [*To the Governess*] Why, dear lady, do you stride so fast that we can see your once-comely calves all the way up to your supremely respectable garters?

GOVERNESS [*stops, extremely angry*]: Why, dear sir, do you open your trap so wide that you make a hole in the outlook?

VALERIO: So that you, dear lady, don't bloody your nose by colliding with the horizon. Thy nose is as the tower of Lebanon which looketh towards Damascus.[23]

LENA [*to the Governess*]: Dearest, tell me, is the way so long?

LEONCE [*dreaming to himself*]: Oh, every way is long! The ticking deathwatch in our breast is slow, each drop of blood is measured in its pace, our entire life's a creeping fever. For tired feet, every way is long . . .

LENA [*who has listened to him with anxious thoughtfulness*]: And for tired eyes every light's too harsh, for tired lips every breath too hard, [*smiling*] for tired ears every word too much. [*Enters the inn with the Governess.*]

LEONCE: Oh, dear Valerio, couldn't Hamlet's words be mine as well: 'Would not this, sir, and a forest of feathers, with two Provençal roses on my razed shoes, get me a fellowship in a cry of players?'[24] I do think I said it with perfect melancholy. Thank God I'm beginning to be delivered of my melancholy. The air is no longer so clear and cold, the heavens descend and fold me in their hot embrace, and welcome droplets fall at last. – Oh, that voice: 'Is the way so long?' Many voices speak over the earth and you think they speak of other things, but this one I have understood. It rests upon me like the spirit that hung over the waters before the coming of the light. Such ferment in the deepest depths, such burgeoning of life within me – oh how the voice goes coursing through the very air – 'Is the way so long?' [*Exit.*]

VALERIO: No. The way to the madhouse is not so long, it's easy to find, I know every footpath, side-road and highway. Already I can see him heading that way along an avenue of trees on an ice-cold day in the middle of winter, holding his hat beneath his arm and stepping amongst the barren trees and their longdrawn shadows, fanning his face with his pocket handkerchief. – He's mad, quite mad. [*Follows him off.*]

Scene 3: A room

LENA, *the* GOVERNESS.

GOVERNESS: Don't think about the creature!

LENA: He was so old beneath his golden curls. Spring on his cheeks, and winter in his heart. How sad.[25] A tired body can always find a pillow, but when the spirit is tired, where shall it rest? A terrible thought occurs to my mind: I believe there are

people unhappy, incurably unhappy, simply because they *exist*.
[*She gets up.*]

GOVERNESS: Where are you going, my child?

LENA: I want to go down to the garden.

GOVERNESS: But listen –

LENA: But listen – you know what I'm like: I should really have
been planted in a flowerpot. I need dew and night air as
the flowers do. Do you hear the gentle chorus of the evening? The
way the day is lulled to sleep by the song of crickets, the scent
of gillyflowers! I can't stay cooped up here. The walls of the
room are collapsing on top of me.

Scene 4: The garden. Night and moonshine

LENA *sitting on the grass.* VALERIO *some way off.*

VALERIO: It's all very lovely, nature is – but it'd be a damned
sight lovelier without gnats to sting you, bed-bugs to bite you,
or deathwatch beetles ticking in the walls. And what a din! –
In there, people snoring, out here, frogs croaking; house-crickets
racketing inside, field-crickets racketing outside. Well, dear
lawn, I'm all forlorn. [*He lies down on the grass.*]

LEONCE [*enters*]: Oh night, as balmy as the first that sank on
Paradise. [*He notices the Princess and silently draws near to her.*]

LENA [*to herself*]: A songbird twittered in its dreams, the night
slips deeper into sleep, her cheek grows paler, her breath more
quiet. The moon is like a sleeping child, its golden curls have
tumbled over its tender face. – Oh, its sleep is death. Look: a
dead angel lying on his cushion of black, with stars for candles
all around him. Poor child, are the bogeymen coming to get
you? Where's your mother? Won't she give you one last kiss?
Oh the sadness of it – dead, and so alone.

LEONCE: Arise in your dress so white and walk through the
night behind the corpse to sing its threnody.[26]

LENA: Who speaks?

LEONCE: A dream.

LENA: But dreams are blessed.

LEONCE: Then dream yourself blessed and let me be your blessed dream.

LENA: The most blessed dream of all is death.

LEONCE: Then let me be your angel of death, and let my lips descend like angels' wings upon your eyes. [*He kisses her.*] You beautiful corpse, you lie so sweetly on the sombre pall of night that even nature turns her back on life, and falls in love with death.

LENA: No, leave me be! [*She jumps up and rushes away.*]

LEONCE: Too much! Too much! All my being is in this single moment. Now die. More is impossible. Out of chaos comes creation, bursting forth towards me, so alive and new, so radiant with beauty. The earth is a chalice of darkest gold: oh how the light within it effervesces, spills over the rim in streams, and from its sparkling bubbles all the stars appear. My craving lips reach out to drink – and this one taste of bliss makes me a precious vessel. And now into the deep, most holy cup! [*He makes to throw himself in the river.*]

VALERIO [*leaps up and grabs him*]: Hold it, your serene Serenitude!

LEONCE: Let me go!

VALERIO: Promise to let up and let well alone, and I'll let you go!

LEONCE: Blockhead!

VALERIO: Your Highness, have you really not outgrown such romantical posturing? You're like a half-baked lieutenant tossing his glass over his shoulder as soon as he's drunk to his sweetheart's health.

LEONCE: Perhaps you're right!

VALERIO: Don't worry though. Even if you won't be sleeping *under* the grass tonight, you might as well sleep *on* it. It would be a second attempt at suicide if you used one of the beds in that place. You lie on the straw like a corpse, but the fleas soon tell you you're alive.

LEONCE: All right, why not. [*He lies down in the grass.*] Good God, man, you've deprived me of the most beautiful suicide. Never in my life shall I find such a perfectly suitable opportunity, and the weather is *so* ideal. I'm already quite out of the mood. This fellow here with his yellow waistcoat and skyblue trousers[27] has ruined the entire thing. – Pray God for a sound and dreamless sleep.

VALERIO: Amen to that. – As for me, I've saved a human life, and my good conscience will keep me warm tonight. Here's to you, Valerio!

ACT III

Scene 1

LEONCE, VALERIO.

VALERIO: Get married? Since when has your Highness been aiming for the eternal treadmill?

LEONCE: Do you realize, Valerio, that even the lowliest of people have so much within them that a whole lifetime is far too short to ever love them enough? In any case, why spoil the fun of those that fondly imagine there's nothing so sacred and beautiful that they shouldn't try to make it even more so. There's a certain pleasure to be had from such harmless arrogance. Why deprive them of it?

VALERIO: Very humane and philobestial. But does she know who you are?

LEONCE: She knows she loves me, that's all.

VALERIO: And does your Highness know who *she* is?

LEONCE: What a fool you are! Try asking a carnation or dewdrop its name.

VALERIO: At least that means she's *something*, if that's not too indelicate, or too reminiscent of a police description. – But let's see, how can we manage it? Hm! – Listen, Prince, will you make me Chief Minister if, this very day and in the presence of your father, you are fully, formally and officially spliced to this nameless, ineffable wonder? Word of honour?

LEONCE: Word of honour!

VALERIO: That poor devil Valerio most humbly takes leave of His Ministerial Excellency Lord Valerio of Valerium.– 'I know thee not, old man! I banish thee on pain of death!'[28] [*He runs off,* LEONCE *follows him.*]

Scene 2: Open area in front of King Peter's palace

LOCAL PREFECT, SCHOOLMASTER, PEASANTS *in their Sunday best, holding fir branches.*

PREFECT: Well, Schoolmaster, how are your people holding up?

SCHOOLMASTER: They are holding up so well in their agony that they've been holding on to one another for quite some time now. They're guzzling alcohol like mad – otherwise they couldn't possibly hold out so long in this heat. Keep it up, you lot! Hold your fir branches straight up in front of you, so people think you're a forest and take your noses for strawberries, your tricorns for antlers and your shiny backsides for moonlight amidst the trees. And don't forget, whoever's at the back must keep running to the front, so it looks as if there are twice as many of you.

PREFECT: Just remember, Schoolmaster, you stand for sobriety!

SCHOOLMASTER: Stands to reason, except that I can scarcely stand for sheer sobriety.

PREFECT: Listen here, you people! It states in the official programme that all subjects without fail must voluntarily place themselves along the road wearing clean clothes, a contented expression and a well-fed air. Don't let us down, do you hear!

SCHOOLMASTER: Be steadfast now! Don't scratch behind your ears or blow your nose with your fingers while the royal pair are driving past, and whip up a suitable show of emotion or you'll be getting a taste of the whip yourselves. Show some appreciation of your generous treatment – after all, you've been carefully positioned downwind of the kitchen so that just for once in your life you catch a whiff of roast meat. Have you remembered your lesson? Have you? *Vi –!*

THE PEASANTS: *Vi –!*

SCHOOLMASTER: *– vat!*

THE PEASANTS: *– vat!*

SCHOOLMASTER: *Vivat!*

THE PEASANTS: *Vivat!*

SCHOOLMASTER: There you are, Mr Prefect, sir. You can see how intelligence is on the increase. Just think: it's *Latin*! But in addition this evening we'll be giving a transparent gala-ball by dint of all the holes in our jackets and trousers, and we'll punch each other's heads so we have bruises for cockades.

Scene 3: Grand stateroom

LADIES *and* GENTLEMEN *in full finery, carefully grouped.*
MASTER OF CEREMONIES *with sundry* SERVANTS *in the foreground.*

MASTER OF CEREMONIES: What a miserable fiasco. Everything's getting ruined. The roasts are shrivelling. The congratulations are turning sour. The stand-up collars are drooping like melancholy pig's-ears. The nails and beards of the peasants are already growing long again. The soldiers' hair-dos are starting to collapse. Of the dozen maids of honour there's not one that wouldn't rather be horizontal than vertical. In their little white dresses they look like tired angora rabbits, and the Court Poet goes grunting and shuffling around them like a fretful guinea pig. The officers of the guard are visibly wilting. [*To a servant*] Tell that young teacher he'd better send his boys for a piddle. The poor Court Chaplain! The tail of his coat has such a melancholy droop. I do believe he has ideals and is busily transforming all the chamberlains into chamber pots. He's quite worn out from all this standing.

SECOND SERVANT: All flesh is weak when it comes to standing. Even the Court Chaplain has become thoroughly got down since he first got up.

MASTER OF CEREMONIES: The ladies are glistening with so much sweat they look like mobile salt machines, their necklaces look like crystallized salt.

SECOND SERVANT: At least they're trying to make themselves comfortable. No one could accuse them of taking too much on their shoulders. Though not open-hearted, they're certainly bare-chested.

MASTER OF CEREMONIES: Yes, they're like maps of the Ottoman empire: you can see the Dardanelles and the Sea of Marmara! Get cracking, you scoundrels! Keep watch by the windows! His Majesty's coming.

Enter KING PETER *and the* PRIVY COUNCIL.

PETER: So the Princess has disappeared as well? Is there still no trace of my beloved heir? Have my orders been followed? Are the borders being watched?

MASTER OF CEREMONIES: Yes, your Majesty: the view from this room here allows us to keep the most rigorous watch. [*To the First Servant*] What have you seen?

FIRST SERVANT: A dog's run right through the kingdom in search of his master.

MASTER OF CEREMONIES [*to another servant*]: And you?

SECOND SERVANT: Someone's out walking on the northern border, but it's not the Prince – I'd recognize him from here.

MASTER OF CEREMONIES: And you?

THIRD SERVANT: Begging your pardon, Sir: nothing.

MASTER OF CEREMONIES: That's not very much. And you?

FOURTH SERVANT: Nothing here either.

MASTER OF CEREMONIES: That's even less.

PETER: But my dear Privy Council, did I not make a clear resolution that on this very day my Royal Majesty should be joyful, and the wedding be celebrated? Was this not our most solemn resolve?

PRESIDENT: Yes, your Majesty, that is indeed what the minutes record.

PETER: And wouldn't I be compromising myself most profoundly if I didn't adhere to my own resolution?

PRESIDENT: If it were ever possible for your Majesty to compromise yourself, then this may be a case where you might possibly be compromised.

PETER: Have I not given my royal word? Yes, I shall put my resolution into effect this instant: I shall herewith be joyful. [*He rubs his hands.*] Oh I am full of quite extraordinary joy!

PRESIDENT: We all share your Majesty's feelings, insofar as mere subjects are entitled and able so to do.

PETER: Oh I am quite beside myself with joy. I shall clothe my chamberlains in new red tunics, I shall promote a few cadets to lieutenant, I shall allow my subjects to . . . – but then, what about the marriage? Doesn't the other half of my resolution declare and determine that the marriage shall be celebrated?

PRESIDENT: Yes, your Majesty.

PETER: But what if the Prince doesn't come and the Princess neither?

PRESIDENT: Yes, if the Prince doesn't come and the Princess neither – then – then . . .

PETER: Then what?

PRESIDENT: Then it must be admitted that they cannot marry.

PETER: But stay, is your conclusion truly logical? If . . ., then . . .: quite right. – But what about my word, my royal word!

PRESIDENT: Let your Majesty take comfort from other Majesties. A royal word is a thing – a thing – a thing that is nothing.

PETER [*to the servants*]: Do you still see nothing?

SERVANTS: Nothing, your Majesty, nothing at all.

PETER: And I had resolved to be so full of joy. I wanted to start on the stroke of noon and be full of joy for twelve whole hours. It's making me quite melancholic.

PRESIDENT: Your subjects will be ordered to share your emotions.

MASTER OF CEREMONIES: For the sake of propriety, however, all persons not equipped with a handkerchief are forbidden to shed tears.

FIRST SERVANT: Wait! I can see something! It's a sort of protuberance, a kind of nose, the rest of it hasn't yet crossed the frontier. And I can see a man as well and another two persons of opposite sexes.

MASTER OF CEREMONIES: Which way are they going?

FIRST SERVANT: They're coming closer. They're approaching the palace. They're here.

Enter VALERIO, LEONCE, *the* GOVERNESS *and the* PRINCESS, *wearing masks.*

PETER: Who are you?

VALERIO: I'm not sure I know. [*He slowly removes several masks, one after the another.*] Am I this? Or this? Or this? What a frightening thought: if I keep on removing layer after layer, I might peel myself entirely away.

PETER [*disconcerted*]: But surely you must be *something*?

VALERIO: If your Majesty so commands. But in that case, gentlemen, turn the mirrors to the wall, cover your shiny buttons, and don't look at me like that lest I see my reflection mirrored in your eyes – or I truly won't know any more who I am.

PETER: This fellow is throwing me into total turmoil and deep desperation. I'm calamitously confused.

VALERIO: But what I really wanted to do was to announce to this noble and venerable company the arrival of these two world-famous automata. I would have added that I am perhaps the third and the oddest of them all – *if*, that is, I myself actually knew for certain who I am, though no one by the way should be surprised that I don't, since I myself know nothing of what I say, and don't even know that I don't know, so that it's highly probable that I am simply being *made* to talk like this, and that in reality it is nothing but cylinders, pipes and windbags[29] speaking these words of mine. [*In a mechanical, rasping voice*] Ladies and gentlemen, you see before you two persons of opposite sex, a male and a female, a gentleman and a lady. Nothing but cunning clockwork, nothing but springs and pasteboard. Each of them has the most delicate ruby spring beneath the nail of their left little toe: press it very gently, and the mechanism runs for a full fifty years. They're so perfectly crafted, these people here, that you couldn't distinguish them from ordinary humans if you didn't already know they were paint and pasteboard. They could even be turned into fully fledged members of proper society. They're extremely noble, since they speak with the right kind of accent. They're extremely moral, since they rise by the clock, take lunch by the clock and retire by the clock. They have a good digestion, which is certain proof of a good conscience. They have the most exquisite sense of decorum, since the lady knows no word for trousers, and the gentleman would never dream of going *up*stairs *behind* a woman, or *down*stairs in *front* of one. They're extremely cultured, since the lady can sing all the latest operas and the gentleman wears cuffs. Take note, ladies and gentlemen, they are now at an interesting stage: the mechanism of love is beginning to operate, the gentleman has already carried the lady's shawl a few times, the lady has already rolled her eyes and gazed heavenwards a few times. On several occasions they have both whispered, 'Faith, love, hope!' They already seem to be as good as hitched. All that's needed now is a quick 'Amen'.

PETER [*putting his finger on his nose*]: In effigy, that's it, in effigy! Tell me, President, if someone's hanged in effigy, isn't that just as good as if he were hanged for real?

PRESIDENT: Begging your Majesty's pardon, but it's better by far, since he comes to no harm, yet is hanged all the same.

PETER: That's it, I've got it. We'll celebrate the wedding in effigy. [*Pointing at Leonce and Lena*] That's the Prince, and that's the Princess. I shall carry out my resolution after all: I shall be joyful. Let the bells ring out! Get your congratulations ready! Look lively, Chaplain!

The COURT CHAPLAIN *steps forward, clears his throat, repeatedly raises his eyes towards heaven.*

VALERIO: Begin! Pox, leave thy damnable faces and begin! Come![30]

COURT CHAPLAIN [*in a state of utter confusion*]: If we ..., or rather ..., but on the other hand ...

VALERIO: In consideration whereof and notwithstanding –

COURT CHAPLAIN: For inasmuch ...

VALERIO: – as it came to pass before the creation of the world –

COURT CHAPLAIN: – that ...

VALERIO: – God was desperately bored –

PETER: Do get on with it, dear fellow.

COURT CHAPLAIN [*recovering his composure*]: If it so please your Highness Prince Leonce of Bum, and if it so please your Highness Princess Lena of Piddle, and if it so please you both together, to take each other conjointly and mutually in wedlock, then speak a loud and audible 'Yes'.

LEONCE *and* LENA: Yes.

COURT CHAPLAIN: Then I say, 'Amen'.

VALERIO: Very well done, short and sweet. So that's it then: man and woman created in a trice, with all the beasts of Paradise around them.

LEONCE *takes off his mask.*

ALL: The Prince!

PETER: The Prince! My son! What a disaster! What a deception! [*He rushes towards the Princess.*] Who is this person?! I declare the whole thing null and void!

GOVERNESS [*triumphantly, as she removes the Princess's mask*]: The Princess!

LEONCE: Lena!

LENA: Leonce!

LEONCE: Paradise, Lena – I do believe we fled to Paradise!

LENA: I've been deceived!

LEONCE: *I've* been deceived!

LENA: Oh chance!

LEONCE: Oh providence!

VALERIO: I have to laugh, I really have to laugh. By chance your Highnesses happen to have happened on each other. I hope you'll be happy it happened this way.

GOVERNESS: Fancy me living to see the day! A wandering prince! Now I can die in peace!

PETER: Children, I am moved, so deeply moved I am quite transfixed. I'm the happiest of men! But I hereby transfer my regal powers to you, my son, and from this moment on I shall start to do nothing but think undisturbed. So that I am properly assisted in this arduous task, my son, you will grant me possession of these fountains of wisdom [*pointing to the Privy Council*]. Come, gentlemen, we must think, we must think undisturbed. [*He exits with the Privy Council.*] That man made me so confused just now, I must order my thoughts all over again.

LEONCE [*to all those remaining*]: Gentlemen, my wife and I are most infinitely sorry that you have spent so much time today standing about on our behalf. Your position is so pitiful that we should not wish at any price to make you withstand more standing. Go home now, but don't go forgetting your speeches, your sermons, your verses, for tomorrow we shall calmly and quietly do the whole farce again from beginning to end. Goodbye, goodbye!

Exit all except LEONCE, LENA, VALERIO *and the* GOVERNESS.

LEONCE: There now, Lena, do you see how full our pockets are, full of puppets and playthings? What games shall we play with them? Shall we fit them all out with moustaches and muskets? Shall we stick them in tail-coats, dump them in the dunghill of politics and diplomacy, and settle down with a microscope to study their antics? Or do you fancy a barrel-organ on which sundry aesthetical, milk-white shrewmice dance and caper? Shall we build a theatre? [*Lena leans against him and shakes her head.*] But I know better than that what you really want. We'll have all the clocks in the kingdom destroyed, all calendars banned, then measure the hours and months by the flower-clock alone, by the rhythms of blossom and fruit. And then we'll surround our entire little kingdom with suntrap-mirrors so that winter will be banished for ever, in summer we'll have the warmth of Capri and Ischia, and all through the year we shall wander amongst violets and roses, oranges and bay.

VALERIO: And I shall be Chief Minister and issue a decree that anyone getting calluses on their hands shall be taken into care, anyone working themself sick shall be guilty of a crime, anyone boasting of earning their bread by the sweat of their brow shall be declared insane and a danger to society. And then we shall all lie down in the shade and pray God for macaroni, melons and figs, for melodious voices, classical bodies and a comfortable religion.

WOYZECK

CHARACTERS[1]

Woyzeck *a soldier*[2]
Andres *a soldier*[3]
Marie *Woyzeck's common-law wife*[4]
Child *of Marie and Woyzeck*[5]
Margreth *Marie's neighbour*
The Drum-Major
A Sergeant
Old Man
Showman
The Officer[6]
The Doctor
The Professor (?)[7]
1st Journeyman
2nd Journeyman
Idiot
Jew
Grandmother
Innkeeper
Käthe *woman at the inn*
Policeman

Soldiers, sundry men and women, students,
children, court officials, judge

Scene 1: Open countryside. The town in the distance[8]

WOYZECK *and* ANDRES *are cutting canes in the undergrowth.*[9]

WOYZECK: Yes, Andres: that streak there over the grass, that's where the head rolls in the evenings;[10] someone picked it up once, thought it was a hedgehog. Three days and three nights, and he was lying in his coffin. [*Softly*] Andres, it was the Freemasons, that's it, the Freemasons[11] – quiet!

ANDRES [*sings*]:
> A pair of hares was sitting there.
> Eating the green green grass . . .[12]

WOYZECK: Quiet! Something's moving!

ANDRES:
> Eating the green, green grass
> Till every blade was gone.

WOYZECK: Something's moving behind me, under me [*stamps on the ground*] – hollow, do you hear? Everything's hollow down there. The Freemasons!

ANDRES: I'm scared.

WOYZECK: It's so quiet, so strange. Makes you want to hold your breath. Andres!

ANDRES: What?

WOYZECK: Say something! [*Stares into the distance.*] Andres! How bright it is! Flames are raging through the heavens and a distant roar like mighty trumpets.[13] It's getting nearer! Let's get away. Don't look back.[14] [*Pulls him into the bushes.*]

ANDRES: Can you still hear it, Woyzeck?

WOYZECK: Quiet, all quiet, as if the world was dead.

ANDRES [*after a pause*]: Hear that? There's the drum. We got to go.

Scene 2: The town

MARIE *with her* CHILD *at the window.* MARGRETH. *The tattoo marches by,*[15] *the* DRUM-MAJOR *at its head.*

MARIE [*bobbing the child on her arm*]: Hey lad, tra ra, tra ra! D'you hear? Here they come!

MARGRETH: What a man, like a tree!

MARIE: The walk of him – like a lion!

The DRUM-MAJOR *salutes.*

MARGRETH: Ooh, neighbour, what a friendly sparkle in your eye – that's a novelty, coming from you!

MARIE [*sings*]: Soldiers they're such handsome lads . . .

MARGRETH: Your eyes, there's a real shine in 'em still!

MARIE: What if there is! Take your own to the yid and get 'em polished, perhaps they'll shine too and someone could flog 'em for a couple of buttons.

MARGRETH: That from you? From *you*? Well, missus – or is it 'miss'? – I'm a decent woman, I am, but you, you see clean through seven pairs of leather breeches!

MARIE: Bitch! [*Slams the window shut.*] Don't fret, little 'un. Don't know what they're on about. You're just a poor little tart's kid, and you makes your mum happy with your bastard face. There, there! [*Sings*][16]

> Hey lass what's this for a joke?
> You've got a young kid but no bloke.
> But why in hell's name should I care?
> I'll sing a loud song and just dare:
> Rockabye baby, my lad, heigh ho!
> For me no one else gives a damn.

> Johnny now saddle your horses so white,
> Give them more fodder, oh do.
> Oats they never will eat, oh no,
> Water they never will drink,

Wine, only wine must it be, heigh ho!
Wine, only wine must it be!

Knocking at the window.

MARIE: Who's there? Is that you, Franz? Come in!

WOYZECK: Can't. Time for roll-call.

MARIE: What's up, Franz?

WOYZECK [*mysteriously*]: Marie, it's happened again, lots of things. Is it not written: and behold, there rose up smoke from the land like smoke from a furnace?[17]

MARIE: For Christ's sake, man!

WOYZECK: It followed right behind me as far as the town. Where's it going to end?

MARIE: Franz!

WOYZECK: I've got to go. [*Exit.*]

MARIE: What a bloke! Such a state he's in. Didn't even glance at his own kid. He'll go berserk with all them thoughts of his. Why so quiet, little 'un? Scared are you? It's getting so dark, you'd think you was blind. Strange, that is: no light from the streetlamp. I can't stand it. Gives me the shivers. [*Exit.*]

Scene 3: Stalls, lights, people

OLD MAN. CHILD [*dancing*]:
In this world shall none abide,
All of us we have to die,
And well we know it too!

(MARIE:)[18] Look at that!

(WOYZECK:) Poor man, old man! Poor child, young child! Tears and joy![19] Hey, Marie, d'you want me to carry you?

(OLD MAN:) You have to be a fool with brains to say: world so foolish, world so fine!

SHOWMAN[20] [*in front of a booth*]: Ladies and gentlemen! Consider the creature as God first made it: nothing, just nothing. Add civilization and see what you've got: walks upright, wears trousers and carries a sword.[21] Let's 'ave yer, do a bow! You're a regular lord. Give us a kiss! [*He blows a trumpet.*] A musical devil and no mistake! Roll up, ladies and gentlemen, roll up and see the astronomical horse and the dwarf canary; favourites of the entire crowned 'eads of Europe and members of all known learned societies; tell your fortune they can, anything you like: how long you'll live, how many kids, your illnesses. Shoots with a pistol, this one does, stands on one leg. It's all edication, he's got animal brains, or rather: brainy animality, he's not the pig-stupid sort like some people – present most honourable company excepted. Roll up for the show: the start of the beginning will soon commence.

Observe the forward march of civilization. Everything is making giant strides.[22] A horse, a monkey, a canary. The monkey's already a soldier, though that's not saying much – the bottom-most species of human kind!

Roll up for the show! They're beginning the beginning!

WOYZECK: What d'you reckon?

MARIE: Suits me. Must be real lovely. Just look at his tassles, and the woman's in trousers.[23]

SERGEANT: Hold your horses! See what I see? What a woman!

DRUM-MAJOR: Hell's teeth! Spawn whole regiments of cavalry she could, breed drum-majors by the dozen!

SERGEANT: Just look at the way she carries her head; you'd think her black hair would drag her down like a millstone, and them eyes so black . . .[24]

DRUM-MAJOR: Like trying to see down a well or a chimney. Come on: after 'er!

Scene 4: Inside the booth

MARIE: Look at them lights! Fair blinds you.

WOYZECK: Real sight, that is: like a great black cat with blazing eyes. Christ what a night!

SHOWMAN: Right then, let's 'ave yer! Show us what you can do! Show us what a brainy brute you are! Put human society to shame. Ladies and gentlemen, this animal what you see 'ere with its various appendages is a four-legged member of every

known learned society and a professor at the university,
where he teaches the students riding and fencing. Bit of single
reasoning, that was. Now have a think with your double
reasoning. What do you do when you're thinking double?
Any asses out there amongst our learned assembly? [*The horse
shakes its head.*] How about that for double reasoning? Genuine scientific horsology, that is. No pig-stupid individual, this
one: he's a proper person. A 'uman he is, a 'uman being in
animal form, but a beast, an animal all the same. [*The horse
disgraces itself.*] Go on, put society to shame! There, you see,
the beast is still a part of nature, unspoilt nature. You should
follow his example. Just ask your doctor, it does terrible 'arm
(to keep it in). That's the motto: man, be natural.[25] You're
made of dust, sand, dirt – d'you want to be more than dust,
sand, dirt? There's brains for yer: he can add up all right
but he still can't count on 'is fingers. And why? Just can't
express 'isself, just can't explain things, he's a 'uman bein' in
all but shape! Tell the good people what time it is. Any of
you ladies and gentlemen got a watch? A watch?

SERGEANT: A watch! [*Slowly and ostentatiously pulls a watch from his
pocket.*] There, my friend!

MARIE: Can't miss this! [*She clambers into the front row.* SERGEANT
helps her.]

Scene 5

MARIE *seated, her* CHILD *on her lap, a bit of mirror in her hand.*

MARIE [*Looking at herself in the mirror*]: These stones don't 'alf
shine! Wonder what sort they are? What was it he said? –
Sleep, lad, sleep! Shut your eyes tight [*the child hides his eyes
behind his hands*], go on, tighter, keep 'em like that and stay
quiet or the bogeyman'll get yer. [*Sings*]
> Hey lass now shut up the house
> A gypsy boy's coming at last
> To lead you away by the hand
> Off into gypsy land.

117

[*Looks in the mirror again.*] Bet you that's gold! Our sort don't 'ave much, a dump like this and a broken bit of mirror − but me mouth's just as red as them grand madames' with their bloody great mirrors and their fancy gents what kiss their 'ands; a poor woman, that's what I am. [*The child sits up.*] Quiet, child, shut your eyes, the sandman's coming! See him run along the wall? [*She dazzles him with her mirror.*] Keep 'em shut or he'll look in your eyes and turn you blind.

WOYZECK *enters behind her. She jumps and puts her hands over her ears.*

WOYZECK: What's that you've got?

MARIE: Nothing.

WOYZECK: It's glinting under your fingers for chris'sake!

MARIE: An earring; I found it.

WOYZECK: I've never had such luck: two at one go!

MARIE: So what am I, a tart?!

WOYZECK: It's alright, Marie. − How the lad sleeps. Give him a tug under 'is little arm, the chair's digging into him. His forehead's all shiny with sweat; nothing in the world but work, even in your sleep you sweats. That's us, that is: the bloody poor! Here's some more money, Marie, me wages and a bit from me officer.

MARIE: God bless you, Franz.

WOYZECK: I got to go. Tonight then, Marie. See you.

MARIE [*alone, after a pause*]: I *am* a tart, a no-good tart. If I had a knife I'd do meself in. − But why give a toss in a world like this? Going to the devil it is − man, woman, the whole bloody lot.

Scene 6: The Officer. Woyzeck

OFFICER *in a chair*, WOYZECK *shaving him.*

OFFICER: Steady, Woyzeck, steady; one thing after another. You're making me quite giddy. What on earth am I to do with the spare ten minutes if you finish too early today? Woyzeck, just think, you've still got a good thirty years to live, thirty years! That's 360 months, not to mention the days, the hours, the minutes! What are you going to do with all this vast expanse of time? Pace it, Woyzeck, pace it!

WOYZECK: Yessir!

OFFICER: I get really frightened for the world when I think of eternity. Activity, Woyzeck, activity! Eternal means eternal, it means *eternal*, you must see that; but then again on the other hand it's not eternal, it's a moment, a single moment − Woyzeck, it frightens me when I think that the world revolves in a single day, what a squandering of time, where's it all going to end? Woyzeck, I can't bear to see a millwheel turning any more − it makes me melancholic.

WOYZECK: Yessir!

OFFICER: Woyzeck, you always look so worked up. Good chaps never look like that, good chaps with a nice clear conscience. − Say something, Woyzeck. What's the weather like today?

WOYZECK: Bad, sir, bad; wind.

OFFICER: Yes, yes, I can tell: it's all sort of rushing by out there. Gives me such a turn, a wind like that does − as bad as mice. [*Craftily*] I reckon it's a northerly-southerly.

WOYZECK: Yessir!

OFFICER: Ha ha ha! Northerly-southerly! Ha ha ha! God you're stupid, so abysmally stupid. [*Mawkishly*] Woyzeck, you're a good chap, a good chap − but [*with dignity*] Woyzeck, you've got no morals. Morals, that's when people are moral, do you see. It's such a good word. You've got a child without the blessing of the church, as our reverend padre puts it, without the blessing of the church; it's not me that says so.

WOYZECK: But, sir, the good Lord won't look over the poor little mite to check that a prayer was said before he was made. The Lord spake: Suffer the little children to come unto me.[26]

OFFICER: What did you say? What an odd reply! He's made me all muddled replying like that. And when I say 'him', I mean you, you!

WOYZECK: Poor, that's what we are. Money, you see, sir, it's the money. If you don't have no money. Morality don't get much of a look in when our sort gets made. We're flesh and blood after all. Us lot just don't have a chance in this world or the next; if we ever got to heaven I reckon we'd have to help with the thunder.

OFFICER: Woyzeck, there's no virtue in you, no virtue at all. Flesh and blood? When I lie by the window when it's rained and watch those white stockings go hopping down the street – dammit, Woyzeck – I feel the surge of love. I'm flesh and blood as well, you know. But Woyzeck, virtue, virtue! How else could I ever cope with time? I say to myself again and again: you're a virtuous chap, [*mawkishly*] a good chap, a good chap.

WOYZECK: Yes, sir, virtue, sir! I'm not that far meself. You see, us common folk, we don't have no virtue, all we got is our nature; but if I was a gent with an 'at and a watch and a nice smart coat and could talk all posh, I'd be virtuous alright. Must be a nice thing, sir, virtue. But poor, that's what I am.

OFFICER: Good show, Woyzeck. You're a good chap, a good chap. But you think too much, it eats away at you, you always look so worked up. Our little talk has quite worn me out. Off you go now – and don't run like that; slowly, nice and slowly down the street.

Scene 7

MARIE. DRUM-MAJOR.

DRUM-MAJOR: Marie!

MARIE [*with intensity as she looks at him*]: Walk up and down, go on. – Chest like an ox, beard like a lion . . . There's not another man like you . . . I'm the proudest woman in the whole wide world.

DRUM-MAJOR: You should see me on Sundays with me great plume of feathers and me white gloves, Marie, fair take your breath away; the Prince he always says, 'Now there's a feller!'

MARIE [*mockingly*]: Get away! [*She goes right up to him.*] What a man!

DRUM-MAJOR: And you're some woman. Christ almighty, we could breed little drum-majors like bloody rabbits – let's get started, eh? [*He puts his arm around her.*]

MARIE [*crossly*]: Get your hands off!
DRUM-MAJOR: Wild animal, that's what you are!
MARIE [*vehemently*]: Just touch me!
DRUM-MAJOR: Is that the devil in your eye?
MARIE: Don't care if it is. What the hell.

Scene 8

WOYZECK. *The* DOCTOR.

DOCTOR: I never thought I'd see the day, Woyzeck! Call yourself a man of your word?
WOYZECK: What's wrong, Doctor?
DOCTOR: I saw it, Woyzeck. You pissed in the street, pissed against the wall like a dog. And two groschen every day! It's bad, Woyzeck, the world's turning bad, very very bad.
WOYZECK: But, Doctor, when it's a call of nature!
DOCTOR: Call of nature! Call of nature! Don't give me nature! Have I not proved that the *musculus constrictor vesicae*[27] is subordinate to the will? Nature! Woyzeck, mankind is free, in man individuality attains its most perfect expression as freedom. Can't hold his water! [*Shakes his head, puts his hands behind his back, strides up and down.*] Have you eaten your peas, Woyzeck? I'm going to revolutionize science, I'm going to blow it all sky-high. Uric acid 0.1, ammonium hydrochlorate, hyperoxide. – Woyzeck, surely you're ready for another piss? Just pop inside and have a try.
WOYZECK: I can't, Doctor.
DOCTOR [*with feeling*]: But pissing against the wall! I've got it in writing, a binding agreement, right here in my hand! I saw it, I saw it with my very own eyes, I was just poking my nose through the window letting the sun shine into it so I could make a study of sneezing. [*Makes to attack him.*] No, Woyzeck, I am not angry, anger is unhealthy, it's unscientific. I am calm, quite calm, my pulse is its customary 60, and I am telling you so with the utmost composure. Good God, who's going to bother getting angry with a human, a mere human? If it had

been an interesting lizard dying on me, well . . . But dammit you shouldn't have pissed against the wall –

WOYZECK: You see, Doctor, some people just have that sort of character, that sort of structure to 'em. – But with nature it's different, you see, when it comes to nature [*he snaps his fingers*], it's kind of, what I mean is, for instance . . .

DOCTOR: Woyzeck, you're at it again, you're philosophizing!

WOYZECK [*confidentially*]: Doctor, have you ever caught sight of the other side of nature? Sometimes, when the sun's up high in the middle of the day and it seems like the world is bursting into flames, this terrible voice starts talking to me.

DOCTOR: Woyzeck, you've got an *aberratio*!

WOYZECK [*puts his finger against his nose*]: It's the mushrooms, Doctor. It's all in the mushrooms. Have you noticed the patterns they make on the ground? If only we knew how to read what they say.

DOCTOR: Woyzeck, you have the most beautiful *aberratio mentalis partialis*, category two, such a beautiful example. I'm going to give you a bonus, Woyzeck. Category two: obsessional but otherwise generally rational. Still doing everything as usual? Shaving your officer?

WOYZECK: Yessir.

DOCTOR: Eating your peas?

WOYZECK: Loads of 'em, Doctor. Me woman gets the money for the housekeeping.

DOCTOR: Doing all your duties?

WOYZECK: Yessir.

DOCTOR: You're an interesting case, Woyzeck, an interesting case. You'll be getting a bonus. Keep at it. Show me your pulse. Splendid!

Scene 9: Street

OFFICER. DOCTOR.

OFFICER: Doctor, the horses quite fill me with terror. To think the poor creatures can only get around on their own four legs! Stop hurtling about like that. Stop thrashing around in the air with your cane. You're chasing your own death, that's what you're doing. A good chap with a good conscience doesn't go rushing about the place like that. Not a good chap. [*He grabs the Doctor by his coat.*] Doctor, permit me to save a human life, you're racing about so ... Doctor, I feel so melancholy, I've too much imagination, I can't help sobbing whenever I see my coat hanging on the wall, just hanging there.

DOCTOR: Hm! Puffy, fat, podgy neck, inclined to apoplexy. Yes, my good sir, you're ripe for an *apoplexia cerebralis*, but perhaps you'll get it on just the one side and suffer paralysis in merely half your body, or if you're really lucky it will damage only your brain and you'll turn into a vegetable – those are more or less your prospects for the next four weeks. Incidentally I can assure you that you're a most interesting case, and if God is kind enough to let your tongue become only partly paralysed, we shall conduct the most immortal experiments.

OFFICER: Doctor, don't frighten me, people can die of fright, of sheer fright. I can see them now, standing round my body with hat in hand, but they'll say, 'He was a good man, a good man'. – You diabolical old coffin-nail!

DOCTOR [*holds out his hat*]: What is this, my good fellow? ([*Thrusts hat onto the Officer's head.*]) A numbskull!

OFFICER [*makes a fold in the hat*]: What is this, dear Doctor? ([*Thrusts hat onto the Doctor's head.*]) A crackbrain!

DOCTOR: I shall take my leave, most honourable square-basher!

OFFICER: And the same to you, my very dear coffin-nail!

WOYZECK *comes running down the street.*

OFFICER: Hey, Woyzeck, why on earth are you tearing past like that? Just hold it, Woyzeck; you rush through the world like an open razor, you'll cut us to ribbons; you're running as if you had a regiment of Cossacks[28] to shave, all in a quarter of an hour, and were due to be hanged after the very last hair – but talking of long beards, Woyzeck, what was it I wanted to say? – Long beards ...

DOCTOR: Long beards, hairy chins, Pliny complained of them

even in his day, they should be discouraged among soldiers, and you, you . . .

OFFICER [*continues*]: Eh? Talking of long beards? How's it going, Woyzeck, haven't you found a hair from someone's beard in your soup? Eh? You follow me, don't you? A human hair, from the beard of a sapper? A sergeant? Or perhaps – a drum-major? Eh, Woyzeck? But she's a good sort, your woman is. Doesn't give you the bother that some men have.

WOYZECK: Yessir! What are you trying to say, sir?

OFFICER: What a face the man's pulling! Perhaps it's not in your soup after all; but if you're really quick and pop round the corner, you might just find one on a pair of lips, Woyzeck, on a certain pair of lips. Ah the pangs of love, Woyzeck, I've felt them too. – Good God, man, you're white as a sheet!

WOYZECK: A poor devil, sir, that's what I am – and she's all I've got in the world. If this is a joke, sir –

OFFICER: Joke! I'll give you joke, you scoundrel!

DOCTOR: Your pulse, Woyzeck, your pulse! – small, hard, erratic, irregular.

WOYZECK: The earth's as hot as hell, sir, but to me it's cold, icy cold; hell's cold, d'you want to bet? It ain't possible. Not her! Not her! Impossible!

OFFICER: Do you want to be shot, man, do you want a brace of bullets through the brain? Look daggers at me, would you, and me just trying to help – 'cause you're a good chap, Woyzeck, a good chap.

DOCTOR: Facial muscles tense, rigid, occasional spasms, bearing tense, erect.

WOYZECK: I'm going. Anything's possible. Bloody 'umans! Anything's possible. Nice weather we're having, sir. The sky has such a nice, solid, rough-cast look, it makes you want to bang a nail into it and hang yourself, just because of the tiny line between yes and no, d'you see, sir, yes and no? Is no to blame for yes, or yes for no? I must think it over. [*Exit with large steps, first slowly and then faster and faster.*]

DOCTOR [*goes running after him*]: Phenomenal, Woyzeck! A bonus, a bonus!

OFFICER: Make me quite giddy, these people do: such frantic

haste; the tall one all legs, like the shadow of a spider, the short one all jerky. The tall one's the lightning, the short one the thunder. I'd better get after them. Not that I like to. A good man is grateful and values his life, a good man's not courageous, only cowards are courageous. I only went to war to boost my love of life. How absurd to infer courage from that! Grotesque, quite grotesque!

Scene 10

MARIE. WOYZECK.

WOYZECK [*stares at her fixedly, shakes his head*]: No! I don't see nothing, nothing! Oh, you ought to be able to see it, to grab hold of it with your bare hands.

MARIE [*cowed*]: What's the matter with you, Franz? You're raving mad, Franz.

WOYZECK: A sin so big and so fat. It stinks enough to drive the angels out of heaven. Such a red mouth, Marie. No blisters on it?[29] Goodbye, Marie, you're beautiful as sin. Can mortal sin be so beautiful?

MARIE: You got the fever, Franz, you don't know what you're saying.

WOYZECK: Hell and damnation! – Did he stand right here? – like this? – and this?

MARIE: As the day is long and the world is old, lots of people can stand in the same place, one after another.

WOYZECK: I saw him!

MARIE: You can see a lot if you've eyes and aren't blind and the sun's in the sky.

WOYZECK: With my own eyes!

MARIE [*cockily*]: And what if you did?

Scene 11: The Professor's courtyard

STUDENTS *down below. The* PROFESSOR *at a window in the roof.*

(PROFESSOR:) Gentlemen, I am on the roof like David when he beheld Bathsheba;[30] though all *I* behold are the bloomers drying in the girls' school garden. Gentlemen, we come now to the vital question of the relationship of the subject to the object. If we but take one of those things in which the divine organically affirms itself by becoming so splendidly manifest, and if we investigate its relationship to space, to the earth, to the universe, if, gentlemen, I throw this cat out of the window, how will this being, this essence behave in relation to the centre of gravity and to its own instincts? Hey, Woyzeck, [*bellowing*] Woyzeck!

WOYZECK: Professor, it's biting me!

PROFESOR: You numbskull, you're handling the beast as gently as if it was your own grandmother!

WOYZECK: Doctor, I've got the shakes!

DOCTOR [*extremely pleased*]: Splendid, Woyzeck, splendid! [*Rubs his hands together. Takes the cat.*] What do I see here, gentlemen, but the new species of chicken-louse, a splendid species, considerably different, deeply buried, I shall now ... [*takes out a magnifying-glass*]. A *ricinus*, gentlemen – [*the cat runs off*]. Gentlemen, the beast has no instinct for science. *Ricinus*,[31] come along, the finest examples, bring your fur collars. Then again, gentlemen, you can see something else instead: this human specimen here, d'you see, for three months it has eaten nothing but peas, observe the effects, just feel how irregular the pulse is, here, and notice the eyes.

WOYZECK: Doctor, everything's going dark. [*He sits down.*]

DOCTOR: Cheer up, Woyzeck, just a few more days and it'll all be over; examine him, gentlemen, examine him. [*They feel his temples, pulse and chest.*] By the way, Woyzeck, just waggle your ears for the gentlemen, will you; it's something I've been meaning to show you. Two muscles are in operation here. Hurry up, Woyzeck, hurry up!

WOYZECK: Oh, Doctor!

DOCTOR: You animal, do you want *me* to waggle your ears? Are you trying the cat's trick? There, gentlemen; what we have here is a throw-back to the ass, often brought about by excessive childhood exposure to women and a vulgar mother tongue. How much hair did your tender loving mother tear out for a keepsake then? Your hair has gone so thin these last few days; yes, gentlemen, it's the peas.

Scene 12: The guardroom

WOYZECK. ANDRES.

ANDRES [*sings*]:
>   At the inn you'll find a pretty maid
>   She waits in the garden night and day
>   She waits so bold and bolder . . .

WOYZECK: Andres!

ANDRES: What's up?

WOYZECK: Nice weather!

ANDRES: Sunday sunshine. Music playing outside the town. The women set off a while ago, they're fair on the boil, it's a real to-do.

WOYZECK [*restless*]: Dancing, Andres, they're dancing.

ANDRES: At the Nag's Head and the Star!

WOYZECK: Dancing, dancing.

ANDRES: Let them! [*Sings*]
>   She waits so bold and bolder
>   Until the clock doth midnight say
>   And watches for a soldier.

WOYZECK: I'm all on edge, Andres.

ANDRES: You're a bloody fool!

WOYZECK: I've got to get away. Everything's going round in circles. Their hands, they're so hot. Hell and damnation, Andres!

ANDRES: What d'you want then?

WOYZECK: I got to go.

ANDRES: All because of her?!

WOYZECK: I've got to get away, it's so hot around here.

Scene 13: Inn

Open windows, dancing. Benches in front of the inn. Young men.

1st JOURNEYMAN:
>The shirt on me back: it isn't mine,
>And me soul fair stinks of brandy and wine . . .

2nd JOURNEYMAN: Brother, should I smash an 'ole in your outlook for the sake of friendship? Sod it, I want to smash an 'ole in your outlook. I'm a real man too, y'know. I'm gunna smash every flea on 'is body to death.

1st JOURNEYMAN: Me soul fair stinks of brandy and wine. Even money turns rotten in the end. Forget-me-not, forget-me-not! What a beautiful world we live in, brother! I could fill a barrel to the brim with tears. Wish our snouts was bottles and we could pour 'em down each other's throats.

OTHERS [*in chorus*]:
>A huntsman from the Rhine
>Went riding once through forests fine
>Tally ho, my lads, what fun to hunt
>Across this land so green and wide
>For hunting's surely my delight.

WOYZECK *comes to the window.* MARIE *and the* DRUM-MAJOR *dance past without noticing him.*

MARIE [*as she dances past*]: Go on! Go on!

WOYZECK [*choking*]: Go on! Go on! [*Starts up violently then sinks back onto the bench.*] Go on! Go on! [*Claps his hands together.*] Whirl and spin! Wallow in your filth! Why don't God blow out the sun when he sees the whole world writhing in lechery, men and women, man and beast. They're at it in broad daylight, before your very eyes, like dogs in the street. The bitch! The bitch is hot, so hot! Go on, go on! [*Starts up.*] The bastard! How he gropes at her, gropes at her body, he's got 'er the same as I had 'er once.[32]

1st JOURNEYMAN [*standing on a table, preaching*]: Albeit if a wanderer that stands beholding the river of time, nay even if divine wisdom itself should answer its own question and reply to itself: Wherefore is man? Wherefore is man? – But verily I say unto you, how could the farmer, the cooper, the cobbler, the doctor have earned their living if God had not created man? How could the tailor have made his living if God hadn't made men feel ashamed of their nakedness? And how the soldier if he hadn't blessed them with the urge to fight and kill each other? Therefore be ye not anxious, yea verily, it is milk and honey, but vanity of vanities, all is vanity, even money turns rotten in the end. – In conclusion, dear brethren, let us piss on the cross that a Jew might die.

Scene 14: Open field

WOYZECK: Go on! Go on! Quiet, music! [*Bends towards the ground.*] Ah, what's that? What's that you say? Louder, louder! – Stab, stab the bitch dead? Stab, stab the bitch dead! Shall I? Must I? Can I hear it there too? Does the wind say it too? Will I go on hearing it over and over: stab, stab, stab her dead?

Scene 15: Night

ANDRES *and* WOYZECK *in one bed.*

WOYZECK [*shakes Andres*]: Andres! Andres! I can't sleep, when I shuts my eyes everything goes round and round and I hear the thump of the music, 'Go on! Go on!', then the walls start speaking, can't you hear it?

ANDRES: Alright – let them dance! God save us, amen. [*Goes back to sleep.*]

WOYZECK: 'Stab! Stab!' it keeps on saying, and there's a feeling between me eyes like a knife cutting through.

ANDRES: Glass of schnaps with a powder in it, that's what you need, it'll clear the fever.

Scene 16: Barrack square

WOYZECK: Didn't you hear nothing?

ANDRES: He's in there still with a friend of his.

WOYZECK: He *did* say something!

ANDRES: How the hell do *you* know? How can I tell you? Anyway, he laughed, and then he said, 'Real tasty bit of stuff! Talk about thighs! And hot all over, so bloody hot!'

WOYZECK [*with icy coldness*]: So that's what he said? What was that dream last night? Something about a knife, wasn't it? Don't half have crazy dreams.

ANDRES: Where you going?

WOYZECK: Get wine for me officer. – But what a girl, Andres; real special, she was.

ANDRES: Who was?

WOYZECK: Nothing. See you.

Scene 17: Inn

DRUM-MAJOR. WOYZECK. SUNDRY PEOPLE.

DRUM-MAJOR: A real man, that's me! [*Pounds his chest.*] A man, I tell you. Anyone looking for a fight? Unless you're some piss-drunk God almighty you'd better keep your distance, or I'll ram your nose clean down to your arsehole. I'll – [*to Woyzeck*] hey, you, drink! Real men drink. I wish the world was made of booze, all booze.

WOYZECK *whistles.*

DRUM-MAJOR: Cheeky little runt! D'you want me to yank your tongue right out of yer head and wrap it round your body? [*They fight, Woyzeck loses.*] How much breath should I let you keep? – about as much as an old woman's fart, eh?

WOYZECK *sits down on the bench, exhausted and trembling.*

DRUM-MAJOR: The bleeder can whistle till he's blue in the face. Ha!
    Brandy is me very life,
    Brandy makes you brave!
A WOMAN: Asked for it, didn't 'e?
ANOTHER WOMAN: He's bleeding.
WOYZECK: It's one thing after a-bloody-nother.

Scene 18

WOYZECK. *The* JEW.

WOYZECK: The pistol's too dear.
JEW: Well, you buying or not buying, what you doing?
WOYZECK: How much for the knife?
JEW: Straight, that is, nice and straight. Going to slit your throat
    with it? Well, what you doing? You won't get one cheaper
    nowhere else, do yourself in real cheap, you can, but not for
    free. So what you doing? Get yourself a nice economical death.
WOYZECK: Cut more than bread, that will.
JEW: Two groschen!
WOYZECK: There! [*Exit.*]
JEW: 'There!' As if it was nothing. But it's money. The bastard!

Scene 19

(MARIE. *The* IDIOT.)

MARIE [*leafing through the Bible*]: 'Neither was guile found in his
    mouth'.[33] – O God! Dear God! Don't look at me! [*Turns other
    pages.*] 'And the scribes and Pharisees brought unto him a
    woman taken in adultery, and set her in the midst. – And Jesus
    said unto her, Neither do I condemn thee; go, and sin no
    more.'[34] [*Claps her hands together.*] God! Dear God! I can't. O
    God, just give me strength enough to pray. [*The child huddles
    closer to her.*] Fair cuts me up, the child does. Karl! He just lies
    there sunning hisself!

IDIOT [*lying on the floor counting off fairy-tales on his fingers*]: 'Tis my lord the king that has the golden crown. On the morrow I shall bring milady the queen her child. Said Blood Sausage to Liver Sausage: I beg thee, come! – [*he takes the child and falls silent.*]

MARIE: Franz still hasn't come, not yesterday, not today; it's getting so hot in here. [*She opens the window.*] 'And stood at his feet weeping, and began to wash his feet with tears, and did wipe them with the hairs of her head, and kissed his feet and anointed them with the ointment.'[35] [*Strikes herself on the chest.*] Dead, everything dead! Blessed Saviour, if only I could anoint your feet!

Scene 20: Barracks

ANDRES. WOYZECK *rummaging through his things.*

WOYZECK: This jerkin's not part of me kit, Andres, it might come in handy, Andres. This cross is me sister's and so's the ring, then there's this holy picture, two Bleeding Hearts and all in gold, found it in me mother's Bible, and it says:

> May suffering be my sole reward
> May suffering be my praise to God.[36]
> Lord as Thy flesh was red and raw,
> So let my heart be ever more.

My mother don't feel nothing any more, except when the sunshine warms her hands. What does it matter.

ANDRES [*totally numbed, says to everything*]: Right.

WOYZECK [*pulls out a piece of paper*]: Friedrich Johann Franz Woyzeck,[37] soldier, rifleman in the 2nd Regiment, 2nd Battalion, 4th Company, born Feast of the Annunciation, 20th July, me age today is 30 years, 7 months and 12 days.[38]

ANDRES: Hospital, Franz, that's what you need. Poor sod, you should drink some schnaps with a powder in it, it'd clear the fever.

WOYZECK: Yes, Andres, when the coffin-maker finishes a coffin, no one knows who'll end up inside it.

Scene 21

MARIE *with* GIRLS *in front of the house.*

GIRL:

> The sun shines bright at Candlemas,
> The corn it stands so high.[39]
> They gaily walked along the road,
> They walked out two by two,
> The pipers piping right in front,
> The fiddlers fiddling close behind,
> Her stockings red, so very red . . .

1st CHILD: That's dirty, that is.

2nd CHILD: What you on about?

(3rd CHILD:) What d'you start for?

(2nd CHILD:) Why?

(1st CHILD:) Because!

(2nd CHILD:) But why because?

(3rd CHILD:) Someone's going to sing a song . . . [*She looks around the circle and points at the First Child.*]

(1st CHILD:) I can't!

(ALL THE CHILDREN:) Marie, *you* sing.

MARIE: Come on, you little shrimps! Ring-a-ring-o'-roses! How about King Herod and the babes? Tell us a story, Grandma!

GRANDMOTHER: Once upon a time there was a poor child, had no father and no mother, everyone was dead and there was nobody left in all the world. Everyone dead, and the child went and cried both day and night. And seeing there was nobody left on earth, he[40] wanted to go up to heaven, and the moon gave him such a friendly look, and when in the end he came to the moon, it was a lump of rotten wood, so he went to the sun, and when he came to the sun, it was a withered sunflower, and when he came to the stars, they were tiny golden insects stuck there as though by a butcher-bird on blackthorn,[41] and when he wanted to come back to earth again, the earth was an upturned cookpot, and he was all

alone, so he sat down and cried, and he's sitting there still, all
on his own.[42]

WOYZECK: Marie!

MARIE [*frightened*]: What's the matter?

WOYZECK: Let's go, Marie. It's time.

MARIE: Where to?

WOYZECK: Who knows.

Scene 22

MARIE *and* WOYZECK.

MARIE: But the town's that way. It's dark.

WOYZECK: You'll be staying a while. Come on, sit down.

MARIE: But I got to go.

WOYZECK: You won't be walking your feet sore.

MARIE: You're acting so queer!

WOYZECK: D'you know how long it's been, Marie?

MARIE: Two years come Whitsun.

WOYZECK: D'you know how long we've still to go?

MARIE: I've got to be off, there's dew in the air (I'll catch me
death).[43]

WOYZECK: Are you cold, Marie? But you're warm all the same.
How hot your lips are! Hot, hot, breath of a whore. – Even so
I'd give heaven and earth to kiss them again. Funny: once
you're stony cold you don't *feel* cold no more. You won't feel
cold in the morning dew.

MARIE: What're you saying?

WOYZECK: Nothing. [*Silence.*]

MARIE: Moon's coming up as red as red.

WOYZECK: Like a bloody knife.[44]

MARIE: What are you up to? Franz, you look so pale. [*He pulls
out the knife.*] Franz, stop! For Christ's sake, he . . . – help!

WOYZECK: Take that, and that! Can't you die? There! There!
Still twitching! Not dead yet, not dead? Still twitching? [*Stabs
her repeatedly.*] Dead are you? Dead! Dead! [*People approach; he
runs away.*]

Scene 23: People approach

1st PERSON: Stop!

2nd PERSON: D'you hear? Quiet! Over there!

1st PERSON: Ugh! Over there! What a horrible sound.

2nd PERSON: It's the water, it's calling, it's such a long time since anyone drowned. Let's get away, it's not good to hear it.

1st PERSON: Ugh, there it is again. Like somebody dying.

2nd PERSON: It's scary, all grey and vapours and wreaths of mist, and the humming of insects like cracked bells. Let's get away!

1st PERSON: No, it's too clear, too loud. Up there. Come on.

Scene 24: The inn

WOYZECK: Dance all of you, go on, sweat and stink, the devil'll take you all in the end. [*Sings*]

> At the inn you'll find a pretty maid
> She waits in the garden night and day
> She waits so bold and bolder
> Until the clock doth midnight say
> And watches for a soldier.

[*He dances.*] There, Käthe! Sit yourself down! I'm hot, so hot! [*He takes off his coat.*] That's the way it is, the devil takes the one and leaves the other be. Käthe you're hot! Why's that? Käthe, you'll be stone cold too one day. Better watch yourself. Can't you sing?

(KÄTHE:)

> To Swabia will I never go,
> Long dresses will I never show
> For dresses long and pointed shoe
> Will never for a skivvy do.

(WOYZECK:) No, no shoes; you don't need shoes to go to hell.

KÄTHE [dancing]:

> O fie, dear sir, whatever next!
> Keep your money and sleep alone.

135

(WOYZECK:) Yes that's the truth, I wouldn't want blood on *my* hands!

KÄTHE: What *is* that on your 'and then?

(WOYZECK:) What, me, me?

KÄTHE: Red! It's blood! [*People gather round them.*]

(WOYZECK:) Blood? Blood?

INNKEEPER: Ugh, blood!

WOYZECK: Must've cut m'self I reckon, here on me right hand.

INNKEEPER: How d'you get it on your elbow then?

WOYZECK: When I wiped it off.

INNKEEPER: What, wiped it off your right hand on to your right elbow? Clever bugger, you are!

IDIOT: And then the giant said, Fee fie fo fum, I smell blood so who's spilt some? Ugh! What a stink!

WOYZECK: Hell and damnation, what d'you want? It's none of your business! Out of my way or else I'll ... – Hell and damnation! D'you think I've done someone in? A murderer, me? Why stare at me? Just look at yourselves! Get out of my way! [*Exit, running.*]

Scene 25

WOYZECK, *alone.*

WOYZECK: The knife? Where's the knife? I left it behind. It'll give me away! Closer! Still closer! What sort of a place is this? What's that I can hear? Something's moving. Quiet. Close by here, Marie? Oh, Marie! Quiet. Everything's quiet. (Why so pale, Marie? Why this red necklace around your neck? Who d'you earn the necklace from with all your sins? Black with it you were, black! I've made you go white again. Why does it hang so wild, your black, black hair? Didn't you put it in plaits today?)[45] There's something lying there! – cold, wet, still. Got to get away from here. The knife, the knife; is this it? At last! Someone's coming. – Over there. [*He runs off.*]

Scene 26

WOYZECK *by a pool of water*.

WOYZECK: Here it goes! [*He throws the knife in the water*.] It's sinking in the dark water like a stone! The moon's like a bloody knife! Is the whole world going to give me away? No, it's too close in, when they go swimming – [*he enters the pool and throws the knife further out*]. There! But how about the summer when they dive for mussels? – but no, it'll rust. Someone might recognize it. – Wish I'd broken it in pieces! Is there blood on me still? I need to wash m'self. There's a stain! And there's another!

Scene 27

CHILDREN.

1st CHILD: Come on, Marie![46]
2nd CHILD: What's up?
1st CHILD: Don't you know yet? All the others went ages ago. There's a dead woman out there.
2nd CHILD: Where?
1st CHILD: Right up on the left beyond the ditch, by the red cross.
2nd CHILD: Let's go and see it quick, or they'll take it away.

Scene 28

The IDIOT. *The* CHILD. WOYZECK.

KARL [*holding the child on his lap*]: He's fallen in the water, he's fallen in the water, look, he's fallen in the water.[47]
WOYZECK: Hey lad, Christian.
KARL [*stares at him fixedly*]: He's fallen in the water.
WOYZECK [*tries to cuddle the child, it turns away and screams*]: Oh my God!

137

KARL: He's fallen in the water.

WOYZECK: Christian, you can have a toy soldier. There, there! [*The child pushes him away. To Karl*] Here, get him a toy soldier.

KARL *stares at him fixedly.*

WOYZECK: Giddyup, horsie, giddyup!

KARL [*excited*]: Giddyup, horsie, giddyup, giddyup! [*Runs off with the child.*]

Scene 29

COURT OFFICIALS. DOCTOR. JUDGE.

POLICEMAN: A good murder, a proper murder, a lovely murder, as lovely a murder as anyone could wish, we've not had a murder like this for years.

LENZ

On 20th January Lenz crossed the mountains. Snow on the peaks and upper slopes, down into the valleys grey stone, green patches, rocks and pine-trees. It was cold and wet, the water trickled down the rocks and leapt across the path. The boughs of the pine-trees sagged in the damp air. Grey clouds marched across the sky, but everything so close, and then the mist came swirling up and drifted dank and heavy through the bushes, so leaden, so sluggish. He carried on, indifferent, the way meant nothing to him, now up, now down. He felt no tiredness, just occasional regret that he couldn't walk on his head. A surge swept through his breast at first when the rock seemed to leap away, the grey wood shuddered beneath him, and the mist devoured the shape of things then half revealed their giant limbs; the surge swept through him, he sought for something, as though for lost dreams, but he found nothing. Everything was so small to him, so near, so wet, he would have liked to tuck the earth behind the stove, he couldn't understand that he needed so much time to clamber down a slope, to reach a distant point; he thought he should be able to measure out everything with a few strides. Only sometimes, when the storm cast the clouds into the valleys and they swirled up through the trees, and the voices awoke amongst the rocks, at first like distant rumbling thunder, then arriving with a roar in mighty chords as though they wished in their wild exulting to sing the praises of the earth, and the clouds galloped up like wild whinnying horses, and the sunlight pierced them and came and drew his flashing sword along the sheets of snow so that a bright, blinding light went slicing over the peaks and down into the valleys; or when the storm drove the clouds downwards and tore a hole in them, a light blue lake, and then the wind fell silent and far below a sound like lullabies and church bells rose from ravines and treetops, and a delicate red spread upwards in the dark blue sky, and tiny clouds went past on silver wings, and all the mountain peaks, sharp and solid, flashed and glowed far across the land – then his breast burst, he stood there panting, his body bent forward, his eyes and mouth wide open, he thought he should draw the storm right into himself, embrace all things within his being, he spread and lay over the entire earth, he burrowed his way into the All, it was an ecstasy that hurt; or else he stopped and laid his head in the moss and half closed his eyes, then everything receded far away, the earth beneath him shrank, grew small like a wandering star and dipped into a roaring stream whose limpid depths stretched out beneath him. But these were only moments, and then he stood up, sober, solid, calm, as though a shadow-play had passed before him, no memory remained. Towards evening he reached the crest of the mountains, the snowfields that led down again to the westward plain, he sat a while at the top. It had turned calmer towards evening; the clouds lay solid and motionless in the sky, nothing so far as the eye could see but mountain peaks from which broad slopes descended, and everything so quiet, grey, increasingly faint; he felt a terrible loneliness, he was all alone, completely alone, he wanted to talk to himself, but he couldn't, he scarcely dared breathe, his footfall rang like thunder beneath him, he had to sit down; a nameless fear took hold of him in this nothing, he was in empty space, he leapt to his feet and flew down the slope. Darkness had fallen, heaven and earth had melted into one. It was as though something were following him, as though something terrible would catch up with him, something no human can bear, as though madness were chasing him on mighty horses. At last he heard voices, saw lights, he felt a little easier, he was told it was another half-hour to Waldbach. He walked through the village, the candlelight shone through the windows, he looked in as he passed, children at the table, old women, young girls, the faces all calm and still, it seemed to him as if they were the source of the radiant light, he was filled with ease, he was soon in the vicarage in Waldbach.[1] They were sitting at table, he entered the room; his blond locks hung about his ashen face, his mouth and eyes twitched, his clothes were torn. Oberlin[2] bade him welcome, he took him for a journeyman. 'I don't know who you are, but I bid you welcome.' 'I am a friend of Kaufmann's[3] and bring you his greetings.' 'Your name, if you please?' 'Lenz.' 'Ah yes, let me see, are you not in print? Have I not read a few plays that bear such a name?' 'Yes, but pray do not judge me by that.' The conversation continued, he hunted for words and then rattled them out, but as though on the rack; gradually he grew calm, the homely room and the calm faces emerging from the shadows, the radiant face of a child upon which all light appeared to rest, looking up full of trust and curiosity, glancing at its mother sitting calm, like an angel, in the shadows at the back. He began to talk, recounted where he came from; he sketched all manner of local costumes,[4] they thronged around him full of interest, he was soon at home, his pale child's face, now full of smiles, his knack of bringing his story to life; he grew quiet, he felt as if forgotten faces, figures from long ago, were reappearing from the darkness, old songs came to life, he was away, far away. It was finally time to go, he was led across the road, the vicarage was too small, they gave him a room in the schoolhouse. He went up, it was cold upstairs, a large room, bare, a high bed right at the back, he set his candle on the table and paced up and down, he went over the day in his mind, his journey here, the place itself, the room in the vicarage with its lights and kindly faces, it was like a shadow, a dream, and emptiness overcame him, as it had on the mountain, but he could fill it with nothing any more, the candle had gone out, the darkness swallowed everything; a nameless terror seized him, he leapt up, he ran through the room, down the stairs, in front of the house; but no use, darkness everywhere, nothing, he himself but a dream, random thoughts came ghosting by, he grasped at them and held them tight, he felt as if he had to repeat 'Our Father' again and again; he could find himself no longer, an obscure instinct drove him to save himself, he banged his head against the stones, he ripped his flesh with his nails, the pain began to restore his consciousness, he hurled himself in the fountain, but the water was shallow, he could only splash about. Then people came, they had heard the noise, they called to him. Oberlin came running; Lenz was himself again, the situation was clear to him in every detail, he felt easy once more, he felt ashamed and sorry to have given the good people such a fright, he told them he was accustomed to taking cold baths, and went back upstairs; at last, exhausted, he fell asleep.

All went well the following day. With Oberlin on horseback through the valley; broad slopes funnelling down from on high to form a narrow, winding valley that climbed and twisted far into the mountains, great masses of rock that broadened towards the bottom, few trees, but all of them in grey, grave coppices, a view of the distant countryside to westward and of the chain of mountains that stretched away to north and south and whose peaks stood like a fading dream, still and silent, massive, grave. Huge masses of light that sometimes streamed from the valleys like a river of gold, then clouds that lay on the tallest peak and slowly slipped over the trees and down into the valley or rose and fell in the flashes of sunlight like silver gossamer; no sound, no movement, no birds, nothing but the sighing of the wind, now far, now near. Distant points became visible too, the skeleton of huts, straw-topped planks, grave and black. The people, silent and grave as though not daring to break the peace of their valley, saluted quietly as they rode by. All was bustle in the huts, they thronged around Oberlin, he chided, counselled, consoled; everywhere prayers, eyes full of trust. The people recounted dreams, premonitions. Then straight into practical life, laying out new roads, digging ditches, visiting the school. Oberlin was tireless, Lenz his constant companion, now talking, now working, now lost in contemplation of nature. It all had a benign and calming effect on him, he would often look into Oberlin's eyes, and the mighty peace that comes over us at the sight of nature in repose, in the depths of forests, in melting moonlit summer nights, seemed even nearer to him in these calm eyes, this grave and venerable face. He was shy, but he offered observations, he spoke, Oberlin found his conversation most agreeable, and Lenz's graceful child's face filled him with joy. But he could bear it only so long as there was light in the valley; towards evening he was seized by a peculiar fear, he would have liked to follow the sun; as objects became more and more shadowy, everything seemed to him so dream-like, so horrible, he was filled with the same kind of fear as children asleep in the dark; he felt as though he were blind; his fear now grew, the spectre of madness settled at his feet, the thought that everything existed only as his dream opened before him like a fatal chasm, he clung to objects of every kind, figures rushed by him, he flung himself on them, they were shadows, the life drained out of him, his limbs were quite rigid. He talked, he sang, he recited Shakespeare, he seized at everything that had quickened his blood in earlier days, he tried everything, but cold, cold. Then he had to get out into the open air, the faint light scattered across the night made him feel better as soon as his eyes were used to the dark, he leapt into the fountain, the sharp shock of the water made him feel better, he also secretly hoped to fall ill, he now bathed less noisily. But the more he adjusted to the life, the calmer he became; he helped Oberlin, drew, read the Bible; old, long-dormant hopes reawoke in him; the New Testament seemed so real to him here, and [*words missing*] When Oberlin recounted how an invisible hand had held him on the bridge, how a dazzling light had blinded him in the mountains, how he had heard a voice speak to him in the night, and how God had come to him so completely that he had taken the tokens[5] from his pocket like a child in order to know what he should do, – this faith, this eternal heaven in life, this being in God; now for the first time he understood the Scriptures. The way nature came so close to these people, all in heavenly mysteries, yet not with terrible majesty but as something still known and familiar! – One morning he went out, snow had fallen in the night, bright sunshine lay in the valley, but the landscape beyond half hidden in mist. He soon left the path, up a gentle slope, no trace of footsteps now, along the edge of a pine-wood, the sun etched crystals, the snow was light and fluffy, here and there in the snow faint traces of animals leading into the mountains. The air quite still save a gentle sighing and the rustle of a bird softly shaking the snow from its tail. Everything so quiet, and the white-feathered trees in all directions swaying gently in the deep blue air. He felt steadily more at home, the awesome mass of lines and spaces that sometimes made him feel they were speaking in awesome voice directly to him were veiled from sight, a warm Christmas feeling stole over him, he thought at times that his mother would be sure to appear from behind a tree, larger than life, and tell him she had given him all this as a present; as he went back down, he saw a rainbow of radiance envelop his shadow, he felt as if something touched his forehead, the presence spoke to him. He came down. Oberlin was in the room, Lenz went up to him all serene and told him he would like one day to preach a sermon. 'Are you a theologian?' 'Yes!' 'Good then, next Sunday.'⁶

Lenz went delighted to his room, he began to think about a text for his sermon, a meditative mood came over him, and his nights became peaceful. Sunday morning arrived, a thaw had set in. Drifting clouds, patches of blue, the church stood on a spur of rock a short way up the hill, the churchyard round about it. Lenz stood there as the bell rang out and the worshippers came from every side on the narrow paths leading up and down between the rocks, the women and girls in their grave black costumes, on their prayerbooks the folded white handkerchief and sprig of rosemary. From time to time a splash of sunlight lay across the valley, the warm air slowly stirred, the landscape shimmered in a pool of fragrance, a distant sound of bells, it seemed as though everything were dissolving into a single harmonious wave.

In the tiny churchyard the snow was gone, dark moss amongst the black crosses, a cluster of late roses leaning against the churchyard wall, late flowers, too, peering from the moss, sometimes sunlight, then shadow again. The service began, the voices of the people merged in bright pure harmony; it was like gazing into pure clear water from a mountain spring. The sounds of the singing died away, Lenz began to speak, he was shy, thanks to the music his numbness was gone, all his pain awoke and filled his heart. A sweet sensation of endless well-being crept over him. He spoke simply to the people, all shared his suffering, and it was a comfort to him if he could bring sleep to weeping tired eyes and peace to tortured hearts, if in the face of this existence racked by material needs he could guide this silent suffering towards heaven. He had found more strength by the time he finished, then the voices began to sing again:

> Let in me the sacred passion
> Open all the deepest wells;

> Suffering be my sole reward,
> Suffering be my praise to God.[7]

The surging within him, the music, the pain threw him into turmoil. The whole universe seemed stricken by terrible wounds; it filled him with deep indescribable pain. Then suddenly, a different being: lips divine leaned down towards him, met his own and sucked at them in trembling fervour. He went to his solitary room. He was alone, alone! And then the wellspring roared, the tears came bursting from his eyes in torrents, his body writhed, his limbs convulsed, he felt as though he must dissolve, there seemed no end to this voluptuous bliss; at last it faded, he felt the balm of deep self-pity, he wept for himself, his head sank onto his chest, he fell asleep, the full moon stood there in the sky, his locks tumbled down over temple and face, the tears still clung to his lashes and dried on his cheeks, and so he lay there now alone, and all was calm and still and cold and the moon shone down the whole night through and stood there over the mountains.[8]

The next morning he came down, he told Oberlin quite calmly how his mother had appeared to him during the night: she had stepped from the darkness of the churchyard wall, dressed all in white and with roses at her chest, one white, one red; then she had sunk down in a corner and slowly the roses had grown up above her, she was surely dead; but he felt quite calm.[9] Oberlin then told him how at the time of his father's death he had been alone in the fields and had heard a voice and knew at once that his father was dead, and so it proved when he came back home. This led them further. Oberlin talked of the people up in the mountains, of girls divining water and metals beneath the earth, of men fighting spirits that seized them on mountain-tops; he told him too how once in the mountains he had been put into a kind of sleepwalker's trance by gazing into the fathomless void of a mountain pool. Lenz said that the spirit of the water had come over him and in consequence he had felt something of his essential being. He continued: the simplest, purest kind of human nature was most closely connected to elemental nature; the more refined the mental life and emotions of a person became, the more this elemental sense was blunted; it was no very elevated state in his view, it was insufficiently independent, but he thought it must give a feeling of infinite bliss to be touched by the essential life in each form of nature, to have a soul receptive to stone, metal, water and plants, to be able as though in a dream to take into oneself each being within nature as flowers take in air with the waxing and the waning of the moon.[10]

He voiced more of his beliefs, how he saw in all things an indescribable harmony,[11] a resonance, a blessedness, which in the higher forms of life had numerous means of making itself graspable, audible, apprehensible, but in consequence was all the more attenuated, whereas in the lower forms everything was necessarily more contained, more restricted, but its tranquillity in consequence greater. He pursued this even further. Oberlin stopped him, it took him too far from his simple ways. On another occasion Oberlin showed him colour tokens, he explained the relationship of each colour to mankind, he cited the twelve apostles, each of whom, he said, was represented by a colour.[12] Lenz took this in, developed it further, had anxious dreams, and began, like Stilling,[13] to read the Apocalypse, and devoted himself to reading the Bible.

At about this time Kaufmann came to the Steintal with his fiancée. At first Lenz found the encounter unpleasant, he had made himself such a niche, the little bit of peace was so very dear to him, and now he was faced with someone who reminded him of so much, someone he had to talk to and who knew his history. Oberlin knew nothing of all that; he had taken him in and cared for him; he saw it as an act of God, who had chosen to send him this unhappy man, whom he dearly loved. And they all found it right and necessary for him to be there, he belonged amongst them as if he had always been there, and no one asked where he had come from or where he was going. At table Lenz was back in good spirits, the topic was literature, he was in his element; the idealist period was beginning at the time,[14] Kaufmann was a keen supporter,[15] Lenz was vehement in opposing it. Those writers, he argued, of whom it was said that they reflected reality in fact knew nothing whatever about it, but even they were a good deal more bearable than those who sought to *transfigure* reality. The dear Lord, he said, has surely made the world as it is meant

to be, and I doubt if we can cobble up anything better, our one
aspiration should be to create much as he did. What I demand in
all things is – life, full scope for existence, nothing else really
matters; we then have no need to ask whether something is ugly
or beautiful, both are overridden by the conviction that 'Everything created possesses life', which is the sole criterion in matters
of art. All the same, we meet it only rarely; we find it in
Shakespeare, it speaks to us full-throated in folksongs, fitfully in
Goethe. Everything else can be thrown in the fire. These people
can't even draw a dog-kennel. They are supposed to want idealist
figures, but they have produced nothing to my knowledge but
wooden puppets. This 'idealism' displays the most shameful contempt for human nature. People should try it sometime, they
should enter completely into the life of the meanest of men and
then reproduce it with every twitch of an eyebrow, every wink
and nod, the whole subtle, hardly perceptible play of facial
expression; he had tried something of the sort in *The Tutor* and
The Soldiers.[16] They are the most everyday people in the world;
but the pulse of feeling is the same in almost everyone, the only
difference is the thickness of the covering that it has to pass
through. All you need is the eyes to see and the ears to hear.
Yesterday as I walked up by the valley I saw two girls sitting on
a stone, one putting up her hair, the other helping; and her
golden hair cascading down, and a pale grave face, and so very
young, and her black peasant dress, and the other so helpful, so
full of concern. Even the most intense, most beautiful paintings of
the old German school[17] give scarcely a hint of it. Sometimes one
would like to be a Medusa's head to be able to turn such a
tableau to stone, then shout to everyone to come and look. They
stood up, the beautiful tableau was gone for ever; but as they
clambered down amongst the rocks there was yet another picture.
The most beautiful images, the most resonant harmonies, coalesce,
dissolve. Only one thing abides: an infinite beauty that passes
from form to form, eternally changed and revealed afresh,[18]
though needless to say you can't always capture it and stick it in
museums or put it into music, then summon all and sundry and
have them prattling away, both young and old, and getting all
excited. You need to love mankind to be able to reach the

essential being of each individual, you must consider no one too lowly, no one too ugly, only then can you understand them; the most ordinary of faces makes a deeper impression than any contrived sensation of beauty, and you can let the characters' own being emerge quite naturally without bringing in anything copied from outside where no life, no pulse, no muscles surge and throb. Kaufmann objected that he would find no models in reality for the Apollo Belvedere[19] or Raphael's Madonnas.[20] What does that matter, Lenz retorted, I have to confess that things like that leave me utterly cold. If I work at it within myself, I can doubtless generate feeling of some kind, but it takes a real effort. The writers and artists I like above all are those that most strongly convey the reality of nature, with the result that their work engages my feelings. Everything else troubles me. I prefer the Dutch painters to the Italians, they are the only ones, too, that you can truly grasp; I know only two paintings, both by Dutchmen, that have as much effect on me as the New Testament does; one of them, I don't know who by, is of Christ and the disciples at Emmaus.[21] When you read how the disciples went out: the whole of nature resides in those few words. It is a sombre twilight evening, a monotonous streak of red on the horizon, the road half in darkness, a stranger approaches, they talk, he breaks bread, with their simple humanity they realize who he is, and the divine suffering in his face calls out to them, and they are afraid, for it has grown dark, and they are touched by something beyond understanding, but it is not some ghostly dread; it is like a dead beloved coming up to you in the twilight, just as they used to be – that is how the picture looks with its all-pervading brownish tinge, its still and sombre air of evening. Then another one.[22] A woman sits in her room, prayerbook in hand. All is Sunday-fresh and orderly, the clean sand scattered, so pure and warm and homely. The woman couldn't go to church, and she is saying her prayers at home, the window is open, she sits turned towards it, and it is as though the sound of the bells in the village were floating across the wide, flat landscape into her window, as though she can hear faint echoes of the hymns in the church not far away, and the woman is following the words in her prayerbook. – He carried on speaking in similar vein, they listened attentively, much struck home, he was flushed from all the talking, and he shook his blond locks, now smiling, now grave. It had taken him completely out of himself. After the meal Kaufmann took him to one side. He had received letters from Lenz's father,[23] Lenz was to go home and give him assistance. Kaufmann told him how he was squandering his life here, uselessly wasting it, he should set himself a goal – and so on and so on. 'Leave!' Lenz retorted angrily, 'leave this place? Go home? Go mad there? You know I can't bear it anywhere but here, in this countryside; if I couldn't get out on to a mountain occasionally and see the landscape all around, then come back home and walk through the garden and look inside through the window – I'd go mad! mad! Leave me in peace, for God's sake! A little bit of peace, that's all, now that I'm starting to feel a bit happier. Leave this place? Three words, that's all, and the world is ruined, I don't understand it. We all need something; what could be better than having peace! Climbing ever higher and battling onward, forever spurning what the moment offers, always fasting in order to feast in the future, choosing to go thirsty while bright streams sparkle right before you. Life is bearable now, and I want to stay here. Why? why? Because I feel happy, that's why. What does my father want? Can he give me more? Impossible! Leave me in peace.' He became very angry, Kaufmann walked out, Lenz's mood was soured.

The following day Kaufmann wanted to leave, he urged Oberlin to go with him to Switzerland. What decided him was that he had long known Lavater[24] through correspondence, and wanted also to meet him in person: he agreed to go. They had to wait another day for all the preparations to be made. Lenz was filled with dismay. To escape his infinite torment he had anxiously clung to whatever he could; at various moments he was deeply aware that he was simply accommodating everything to his needs; he treated himself like an invalid child, he was prey to thoughts and mighty emotions that he escaped only at the cost of supreme terror, and then he felt drawn to them again by an infinite force, he shook and trembled, his hair almost stood on end, until with the most colossal effort he prevailed at last. He took refuge in a figure that constantly danced before his eyes –

and in Oberlin; his words, his face were an infinite comfort to him. And so he viewed his impending departure with fear.

Lenz was frightened at the prospect of remaining in the house on his own. The weather had turned mild, he decided to accompany Oberlin up into the mountains. On the other side, where the valleys run down into the plain, they parted. He returned alone. He wandered through the mountains hither and thither, broad slopes funnelled down into the valleys, few trees, nothing but mighty sweeping lines and, further beyond, the distant smoking plain, in the air a mighty rushing, nowhere any trace of man save here and there an empty hut, used by shepherds in the summer, perched forlornly on the mountainside. He grew quiet, perhaps almost in a dream, for him everything melted into a single line, like a wave of water rising and falling between heaven and earth, it was as though he were lying by the edge of an infinite, gently undulating sea. Sometimes he sat down, then he carried on walking, but slowly and in a dream. He sought no path. It was profoundly dark when he came to an inhabited hut on the slopes leading down towards the Steintal.[25] The door was shut, he went to the window where a glimmer of light was shining through. A lamp illumined scarcely more than a single point: its light fell on the ashen face of a girl sitting calmly behind it with half-open eyes, silently moving her lips. Further away in the darkness sat an old woman, singing from a hymnal in a harsh croaking voice. He knocked and knocked, she opened the door; she was half deaf, she gave Lenz food and showed him where he could sleep, continuing all the while to croak her hymn. The girl hadn't stirred. A little while later a man arrived, he was tall and gaunt, traces of grey hair, his face troubled, restless. He stepped towards the girl, she started violently and was suddenly restless. He took a dried herb from the wall and laid the leaves on her hands, this made her more calm and she began in sustained and piercing tones to hum intelligible words. He recounted how he had heard a voice in the mountains and then seen a sheet of lightning above the valleys, it had touched him, too, he said, and he had wrestled with it like Jacob. He threw himself to the floor and prayed in hushed, fervent tones, while the sick girl sang her long-drawn-out phrases that echoed gently before fading away. Then he went to bed.

Lenz dozed off in a dream, then from the depths of sleep heard the ticking of the clock. Amidst the quiet chanting of the girl and the croak of the old woman the whistle of the wind could be heard, now near, now far, and as in a dream the moon, now clear, now veiled, bathed the room in its changing light. At one point the sounds became louder, the girl spoke distinctly and definitely, she said how a church stood on the cliff over on the other side. Lenz looked up, and she was sitting there bolt upright behind the table with wide-open eyes, and the moon cast its silent light upon her features, from which an unearthly glow appeared to radiate, while the old woman continued her croaking – and amidst all this changing and ebbing of light, this hubbub of sounds and voices, Lenz fell at last into a deep sleep.

He woke early, all were asleep in the half-light of the room, even the girl was at rest, lying back in her chair, her hands folded under her left cheek; the ghostly air was gone from her features, she bore instead an expression of indescribable suffering. He went to the window and opened it, the cold morning air struck his face. The house lay at the end of a deep, narrow valley that opened towards the east, crimson rays shot through the grey morning sky into the twilit, mist-clad valley, sparkled on the grey rock and flashed through the windows of the huts. The man awoke, his eyes met a candle-lit picture on the wall, they remained fastened upon it in a fixed and rigid stare, his lips began to move, and he prayed in a voice at first quiet, then loud and ever louder. As he did so people entered the hut and threw themselves to their knees without uttering a word. The girl lay convulsed, the old woman grunted her hymn and gossiped with her neighbours. The people told Lenz the man had come to the district long before, no one knew where from; he was reputed to be a saint, he could see water beneath the ground and summon spirits, and people came to him as pilgrims. Lenz also discovered that he had strayed quite far from the Steintal, he left with some woodcutters who were going that way. He felt glad of the company: it suddenly felt eerie and forbidding in the presence of this mighty figure, who seemed at times to speak in fearsome tones. He was afraid of himself as well should he find himself alone.

He came home. But the previous night had affected him

profoundly. For him the world had been suddenly illumined, and he recognized within himself a stirring, seething fascination for an abyss towards which a relentless force was dragging him. He fell into a frenzy of self-absorption. He ate little, spent most of each night in prayer and feverish dreams. A violent surging within him, then collapse and exhaustion; he would lie there in floods of the hottest tears, then suddenly, possessed by a fit of strength, rise to his feet, cold and indifferent, then his tears felt like ice, he had to laugh. The more he raised himself, the further he fell. Everything streamed back together within him. Glimpses of his earlier state flashed through him and briefly lit up the terrible chaos of his mind. During the day he normally sat in the room downstairs, Madame Oberlin went to and fro, he drew, painted, read, seized on every distraction, jumping abruptly from one thing to another. But he now attached himself especially to Madame Oberlin as she sat there, her black hymnal before her, a house plant close by, her youngest child between her knees; he devoted a lot of time to the child too. He was sitting there once when he suddenly grew anxious, he leapt to his feet and paced up and down. The door was ajar, he heard the maid singing, at first it was a blur, then the words came through:

> In this world can I ne'er be gay,
> My dear beloved is far away.

The effect on him was profound, he seemed almost destroyed at the sound of the words. Madame Oberlin looked at him. He plucked up his courage, he couldn't remain silent, he had to speak. 'Dearest Madame Oberlin, can't you tell me what the girl is doing whose fate weighs so heavily upon me?'[26] 'But, Herr Lenz, I know nothing about it.'

He fell silent again and paced rapidly up and down the room; then he began once again: 'I want to go, do you see; God knows, you're the only people where I could bear it – but even so, even so, I have to leave, go to *her* – but I can't, I mustn't –'. He was extremely agitated, and left the room.

Towards evening Lenz returned, it was growing dark in the room; he sat down near Madame Oberlin. 'You see,' he began again, 'I can picture her walking through the room, singing softly

to herself, every step was music, there was so much happiness in
her, and it flowed over into me, I was always at peace whenever
I looked at her, or she leant her head against me and – God!
God! – I haven't known peace for such a long time [*words missing*]
So wholly a child; it was as though she found the world too big,
she retreated so completely into her own being, she would seek
out the smallest nook in the house and just sit there, as though
her whole happiness were concentrated in a single tiny point, and
then I too would feel the same; at such moments I could have
played like a child. Now I feel so constricted, you see, so terribly
constricted, I sometimes feel as if my hands were pressing against
the sky; oh, I can't breathe! Then I often feel as if I'm experien-
cing physical pain, here on my left side, in the arm I always held
her with. Yet I can't imagine her any more, her picture evades
me, and this tortures me, only occasionally when things seem
utterly bright and clear do I feel really happy again.' – Later he
often spoke to Madame Oberlin of these things, but almost only
in disjointed sentences; she could never find much to say in reply,
but he found it comforting all the same.

Meanwhile his religious torments continued. The more empty,
cold and dead he felt within himself, the greater was his urge to
ignite an inner fire; memories came flooding back of times when
there was a mighty surging throughout his being, when he was
almost overwhelmed by the intensity of his emotions; and now so
dead. He despaired of himself, and then he would fling himself on
his knees, wring his hands, work himself into a frenzy; but dead!
dead! Then he pleaded with God to give him a sign, relentlessly
scoured his innermost being, fasted, lay dreaming on the ground.
On the 3rd of February he heard that a child had died in
Fouday, Friederike by name, he latched onto this fact like an
idée fixe. He withdrew to his room and fasted for a day. On the
4th he suddenly came into the room and went up to Madame
Oberlin, he had daubed ash on his face, he demanded an old
sack; she was filled with alarm, he was given what he wanted. He
wrapped the sack around himself like a penitent and set out for
Fouday. The people in the valley were long since used to him; all
manner of strange stories were current about him. He entered the
house where the child lay. The people within were going about

their business in total indifference; someone pointed to a room, the child lay on a wooden table clothed in a shift and bedded on straw.

Lenz shuddered when he touched her cold limbs and saw her half-open glassy eyes. The child seemed to him so forlorn, and he himself so alone and isolated; he threw himself on top of the corpse; death frightened him, he was seized by an agony of pain, these features, this quiet face were going to rot away, he threw himself to his knees and with all the plangent ardour of despair he prayed that God might give him, weak and wretched creature that he was, a sign, and bring the child back to life; whereupon he huddled down in total concentration, focusing all his will-power on a single point, and thus he remained for a long time, quite rigid. Then he stood and, grasping the hands of the child, said loudly and firmly: 'Arise, and walk!' But the words echoed back from the sober walls as though in mockery, and the corpse stayed cold.[27] He fell to the ground, half-seized by madness, then something drove him to his feet, and he fled into the mountains. Clouds raced across the moon, now blanketing everything in darkness, now revealing the melting, shadowy outline of the landscape in the moonlight. He rushed to and fro. His breast was bursting with the exultation of hell. The rushing of the wind was like a chorus of Titans; he felt as if he could thrust a gigantic fist into heaven and seize God by the scruff of the neck and drag Him bodily through the clouds, as if he could crunch the world to bits with his teeth and spit the pieces in their Creator's face; he cursed, he blasphemed. Thus he came to the crest of the mountains, and the uncertain light spread down into the depths below where lay the huge white masses of stone, and the heavens were an eye of idiot blue, and the moon just stood there, moronic and ridiculous. Lenz laughed out loud, he couldn't help it, and as he laughed the hand of atheism clutched at him and held him fast in a grip completely secure and steady and firm. He no longer knew what had moved him so deeply earlier that day, he was frozen, he decided that sleep was what he wanted, and he strode cold and unshakeable through the ghostly darkness – everything seemed to him empty and hollow, he had to start running, and went to bed.

The next morning a deep horror overcame him at the state he had been in the previous day; he stood now on the brink of an abyss, driven by an insane desire to keep on peering into it, reliving the same agony again and again. Then his fear grew more intense, his sin against the Holy Ghost stood starkly before him.

A few days later Oberlin returned from Switzerland, much earlier than expected. Lenz was dismayed. But his spirits returned once Oberlin began talking of his friends in Alsace, wandering about the room as he did so, unpacking his things and putting them away. He mentioned Pfeffel,[28] exalting the happy lot of a country parson. He also urged him to comply with his father's wishes, to live in accordance with his proper vocation, to return to his home. He told him: 'Honour thy father and thy mother', and other such things. At this Lenz fell into a state of extreme agitation; deep sighs racked his body, tears burst from his eyes, his words were disjointed. 'Yes, but I couldn't bear it. Are you casting me out? In you alone lies the path to God. As for me, I am finished! I am fallen from God, damned for all eternity, the Wandering Jew!'[29] That was what Jesus had died for, said Oberlin, he should turn to Him with fervent devotion, and by so doing he would share in His grace.

Lenz raised his head, wrung his hands, and said: 'Oh my God! Divine consolation!' Then suddenly he asked in an amiable tone: 'What's the girl doing now?' Oberlin told him he knew nothing about it, but wanted to help and advise him in all things, but had to have details of the place and the circumstances and the person involved. Disjointed words were his only reply: 'Oh, she's dead! Is she still alive? You angel, she loved me – I loved her, she deserved it, oh you angel! Damned jealousy, I sacrificed her – she loved another man too[30] – I loved her, she was worthy of it – Oh dear kind mother, she loved me too. I'm a murderer.' Perhaps these people were all still alive, replied Oberlin, perhaps quite contented; but however that may be, it was certain that if he gave himself fully to God, He would heed his prayers and his tears and do such goodness unto them that the benefit he brought them might far outweigh whatever harm he had done. At this he grew steadily calmer, and returned to his painting.

He came back again in the afternoon. Over his left shoulder he had a length of fur, in his hand a bundle of birch-rods that someone had asked Oberlin to give to him with a letter. He offered the rods to Oberlin and begged him to beat him. Oberlin took the rods from his hand, kissed him several times on the mouth, and said these were the only strokes he could give him; he should try to be calm, and should settle his business with God alone; all the beatings in the world would not take away even one of his sins; Jesus had taken care of that, he should turn to Him. Lenz went away.

At supper, as usual, his mood was quite melancholy. He talked none the less of many different things, but rapidly and anxiously. At midnight Oberlin was woken by a noise. Lenz was rushing through the courtyard repeatedly shouting the name 'Friederike' in a hollow, strident voice heavy with confusion and despair, he then threw himself in the fountain, splashed around, scrambled out, up to his room again, back to the fountain, up, down, up, down several times more; at last he settled. The maids who slept in the nursery below him said that often, but especially that night, they had heard a clamour that they could only compare to the cry of a snipe. Perhaps it was the sound of him wailing, in a hollow, terrible, despairing voice.

The next morning Lenz failed to appear at his customary time. In the end Oberlin went up to his room, he was lying in bed, tranquil and motionless. Oberlin had to enquire again and again before an answer came; eventually he said: 'Yes, Reverend, it's boredom you see, boredom! It's all so boring. I don't even know what to say any more. I've already drawn pictures of all the people on the wall.' Oberlin told him he should turn to God; at that he laughed and said: 'Yes, if I had the good fortune to discover a pastime as cosy as yours, I'm sure I could manage to fill the time. Everything comes of idleness. Most people pray out of boredom, others fall in love out of boredom, some turn to virtue, others to vice – and for me there is nothing, nothing, not even suicide: it's just too boring!'[31]

> Oh God amidst Thy radiant light,
> Amidst Thy midday heat so bright,
> My waking eyes are grown so sore.
> If only night would come once more.'

Oberlin glared at him angrily and made to go. Lenz darted after him, looked at him with haunting eyes, and said: 'There, you see, it's suddenly come to me, if only I could determine whether I'm awake or dreaming: such a vital question, we shall have to explore it' – then he darted back to bed.

That afternoon Oberlin wanted to pay a visit in the neighbour-hood; his wife had gone ahead and he was about to leave when there was a knock at his door and Lenz came in with body bent forward, head hung down, ash smeared over the whole of his face and parts of his clothing, and clutching his left arm with his right hand. He begged Oberlin to pull his arm, he had put it out of joint, he had jumped out of the window, but since no one had seen it, he wanted no one to know. Oberlin was aghast, but said nothing and did Lenz's bidding, while instantly writing to the schoolmaster at Bellefosse, Sebastian Scheidecker, telling him to come and giving him instructions. Then he rode on his way. The man came. Lenz had often met him and had grown quite attached to him. He pretended he had wanted to talk to Oberlin, then made as if to leave. Lenz begged him not to go, and so they stayed together. Lenz suggested a walk to Fouday. He visited the grave of the child he had tried to raise from the dead, knelt down repeatedly, kissed the mound of earth, appeared to be praying, though in deep confusion, tore off part of the flower on the grave as a keepsake, went back to Waldbach, turned around again, with Sebastian the schoolmaster always beside him. Sometimes he walked slowly, complaining of great weakness in all his limbs, then he would rush along in frantic desperation, the countryside frightened him, he felt so enclosed that he was afraid of bumping into everything. An indescribable feeling of unease overcame him, he began to find his companion a burden, perhaps, too, he had guessed his real purpose and was trying to get rid of him. Sebastian played along with him, but secretly managed to alert his brother, and Lenz now had two people guarding him instead of one. He led them here, there and everywhere, eventually he took the path back to Waldbach, as they neared the village he turned in a flash and went bounding like a stag in the direction of Fouday. The men chased after him. While they were searching for him in Fouday two shopkeepers came and told them of a stranger held captive in one of the houses who claimed he was a murderer but surely couldn't be. They ran to the house, and found it so. At the furious insistence of Lenz himself a terrified young man had tied him up. They untied him and took him safely back to Waldbach, where Oberlin had meanwhile returned with his wife. He looked confused, but noticing how kindly and lovingly he was greeted, he recovered his spirits, his face relaxed, he thanked his two escorts most gently and kindly, and the evening passed in unruffled calm. Oberlin implored him to give up his bathing, to stay calmly in bed the whole night through, and if he couldn't sleep, to talk to God. He gave his word, and duly kept it that following night, the maids heard him praying almost all night long. – The next morning he came to Oberlin's room with a cheerful expression. After they had chatted on a variety of topics, he suddenly remarked with the utmost amiability: 'Dear Reverend, that girl that I spoke of is dead, yes dead, poor angel.' 'How do you know?' 'Hieroglyphs, hieroglyphs –' and then again, with his eyes lifted heavenwards: 'Yes, dead – hieroglyphs.' That was all he would say. He sat down and wrote some letters, then gave them to Oberlin with the request that he add a few lines.

Meanwhile his condition had grown ever more hopeless. The peace he had derived from the proximity of Oberlin and the tranquillity of the valley had gone completely; the world that he had wanted to enjoy was irredeemably fractured. He had no love, no hate, no hope, just a terrible emptiness and the frantic, agonizing urge to fill it. He had *nothing*. Whatever he did, he did quite consciously, and yet he was driven by an inner compulsion. When he was on his own, he felt such terrifying loneliness that he continually talked out loud to himself, then his fear redoubled and he imagined he was hearing the voice of a stranger. In conversation he often stumbled, seized by indescribable fear, he had lost the end of his sentence; he then felt obliged to hang on to the last word he had spoken and repeat it again and again, only with great difficulty could he suppress such impulses. The good people were deeply troubled when sometimes in calm moments he would be sitting with them talking quite normally, then suddenly stop with a look of unspeakable fear on his face, grip the arm of whoever was nearest to him, and only slowly come to himself again. When he was alone, or reading by himself, it was even worse, his entire mind would become stuck on a single thought; if he began thinking of someone else, or saw them vividly in his imagination, he felt as if he was becoming them himself, he became utterly confused, at the same time he had a boundless urge to make free in his mind with everything around him – nature, people (except for Oberlin), and all quite coldly, as if in a dream; it amused him to up-end houses and stand them on their roofs, to take people's clothes off and put them back on, to dream up the craziest pranks. Sometimes he felt an irresistible urge to enact whatever fantasy he happened to have in mind, then his face would twist into terrible grimaces. On one occasion he was sitting next to Oberlin, the cat was lying on the chair opposite, suddenly his eyes turned stony, he transfixed the animal with an unwavering stare, then slowly slid from his chair, the cat did the same, as if bewitched by his gaze, it was stricken with terror, it bristled and snarled, Lenz, his face horribly contorted, snarled in return, both leapt at each other as if in desperation, until at last Madame Oberlin arose to separate them, whereupon he felt deeply ashamed once more. His nocturnal troubles intensified to the most terrible degree. Only with the greatest difficulty could he get to sleep, having first attempted to fill the dreadful emptiness. Then between sleep and waking he fell into a terrifying state; he bumped against something hideous, horrific, madness seized hold of him, he would start up in bed pouring with sweat and screaming horribly, only gradually coming to himself again. He could retrieve himself on such occasions only by proceeding from the simplest things. It wasn't really he that did it but some powerful instinct for self-preservation, it was as if he were double and one side of him were calling out to the other in an effort to save it;[32] shaking with fear he would recite poetry and stories until he recovered his composure.

He suffered these attacks in the daytime too, and they were then much worse, for the light had previously been his safeguard. He felt at such moments as if he alone existed, as if the world existed only in his imagination, as if there were nothing but him, as if he were Satan, damned in all eternity, alone on the rack of his imagination. He rehearsed his past life in a hectic frenzy and then gave his verdict: 'logical, logical'; the pronouncements of others were 'illogical, illogical'; it was the gaping abyss of incurable madness, a madness through all eternity. He was galvanized at times by an instinctive urge to keep hold of his mind; he threw himself into Oberlin's arms, clung on to him as though wanting to melt into his body, he was the only being that had life for him, the only one in whom life stood revealed once more. Gradually Oberlin's words brought him to himself again, he knelt there before him, his hands in Oberlin's, his head in his lap, dank with cold sweat, the whole of his body trembling and heaving. Oberlin felt infinite compassion, the family knelt and prayed for him in his wretched misery, the maids fled, seeing in him a man possessed. And when he grew calmer, his grief was like a child's, he sobbed, he felt the deepest self-pity; these were also the moments of his deepest happiness. Oberlin spoke to him of God. Lenz quietly drew back, looked at him with an expression of infinite suffering, and finally said: 'But me, if I were almighty, do you see, if I were omnipotent, I couldn't bear people suffering, I would save them, save them;[33] I want nothing but peace, peace, just a little peace and the chance to sleep.' This was blasphemy, said Oberlin. Lenz gave a desolate shake of the head. The half-hearted attempts at suicide that he kept making were not really serious; it was not so much a desire for death – death held for him neither peace nor hope – but rather the attempt, at moments of extreme terror or a vacant stillness close to un-being, to restore his equilibrium through physical pain. His happiest moments were those when his mind seemed rapt in a flight of lunatic fancy. At least it brought him a little peace, and the crazed look in his eye was not so terrible as his fear and desperate hunger for salvation, the infinite agony of his inner turmoil! Often he would bang his head against the wall, or cause himself physical pain in some other way.

On the morning of the eighth he remained in bed, Oberlin went up; he was lying almost naked on the bed in a state of severe distress. Oberlin wanted to cover him up, but he responded with an anguished lament at how heavy everything was, so heavy, he didn't think he could walk, never before, he said, had he felt the monstrous weight of the air. Oberlin tried to raise his spirits. But his condition stayed the same, and remained so throughout most of the day; he also took no food. Towards evening Oberlin was called to a sick-bed in Bellefosse. The weather was mild and the moon was shining. On the way back he met Lenz. He seemed quite rational and talked calmly and amiably. Oberlin begged him not to go too far, he gave his word. Walking away he suddenly turned, came right up to Oberlin again, and said rapidly: 'You see, Reverend, I would be alright if only I didn't have to hear it any more.' 'But what, dear friend?' 'Do you really hear nothing? Do you not hear the terrible voice screaming around us on every side, the voice known commonly as silence? Since I came to this silent valley I have heard it all the time, it won't let me sleep, oh yes, Reverend, if only I could sleep again.' He went on his way, shaking his head. Oberlin returned to Waldbach and was about to send someone after him when he heard him going up the steps to his room. A moment later there was a thud from the courtyard, so loud that it seemed to Oberlin it could not possibly be caused by someone falling. The nursemaid came in, deathly white and trembling all over [*substantial passage missing*][34]

He sat in the carriage in cold resignation as they travelled west along the valley. He didn't care where they were taking him; several times when the carriage nearly toppled on the bad roads, he just sat there, quite calm; he was utterly indifferent to all that happened. This remained his condition all the way back through the mountains. Towards evening they reached the Rhine valley. They drew further and further away from the mountains that now rose into the red of evening like a deep-blue crystal wave upon whose floods of warmth the russet glow of evening played; across the plain at the foot of the mountains lay a gossamer of shimmering blue. It grew dark as they came closer to Strasbourg; a full moon high in the sky, distant objects all dark and vague, only the hill close by in sharp relief; the earth was like a goblet of gold over which the golden waves of moonlight foamed and tumbled. Lenz stared out, impassive, without a flicker of recognition or response, except for a turbid fear that grew as more and more things disappeared in the darkness. They had to stop for the night; he made several more efforts to harm himself, but he was too closely guarded. The following morning, in dull, rainy weather, he arrived in Strasbourg. He seemed quite rational, he talked to people; he did everything as others did, but there was a terrible emptiness within him, he felt no fear, no longing any more; he saw his existence as a necessary burden. – Thus he lived for the rest of his days.[35]

THE HESSIAN MESSENGER

GEORG BÜCHNER / LUDWIG WEIDIG

THE HESSIAN MESSENGER [1]

First Message [2]

Darmstadt, July 1834 [3]

Preface [4]

The aim of this pamphlet is to convey the truth to the people of Hessen, but they that speak the truth are hanged; yes, even they that read the truth may well suffer punishment from perfidious judges. Recipients of the pamphlet must therefore observe the following precautions:

1. They must conceal the pamphlet from the police, carefully and well away from their homes;
2. they should pass it on only to trusted friends;
3. they should pass it only anonymously to anyone they do not trust as they trust themselves;
4. should the pamphlet none the less be found in the possession of someone who has read it, he must declare that he was about to hand it to the district authorities;
5. anyone not having read the pamphlet when it is found in his possession is, of course, guiltless.

Peace to the peasants! War on the palaces! [5]

In the year 1834 it might seem as if the Bible stood convicted of lying. It might seem as if God created peasants and labourers on the fifth day, and princes and gentry [6] on the sixth, and as if the good Lord said to the latter, 'Have dominion over every creeping thing that creepeth upon the earth', [7] and counted peasants and burghers amongst the worms. The life of the gentry is one long Sunday, they live in fine houses, wear elegant clothes, have over-fed faces and speak their own language; but the people lie before them like dung on the fields. Behind the plough go the peasants, but behind the peasants go the gentry, driving them on together with the oxen, stealing the grain and leaving them the stubble. The life of the peasant is one long work-day; strangers devour his land in his presence,[8] his whole body is a callus, his sweat is the salt on the gentry's table.

In the Grand Duchy of Hessen there are 718,373 inhabitants, who each year pay 6,363,364 gulden to the state, as follows:

1.	Direct taxes	2,128,131	gulden
2.	Indirect taxes	2,478,264	"
3.	Crown lands	1,547,394	"
4.	Regales[9]	46,938	"
5.	Fines	98,511	"
6.	Sundry sources	64,198	"

6,363,363 gulden [10]

This money is a tithe of blood squeezed from the body of the people. Some 700,000 people sweat, groan and starve because of it. It is extorted in the name of the state, the extortioners cite the government, and the government claim it is necessary for maintaining order in the state. Now what kind of a mighty thing is this: the state? If a number of people live in a country, and regulations or laws exist which all must follow, then they are said to form a state. The state is therefore *everyone*; the state is regulated by laws which ensure the well-being of *all*. – Now see what they have made of the state in the Grand Duchy of Hessen; see what it means to 'maintain order in the state'! 700,000 people pay six million for it, in other words they are turned into plough-horses and oxen to enable them to live in order. To live in order is to starve and be plundered.

Who then are they that have fashioned this order and are vigilant in maintaining it? They are the Grand Ducal government. The government consists of the Grand Duke and his highest officials. All the other officials are men who are charged by the government with keeping in place the order they have fashioned. Their number is legion: State Officials and Government Officials, District Officials and Local Officials, Church Officials and School Officials, Tax Officials and Forestry Officials, etc., with their entire armies of secretaries, etc. The people are their flock, whom they herd, milk and flay;[11] the clothes on their back are the skin of peasants,[12] the spoil of the poor is in their houses;[13] the tears of widows and orphans are the fat on their faces; their rule is unfettered and they urge servitude on the people. It is to them that you pay 6,000,000 gulden in taxes; in return they suffer the burden of governing you, that is to say of getting you to feed their faces and robbing you of your human and civil rights. See what a fine harvest is reaped from your sweat.

1,110,607 gulden are paid to the Ministry of Justice and the Interior. In return you get a hotchpotch of laws, an accumulated jumble of arbitrary ordinances from every century, mostly written in a foreign tongue. The foolishness of all previous generations has thereby been passed down to you, the great weight that stifled them has shifted to you. The law is the property of an insignificant class drawn from the aristocracy and the academies who rule by a right that they themselves have invented. Their 'justice' is simply a means of keeping you in order, so that you can be the more easily oppressed and exploited; it delivers judgements of which you understand nothing according to laws you do not comprehend and principles you do not know. It is incorruptible simply because it makes sure that it is paid so dearly that it needs no bribes. But most of its minions have sold themselves body and soul to the government. Its padded armchairs stand on a money-mountain of 461,373 gulden (such is the cost of courts and prisons). The uniforms, cudgels and swords of its inviolable servants are trimmed with the silver of 197,502 gulden (such is the cost of the police in general, the constabulary, etc.). For centuries in Germany justice has been the whore of the German princes. Any path you take to the law you must pave with silver, and you pay for its verdicts with poverty and humiliation. Think of the stamp taxes, think of your bowing and scraping in government offices and the hours spent waiting outside the door. Think of the fees paid to clerks and bailiffs. You can go to court against your neighbour for stealing a potato; but try going to court over the theft perpetrated daily against your property by the state in the name of dues and taxes, so that a horde of useless officials can grow fat on your sweat: complain that you are subject to the whims of a pot-bellied clique, and that these whims are called laws; complain that you are the plough-horses of the state; complain that you have been deprived of your human rights: where are the courts that will hear your complaints, where the judges that would give you justice? – The jangling chains of your fellow-citizens from Vogelsberg who were dragged off to Rokkenburg will give you your answer.[14]

And if at last some judge or other official from amongst the few that set justice and the common good above Mammon and their bellies should try to help the people instead of harming them, he himself will suffer harm from the prince's chief minions.

For the Ministry of Finance: 1,551,502 gulden.

With this the treasury officials and the sundry ranks of tax gatherers are paid. For this your heads are counted, the yield of your fields calculated. Everything is taxed: the ground beneath your feet, the morsel between your teeth. For this the worthy gentlemen sit comfortably together in their dress-coats and the people stand before them bowed and naked; they run their hands over thigh and shoulder to gauge what additional burden they can bear, and if they are merciful, then only as one spares an ox to keep it serviceable.

For the military you pay 914,820 gulden.

For that your sons get a brightly coloured coat on their back, a gun or a drum over their shoulder, and can fire into the air once a year in the autumn[15] – and recount how the gentlemen of the court and the ill-bred brats of the nobility take precedence over the children of decent folk and go gallivanting along with them through the broad streets of the town to the sound of drums and trumpets. For those 900,000 gulden your sons must swear allegiance to the tyrants and stand guard over their palaces. With their drums they drown out your sighs, with the butts of their rifles they smash your skulls if you dare to think that you are free human beings. They are murderers who murder in the name of the law to protect robbers who rob in the name of the law – think of Södel! At Södel your brothers and sons were the murderers of their brothers and fathers.[16]

For pensions: 480,000 gulden.

For this the officials are put comfortably out to grass when they have served the state faithfully for a certain period – that is, when they have been zealous henchmen in the regular round of exploitation and oppression known as law and order.

For the Ministry of State and Council of State: 174,600 gulden.

It is surely true of all Germany these days that those closest to the princes are the biggest rogues, at least it is true of this Grand Duchy: any honest man who joins a Council of State is unfailingly ousted. Even if an honest man *were* these days to become and remain a minister, the way things are in Germany he could only be a puppet manipulated by the prince, himself a ridiculous puppet manipulated in his turn by a valet or a coachman or the coachman's wife and her lover or the coachman's stepbrother or all of them together. Things in Germany are just as the prophet Micah describes them in chapter 7, verses 3 and 4: 'The mighty utter their mischievous desire: so they wrap it up. The best of them is as a brier: the most upright is sharper than a thorn hedge.' You have to pay dearly for the briers and the thorn hedges; for on top of everything else you have to pay 827,772 gulden for the Grand Ducal household and the court.

The institutions and people of whom I have so far spoken are but instruments and servants. They do nothing in their own name; at the foot of their letters-patent stands the letter L, signifying *Ludwig* by the grace of God, and it is with reverence that they speak the words: 'In the name of the Grand Duke'. This is their battle-cry when they sell off your implements, round up your cattle, throw you in prison. 'In the name of the Grand Duke,' they say, and the person thus named is called 'inviolable', 'sacred', 'sovereign', 'Royal Highness'. But go close to this altogether human being and look beyond his princely garb. He eats when he is hungry, sleeps when he is tired. See, he crawled into the world as soft and naked as you, he will be carried out of it as stiff and rigid as you[17] – and yet he stands there with his foot on your neck, has 700,000 people pulling at his plough, has ministers who must bear responsibility for whatever he does, has power over your property through the taxes he imposes and over your lives through the laws he proclaims; he is surrounded by noble lords and ladies called 'the court', and his divine power is passed on to his children, born of women from stock as superhuman as his own.

Woe upon you, you idolaters! You are like the heathen who worship the crocodile that tears them limb from limb. You give him a crown, but it is a crown of thorns that you press upon your own head;[18] you put a sceptre in his hand, but it is a rod with which you are beaten; you place him on your throne, but it is a rack on which you and your children are tortured. The prince is the head of the leech that crawls all over you, the ministers are its teeth, the officials its tail. The hungry bellies of all the high and mighty gentlemen to whom he gives the top offices are cupping-glasses with which he bleeds the country dry. The L at the foot of his edicts is the mark of the beast[19] that is worshipped by the idolaters of our epoch. The mantle of the prince is the carpet upon which the lords and ladies of court and nobility cavort in their lechery, disguising their sores with orders and ribbons and swaddling their cankered bodies in costly clothes. The daughters of the people are their maids and whores, the sons of the people their lackeys and soldiers. Go to Darmstadt and see what a fine time the gentlemen have at your expense, then tell your starving wives and children what a boon your bread has been for alien bellies, tell them of the fine clothes dyed with their sweat, of the elegant ribbons fashioned from the skin of their calloused hands, tell them of the magnificent houses built from the bones of the people. Then crawl back into your smoky hovels and bend to your labour on your stony fields so that your children too can one day make the journey when some crown prince and princess are about to give succour to some other crown prince, and then through the wide-open glass doors they can see the tablecloth off which the gentlefolk eat, and smell the lamps that are fuelled with the fat of peasants' bodies. All this you tolerate because scoundrels tell you that 'this government is ordained of God'.[20] This government is ordained not by God but by the Father of Lies.[21] These German princes do not represent rightful authority, but have themselves for centuries despised and ultimately even betrayed rightful authority as vested in the German Emperor, who used to be freely chosen by the people. The power of the German princes derives not from the choice of the people, but from treachery and deceit, and hence their ways and doings[22] are accursed of God; their wisdom is falsehood, their justice extortion.[23] They trample the land[24] and grind the faces of the poor.[25] You blaspheme against God if you call any of these princes 'the Lord's Anointed':[26] this could only mean that God had anointed the devil and given him to rule over German soil. Germany, our beloved Germany, has been torn asunder by these princes, they have betrayed the Emperor chosen in freedom by our forefathers, and now these traitors and torturers demand loyalty from you! But the reign of darkness is nearing its end. A little while,[27] and Germany, at present so cruelly exploited by the princes, will arise again as a republic with rulers chosen by the people. Holy Scripture says: 'Render unto Caesar the things which are Caesar's'.[28] But what is due to these princes, these traitors? – *the fate of Judas!*

For the Parliamentary Assembly: 16,000 gulden.[29]

In the year 1789 the people of France were tired of being the king's ill-treated milch-cow. They rose up and called on men whom they trusted, and these men came together and declared that the king was human like anyone else; that he was simply the prime servant of the state; that he must answer to the people; and that he could be called to account and punished if he performed his duties badly. They then declared the rights of man: 'No one shall inherit privileges or entitlements by virtue of birth, no one shall inherit privileges by virtue of property. Supreme authority resides in the will of all or of the majority. This will is the law, it is manifested through the deputies or the representatives of the people, they are elected by everyone and everyone can be elected; these elected representatives express the will of those that elected them, hence the will of a majority of them corresponds to the will of a majority of the people; the sole task of the king is to implement the laws that they have passed.'[30] The king swore loyalty to this constitution, but he betrayed the people, and the people dealt with him as befits a traitor. Then the French abolished the hereditary monarchy and freely chose a new form of supreme authority, as is the right of every people in accordance with reason and Holy Scripture. The men who were to serve as guardians of the law were chosen by the assembly of the people's representatives, and constituted the new supreme authority. Thus both government and legislature were elected by the people, and France had become a free country.

But the other kings were horrified at the might of the French people, reckoning that this first royal corpse might cause them all to trip and break their necks, and that the Frenchmen's call to freedom might rouse their own maltreated subjects. With the help of huge quantities of cavalry and equipment, they attacked France from every side, and a large proportion of the country's aristocracy rose up and joined the enemy. This enraged the people and they arose and were exalted in their strength.[31] They crushed the traitors and destroyed the hireling armies of the kings. The newborn freedom grew apace in the tyrants' blood and the sound of its voice made thrones quake and their peoples rejoice.[32] But the French themselves traded their freedom for the fame that Napoleon offered them, and set him on an emperor's throne. Whereupon the Almighty had the Emperor's army freeze to death in Russia and scourged France with the Cossacks' knout and made the fat-bellied Bourbons kings again, in order that France might turn from her idolatry of hereditary monarchy and serve the true God[33] that made men free and equal. But when the time of her punishment was done, and brave men drove the treacherous King Charles the Tenth from the country in July 1830, France, having regained her freedom, even now resorted to 'limited' monarchy, and made a new rod for her own back in the person of that hypocrite Louis Philippe. But there was great rejoicing in Germany and all Europe when Charles the Tenth was driven from the throne, and throughout the German lands the oppressed made ready to fight for their freedom. So the princes put their heads together to see how they could escape the wrath of the people, and the cunning amongst them said: 'Let's yield part of our power in order to keep the rest.' And they went before the people and said: 'We will *give* you the freedom you are ready to fight for'. – And trembling with fear they threw them a few crumbs and spoke of their graciousness. Unfortunately the people trusted them and went about their peaceful business again. – Thus Germany was deceived as France was.

For what *are* these new constitutions in Germany? Nothing but chaff from which the princes have beaten all the grain for themselves. What are our parliamentary assemblies? Nothing but lumbering carts that might possibly serve once or twice to block the rapacity of the princes and their ministers, but which can never be built into a secure bastion of German freedom. What are our electoral laws? Nothing but an infringement of the civil and human rights of the majority of Germans. Think of the electoral law in this Grand Duchy, whereby no one can be elected who does not possess substantial wealth, no matter how upright and well disposed – and yet *Grolmann* could be elected, a man who wanted to rob you of two million gulden.[34] Think of the Grand Duchy's constitution. – According to its provisions the Grand Duke is inviolable, sacred and unaccountable. His rank and office remain within his family by heredity; he has the right to make war, and has exclusive control over the army. It is he that convenes, suspends or dissolves the Assembly. Its deputies may not table laws themselves, but instead must request them of the prince, and it lies wholly within his discretion whether to grant a law or refuse it. He remains in possession of almost unlimited power; the only thing he cannot do is make new laws or impose new taxes without the approval of the Assembly. But he either does not bother with this approval, or else he contents himself with the old laws, which are the product and embodiment of traditional monarchic power, so that he has no real need of new laws. Such a constitution is a wretched, miserable thing. What can be expected of deputies that are tied to such a constitution? Even if there were no traitors or cowards amongst them, even if every one of them were a resolute friend of the people?! What can be expected of deputies who are scarcely even able to safeguard what pathetically little there is of this wretched constitution! – The sole resistance they were capable of offering was to refuse the two million gulden that the Grand Duke wanted to extract from his already over-burdened people in order to pay his debts. But even if the Assembly of the Grand Duchy were to have sufficient rights, and even if the Grand Duchy, but this Duchy alone, were to have a true constitution, its glory would soon be over. The vultures in Vienna and Berlin would reach out with their hangman's talons and wipe the infant freedom from the face of the earth.[35] The battle for freedom must be fought and won by the entire German people. And that moment, beloved countrymen, is not far off. – The Lord has delivered the beautiful land of

Germany – for centuries the most magnificent realm on earth – into the hands of foreign and native oppressors because the heart of the German people had turned from the freedom and equality of their forefathers and from their fear of the Lord; because you had yielded yourself up to idolatry of the many little masters, petty dukes and pocket-sized kings.

The Lord broke the rod[36] with which the foreign oppressor Napoleon sought to drive all before him, and through the hand of the people He will also break the false idols of our own German tyrants. These idols may sparkle with gold and jewels, medals and insignia, but *the worm within them dieth not,*[37] *and their feet are of clay.*[38] God will give you strength[39] to smite these feet of clay as soon as you have turned from the error of your way[40] and acknowledged the truth:[41] 'that there is but one God[42] and none others before him, calling themselves Highness and Most High,[43] sacred and unanswerable; that God made all men free and equal in their rights, and that no government has the blessing of God except that which rests on the trust of the people and is explicitly or implicitly chosen by the people; that by contrast any government that exerts power over a people without the right to do so is of God only inasmuch as the devil is also of God, and that obedience to such a devil's government is valid only until its devil's power can be broken; that God, having united a people through a single language into a single body,[44] will take those that brutally tear it apart and hack it into four or even thirty pieces,[45] and eternally punish them in this world and the next as tyrants and murderers of the people, for it is written in Scripture: What God hath joined together, let not man put asunder;[46] and that the Almighty, who can turn a desert into a paradise,[47] can also turn a land full of travail and affliction[48] back into such a paradise as our beloved Germany used to be until its princes tore it to pieces and stripped it clean.'

Because the German empire was decayed and rotten, and the Germans had turned from God and freedom, God made the empire crumble into nothing in order to regenerate it anew as a state built on freedom. He has given power for a while to the 'messengers of Satan'[49] that they might beat Germany with their fists, he has given power to 'principalities and powers that rule in

the darkness of this world, to spirits of wickedness in high places'
(Ephes. 6)[50] that they might torment both burghers and peasants
and suck their blood and do their mischief to all who love justice
and freedom more than injustice and servitude. – But their day is
done!

Look at that monster marked by God, King Ludwig of Bavaria,
that blasphemer who forces honest men to kneel before his image,
and has all who bear witness to the truth cast into dungeons by
his perfidious judges; a swine who wallowed in every sink of vice
throughout Italy; a wolf who gets his perfidious parliament to
approve a permanent allowance of five million a year for his
court of Baal[51] – then ask: 'Is such a government blessed by
God?'

> Ha! So you govern in the name of God?
> God bestows blessings;
> *You* rob and flay and imprison your subjects,
> You tyrant, you are not of God![52]

I tell you, his and his fellow-princes' day is done. God, who
through these princes has smitten Germany for her sins,[53] will
heal her again[54] – 'He shall tear out the briers and thorns and
burn them together' (Isaiah 27:4).

Just as the hunchback with which God marked this King
Ludwig no longer increases,[55] so too shall the monstrous deeds of
these princes no longer increase. Their day is done. The Lord will
utterly destroy their strongholds, and life and energy and the
blessing of freedom will flourish anew in Germany. The princes
have turned the soil of Germany into a place of carnage, as
described by Ezekiel in chapter 37: 'The Lord set me down in the
midst of the valley which was full of bones, and lo, they were very
dry.' But what does the Lord say to these dry bones: 'Behold, I
will lay sinews upon you, and will bring up flesh upon you, and
cover you with skin, and put breath in you, and ye shall live; and
ye shall know that I am the Lord.' And the word of the Lord
shall prove to be true of Germany also, as the prophet spake:
'Behold, there was a noise and a shaking, and the bones came
together, bone to his bone. – Then the breath came into them,
and they lived, and stood up, an exceeding great army.'

As it is written in the book of the prophet, so too has it been in Germany until now: your bones are dry, for the 'order' in which you live is rank exploitation. In the Grand Duchy you pay six million to a handful of people whose arbitrary rule controls your life and your property, and it is the same too for all the others in this torn and abject land of Germany. You *are* nothing, you *have* nothing! You have no rights. You must give whatever your insatiable oppressors demand, bear whatever burden they place on your shoulders. As far as a tyrant's eye can see – and Germany has some thirty such – both land and people are becoming as dry bones. But as it is written in the book of the prophet, so shall it soon be in Germany: the day of resurrection is not far off. There shall be a noise and a shaking amongst the bodies on the battle-field, and there shall be a great army of warriors that are risen anew.

Lift up your eyes[56] and count the tiny number of your oppressors, who are strong only because of the blood that they suck from you, and because you submissively lend them the strength of your arm. There are perhaps 10,000 of them in the Grand Duchy, and 700,000 of you; and the ratio of the people to their oppressors is the same in the rest of Germany too. Yes, they threaten you with all the weapons and horsemen of the kings, but I say unto you:[57] he that raises his sword against the people shall perish through the sword of the people.[58] Germany today is a place of carnage: soon it will be a paradise. The German people are *one* body, you are a limb of that body. It matters not which part of the seeming corpse first begins to twitch. When the Lord gives you a sign[59] through the men whom He uses to lead the peoples from servitude to freedom, then rise up, and the entire body will rise again with you.

For many long years you have bowed to your labour in the thorn-fields of servitude;[60] you will sweat for a hot summer in the vineyard of freedom, then be free even unto the thousandth generation.[61]

You have laboured all your life at digging the soil, now you shall dig your tyrants' grave. You built their fortresses, now you shall destroy them and build the house of freedom. You shall be able to baptize your children in freedom with the water of life.[62]

And until the Lord calls you through His messengers and His signs, be watchful and prepare in spirit for the battle, saying this prayer[63] and teaching it to your children: 'Lord, destroy the rods of our oppressors[64] and let Thy kingdom come unto us,[65] the kingdom of justice. Amen.'

ON CRANIAL NERVES[1]

Introductory section of the 'Trial Lecture' delivered by Georg Büchner at Zurich University on 5 November 1836.

Esteemed audience!

In the field of the physiological and anatomical sciences we are confronted by two conflicting basic views, which even bear a national stamp in that one is dominant in England and France, the other in Germany. The one considers all phenomena of organic life from a *teleological* standpoint;[2] it sees the solution to the riddle in the purpose, the effect, the usefulness of the way an organ functions. It knows the individual only as something that is meant to achieve a purpose beyond itself, and only as something dedicated to holding its own – partly as an individual, partly as a species – against the world around it. For the proponents of this view, every organism is a complex machine provided with functional devices enabling it to survive over a certain span of time. The revealing in mankind of the purest and most beautiful forms of nature, the perfectness of the noblest organs, in which the spirit seems almost to break through the barrier of matter, to dance behind the slenderest of veils – these things are to them merely the optimal attributes of such a machine. For them, the skull becomes a special vault-like structure equipped with buttresses, dedicated to protecting its inhabitant, the brain; cheeks and lips become an apparatus for chewing and breathing; the eye becomes a complex lens; eyelid and eyelashes become its protective curtain; as for tears, they are simply the water-droplets that keep it moist. One sees what a far cry it is from that to the enthusiasm with which *Lavater*[3] praises his good fortune in being able to speak of something as divine as lips.

The teleological method goes round in an endless circle in assuming the effects of organs to be their purpose. It says, for instance: if the eye is to perform its function, then the cornea must be kept moist, and a lachrymal gland is accordingly necessary. The latter is thus present in order to keep the eye moist, and this explains why the organ came into being; no further question needs to be asked. The opposing view on the other hand says: the lachrymal gland is not there in order to keep the eye moist, but rather the eye becomes moist because there is a lachrymal gland; or, to give another example: we do not have hands in order that we can grasp things, but rather we grasp things because we have hands. The *greatest possible fitness for purpose* is the sole law of the teleological method; but then one naturally asks, What is the purpose of this purpose? – and equally naturally the teleologist can answer each successive question only by going round in an infinite circle.[4]

Nature does not operate according to purposes, it does not consume itself in an infinite series of purposes each of which is conditioned by another; on the contrary, in all its manifestations it is directly, immediately *sufficient to itself*. Everything that exists, exists for its own sake. To seek the law of this existence is the aim of that viewpoint that is opposite to the teleological, and which I shall term the *philosophical*. Everything that is *purpose* to the former is *effect* to the latter. At the very point where the teleological school's answer is done, the question begins for the philosophical one. The answer to this question, which confronts us at every turn, can only be found in a fundamental law informing the entire organic world; for the philosophical method, therefore, the entire physical existence of the individual, rather than being constituted for the purpose of its own survival, becomes the manifestation of a primordial law, a law of beauty,[5] which produces the highest and purest forms from the simplest outlines and patterns.[6] For the philosophical school, everything, form and matter alike, is bound by this law. All functions are its effects; they are not determined by purposes beyond themselves, and their so-called purposive interaction is none other than the harmony that necessarily prevails amongst the manifestations of a single law, the effects of which naturally cannot be mutually destructive.

The search for such a law led automatically to those two wellsprings of knowledge that have ever been the heady drink of enthusiasts for absolute knowledge: the intuition of the mystic, and the dogmatism of the rationalist.[7] As to whether it has ever proved possible to bridge the gulf between the latter and natural life as we directly apprehend it: any critique must answer no. A priori philosophy[8] still dwells in a bleak and arid desert; a very great distance separates it from green, fresh life, and it is highly questionable whether it will ever close the gap. Notwithstanding the intellectual finesse of its attempts to progress, it has to resign itself to the recognition that the point of its struggle lies not in the achievement of its goal, but in the struggle itself.

Now although no absolutely satisfactory conclusion was achieved, the impetus of these various efforts was none the less sufficient to give the study of nature a quite different shape. Though one may not have discovered the spring-head itself, at many points one could hear the stream roaring deep below, and in places the water leapt up fresh and clear. In particular, botany and zoology, physiology and comparative anatomy all enjoyed significant progress. Amongst the vast accumulation of material, laboriously gathered over a period of centuries, and scarcely even ordered into a catalogue, simple and natural groups took shape; a chaos of strange forms with the most outlandish names resolved into the most beautiful and harmonious proportion; a mass of things that previously weighed on the memory as discrete, widely separated facts, moved into relationship with each other, developed into distinct groupings, or resolved into polarities. Although no complete picture has yet been achieved, coherent parts of it have none the less emerged, and the eye, so easily tired by a jumble of disconnected facts, dwells with delight on such beautiful details as the metamorphosis of the plant out of the leaf; the derivation of the skeleton from the vertebra; the metamorphosis, even metempsychosis of the foetus during its life in the womb;[9] Oken's notion of representation in the taxonomy of the animal kingdom[10] – and so on. In comparative anatomy everything was striving towards a certain unity, towards the tracing of all forms back to the simplest primordial type.[11] The position was quite clear regarding the significance of the structures of the vegetative nervous system for the formation of the skeleton; solely in respect of the brain has it not so far proved possible to achieve such a happy outcome. Once Oken had stated that 'the skull is a spinal column',[12] then one also had to say that the brain is metamorphosed spinal cord, and that the nerves of the brain are spinal nerves. How to prove this in actual practice has so far remained a profound puzzle. How can the masses of the brain be traced back to the simple form of the spinal cord? How can the nerves of the brain, so complex in both their origin and their course, be compared to the nerves of the spine, which originate so evenly via the double row of roots along the spinal cord, and follow such a simple and regular course? How, finally, can one demonstrate the relationship of the nerves of the brain to the cranial vertebrae? Several attempts have been made to answer this question.[13] [. . .]

SELECTED LETTERS

To his family

Strasbourg, [after 4 December] 1831

(. . .)[1] When the rumour spread that Ramorino[2] would pass through Strasbourg, the students immediately started collecting money and decided to go out to meet him with a black flag. The news finally reached here that Ramorino would arrive in the afternoon with generals Schneider and Langermann.[3] We gathered at once in the Academy; but when we tried to march through the city gate, the officer in charge, who had received orders from the government not to let us pass with the flag, had the guard take up position with their guns to prevent us going through. But we forced our way through all the same, and three or four hundred of us stationed ourselves by the great bridge over the Rhine. We were joined by the National Guard.[4] Ramorino finally appeared, accompanied by a mass of people on horseback; a student makes a speech, which Ramorino replies to, a National Guardsman does likewise. The National Guard gather round his carriage and start to pull it; we place ourselves with the flag at the head of the procession, which is preceded by a large band. Thus we march into the city, accompanied by a huge mass of people all bawling the Marseillaise and the Carmagnole;[5] shouts ring out on every side: 'Vive la liberté! Vive Ramorino! A bas les ministres! A bas le juste milieu!'[6] The city itself is all lit up, at the windows are ladies waving handkerchiefs, and Ramorino is led in triumph to the inn, where our man bearing the flag hands it over to him with the wish that this flag of mourning might soon turn into Poland's flag of freedom. Thereupon Ramorino appears on the balcony, expresses his thanks, there are shouts of *Vivat!* – and the comedy is done.[7] (. . .)

To his family

Strasbourg, December 1831

(. . .) It looks desperately like war.[8] If it *does* come to a war, there'll be Babylonian confusion in Germany especially, and heaven knows how the song and dance would end. *All* can be gained and *all* can be lost. But if the Russians cross the Oder I'll grab a gun, even if I have to do it in France. May God have mercy on the most utterly serene and anointed dunderheads; they'll hopefully find no more mercy on earth. (. . .)

To his family

Strasbourg, December 1832

(. . .) I almost forgot to mention that the place is being put in a state of siege (because of the troubles in Holland).[9] Cannons constantly go rattling past below my window, troops are exercising on all the public squares, and guns are being mounted on the city walls. I've no time now to write you a political treatise, and anyway it wouldn't be worth the effort, the whole thing after all is just a comedy. The King and his councils rule, the people applaud and pay. (. . .)

To his family

Strasbourg, 5 April 1833

Today I received your letters with the stories from *Frankfurt*.[10] My opinion is this: if anything can help in this age of ours, it is *violence*. We know what to expect from our princes. Every concession they have made they were driven to by necessity. And even their concessions were flung down like favours granted to a cringing petitioner, like some miserable toy aimed at making that gawping idiot the *people* forget how tightly swaddled it is. Only a German could have the ineptitude to play at toy soldiers with a tin gun and a wooden sword. Our parliamentary assemblies are a mockery of common sense; even if we lumbered on with them for another whole age and then totted up the results, the people would end up paying more dearly for the fine speeches of its representatives than the Roman emperor that paid 20,000 gulden to his court poet for a couple of unfinished lines. These young people are condemned for using violence. But are we not constantly subjected to violence? Because we are born and bred in a dungeon we no longer even notice that we are stuck in a hell-hole chained hand and foot and with gags in our mouths. What on earth do you mean by 'lawful state of affairs'? A 'law' that turns the great mass of citizens into beast-like slaves in order to satisfy the unnatural requirements of an insignificant and degenerate minority? And this law, sustained by brute force through the military and by the mindless cunning of its spies[11] – this law is *violence, constantly* and *brutally* perpetrated against justice and common sense, and I shall fight it with *word* and *deed* wherever I can. If I have taken no part in what has happened so far, and take *no part* in what might happen in the future, this is out of neither disapproval nor fear, but only because I consider revolutionary activity of any kind to be a futile undertaking in present circumstances,[12] and because I do not share the delusion of those who see in the Germans a people ready to fight for their rights. This insane view generated the events in Frankfurt, and the mistake cost very dear. Making mistakes is no sin, incidentally, and German apathy is truly such as to confound even the most careful calculation. I pity the poor wretches with all my heart. Were none of my friends involved in the affair?[13] (. . .)

To his family

Strasbourg, June 1833

(. . .) Although I shall always act according to my principles, I have *recently* come to realize that only the imperative needs of the great mass of the people can bring about change,[14] and that all the beavering and bellowing of *individuals* is futile and foolish. They write: no one reads them; they shout: no one hears them; they act: no one helps them. You can well imagine that I won't be getting myself involved in Giessen's back-room politics and childish revolutionary antics.[15]

To August Stöber

Darmstadt, 9 December 1833

[. . .] I'm throwing myself into philosophy with all my might, the contrived language is repulsive, I think we should find human words for human concerns;[16] but it doesn't bother me, I laugh at my silliness and reckon that at bottom there are no problems to crack anyway except hollow ones. But then one has to ride through life on a donkey of some kind, so in the name of God I'm saddling mine; feeding it doesn't worry me, there'll be no shortage of thistles so long as books are still printed. [. . .]

The political conditions could drive me mad. The poor people tamely haul the cart on which the princes and liberals act out their ludicrous comedy. I say a prayer every evening to ropes and street-lights. [. . .]

To his family

Giessen, February 1834

(. . .) *I feel contempt for no one*, least of all because of their intellect or education, since no one can prevent himself becoming a fool or a criminal; since we would presumably all be equal if our circumstances were equal; and since circumstances lie beyond our control. *Intellect* is in any case only a very minor aspect of our inner being, and education only a form it very randomly acquires. Anyone who accuses me of such contempt is claiming that I would trample someone underfoot because he wore a threadbare coat. You would never think anyone capable of physically carrying out such a cruel act, yet I am accused of carrying it out in the mind – an even crueller act. I can call someone a fool without *despising* him for it. Foolishness is one of the general attributes of human life. I can't do anything about the fact that it exists, but no one can stop me from calling the things that exist by their proper name, and avoiding whatever I find disagreeable. To be hurtful to someone is cruel – but whether to seek their company or avoid them is entirely for me to decide. *That* is the explanation for my treatment of old acquaintances; I was hurtful to nobody, and spared myself a great deal of boredom; if they consider me arrogant for not enjoying their pleasures and pursuits, then that is unjust; I myself would never dream of making such an accusation against anyone on that basis. People call me a *mocker*. It's true that I often laugh, but I don't laugh at the *way* people are human, only at the *fact* that they are human, which they can't do anything about anyway, and at the same time I laugh at myself, since I share their fate. People call that mockery, they can't bear anyone acting the fool and calling them *du* like an old familiar;[17] they themselves are contemptuous, mocking, arrogant in seeking foolishness only *outside themselves*. I do admittedly have mockery of a different kind in me – not that of contempt but that of hatred. Hate is just as legitimate as love, and I harbour it to the fullest degree against those who are *truly* contemptuous. There are large numbers of such people who, possessed of a ludicrous façade called 'breeding' or a clutter of dead knowledge called 'learning', sacrifice the great mass of their brothers on the altar of their own contemptuous egotism. To behave like an aristocrat is to show the most shameful contempt for the holy spirit in man, and I attack such people with their own weapons: arrogance against arrogance, mockery against mockery. – You would do better to see what my bootblack thinks; he would surely be an ideal target for my 'arrogance', and my 'contempt' for the uneducated and less intelligent. I beg you, ask him sometime. . . You surely don't think me capable of anything so ridiculous as condescension. I still trust that I have cast more looks of compassion towards the suffering and the oppressed than I have spoken bitter words to the cold-hearted and the supercilious – (. . .)

To Minna Jaeglé [18]

[Giessen, February 1834]

(. . .) I yearn for a letter. I'm alone, as though in the grave; when is your hand going to wake me?[19] My friends are abandoning me, we scream in each other's ears like the deaf; I wish we were dumb, then we could just gaze at each other, and for some time now I've scarcely been able to look fixedly at anyone without tears appearing. This is a disease affecting the fluid in the eye that often also occurs in connection with staring. They say I'm mad because I said I would arise again in six weeks, but first ascend into heaven – by stagecoach, that is.[20] Goodbye, dear heart, and don't go away from me. Mistress Melancholy is trying to take me from you: I lie in her lap the whole day long; poor heart, I fancy you're paying me back in the very same coin. (. . .)

To Minna Jaeglé

[Giessen, on or before 7 March 1834]

(. . .) My first lucid moment for a week. Ceaseless headaches and fever, at night just an hour or two of fitful sleep. I never get to bed before two, then repeatedly jerk awake, and a sea of thoughts floods through me, drowning all my senses. My silence torments you, and me too, but I just couldn't help myself. Dear, dear heart, do you forgive me? I have just come in from outside. A single resonant tone from a thousand larks bursts through the brooding summer air, a heavy bank of cloud wanders over the earth, the booming wind rings out like its melodious tread. The spring air freed me from my frozen, rigid state. I was horrified at myself. A sense of being dead continually pervaded me. Everyone's face was the face of death, with glassy eyes and waxen cheeks, and then, when the whole machinery began to grind away with jerking limbs and grating voice, and I heard the same old barrel-organ tune go tralala and saw the tiny prongs and cylinders bob and whirr in the organ-box – I cursed the concert, the box, the melody – oh, poor screaming musicians that we are – could it be that our cries of agony on the rack only exist to ring out through cracks between the clouds and, echoing on and on, die like a melodious breath in heavenly ears? Could it be that we are the victims roasted in the belly of Perillus' bull, whose screams as they die ring out like the jubilant roars of the bull-god as it is consumed in the flames?[21] I am not blaspheming. But mankind blasphemes. And yet I am punished: I am afraid of my voice and also – my mirror. I could have sat as a model for Herr Callot-Hoffmann,[22] don't you think, my darling? It would have earned me some travel-money. I can tell, I am beginning to become truly interesting –

The vacation begins a fortnight tomorrow. If they refuse me

permission, I'll leave in secret.[23] I owe it to myself to end this
unbearable state of affairs. My capacity to think is completely
shattered. I find work impossible. I'm possessed by a brooding
gloom in which scarcely a single lucid thought takes shape. My
inmost being is wasting away; if only I had a way of expressing
what is within me, but I have no scream for my pain, no hurrah
for my joy, no song for my ecstasy. This muteness is my eternal
punishment. I've told you a thousand times: don't read my letters
– such cold, torpid words. If only I could bathe you in a single
full, rich sound, instead I drag you into my desolate labyrinth.
You sit there now alone with your tears in your dark room, but
soon I'll come to you. For the last two weeks your image has been
constantly before me, I see you in every dream. Your silhouette
floats before me all the time like the shimmering after-image
when one's gazed at the sun. I yearn for the bliss of sensation –
and shall have it soon, very soon, with you.

To Minna Jaeglé

[Giessen, after 10 March 1834]

There are no mountains here that give a clear view. Just hill after
hill and wide valleys, everything so ordinary, so dreary; I can't
get used to this sort of landscape, and the town is repulsive. It's
spring here. I can keep replacing your bunch of violets, it's
immortal like the Lama. So what is the good city of Strasbourg
doing, sweet child? All sorts of things are happening there, and
you tell me not a word. Je baise les petites mains, en goûtant les
souvenirs doux de Strasbourg –

'Prouve-moi que tu m'aimes encore beaucoup en me donnant
bientôt des nouvelles.' And I made you wait! Over the last few
days I've picked up my pen again and again, but I just couldn't
manage a single word. I've been studying the history of the
French Revolution.[24] I felt as though utterly crushed by the
hideous fatalism of history. I find in human nature a terrible
sameness, in human circumstances an ineluctable violence vouch-
safed to all and to none. Individuals but froth on the waves,
greatness a mere coincidence, the mastery of geniuses a dance of
puppets, a ridiculous struggle against an iron law that can at best

be recognized, but never mastered. I wouldn't dream any more of bowing down before the prancing show-offs and hangers-on of history. My eye has grown accustomed to blood. But I'm no guillotine blade. 'Must' is one of those words by which mankind was damned from the very beginning. The saying, 'It must needs be that offences come, but woe to that man by whom the offence cometh', is horrifying. What is it in man that lies, murders, steals?[25] I can't bear to take the thought any further. But if only I could lay this tortured heart of mine on your breast! B. will have reassured you about my condition,[26] I wrote to him. I curse this healthy state I'm in. I was burning hot, my fever covered me with kisses and embraced me as if with lover's arms. The darkness surged above me, my heart swelled with endless longing, stars came bursting through the blackness, and hands and lips bent down towards me. And now? And otherwise? I don't even have the ecstasy of pain and longing.[27] Since crossing the Rhine, I've been as though destroyed inside, not a single feeling stirs within me. I'm an automaton; my soul has been taken from me. [. . .] – You ask if I yearn for you. Do you call that yearning: being able to exist only in a single point and then, once torn away from it, feeling nothing but misery? Answer me, please answer me. Are my lips so cold? (. . .) – This letter is a charivari: I'll console you with another.

To his family

Giessen, 5 August 1834

(. . .) – I think I told you that *Minnigerode* was arrested half an hour before I left, they took him to Friedberg. I've no idea what's behind his arrest.[28] Apparently our sharp-witted University Proctor[29] took it into his head that there was some connection between my journey and Minnigerode's arrest. On getting back here I found my cupboard *sealed*, and was informed that my papers had been searched. At my insistence the seals were removed at once, and my papers were returned as well (just letters from you and friends), the only things kept back were various letters in French [. . .], probably because they first had to get hold of a language teacher in order to read them. I'm filled with indignation at such behaviour, it makes me feel sick when I think of my most sacred secrets in the hands of these squalid characters. And all that – do you know why? Because I left on the same day that Minnigerode was arrested. On a vague suspicion they trampled on my most sacred rights, and then had the gall to demand proof about my journey!!! Needless to say I could give it with the greatest of ease; I have letters from B.[30] that confirm every word that I had said, and amongst my papers there wasn't a *single* line that could have compromised me. You needn't feel the slightest worry about any of this. I'm at liberty, and there is no chance of them finding any reason to arrest me. I just feel so indignant at the action of the courts in invading one's most sacred family secrets at the suspicion of a possible suspicion. [. . .] I'm going to talk to some lawyers to see if there isn't some legal redress for such an infringement of one's rights! (. . .)

To Karl Gutzkow[31]

[Darmstadt, 21 February 1835]

Sir,
Perhaps you know from observing others – or perhaps, more unfortunately, from your own experience – that there is a degree of misery that makes one lose sight of all polite considerations and feelings. There *are* people, it is true, who maintain that in such circumstances one should go out into the world and starve, but I could refute that by citing a recently blinded army captain I met in the street, who said that he would shoot himself if he weren't forced to support his family by staying alive and earning his pay. That is terrible. I'm sure you will appreciate that there are similar circumstances that prevent one from turning one's body into a sheet anchor and throwing it overboard from the wreck of this world, and you will therefore not be surprised at my throwing open your door, bursting into your room, aiming a manuscript at your chest, and demanding alms. What I beg of you is that you read the manuscript as quickly as possible and – *if your conscience as a critic allows you to do so* – commend it to Herr Sauerländer,[32] and send me an answer straightaway.

About the work itself, I can only say that unhappy circumstances compelled me to write it in five weeks at most. I say this to influence your judgement of the author, not of the drama in itself. I don't know myself what to make of it, I only know that I have every reason to feel shamed by history; but I console myself with the thought that, except for Shakespeare, all writers are made to look like schoolboys by history and nature.

I beg you again to answer quickly; if the outcome is favourable, then a few lines from your hand, if they get here before next Wednesday, can rescue an unhappy man from a very miserable situation.

If perhaps you are taken aback by the tone of this letter, then bear in mind that I find it easier to beg in rags than appear in a frock-coat with a formal petition; and almost easier to say 'La bourse ou la vie!' with a pistol in hand, than to whisper 'God bless you!' with trembling lips.

G. Büchner

To his family

Weissenburg, 9 March 1835

I have just arrived here safe and sound. The journey passed quickly and comfortably. So far as my personal safety is concerned, you need have no worries at all. On the basis of completely reliable reports that have come through, I am also quite sure that I shall be permitted to remain in Strasbourg. (. . .) Only the most pressing reasons could force me to leave both home and homeland in such a manner. . . I could readily have faced our political inquisition; I had nothing to fear from the outcome of an investigation,[33] but everything to fear from the investigation itself. (. . .) I am quite sure that after two or three years there will no longer be any obstacles to my returning. Had I stayed, I would have spent that period in a Friedberg dungeon,[34] then left it destroyed in body and mind. I saw this so clearly, I was so completely certain of it, that I chose the great but lesser evil of voluntary banishment. My hands, and my head, are now free of chains. (. . .) Everything now rests in my own hands. I shall pursue my study of the medical-philosophical sciences[35] with the greatest energy, and there is still plenty of scope in this particular area for solid achievement, and our era is especially well suited to giving recognition to such things. Since crossing the border I feel a new zest for life; I am now completely on my own, but that is exactly what gives me my extra strength. It is such a wonderful relief to be free of the constant secret fear of arrest and other forms of judicial persecution that constantly afflicted me in Darmstadt. (. . .)

To his family

Strasbourg, 20 April 1835

(. . .) A sad piece of news reached me this morning. A refugee from the Giessen area arrived here; he told me that several people in the Giessen area have been arrested, and that a printing-press was found at the house of one of them; furthermore my friends *A. Becker* and *Klemm*[36] have been taken in, and Rector *Weidig*[37] is under investigation. [. . .] I am now gladder than ever to be out of it, they wouldn't have spared me on any account. (. . .) I am facing my future with complete calm. If need be I could live from my writing. (. . .) I have been asked to send in reviews of the new French books to the Literary Supplement,[38] they are well paid. I would earn far more if I were prepared to devote more time to it, but I am determined *not to give up my programme of study*. (. . .)

To his family

5 May 1835

[. . .] [Gutzkow] is in Berlin at the moment, but he must be coming back soon. He seems to think a lot of me, I'm very glad about that, his Literary Supplement is very well regarded. (. . .) He will be coming here in June, so he tells me. I found out from him that several extracts from my drama have appeared in *Phönix*,[39] he assured me too that the periodical had done itself a lot of credit as a result. The full play should be coming out soon. In case you happen to see it, I beg you to bear in mind when forming your judgement that I had to remain true to history and show the men of the Revolution as they actually were: bloody, dissolute, energetic and cynical. I regard my drama as a historical portrait that must correspond exactly to its original.[40] [. . .] The King's birthday passed very quietly, no one bothers about such things, even the republicans are staying calm; they don't want any more riots, but their principles are gaining more and more followers every day, especially among the younger generation, and thus the government will probably disintegrate little by little all on its own, without a violent revolution. (. . .) *Sartorius*[41] has been arrested, *Becker* too. Today I have also learned of the arrest of Herr *Weidig*, and Pastor *Flick* in Petterweil.[42] (. . .)

To Wilhelm Büchner[43]

[Strasbourg, 1835]

(. . .) I wouldn't say that to you if I believed that there was even the remotest chance at present of a political revolution. I have been completely convinced for six months now that nothing can be done, and that anyone who sacrifices himself in *present* circumstances is throwing himself away like an idiot. I can't go into details, but I know how things are, I know how weak, how insignificant, how fragmented the liberal party is, I know that appropriate, co-ordinated action is impossible, and that any attempts at such action can have not the slightest effect. (. . .)

Addressee unknown

[Strasbourg, 1835]

(. . .) My close acquaintance with the activities of the German revolutionaries abroad has convinced me that nothing whatever can be hoped for from this quarter either. A Babylonian confusion reigns amongst them that will never be resolved. Time is our only hope! (. . .)

To Karl Gutzkow

[Strasbourg]

(. . .) The whole revolution has already divided into liberals and absolutists, and it is the uneducated and poor class that has to swallow the consequences. The relationship between the poor and the rich is the only revolutionary element in the world, hunger alone can be the goddess of freedom, and only a new Moses inflicting the Seven Plagues of Egypt upon us could be our Messiah. Fatten the peasants, and the revolution will die of apoplexy. Put a chicken in the pot of every peasant, and the Gallic cockerel will drop down dead. (. . .)

To his family

Strasbourg, 28 July 1835

(. . .) I live here completely unmolested; a requisition did arrive some time ago from Giessen,[44] but the police appear to have ignored it. (. . .) It troubles me deeply when I think of Darmstadt; I see our house and the garden, and then, quite involuntarily, the appalling gaol. The poor wretches! How is it going to end? Just the same as in Frankfurt, probably, where one after another they died and were secretly buried. A death sentence, then the scaffold: what's wrong with that? You are dying for your cause. But to be slowly destroyed in prison like that! It's horrible! [. . .]

To his family

Strasbourg, 28 July 1835

(. . .) I must say a few words about my drama.[45] First, I must mention that the permission I gave for some changes to be made was gravely abused.[46] Omissions and additions on almost every page, and almost always extremely detrimental to the overall effect. Sometimes the meaning is seriously distorted or even completely lost, with sheer nonsense in its place. What is more, the book is teeming with the most appalling printing errors. No proofs were sent to me. The title is completely outrageous,[47] and my name appears under it, which I had expressly forbidden – *and* it was absent from the title page of my manuscript. What's more, the proof-reader has put some obscenities into my mouth that I would never have uttered in my life.[48] I have read Gutzkow's glowing reviews, and in the process noticed to my delight that I have no inclinations to vanity. As to the so-called immorality of my book, by the way, my reply is as follows: the dramatist is in my view nothing other than a historian, but is *superior* to the latter in that he *re-creates* history: instead of offering us a bare narrative, he transports us directly into the life of an age; he gives us characters instead of character portrayals; full-bodied figures instead of mere descriptions. His supreme task is to get as close as possible to history as it actually happened. His play must be neither more *moral* nor more *immoral* than *history itself*; but history was not created by the good Lord to serve as reading material for young ladies, so no one should take it amiss if my drama is just as ill suited for such a purpose. I can't possibly turn Danton and the bandits of the Revolution into heroes of virtue! If I wanted to convey their depravity, then I had to let them be depraved; if I wanted to show their godlessness, then I clearly had to let them speak like atheists. If a few indecent expressions occur, then think of the notoriously obscene language of that era, of which the words I give my characters to say are but a pale reflection. The only other thing one might criticize is my choice of subject matter. But this objection has long been refuted. Accept it as valid, and you would have to condemn the greatest masterpieces of literature. The writer is no preacher of morality, he invents and creates characters, he makes past ages live again, and people can learn just as well from that as from the study of history and from their observation of what happens around them in real life. If *that* was one's view, then one would have to forego the study of history because of the very many immoral things recounted in it, go blindfold down the street because of all the vulgarities one might see there, and scream blue murder against God for having created a world so full of obscenities. If incidentally anyone wanted to tell me that a writer should show the world not as it is, but as it ought to be, then my answer is that I don't want to make it any better than the good Lord did, who no doubt made the world just as He meant it to be. As for the so-called Idealists, I consider that they have produced almost nothing but puppets with sky-blue noses and affected rhetoric, but not human beings of flesh and blood whose sorrow and joy I can share emotionally and whose deeds and actions fill me with revulsion or admiration. In a word, I have great respect for Goethe and Shakespeare, but very little for Schiller.[49] It goes without saying,

by the way, that extremely unfavourable reviews will appear in
due course, for governments have to get their paid hacks to prove
that their opponents are either stupid or immoral.[50] Incidentally I
don't by any means consider my play to be perfect, and will
gratefully accept any genuinely aesthetic criticism – [. . .]

To his family

Strasbourg, 17 August 1835

I know nothing of any subversive goings-on.[51] I and my friends
are all of the opinion that for now we must entrust everything to
time; incidentally, the way that the princes are abusing their
newly regained power can only work to our advantage [. . .]

To his family

Strasbourg, October 1835

(. . .) I have acquired all sorts of interesting material here about a
friend of Goethe's, an unfortunate writer by the name of *Lenz*,
who lived here at the same time as Goethe and went half mad.
I'm thinking of publishing an essay about him in the *Deutsche
Revue*.[52] I am also casting around for material for a dissertation on
a topic in philosophy or natural history.[53] Another sustained
period of study, and my way will be clear. There are people here
who prophesy a brilliant future for me. I have no objections.

To Karl Gutzkow

[Strasbourg, late 1835]

[. . .] My brain is being addled by the study of philosophy;[54] I am
getting to know the paltriness of the human mind from yet
another side. But so be it! If we could only imagine that the holes
in our trousers were palace windows, we could live like kings; as
it is, we're miserably cold.

To his family

Strasbourg, 1 January 1836

[...] As for me, by the way, I don't by any means belong to *Young Germany*, the literary party led by Gutzkow and Heine.[55] Only a total misunderstanding of our social conditions could make people believe that a total restructuring of our religious and social ideas could be achieved through the medium of topical literature. Nor do I share *in any way* their views on *Christianity and marriage*, though I do get angry when people who have sinned a thousand times more in practice than those have in their *theories* immediately start pulling moral faces and cast stones at young and serious talents. I go my own way and am sticking to the field of drama, which has nothing to do with these disputes; I draw my characters in such a way as to make them true, as I see it, to nature and history and laugh at people who want to make me responsible for their morality or immorality. I have my own ideas about these things. [...]

To Karl Gutzkow

Strasbourg [1836]

[...] By the way, to be quite honest, you and your friends don't seem to me to have followed exactly the wisest course. Reform society by means of *ideas* deriving from the *educated* class? Impossible! Our age is purely *material*; if you had ever taken a more directly political approach, you would soon have reached the point where reform would have come to a halt all on its own. You will never bridge the gulf between the educated and uneducated classes of society.

I have become convinced that the educated and prosperous minority, whilst keen to wrest concessions for itself from those holding power, will never be willing to give up its own barbed relationship to the great mass of the people. And the masses themselves? For them there are only two levers: material poverty and *religious fanaticism*. Any party adept at applying these levers will carry the day. Our age needs weapons and bread – and then a *cross* or some such. I believe that in social matters one must start from an absolute principle of *justice*, seek the development of a new life and spirit in the *people*, and let the decrepit society of today go to the devil. What's the point of such a creature going lumbering on? Its entire life consists solely in attempts to escape the most appalling boredom. May it die out – that's the only new experience it is capable of having. (. . .)

To Eugen Boeckel

Strasbourg, 1 June [1836]

[. . .] A propos, [Minna] has given me your two letters, with your seals still intact; all the same, I would have considered it more becoming if for propriety's sake you had put your letter in an envelope; if it wasn't meant for the eyes of a lady, then it was unbecoming to address it to a lady; with an envelope it is rather different. I hope you'll forgive me this small rebuke.[56] [. . .]

To Wilhelm Büchner

Strasbourg, 2 September 1836

(. . .) I'm perfectly happy within myself, except when we get continual rain or a north-westerly wind, when I become one of those people who are capable, having removed one stocking of an evening before going to bed, of hanging themselves right there and then because it's too much effort to take off the other one. (. . .) I have decided to commit myself completely to the study of the sciences and philosophy, and will soon be going to *Zurich*, where, in my capacity as a superfluous member of society, I shall give lectures to my fellow human beings on something likewise extremely superfluous, namely German philosophical systems since Descartes and Spinoza. Meanwhile I am busily getting a number of people to kill or marry each other on paper,[57] and am praying for a publisher with no brains, and a large public with as little taste as possible. One needs courage for many things under the sun, even to be a lecturer in philosophy.[58] (. . .)

To his family

Strasbourg, September 1836

(. . .) I haven't sent off my two dramas yet, I'm still dissatisfied with various bits, and don't want the same thing to happen to me as happened the first time. They are pieces of work that you can't get finished by a particular date, like a tailor making a suit. (. . .)

To his family

Zurich, 20 November 1836

(. . .) As regards politics, you needn't worry at all. For goodness' sake don't pay any attention to the fairy-tales in our newspapers. Switzerland is a republic, and since people generally don't know anything better than to say that 'all republics are impossible', so they feed the good Germans with daily stories of anarchy, murder and mayhem. You will be surprised when you visit me. All along the way – friendly villages with pretty houses, and then the nearer you get to Zurich, and especially along the lake – prosperity on every hand; even the physical appearance of the villages and little towns is beyond the ken of people in our country. The streets here aren't full of soldiers, aspiring civil servants and idle state officials, and you don't run the risk of being knocked down by an aristocrat's carriage; instead of that, everywhere you see a healthy, vigorous people, governed at little cost by a simple, good, truly *republican* government, maintained through a tax on *wealth*, a kind of tax that would be universally shouted down in Germany as the height of anarchy. (. . .)

Minnigerode is dead, so I gather from a letter – which is to say that he was slowly tortured to death for three long years.[59] Three years! In the Terror in France at least you were despatched in a matter of hours: first the sentence, then the guillotine! But three years! We have a truly humane government: they can't bear the sight of blood. And so there are some forty people still in gaol, and that's not anarchy, that's law and order, and these gentlemen wax indignant when they think of anarchic Switzerland! By God, these people are taking out a massive loan, which may one day be recovered from them with heavy interest, very heavy – (. . .)

To Wilhelm Büchner

Zurich, end November 1836

(. . .) I sit by day with my scalpel, by night with my books. (. . .)

To Minna Jaeglé

[Zurich] 13 January 1836

Dear child! (. . .) I'm counting the weeks to Easter on my fingers, I feel more and more desolate. It was alright at the beginning: new surroundings, people, circumstances, activities – but now that I'm used to everything, and everything happens according to a familiar routine, I can't escape from myself any more. I keep half-seeing you between the fish-tails and frogs' toes, etc. Isn't that even more touching than the story of Abelard, when Héloïse kept inserting herself between his lips and his prayers? Oh, I'm becoming more poetic every day, all my thoughts are swimming in pure alcohol. Thank God, I'm dreaming a lot at night again, my sleep isn't so heavy any more.

To Minna Jaeglé

[Zurich] 20 January 1837

(. . .) I caught a cold and went to bed. But I'm better now.[60] When you're a little unwell like that you have such an enormous urge to be lazy; but the millwheel goes on turning without pause or peace. (. . .) Today and yesterday I've allowed myself a bit of a rest and am not doing any reading; tomorrow it's the same old slog, you won't believe how regular and steady my routine is. I tick along almost as predictably as a Black Forest clock. But it's good all the same: peace after all my hectic brain-work, and on top of that there's the pleasure I take in creating my poetic stuff. Poor Shakespeare was a scribe during the day and had to write his plays at night, and I that am not worthy to loose his shoe am far better off – (. . .) Could you learn those *folksongs* by Easter-time if it wouldn't be too much to ask of your health? One doesn't hear anyone singing here; the *people* don't sing, and you know how I love those women who bawl or whimper a few notes at soirées and concerts. I feel ever closer to the people and to the middle ages, it seems clearer to me every day – and you *will* sing the songs, won't you? I get half homesick if I sing one of the tunes to myself. (. . .) Every evening I sit for an hour or two in the casino;⁶¹ you know how specially fond I am of beautiful rooms and lights and having people around me. (. . .)

To Minna Jaeglé

[Zurich, 1837]

(. . .) I shall be having *Leonce and Lena* and two other plays published in a week at the outside.⁶² (. . .)

To Minna Jaeglé

[Zurich] 27 January [1837]

Dear child, you are full of tender worries and will end up ill with fright; I almost think you will die – but *I* have no wish to die and am as healthy as ever.⁶³ I think my fear of how I might be looked after here has made me get well again. In Strasbourg it would have been altogether pleasant and I would have gone to bed with the utmost contentment for an entire fortnight, rue Saint-Guillaume no. 66, up to the first floor and turn left, in a not quite tiny room with green wallpaper! Would I have rung the doorbell in vain? I'm feeling reasonably well today, I'm still feasting off yesterday, the sun was big and warm in the clearest of skies – and then I put out my light and hugged a noble soul to my breast, namely a tiny little landlord who looks like a drunken rabbit and has rented me a large elegant room in his magnificent house just outside the city. Such a noble man! The house isn't far from the lake, the water is right in front of my windows, and on every side the Alps, like sun-sparkling clouds. – Are you coming soon? The spirit of youth is gone from me, and I'll get grey hairs otherwise, I need very soon to drink in new strength from your inner happiness and your divine naturalness and your lovely frivolity and all your wicked attributes, you wicked girl. Addio piccola mia! –

NOTES

DANTON'S DEATH

Büchner's first play – which he must have been gestating for some considerable time – was written out in his father's house in Darmstadt in the first weeks of 1835. He sent a completed manuscript to the oppositional author and publicist Karl Gutzkow on 21 February, claiming in the accompanying letter (see p. 197) that he had been compelled by 'unhappy circumstances' to complete it 'in five weeks at most'. The circumstances were indeed oppressive: Büchner's always poor relationship with his father was at its lowest ebb, and he had to go to inordinate lengths to keep his writing secret; the grim fiasco of *The Hessian Messenger* had given him much to think about concerning revolutionary ideals and realities; more urgently, it had made him the object of close police interest and surveillance, so that he lived in constant and well-founded fear of arrest and sequestration (a ladder was kept permanently propped against the garden wall, and less than a fortnight after finishing the play he duly fled across the frontier to Strasbourg, followed in due course by a 'Wanted' notice). On top of all this he was desperately short of money.

Following Gutzkow's commendation the play was published later the same year, but only in bowdlerized form (even so, it is remarkable that it got through the severe censorship then prevailing). No definitive edition was ever published in Büchner's lifetime, and modern editions are based on three main sources: a complete autograph manuscript, which may or may not have been the final version as given to the printer; and two separate copies of the bowdlerized edition of 1835, both with detailed corrections in Büchner's own hand, which he sent to friends.

Even had it been written by a renowned and practised playwright, *Danton's Death* would have been an extraordinary achievement; coming from a 21-year-old medical student with no known experience of the theatre, it was a phenomenal début. No writer in any language has treated the French Revolution more vividly or more penetratingly than Büchner does here; and it would be difficult to find any play that illuminates the political-historical process more subtly or more provocatively. Although not staged until 1902, *Danton's Death* has long since established itself at the heart of the German theatre repertoire, and is one of the very few pre-twentieth-century German plays to be regularly performed abroad.

The historical background

The action of the play covers a crucial period of thirteen days during the last violent spasm of the Revolution proper, and its towering symbol is the guillotine: on the first day (24 March 1794) Hébert and his hard-left *enragés* are liquidated (off-stage); on the final day (5 April) Danton and the soft-left *indulgents* are likewise eradicated (on-stage); Robespierre and his Jacobin faction are left in sole power – but their own destruction will follow within weeks (on 28 July), and is repeatedly foreshadowed within the play. What Büchner shows us here is in a sense the critical climax of revolutionary radicalism: the point at which its failure is starkly, unmistakably evident (especially in the gnawing *hunger* that is one of the play's most insistent motifs); the point, too, at which its extinction becomes increasingly certain as the Terror becomes ever more extreme. Before long the essential determining forces and interests of the pre-revolutionary period – in particular those of money and property – will assert themselves anew, and will inaugurate a long period of ever more reactionary Restoration throughout most of Europe – a period that was still in full swing in Büchner's own day, with its hated minions literally standing watch in the street outside the Büchner house in Darmstadt while the play was being covertly, frenetically penned within.

The many historical references in the text are briefly explained in the notes. But for a comprehensive (and very lively) account of the Revolution as a whole, readers are recommended to read Simon Schama's *Citizens. A Chronicle of the French Revolution* (New York and London, 1989).

Büchner's own sources were manifold, and have probably not yet all been traced. The two principal ones were: Carl Strahlheim (pseudonym for Johann Konrad Friederich), *Die Geschichte unserer Zeit* (Stuttgart, 1826; a part-work of 120 numbers, grouped into thirty volumes, plus numerous supplements and special numbers); Louis Adolphe Thiers, *Histoire de la Révolution française* (Paris, 1823–4; 10 vols.). Büchner did not use his sources simply for the purposes of general background: more than a sixth of the play consists of quotations, either verbatim or in paraphrase (cf. note 7). For the most convenient and detailed guide presently available, see Thomas Michael Mayer's edition of the play, in which he identifies all known borrowings, gives their source, and indicates whether the borrowing is a direct quotation or a paraphrase (in Peter von Becker (ed.), *Georg Büchner: Danton's Tod. Die Trauerarbeit im Schönen*; Frankfurt, 1980).

The dramatis personae

All the named individuals in Büchner's list of characters are taken from history, except Simon the Prompter and the three prostitutes, Rosalie, Adelaide and Marion. For the sake of convenience, all are alphabetically listed here with a brief description – together with Amar and Vouland, who appear in III.8, but were omitted from Büchner's list, presumably by mistake. (Information on other historical figures, i.e. those that are simply referred to in the text, is given at the appropriate point in the notes.) The spelling of names in the headings reflects Büchner's own usage (which is often non-standard).

Amar: Jean-Baptiste André Amar (1755–1816), a lawyer (like the great majority of the revolutionaries detailed here); President of the National Convention in April 1794 and *rapporteur* of the Committee of General Security; a notoriously zealous and draconian participant in the Terror. He turned against Robespierre in July 1794, and contributed to his downfall. He was nevertheless denounced in the post-revolutionary Convention in April 1795 ('L'infâme Amar', 'ce tigre des comités révolutionnaires') and duly arrested. After various ups and downs he managed to live out the rest of his days in careful obscurity.

Barrère: Bertrand Barère de Vieuzac (1755–1841), a brilliant lawyer, then a journalist and revolutionary politician, twice elected to the Committee of Public Safety. He became notorious for his knack of always putting himself on the winning side, and was said to have had two alternative speeches in his pocket at the meeting of the National Convention on 27 July 1794 that sealed the Jacobins' fate. He was arrested by the post-revolutionary Thermidorians and sentenced to deportation in 1795, but managed to escape from the holding-prison. He later made fawning obeisance successively to Napoleon, Louis XVIII and Louis-Philippe. His pangs of conscience (III.6) are Büchner's own invention.

Billaud Varennes: Jacques-Nicolas Billaud-Varenne (1756–1819), another lawyer; a participant in the September massacres, and a particularly bloodthirsty practitioner of the Terror. Having been one of Robespierre's most fervent supporters, he became a chief architect of his downfall in July 1794. Along with Barère and his friend Collot d'Herbois he was sentenced to deportation in 1795, and never returned from exile in South America.

Chaumette: Pierre-Gaspard Chaumette (1763–94); another participant in the September massacres, he was a leading member of the Paris Commune. He chiefly became known for his strenuous efforts to replace Christianity with the cult of Reason. In November 1793 he organized the notorious *Fête de la Raison* in Notre-Dame (recycled for the purpose into a *Temple de la Raison*). Although not himself an *enragé*, he was suspected of posing a similar threat and was guillotined on 13 April 1794, shortly after the Dantonists.

Collot d'Herbois: Jean-Marie Collot d'Herbois (1750–96), originally an actor and minor playwright, became a particularly savage exponent of the Terror, most notoriously when he dealt with the counter-revolution in Lyon by ordering over two thousand summary executions. With his friend Billaud-Varenne he was instrumental in Robespierre's downfall, most notably when, as President of the Convention, he refused to allow Robespierre to speak at the decisive meeting of 27 July 1794. He was sentenced to deportation with Barère and Billaud-Varenne in 1795, and died in Guyana the following year.

Danton (Georges): Georges Jacques Danton (1759–94) was a lawyer, and son of a lawyer. He made his name first through his oratory at the Cordelier and Jacobin clubs in 1791, earning the nickname *le Mirabeau de la canaille* ('the Mirabeau of the mob'). In 1792 he was Minister of Justice. In April 1793 he became a member of the newly created Committee of Public Safety, and for three months was in effect its leader, and thus virtual head of the revolutionary government. He tried to pursue a policy of compromise and diplomatic negotiation vis-à-vis the foreign powers beleaguering the country, but this policy was doomed from the outset, since the enemy powers held all the trumps; in July 1793 he was not re-elected to the Committee. Seeing stabilization as the only viable option for the Revolution, he soon came to be identified with the *indulgents*, and although he strongly supported the Jacobins in their opposition to the ultra-radical *enragés* under Hébert, he was increasingly regarded in early 1794 as a threat as the natural focus of moderatist opposition. He was duly arrested, condemned to death, and immediately guillotined on 5 April 1794.

Danton was an extremely complex character about whom historians still tend to differ. Powerfully built with a bull-like head and a deep, strong voice, he was one of the Revolution's most mighty orators; an inspiring leader with a common touch unequalled by any of his fellow revolutionaries; a man of immense intelligence, energy and charisma. But he was a keen devotee of money and the sensual pleasures of life; he was suspected of embezzling large sums while Minister of Justice; prior to the abolition of the monarchy he almost certainly acted as a paid informer of the royal court. He was mercurial in temperament, and slipped easily from fervour to apathy.

Danton (Julie): Büchner's Julie is to all intents and purposes an invention of his own. Danton did indeed have a (second) wife at the time of his death, Sophie (also recorded as Louise and Sébastienne-Louise), née Gély – whom he probably married on his beloved first wife's advice in order to secure a mother for their two sons. Barely fifteen on her marriage to Danton in July 1793, she remarried three years after his death, and lived on until 1856 (outliving Büchner himself by almost twenty years).

Desmoulins (Camille): Camille Desmoulins (1760–94) was yet another lawyer (though hindered in his profession by a stutter), and one of the most influential pamphleteers and journalists of the Revolution. Though friendly with Robespierre (they had been at school together), he was particularly close to Danton, serving for instance as his Secretary-General at the Ministry of Justice. He began publishing his new journal, *Le Vieux Cordelier*, in December 1793, first attacking the *enragés* under Hébert, but then increasingly attacking the Robespierreans and supporting the *indulgents* – a stance that rapidly cost him his life. The passionate devotion to his wife depicted in the play is authentic.

Desmoulins (Lucile): Lucile Desmoulins (1771–94) did not in reality go mad over the arrest and condemnation of her husband, but efficiently took all possible steps to save his life, including writing a pleading letter to Robespierre. She did not go out and heroically invite her own death: she was picked up on trumped-up charges of complicity in plots to free her husband and guillotined eight days after him (with Chaumette and Dillon) on 13 April 1794.

Dillon: Arthur, comte de Dillon (1750–94) was from an aristocratic family of Anglo-Irish extraction, originally exiled to France following the 1688 revolution. A soldier in the French army from the age of fourteen, Dillon became a general who continued to serve during the Revolution, but remained a committed royalist at heart. He was arrested on conspiracy charges in July 1793; after the Dantonists' arrest he was accused of hatching further plots from his prison cell and guillotined on 13 April 1794 – not before shouting 'Vive le roi!'

Dumas: René François Dumas (1757–94), originally a priest, and then a lawyer. Although described in Büchner's list of characters as a President of the Revolutionary Tribunal, he was in fact Vice-President at the time of the play: notorious as a fanatical bully, he was made President immediately after the Dantonists' trial in place of Herman, who was considered too soft. He remained loyal to Robespierre, attempting to rally support for him in the final days, and was duly guillotined with Robespierre, Saint-Just and the others in the first batch of Jacobin executees on 28 July 1794.

Fabre d'Eglantine: Philippe Fabre (1750–94), a minor poet and playwright (and deviser of the revolutionary calendar); he gave himself the name Fabre d'Eglantine after supposedly winning a prize – a gold eglantine (wild rose) – in a literary competition. He was accused of forgery and corruption following the scandal concerning the Compagnie des Indes (see note 58), and was guillotined with the Dantonists on 5 April 1794. He was particularly close to Danton, and it was Danton's defence of his friend after the latter's arrest that first exposed him to attack.

Fouquier Tinville: Antoine-Quentin Fouquier-Tinville (1746–95), a lawyer. He became Public Prosecutor in the Revolutionary Tribunal in March 1793, and ruthlessly attacked all who appeared in the dock (including Camille Desmoulins, who was not only a friend but also a relative). He was himself tried after the downfall of Robespierre, and guillotined on 7 May 1795.

Hérault-Séchelles: Marie Jean Hérault de Séchelles (1759–94), a lawyer from a distinguished aristocratic family, he enthusiastically embraced the Revolution from the outset. President of the National Convention at the time of the Jacobin coup of 2 June 1793, he became a member of the Committee of Public Safety, and was mainly responsible for drafting the new constitution of June 1793. With his genial wit, aristocratic background and striking good looks, and his undisguised fondness for a luxurious life-style that he could easily afford, he readily attracted envy and suspicion. He was guillotined with Danton and the others on 5 April 1794; he had in fact already been imprisoned on 17 March, a week before Büchner's play begins.

Herrmann: Armand Herman (1749–95), a lawyer who became President of the Revolutionary Tribunal until replaced by the even more ruthless Dumas; in the last few weeks of Robespierre's regime he became in effect a government minister. Arrested a few days after Robespierre's execution, he was condemned by his own court and guillotined with Fouquier-Tinville on 7 May 1795.

Lacroix: Jean-François Delacroix (1753–94), normally known during the Revolution simply as Lacroix. A member of the first Committee of Public Safety, he was a close associate of Danton's. He had a dubious reputation: he was suspected of having enriched himself while on a government mission to the armies in the

Austrian Netherlands (Belgium) in 1792; and in January 1794 he was accused of being mixed up with the renegade general Dumouriez (see note 75). He was guillotined with the other Dantonists on 5 April 1794.

Laflotte: Alexandre de Laflotte (1766–?), a minor and obscure figure in the history of the Revolution. A lawyer by training, he served as a diplomat in Genoa and Florence, but was arrested on 30 March 1794, and promptly made the denunciation reflected in III.5 – a denunciation which, though essentially baseless, led to a wave of arrests and executions (not least that of Lucile Desmoulins).

Legendre: Louis Legendre (1752–97); a butcher by trade, he joined the Jacobin and Cordelier clubs, and became a member of the Committee of General Security. A close friend of Danton's, he supported him at first (see II.7), but then abandoned him out of fear of Robespierre. After the latter's fall he was conspicuously zealous in rooting out the remaining Robespierreans.

Mercier: Louis Sébastien Mercier (1740–1814), a successful author in the pre-revolutionary period, best known for his eight-volume *Tableau de Paris*. Always a moderate, and a dedicated opponent of the Jacobins, he was arrested as a Girondin in October 1793 and sweated it out in gaol for many months (in La Force, not the Luxembourg as Büchner has it in III.3). Acquitted, he went on to become a maverick professor of history. Büchner knew of him through *Le nouveau Paris*, his six-volume sequel to the *Tableau de Paris*, published in 1799, and Mercier is unique in being both a character within the play and also one of its sources.

Paris: Félix Paris, an extremely minor and obscure figure. As a clerk to the Revolutionary Tribunal he had advance knowledge of the warrant for Danton's arrest, and warned him accordingly.

Payne: Thomas Paine (1737–1809) went from England to America in 1774 after meeting Benjamin Franklin, and became one of the most influential advocates of American independence. His defence of the French Revolution, *Rights of Man*, became an immediate sensation when he published it in London in 1791. Having fled from England to France, he was declared a French citizen and elected to the National Convention in September 1792 (the only Englishman to enjoy that questionable honour). A moderate, he was imprisoned in January 1794, and not released until November, several months after the Robespierreans' downfall. The first part of his famous work *The Age of Reason* appeared while he was still in prison in 1794, and the second part in 1796. It is virtually certain that Büchner had not read *The Age of Reason*, but knew only of its notoriety: although infamous as an atheist, Paine – a Quaker by upbringing – was in fact a convinced deist (and in 1798 published his *Atheism Refuted*, a 'discourse to prove the existence of God').

Philippeau: Pierre Nicolas Philippeaux (1756–94), yet another of the countless revolutionary lawyers, he became a journalist and a member of the National Convention. A Dantonist, he was repeatedly attacked in the Jacobin and Cordelier clubs and in the Convention – by Hébert, Robespierre, Momoro, Collot d'Herbois and others – before sharing Danton's fate on 5 April 1794. There is little basis in Büchner's sources for the religious faith and serenity that characterize him in the second half of the play.

Robespierre: Maximilien-François-Marie-Isidore de Robespierre (1758–94), a lawyer and son of a lawyer. Although a representative in the various national assemblies from the Estates-General of 1789 onwards, and an exceptionally prolific speaker, Robespierre developed his power base mainly through the Club des Jacobins and also the Paris Commune. Having called on the masses to rise against the Girondin regime in May 1793, he became the key leader of the dictatorship that rapidly ensued after the Jacobins' seizure of power on 2 June 1793, and which led in due course to the ever more bloody Reign of Terror. Having dealt with the ultra-radicalist threat of the *enragés*, particularly the faction centred on Hébert, he turned his attention to the moderatist threat posed by the *indulgents*: within a fortnight of the Hébertistes' liquidation, the Dantonists were arrested, condemned and guillotined. Although Robespierre was elected President of the National Convention on 4 June 1794 by a colossal majority (216 of the 220 votes), opposition to him grew rapidly in the following weeks, and he was declared *hors la loi* on 27 July, then guillotined without trial the following day.

Robespierre could scarcely have been more different from his victim and erstwhile colleague, Danton (they accordingly make a superbly theatrical contrast in Büchner's play). Physically Robespierre was slight and bony; his voice was curiously thin and high-pitched; he wore steel-rimmed spectacles, powdered hair and impeccably clean but sombre clothes. Unmarried, he lived a famously plain and frugal life. He was devoid of passion, but a man of unshakeable principle and integrity; a rigorous deist and Rousseauist, much given to Roman virtues and righteous indignation; a highly effective orator who swayed his audience not through gutsy flamboyance, but through an implacable Cornelian rhetoric, perfectly measured and calculated. Robespierre has always been a controversial figure, tending to be attacked by the right as a leftist and by the left as not leftist enough. In the Restoration period following the Revolution he was almost exclusively denigrated, and Büchner's own sources were very largely negative in the image they conveyed.

Saint-Just: Louis-Antoine-Léon de Saint-Just (1767–94), a lawyer, and the youngest of the Jacobin revolutionaries (only twenty-six at his death). A fervent disciple of Robespierre's from the earliest days of the Revolution, he became his protégé, friend and chief henchman. Of all the Robespierreans he was the most radical in his ideology, and the most decisive, ruthless and single-minded in his actions. Although because of his youth he exercised power for a relatively short time, he rapidly made himself one of the most dreaded men in France, and in the process anticipated twentieth-century totalitarianism more clearly than anyone else in the Revolution.

Vouland: Jean-Henri Voulland (1751–1801), a lawyer from a Protestant background; he held office as both Secretary and President of the Convention, and became a member of the Committee of General Security. He was a committed exponent of the Terror, but disliked Robespierre both personally and because, as an atheist, he disapproved of Robespierre's campaigns against de-christianization in favour of deism. He helped to overthrow the Jacobins in July 1794, but was subsequently twice arraigned for his role in the Terror (he was acquitted the first time and amnestied the second).

Notes

Reference is occasionally made in these notes to 'Lehmann', with volume and page numbers; this relates to Werner R. Lehmann's edition of Büchner's work: Georg Büchner, *Sämtliche Werke und Briefe*, vols. I and II (Hamburg and Munich, 1967ff.).

1. *Deputies: Députés* in the National Convention.
2. *members of the Committee of General Security:* Both Amar and Vouland were omitted – presumably by accident – from Büchner's list of characters.
3. *HERAULT-SECHELLES ... at the feet of JULIE:* This first scene of Büchner's theatre is provocative enough in its content. (Is there another play in any language or period that evokes the vulva in its opening sentences?) But it is no less provocative in its dramaturgy: the initial sub-scene offers no conventional exposition, nor any triggering of the action; its 'private' rather than 'public' setting is startling; its 'split-screen' structure forces the spectator to watch two sharply contrasted points of interest at the same time; the opening stage direction makes the central figure literally marginal, and also puts him physically low down on the stage. The scene is unimaginable on the nineteenth-century stage. Even today it takes an imaginative director to meet its challenge.
4. *... the very fibres of each other's brain:* No sooner has the curtain gone up than we are offered a perfect example of one of Büchner's most powerful theatrical techniques, whereby contrary messages are simultaneously conveyed: what we *hear* is a savagely graphic evocation of separateness, isolation; what we *see* is a kind of emblematic togetherness, with Danton at Julie's feet, his head in her lap. There is of course a very different kind of separateness enacted on the stage: that which marks off the two lovers from the louche crew around the gaming table.
5. *your red bonnet:* The *bonnet rouge* or *bonnet de la Liberté* had rapidly become one of the most potent emblems of the

Revolution, and in August 1792 had been enshrined on the official Seal of State as the headgear crowning the figure of Liberty. By 1793–4 the wearing of a red bonnet was almost *de rigueur*.

6. *St Jacob:* 'Saint Jacob' is a translator's compromise. Literally speaking it would need to be 'Saint James', but the reference to the Jacobins in Büchner's word 'Jakob' would then be lost.

   The Jacobins were so called because they met in a former Dominican or 'Jacobin' monastery near the rue Saint-Honoré; the Paris Dominicans had long been popularly known as Jacobins because their main base in Paris was in the rue Saint-Jacques.

7. *... Such classical republicans:* These opening lines of Camille Desmoulins are 'authentic' in the sense that Büchner quotes them almost verbatim from his source, Thiers (*Histoire de la Révolution française*), who in turn was quoting from Desmoulins's political journal *Le Vieux Cordelier*. Büchner's persistent use of such documentary or semi-documentary material is one of the play's most crucial and distinctive characteristics. To some extent this clearly was deliberate authenticism in accordance with his claim to his parents that he regarded the dramatist as being essentially a historian whose 'supreme task is to get as close as possible to history as it actually happened' (letter of 28 July 1835; see p. 202); but it is one of the most provocative aspects of Büchner's creativity that it fed to an extraordinary degree on material borrowed from elsewhere.

8. *the Hébertistes:* The Hébertistes under Jacques-René Hébert were a super-radical faction that had threatened the Jacobin radicals as it were from the 'hard left'. On this day, 24 March 1792, Hébert was liquidated with various of his followers – leaving the Jacobins free to deal with the threat from the 'soft left' posed by the Dantonist moderates.

9. *the Decemvirate:* A term for the Committee of Public Safety, which the Jacobins had taken over and turned into their central power base. The use of Latin words, notions and models was extremely common in this period as the revolu-

tionaries sought to authenticate their doings with republican labels from classical antiquity.

The *Decemviri* were originally the commission of ten men set up in 451 BC to formulate a new code of laws for the Roman state.

10. *the lawyer from Arras:* Robespierre.

11. *the Genevan clockmaker:* Jean-Jacques Rousseau (1712–78), born in Geneva as the son of a watchmaker.

12. *Marat's estimate of the number of people that need to be killed:* In his paper *L'Ami du Peuple* Marat had declared (in 1790) that 'five or six hundred' chopped-off heads would ensure 'peace, liberty and happiness' for France.

13. *The Clemency Committee:* A 'Clemency Committee' had been proposed a few months earlier by Camille Desmoulins in *Le Vieux Cordelier*.

14. *The revolution has reached the stage where it must be reorganized:* This speech and the following one graphically summarize the contrary positions and aspirations of the Dantonists and Jacobins. As such they bring into sharp focus an alluring and highly contentious question: whose side is Büchner on? There is no straightforward answer. Büchner certainly wanted to see the fundamental 'social revolution' that Robespierre speaks of in I.6; but the revolutionary reality is a Terror both bloody and – as the play consistently demonstrates – utterly futile. He certainly shared the specific ideals expressed here through the medium of Hérault and Camille; but he knew that there was no more scope for their realization under revolutionary despotism than under monarchic despotism – hence the mordant question he has Danton pose: 'So who's going to bring about all these wonderful things?'

15. *Divine Epicurus:* The tone is flippant but the reference is serious. Epicureanism is popularly understood as 'devotion to a life of ease, pleasure and luxury' (*OED*), but properly speaking it is a rigorous system of moral philosophy – one that is conveniently summarized by Büchner himself in his excerpts from a standard philosophy handbook of the day (see Lehmann, II.403–9). Epicureanism is the direct anti-

thesis of Robespierrean puritanism in that it sees good and evil not as quasi-metaphysical absolutes, but as matters of practicality: virtue is the practical means whereby each individual strives for the 'highest good', which is happiness (Lehmann, II.404); wrongness is any kind of behaviour that infringes the rights of others, thus infringing the compact that joins individuals in a society (Lehmann, II.405).

16. *sweet-arsed Venus:* A reference to the so-called 'Callipygean Venus', now in Naples museum. 'Callipygean' is from a Greek epithet traditionally applied to Aphrodite (Venus), meaning 'beautiful buttocks'.

17. *Chalier:* Joseph Chalier, a revolutionary leader in Lyon, had been executed there in June 1793 by counter-revolutionary forces, and had rapidly acquired the status of a saint and martyr of the Revolution, to the extent that his bust was enshrined on the altar of a (dechristianized) Paris church.

18. *We want naked gods and priestesses ... guardians of the Republic:* These three sentences, together with Hérault's 'lawyer from Arras – Genevan clockmaker' speech and the first two sentences of Philippeau's 'Marat' speech, were all added in the margin of Büchner's manuscript. They were clearly directly inspired by a passage in Heinrich Heine's *Zur Geschichte der Religion und Philosophie in Deutschland*, published in January 1835 – i.e. when Büchner was in the middle of writing his play. For good measure Büchner also inserts a direct quotation from a poem by Sappho.

19. SIMON *the prompter:* On the face of it, it might seem bizarre that Büchner should make this first 'ordinary' representative of the people not ordinary at all, but a theatre-prompter, and one much given to hamming. But in fact Simon inaugurates an important dimension of the play: not only do we encounter discourse on the actual theatre, and metaphors from the theatre, but we are also repeatedly confronted with the theatricality of the Revolution itself, with the extraordinary power of histrionic declamation directed at an excitable and mercurial (on-stage) audience, be it in the street, the Jacobin Club, the National Convention, the courtroom. It is one of Büchner's most

revolutionary achievements to show history being made by the makers of speeches. As he will have Mercier say in III.3: 'Look around you: what you see is what you've said – a precise translation of all your words. These miserable wretches, their executioners, the guillotine: they are your speeches come to life.'

20. *Virginius:* When the beautiful Virginia was consigned into slavery by the lustful Decemvir Appius Claudius, her father, Lucius Virginius, ensured that she remained both free and virtuous by the expedient of stabbing her to death (an act that precipitated the downfall of the Decemvirate – see note 9).

21. *Lucretia:* 'Lucretia' doesn't fit here: Büchner must have meant Virginia (see preceding note). Lucretia was raped by a cousin-in-law, Sextus, son of Tarquinius Superbus, and to erase her dishonour stabbed herself to death.

22. *Appius Claudius:* See note 20.

23. *The King with his veto:* Under the 1791 constitution the King retained the right of veto in the Legislative Assembly. The 1791 constitution was abolished in September 1792 and the Assembly replaced by the National Convention.

24. *the Girondists:* The moderate *Girondins* (so called because they were associated with the Gironde area of France) held power in 1792, but were increasingly threatened by the radicals. Following a brief popular revolt they were ousted by the Jacobins in the coup of 2 June 1793 (see note 31); most were liquidated in October of the same year.

25. *in August and September:* On 10 August 1792 the Tuileries were stormed and the Royal Guard massacred. In September, in the general hysteria stirred up by the threat from the Austrian and Prussian armies, the prisons of Paris were invaded and at least 1,400 inmates (more than half the total prison population) systematically butchered over a period of several days (2–6 September) – an episode that 'has no equal in atrocities committed during the French Revolution by any party' (Schama, *Citizens*, p.631).

26. *Aristides:* Aristides was an Athenian soldier and statesman, nicknamed 'the Just' – a nickname likewise applied to Robespierre.

27. *dear Baucis:* Baucis and Philemon were the Darby and Joan of classical antiquity. Though poor and old, they were unwaveringly happy and devoted.

28. *Porcia:* Porcia was the fiercely republican daughter of Cato of Utica, and wife of Caesar's assassin Marcus Brutus; she committed suicide on the death of her husband (see note 33).

29. *MESSENGER FROM LYON:* The messenger is nameless and never reappears – but his speech, brilliantly conceived and placed by Büchner, conveys the prevailing political mood with maximum force and economy. The Jacobins may have prevented themselves being 'out-Jacobined' by the Hébertistes, but there is still a powerful tide running in favour of continued radicalism. Robespierre and Saint-Just will ride this tide with great skill throughout the play – even if, soon afterwards, they will be wrong-footed and destroyed when the tide changes direction.

30. *Ronsin:* As commander of the revolutionary army Ronsin had crushed the counter-revolutionary forces in Lyon in 1793, but became an Hébertiste and was one of the group whose execution is referred to (by Philippeau) in I.1.

31. *May 31st:* On 31 May 1793 the Paris Sections began a revolt against the Girondins and their control of the National Convention; the Jacobins duly seized power on 2 June.

32. *Gaillard:* Another Hébertiste, Gaillard committed suicide.

33. *the dagger of Cato:* Cato of Utica killed himself rather than yield to the corrupt Julius Caesar and thus sully his own pure principles. This and the 'cup of Socrates' reference in the following line both derive from Büchner's sources. But they contribute to the very marked theme of suicide that reverberates throughout the play, curiously echoing Büchner's school essays with their rapt concentration on the topic, and particularly on the notion of the 'noble', 'self-sacrificing' suicide ('Heroic Death of the Four Hundred Pforzheimers', 'On Suicide', 'Address in Defence of Cato of Utica'). Cf. note 61.

34. *ROBESPIERRE:* Well over half this speech is borrowed, largely verbatim, from Büchner's sources. The only original

paragraphs are the first (wholly) and the fifth and sixth (substantially). It is fascinating to see what Büchner is concerned to stress in these added paragraphs. In the first he shows Robespierre as someone who is by no means simply driven by history, but has cunningly waited for exactly the right moment to strike. In the fifth and sixth he massively increases the emphasis on vice and corruption. In surface terms this is a major plot element (Robespierre's insistence on 'virtue' is what dooms Danton – and ultimately Robespierre himself: cf. p. 56). But it is also one of Büchner's deepest and most powerful creative obsessions: a sense of rampant depravity and corruption underlies *The Hessian Messenger* and *Woyzeck* just as much as it does *Danton's Death*.

35. *One of these factions:* The Hébertistes.

36. *another faction:* The Dantonists.

37. *a shameless parody of Tacitus:* In his journal *Le Vieux Cordelier* Camille Desmoulins had made a thinly veiled attack on the radicals by citing Tacitus' descriptions of the emperor Tiberius and his tyrannical rule.

38. *the Catiline conspiracy:* Catiline was a notoriously cruel and degenerate patrician who mounted a sustained and dangerous conspiracy against the state, ultimately foiled by Cicero; the conspiracy is described by Sallust in his *Bellum Catilinae*. Thus, if Camille can suggest that Robespierre is a tyrannical Tiberius, then Robespierre can retort that Danton is a degenerate and traitorous Catiline.

39. *the Palais-Royal:* Now largely the home of government offices, the Palais-Royal has had a chequered history. A large complex of grand buildings, courtyards and gardens, it was at one time the palace of Louis XIV. By the 1780s it included cafés, shops, theatres, freak-shows, waxworks, etc., and its southern side had become notoriously louche, the haunt not only of pickpockets, prostitutes and gamblers, but also of political agitators; in effect, it was the unofficial centre of opposition. It was here, for instance, that Camille Desmoulins famously incited a major disturbance on 12 July 1789, which led to the storming of the Bastille two

days later. It is here too, within the play, that Saint-Just will encounter Danton fraternizing dangerously with the sans-culottes (I.6, p. 25).

40. *like Medea her brother:* Fleeing with Jason and the Golden Fleece on the *Argo*, Medea was hotly pursued by her father Aeëtes, but hit on the brilliant idea of killing and dismembering her brother Apsyrtus and chucking the bits into the sea: Aeëtes duly stopped to recover them, enabling Medea to make good her escape.

41. *DANTON, MARION:* This is arguably the most startling, most disturbing scene (or part-scene) that Büchner ever wrote. Marion's speech is narrative, not drama; it retards the surface plot and shifts the spotlight completely away from the central figure to a character who never otherwise appears and is never otherwise referred to. And yet it is the second-longest original (as opposed to historically sourced) speech that Büchner ever wrote; it creates a theatrical 'micro-climate' of extraordinary intensity; and it deals with some of Büchner's deepest obsessions, longings and fears. As such it is part of a larger rhythmic – and theatrically highly effective – pattern whereby the spectator is constantly being confronted with sharply differentiated scenes ranging from the maximally private to the maximally public. Nothing like this had ever been written in German literature before; indeed nothing like it will be conceived for many decades to come, and even then it will be a latter-day disciple of Büchner's, Frank Wedekind, that takes up the torch.

42. *Adonis:* Adonis was a youth of extraordinary beauty, the beloved of Venus (Aphrodite), who was killed by a wounded boar, whereupon blood-red flowers (anemones, not roses) sprang from the drops of his blood.

43. *crystals of mercury:* Syphilis was routinely treated with doses of the poison mercuric chloride. The implication here and in the subsequent references is that syphilis is rampant, and that behind the alluring façade lurk disease and corruption.

44. *Fabricius:* After an aristocrat surnamed Pâris had made the name notorious through his assassination of Le Peletier in January 1793, Félix Paris preferred to call himself 'Fabri-

cius'. The Roman consul Fabricius was a legendary epitome of probity and frugality.

45. *Brutus ... his own sons:* Lucius Junius Brutus delivered his own two sons to justice for conspiring against the state, and made a point of watching their grisly execution. This deed had typically been glorified in what amounted to a propaganda painting by Jacques Louis David (cf. note 64).

46. *like Saturn ...:* Saturn (a mythical king of Sicily) was identified by the Romans with the Greek god Chronos, lord of the universe until displaced by his son Zeus. To try to avoid this fate Chronos/Saturn devoured his children as each was born (but his wife cannily slipped him a swaddled-up rock in place of the infant Zeus, who was thus able to survive).

47. *they won't dare:* Büchner took this detail from his sources.

48. *the great hero of September:* See note 66.

49. *Tarpeian Rock:* The Tarpeian Rock was a cliff on the Capitoline Hill in Rome from which traitors and murderers were traditionally flung to their death. It was a much-used motif in the rhetoric of the Revolution.

50. *Scene 6: A room:* Danton and Robespierre did indeed have a final confrontation (on 29 March 1794), but Büchner gives it a content entirely of his own making.

51. *We are all Epicureans ... does us good:* The argument of the two men is clearly central to the specific plot and conflict of the play, but it also reflects an anguish within Büchner himself – an anguish so fundamental that it shapes his works at many of their most critical junctures. Are human beings free to act and to choose? Or simply driven, either by external forces of history, etc., or else by the inner compulsions of their own nature? And the crucial corollary: do they bear responsibility for their actions? The issue was already raised through Marion's statement-plus-question, 'It's simply my nature – can anyone escape it?' And it will surface repeatedly in the rest of the play – not least in Danton's (unhistorical) agony over his role in the September massacres (II.5).

52. *Why can't I drive ... a matter of chance:* In this magnificent

final paragraph of the monologue Büchner imagines in Robespierre the deepest private anguish – which centres again on precisely the problem outlined in the preceding note. Robespierre tries to escape responsibility for his acts ('Who would blame us?'), but the bloody finger 'points and points'. The parallelism between this and Danton's 'September' scene (II.5) is remarkable: the same essential inner struggle, the same imagery, the same setting (by a window at night).

53. *his pathetic rag:* Camille's journal *Le Vieux Cordelier. Danton's Death* is surely the first play in world literature in which the fate of a main character is sealed by his political journalism.

54. *Couthon:* Georges Couthon was a member of the Committee of Public Safety. He ended up on the guillotine with Robespierre and Saint-Just on 28 July 1794.

55. *Collot:* Collot d'Herbois, see p. 212.

56. *Saint Denys:* St Denys (or Denis) was the first bishop of Paris. According to Gregory of Tours, he was beheaded on Montmartre hill in AD 258, then walked to his burial place carrying his head under his arm. Büchner borrowed the reference from his sources. (The name should be pronounced on stage in its French form; a titter is otherwise likely.)

57. *He's a widow that's buried several husbands already:* The historical Barère (see p. 212) was notorious for changing sides whenever it seemed expedient. See also the monologue that Büchner gives him at the close of III.6, and note 106.

58. *We'll have forgers for hors d'oeuvre and foreigners for dessert:* Büchner took this detail from his sources: a Spaniard and a Dane were arraigned on criminal charges with the Dantonists, as were a group of Jacobins who had attempted a massive stock-market swindle by falsifying a crucial government document concerning the dissolution of the Compagnie des Indes in 1793. Political prisoners were frequently tried with common criminals: it conveniently clouded the issues and ensured the taint of guilt by association.

59. *the Commune is busy doing penance:* Having switched allegiance to the Jacobins, the Paris Commune were anxious to make amends for their previous support of the Hébertistes.

60. *31st of May:* See note 31.

61. *I would rather be guillotined than guillotine others:* This is arguably one of the most crucial lines in the play. It suggests that, at one level at least, Danton is to all intents and purposes committing suicide, and doing so as a deliberate and *moral* act – like Cato of Utica. In a fundamental sense the 'corrupt' and 'degenerate' Danton is more virtuous by far than the 'incorruptible' Robespierre . . .

62. *Cornelia:* It had become common for people to adopt Latinate forenames to demonstrate their republican credentials. Cornelia, the mother of the Gracchi, was a particularly popular figure at the time as a paragon of Roman motherly virtue.

63. *Oh what fun . . . like dogs in the street:* This speech (which Büchner added in the margin of his manuscript) has often been seen as expressing cynical delight on Danton's part at the crude sexuality of the whores and their clients. But it is surely a cry of terrible and desperate rage – a cry that will be closely echoed when Woyzeck sees Marie and the Drum-Major dance past at the inn: 'Why don't God blow out the sun when he sees the whole world writhing in lechery, men and women, man and beast. They're at it in broad daylight, before your very eyes, like dogs in the street' (see p. 128).

64. *David:* Jacques Louis David, a Jacobin and friend of Robespierre's, was the foremost artist of the revolutionary period. His *Marat assassiné* is perhaps the most famous image of the Revolution (here, too, David painted the corpse while it was practically still warm).

65. *We shared a desk at school:* At the famous Collège Louis-le-Grand in Paris.

66. *– September! –:* Danton was Minister of Justice at the time of the September massacres in the prisons. He did not instigate the butchery, but he knew it was due to happen, refused to prevent it, and, once it had begun, allegedly justified it as an 'indispensable sacrifice' (see Schama, *Citizens*, pp. 629ff.). Whatever the historical Danton's responsibility for events, what matters in the play is his

screaming, inescapable conscience – and this was entirely Büchner's invention.

67. *The man on the cross. . . that whores, lies, steals, murders:* This passage echoes Büchner's famous letter to Minna Jaeglé of March 1834 (see pp. 195f.). In the context of the play, however, the passage has a very specific function: far from being an apodictic statement by the author, it is the rhetorical climax to a breathtaking exercise in casuistry in which Danton, ably abetted by his wife, contrives to drown the voice of his conscience with a flood of convenient rationalizations and excuses. Robespierre in the face of *his* conscience tried to shift the blame – 'Are our actions not like those in a dream [. . .]? Who would blame us for that?' – and Büchner now has Danton ask a similarly pleading question: 'Who'd ever curse the hand on whom the curse of "must" has fallen?' Mankind as 'puppets' manipulated by 'unknown forces', as 'mere swords in the hands of warring spirits': this perspective of Danton's on his own past actions is precisely that – a *perspective*, and a very expedient one at that. It is certainly not the 'message' of the play, as has so often been claimed.

68. *Let's go and get him:* Danton and his friends were arrested during the night of 29–30 March 1794.

69. *France's saviour in 1792:* Danton had quickly and effectively organized troops to face the Austrian and Prussian armies.

70. *Last night . . . to have his say:* This entire speech is borrowed from Büchner's sources.

71. *special privileges:* The 'privileges' implied here mean parliamentary immunity. This was a burning issue in the period: one of the most detested aspects of monarchy was the principle of inviolability, or immunity from the law (cf. the next speech but one!). *The Hessian Messenger* contains several bitter allusions to it in the context of 1830s Hesse and its continuing semi-feudal regime.

72. *ROBESPIERRE:* Except for the final sentence this entire speech is assembled verbatim from Büchner's sources.

73. *Chabot, Delaunay and Fabre:* The 'forgers' referred to in I.6 (see note 58).

74. *Lafayette:* The same Lafayette that had been lionized for his participation in the American War of Independence in 1777–9, and who was later to welcome the new king, Louis-Philippe, to Paris in 1830 (he died in 1834, shortly before Büchner wrote his play). In 1792 he had been forced to flee abroad because of his support for constitutional monarchy.

75. *Dumouriez:* Dumouriez was a notable general who tried to turn his army against the Jacobin threat in Paris in early April 1793 and was forced to flee to Austria (accompanied by the future Louis-Philippe).

76. *Brissot:* Jacques Pierre Brissot, the leader of the Girondins; he was guillotined in 1793.

77. *the committees:* The Committee of Public Safety and the Committee of General Security.

78. *14th of July:* The storming of the Bastille on 14 July 1789.

79. *the daughters of Pelias:* Büchner's choice of this particular classical allusion perhaps obliquely indicates his own critique of the Terror: on the advice of Medea, Pelias' daughters attempted to rejuvenate him by cutting him up and boiling the bits – but ended up, unsurprisingly, with a heap of bones. Again and again throughout the play, Büchner emphasizes that the Terror has achieved precisely nothing: the masses remain as hungry and ill-clad as ever they were, and Saint-Just's enthusiastically applauded talk of 'humanity reborn' is insistently belied.

80. *The Luxembourg: a room with prisoners:* The Luxembourg Palace served as an important prison during the Revolution.

81. *CHAUMETTE . . . OTHER PRISONERS:* . . . Intellectually this scene is the most complex and subtle in the play. Theatrically it is a disaster unless its *comic* structure is recognized and exploited – Payne's 'catechism' of the hapless Chaumette is virtually a play within a play: Payne and Mercier constitute a two-man act running rings around their stooge. Büchner even provides an on-stage audience (the other prisoners), who can be used effectively to cue an appropriate response in the real audience.

82. *Anaxagoras:* A fanatical atheist, Chaumette liked to style

himself after the Athenian philosopher Anaxagoras, who
was accused of irreligion and went into voluntary exile.

83. *The tiniest spasm . . . torn asunder:* This echoes one of the
most telling passages in Büchner's lengthy commentary on
the thought of Spinoza, where he deals with the latter's
proposition that God exists necessarily, since, for Spinoza,
the primacy of the mind is such that if we *think* God, then
God must exist. Büchner retorts: 'But what compels us to
think an entity that can be thought of only as being?' and
he continues a few lines later:

If one accepts the definition of God, then one must admit the
existence of God. But what justifies us in making this defini-
tion?
Reason?
It knows imperfectness.
Feeling?
It knows pain. (Cf. Lehmann, II.236–7.)

The phenomenon of pain and suffering was central for
Büchner – and he was deeply ambivalent in his attitude to it.
His treatment of the issue in *Lenz* is particularly revealing: he
has Lenz tell Oberlin (with an expression of 'infinite suffering'
in his face) that if he were omnipotent he could not bear to see
suffering, and would intervene to stop it; yet it is an experience
of 'deep indescribable pain' that triggers in Lenz his most
intense and mystical experience of divine communion (see p.
147). There is nothing truly surprising in the famous words
that Büchner is said to have uttered just before dying: 'We do
not have too much pain, we have too little, for through pain
we enter into God.' (Cf. the words that Büchner puts into
Lena's mouth on her very first appearance in the comedy:
'My God, my God, is it really true that redemption comes
only through our own pain?'; see p. 92).

84. *Madame Momoro:* Sophie Momoro, the beautiful wife of the
powerful Hébertiste printer-publisher Antoine François
Momoro; a former actress, she had played the part of the
Goddess of Reason in Chaumette's *Fête de la Raison* in
November 1793. She was executed with the Hébertistes on
24 March 1794.

85. *groinful of rosaries:* Chaumette is being doubly mocked: not only are Catholic rosaries being imputed to an atheist, but these 'rosaries' are a symptom of syphilis (strings of nodular enlargements in the lymphatic glands of the groin).

86. *this dove-winged mastiff:* Mercier's oxymoron highlights a central paradox of the play – one that is all too easily lost on the reader/spectator: the Danton that we see almost all through the play is a 'dove-winged' and above all *torpid* creature, but all his fellow revolutionaries on the stage, friend and foe alike, know him as a raging 'mastiff', a man whose energy and eloquence made him one of the mightiest forces of the Revolution. It is no easy task, but an actor has to suggest the 'mastiff' element as well as Danton's prevailing mood of lethargy and resignation – and not only in the courtroom scenes.

87. *the twenty-two Girondists:* See note 24.

88. *The might of the people and the might of reason are one and the same:* Hérault de Séchelles had made this pronouncement as President of the Convention at the time of the uprising against the Girondins.

89. *Well, Procurator-General of the Streetlamp ... the prospects for France:* In September 1789 Camille Desmoulins published his famous pamphlet *Discours de la Lanterne aux Parisiens*, in which the citizens of Paris were supposedly addressed by the Place de Grève streetlamp used in July for summary executions; as a result, Desmoulins was nicknamed 'le procureur général de la lanterne' (*procureur* in this context means 'public prosecutor'). The point being made here is part of the play's insistent leitmotif that all the butchery of the Revolution has achieved nothing whatsoever.

90. *Leroi:* Leroi and the other four jurors named here were all derived from Büchner's sources.

91. *Like Bayezid with his pyramids:* The reference is presumably to Bayezid I, Ottoman sultan from 1389 to 1402, nicknamed 'the Thunderbolt'; though it is not clear what Büchner had in mind with his reference to Bayezid's 'pyramids'.

92. *Mirabeau:* A key leader of the Revolution in its early

stages, Mirabeau fell into disgrace after his death when it was discovered that he had been in the pay of the monarchy.

93. *Orléans:* The Duke of Orléans, a relative of the King, joined the Revolution and became known as 'Philippe Egalité'. He voted for the King's execution, but duly followed him onto the scaffold in November 1793 when he was suspected of wanting the throne for himself.

94. *Remember Marat:* Marat was put before the Revolutionary Tribunal by the Girondins in April 1793, but was acquitted by popular acclamation.

95. *Champ de Mars:* A petition was got up against the King at the Champ de Mars on 17 July 1791; several people were shot and killed in the ensuing confrontation between the crowd and the National Guard. This episode soon came to be viewed as the beginning of popular republicanism.

96. *21st of January:* The King was executed on 21 January 1793.

97. *[Loud applause]:* Schama remarks that the surviving records, though incomplete, indicate that Danton 'spoke nearly the whole day and with stupendous effect, brushing off the charges against him like insects crawling up his clothes' (Schama, *Citizens*, p. 818).

98. *Sainte-Pélagie:* Originally a convent, Sainte-Pélagie was a notoriously horrible prison during the Revolution.

99. *a Tarquin:* It was a Tarquin – Sextus, son of the tyrant Tarquinius Superbus – who raped Lucretia (and thereby precipitated his father's overthrow); see note 21.

100. *Like Jupiter with Semele:* Semele was turned to ashes when she compelled her lover Zeus (Jupiter) to prove his divinity by appearing before her in all his majesty of thunder and lightning.

101. *bad lot ... good lot:* Cf. Robespierre's final oration in the National Convention, two days before his execution: 'I know only two parties, that of good citizens and that of bad citizens.' On an earlier occasion Saint-Just had characteristically declared: 'There are only two kinds of citizens: the good and the bad. The Republic owes to the good its protection. To the bad it owes only death.'

102. *When are you coming for some more fun at Clichy:* Büchner's sources recounted that members of the committees of Public Safety and General Security routinely indulged in orgies at country houses at Clichy, near Paris, and that Barère ran a prostitute-mistress there, 'la Demahy'.

103. *Demahy:* See preceding note.

104. *[a fanatic without balls]:* This phrase is not Büchner's, but is tacked on here for the sake of clarity, especially in stage productions.

105. ... *[Exit BILLAUD and COLLOT]:* This exchange following Saint-Just's exit is especially revealing. In plot terms, it points beyond the end of the play to Robespierre's downfall (he was declared an outlaw on 27 July 1794, and summarily guillotined the following day, only three and a half months after the liquidation of the Dantonists). Far more important is the fact that Büchner bends history by making lechery and corruption the driving force behind his overthrow. The real-life dynamics of the Jacobins' removal were much more complex. But here as so often, what Büchner projects is a terrible vision of rampant sexuality, disease, corruption, whereby the virtuous Robespierre's own Jacobin accomplices are themselves syphilitic libertines.

106. *I was doomed for sure:* In his manuscript Büchner added and then deleted an extra sentence at the end of Barrère's monologue: 'Come, my conscience, we're still getting on very well with each other.' Barrère's struggle with his conscience is characteristically Büchner's own invention.

107. *The Conciergerie:* The Conciergerie was the foulest of all the revolutionary prisons, and also the most feared, not least because condemned prisoners were kept there pending their execution.

108. *In nothingness ... But I'm an atheist:* Büchner has Danton play desperate games with logic here in a syllogism whose third part remains unspoken: if God is nothingness, and Danton an atheist, then Danton cannot believe in nothingness, cannot be a nihilist. The game is continued, but in the most sardonic terms, in the ensuing paragraphs: if

Something cannot become Nothing (see next note), then let's imagine that Nothing became Something – and Büchner projects the comic-appalling vision of all creation being the product of Nothing's bloody suicide.

109. *'something can't become nothing'*: Cf. Büchner's commentary on Spinoza: 'it being impossible for *something* to become *nothing* [. . .]' (see Lehmann, II.237).

110. *the Wandering Jew:* The Jew Ahasver is said to have turned away Jesus on his way to Golgotha, whereupon he was condemned to wander without rest for all eternity.

111. *. . . Committee of Public Safety:* Almost all the scene up to this point is borrowed, largely verbatim, from Büchner's sources.

112. *still a traitor:* Lafayette, as Commander of the National Guard, had led the royal family back to Paris from their Versailles stronghold on 6 October 1789. Concerning Lafayette as a traitor, see note 74.

113. *The instincts of a tiger:* Dumas was known as 'le tigre'.

114. *The Revolutionary Tribunal . . . cut her out of my life:* This detail is authentic. Dumas's wife was sentenced to death by his own Tribunal (but saved in the event by the Jacobins' downfall).

115. *Life, Death and Immortality:* Edward Young's *The Complaint, or Night Thoughts on Life, Death and Immortality* had been translated into several European languages, and Büchner's sources mention it as one of the things Camille had with him in prison.

116. *La Pucelle:* Voltaire's mock-heroic poem *La Pucelle d'Orléans*, a cheerfully salacious burlesque on the legend of Joan of Arc.

117. *it's quarantine for you:* Again Büchner intensifies his projection of revolutionary Paris as a place of ubiquitous fornication and disease.

118. *nous ferons des vers:* Vers means both 'lines (of verse)' and 'worms'. Thus: 'We will make verse/worms.'

119. *my legs to Couthon:* Cf. note 54. Couthon was a cripple.

120. *his Clytemnestra:* With her lover Aegisthus, Clytemnestra murdered her husband Agamemnon on his return from the Trojan war.

121. *provided some latter-day Samson turns up to brandish our jawbones:*
See Judges 15:15: Samson killed a thousand enemies with
the jawbone of an ass.

122. *But we are the poor musicians . . . in heavenly ears:* Cf. Büchner's
letter to Minna Jaeglé of early March 1834 (see p. 194).

123. *[She dies.]:* Julie's suicide is one of Büchner's most spectacular departures from history. In truth, Danton's second wife
remained very much alive, remarrying in 1797 – and
outliving Büchner himself by almost twenty years.

124. *the 'Carmagnole':* The 'Carmagnole' appeared anonymously
soon after the storming of the Tuileries on 10 August 1792,
and rapidly became one of the great inspirational anthems
of the Revolution, alongside the 'Marseillaise'. (Cf. Büchner's earliest extant letter, p. 189.) The music and the
original French words are reproduced in *Georg Büchner. Der
Katalog* (Basel, Frankfurt, 1987), catalogue of the September 1987 Büchner exhibition in Darmstadt.

125. *Go on, quote the Bible . . . down the mountainside:* There is an
oblique reference in this exchange to the 'Mountain' (*la
Montagne*), i.e. the Robespierrean faction in the National
Convention, so called because it sat in the benches high up
against the wall of the chamber (the group that sat lower
down were known as *la Plaine*).

126. *Charon:* In Greek mythology, Charon ferried the dead
across the Styx to Hades.

127. *We've 'eard that one before! 'ow boring:* A hyper-subtle joke:
the real crowds had indeed heard Lacroix's *bon mot* before: the
Girondin Lasource had shouted it out at his execution in
October 1793.

128. *Festival of the Constitution:* On 10 August 1793 Hérault de
Séchelles presided over an elaborate processional pageant,
devised by the painter David, to celebrate the new constitution. The second station of this pageant was a triumphal
arch in the Boulevard des Italiens glorifying the *poissardes*,
the women who had helped to winkle the King out of
Versailles in October 1789 (cf. note 112).

129. *Long live the King:* Lucile's cry is not, of course, a political
declaration, but an act of suicide. Here, as with Julie's

suicide, Büchner departs from history: the real Lucile was
sought out and arrested on the pretext of the 'fairy-tales'
(cf. p. 55) alleging her involvement in a plot to liberate
the Dantonists.

LEONCE AND LENA

Early in 1836 the Stuttgart publisher Cotta advertised a substantial prize of 300 gulden 'for the best one- or two-act comedy in
prose or verse'. Although the deadline was 1 July 1836, Büchner
was probably not able to start work on his comedy until the
beginning of June (his scientific activities preoccupied him almost
exclusively in the preceding months, and he only finalized his
Mémoire sur le système nerveux du barbeau on 31 May). Despite
finishing his competition manuscript astonishingly quickly, he
none the less missed the (extended) deadline, and the package
containing his entry was promptly returned to him unopened. In
the remaining few months of his life he evidently worked further
on the play, in the process expanding it to three acts
(the version submitted to Cotta must have had two acts at most,
as stipulated in the prize conditions); and only very shortly before
the onset of his fatal illness he told Minna Jaeglé in a letter that
he would be 'having *Leonce and Lena* and two other plays published
in a week at the outside' (see p. 208 and the corresponding note).
One implication of this time-scale is that Büchner must have
written *Leonce and Lena* and *Woyzeck* virtually in parallel – but
despite the strident contrast in genres, this simultaneity is not so
startling as it might appear: *Leonce and Lena* is no whit less serious
than *Woyzeck*, and *Woyzeck* often no less comic than *Leonce and
Lena*; more fundamentally, the two plays can readily be seen as
inverse images of each other (and thus would make a spectacular
double-bill, with the same actors playing corresponding roles in
both plays).

Of all Büchner's texts *Leonce and Lena* is the least definitive.

Whatever the massive problems presented by the *Woyzeck* manuscripts, at least they still exist: *no* substantial manuscripts of *Leonce
and Lena* have survived. Büchner must have written at least two
complete versions – the competition entry and a final revised
version – and a complete fair copy was written out by Minna Jaeglé
for the use of Karl Gutzkow. All these manuscripts have disappeared without trace. Only three manuscript fragments are currently known: an incomplete version of Act I, Scene 1, almost
certainly belonging to an early, superseded draft of the play; a
single sheet of paper containing short to extremely short snatches
of discrete scenes; and a sheet containing five heavily crossed-out
lines by Valerio (the sheet was then used by Büchner for his
Descartes commentary). As a result, modern editions have to rely
almost entirely on the printed versions published after Büchner's
death by Gutzkow (1838) and by his brother Ludwig (1850). As in
the case of their *Lenz* editions, Gutzkow based his version on a
'clean copy' written out by Minna, while Ludwig Büchner either
used the same Minna copy or else perhaps had Georg Büchner's
own original manuscript at his disposal. Unfortunately, however,
both these editions present serious problems: Gutzkow had a low
opinion of the play, and chose to leave out almost the whole of
Act I, providing instead a kind of summarizing paraphrase of his
own; Ludwig Büchner for his part clearly bowdlerized the text
without compunction, removing or rewriting anything that
seemed to him morally or politically undesirable. In consequence
there is no truly authentic text (a neat poetic irony, as we shall
see). The best text currently available is Thomas Michael Mayer's
fine scholarly edition of 1987, which essentially gives Gutzkow's
version, fully supplemented throughout by the manuscripts and
by Ludwig Büchner's version; it is Mayer's edition that forms the
basis of this present translation.

Büchner's habit of borrowing creatively from other people's
writing acquires a distinctive new slant in *Leonce and Lena*. Whereas
in the other works he draws on specific non-fiction accounts of
specific real-life events, in his comedy he draws on all manner of
literary models, thereby producing not the powerful sense of reality
so often characteristic of *Danton's Death*, *Lenz* and *Woyzeck*, but an
equally powerful sense of *non*-reality, of a kind of shimmering but

free-floating and constantly changing bubble, chiefly conjured up through a dazzling collage of quotations, allusions, echoes, puns and mood shifts that leave the reader/spectator rapt but disconcerted. The range of references is astonishing: one commentator (Walter Hinderer) mentions Shakespeare, Sterne, Musset, Goethe, Holberg, Tieck, Brentano, Jean Paul, Friedrich Schlegel, Bonaventura and the *commedia dell'arte* as just *some* of Büchner's sources. This unremitting 'derivativeness' is no doubt what chiefly caused Gutzkow and many after him to disparage the play as lightweight and inconsequential; but critics have more recently come to appreciate that Büchner's inspired and unprecedented technique of collage is what gives the play its unique appeal and power. In a nutshell, one might say that Büchner makes virtuoso use of the inauthentic to convey a desperate search for authenticity. At the outset of his work, in the very first speech of *Danton's Death*, Büchner instantly raised the problem when he had Danton point the finger at the duplicitous dealings of the 'pretty lady', and then wryly comment that 'you could make a man fall in love with lies'. Leonce's misfortune at the start of the play is that he sees the world as offering nothing but lies, pretences, masks, disguises – not least his own preordained fate as a neatly trimmed and packaged princeling doomed to follow robotically in the footsteps of his robotic father. Is there any solution? In *Danton's Death*, *Lenz* and *Woyzeck* the crises and outcomes are clear, definitive, irreversible. We have no such luck in Büchner's comedy: its radical playfulness and ironic shifts deprive us of any certainty. We are not even allowed any real sense of place: where on earth *are* these minuscule kingdoms of 'Bum' and 'Piddle'? Are we meant to see Leonce negatively (e.g. as an idle parasite) or positively (e.g. as a genuine spirit struggling to escape his royal straitjacket)? Are we to believe in the instantaneous explosion of love between Leonce and Lena, and in Leonce's sense of a sudden and absolute totality of being? Do they really escape the marital cage ordained for them? Do they flee it only to enter it? Do they ultimately transcend it? Is the utopian ending serious? – There is no end to such questions in this most teasing and in many ways most disturbing of Büchner's works.

Notes

1. *Preface:* The enigmas of the comedy begin at once with this curious 'Preface'. For one thing, both 'quotations' are inauthentic, there being no trace of them in the works of their alleged authors – a lovely touch as the curtain-raiser to a play stuffed full of quotations and preoccupied with problems of authenticity. Then there is the question of what Büchner meant by his pseudo-quotations. They translate as 'And fame?' 'And hunger?' – a wry reference perhaps to the contrary fates that awaited him if he won, or did not win, the prize in the Cotta play competition.

2. *A garden:* The contrastive pattern of the play suggests that this is a French-style garden, enclosed, artificial and formal, at the furthest possible remove from the natural landscape within which Leonce and Lena meet in Act II. This is also suggested by history: minor German potentates were much given to aping such markers of French monarchic grandeur.

3. *Oh, Dr Cantharides, I'm desperate for an heir:* Cantharides – the dried beetle *cantharis vesicatoria*, or Spanish Fly – was widely regarded as an aphrodisiac. (The word is spoken with four syllables, the second one carrying the stress – as in 'Hesperides'.)

4. *Peter:* King Peter is a walking parody of rationalist philosophy and what Büchner saw as its futility and remoteness from life. In the dismissive words of the 'Trial Lecture': 'A priori philosophy still dwells in a bleak and arid desert; a very great distance separates it from green, fresh life, and it is highly questionable whether it will ever close the gap' (see p. 185). Descartes and his followers, especially Spinoza, gave absolute primacy to reason; for them, being is mediated and authenticated solely by the mind: 'I think, therefore I am.' For Büchner, being is directly known to us *without* any mediation through the mind; indeed, it is wholly *inaccessible* to the mind, the operations of which are merely a 'secondar~' activity of the self:

The basic characteristic of all unmediated truth is postulation and affirmation pure and simple, without its being mediated in any way, nor even touched in any essential respect, by the secondary activity of thought. The question arises: does the philosophizing self exist? In Descartes's terms, he cannot think if he does not exist, therefore he exists; in terms of unmediated knowledge, he exists before he philosophizes, i.e. it is positively given within our awareness that the self exists, and this being is inaccessible to thought, indeed the latter can attain to no positive affirmation of it whatsoever.

(Quotation translated from Büchner's Descartes commentary (Lehmann, II.140).) In King Peter, Büchner presents the comic but subtly frightening spectacle of a man in whom the 'secondary activity' of thought has not merely become primary, but has become his sole mode of being – with the result that he *has* no being in the true sense. Whereas Leonce in Scene 1 was desperate to become someone else, King Peter in Scene 2 is desperate that he might *be* someone else (see his last but one speech in this scene).

5. *to bring the glorious banquet . . . their dying agony:* Büchner uses the same image in *Danton's Death*: cf. p. 69.

6. *epicureans:* Cf. p. 221, note 15.

7. *do you know what Nero and Caligula were? I know:* This enigmatic allusion to the two most infamously cruel of Roman emperors rings strange in a comedy, but it helps to signpost the gravity of the crisis personified in Leonce beneath the comic mask. If Leonce professes to understand Nero and Caligula, it is surely because he, too, feels driven to cruelty – driven by an existential *ennui* that has radically alienated him from himself and from the world, to the point that he lacerates himself and those around him: first the Tutor, and then poor Rosetta, whom he consciously treated like some 'Roman' (Nero or Caligula perhaps?) deliberately putting fish to death to savour 'all the colours of their dying agony'.

8. *Adonis:* See p. 226, note 42.

9. *Cape of Good Hope:* Büchner's German makes a pun on the euphemism *guter Hoffnung sein* (literally 'to be of good hope'),

meaning 'to be pregnant'. Büchner's myriad puns in *Leonce and Lena* are difficult to render at the best of times . . .

10. *horns on their heads:* Horns are the traditional symbol of the cuckold.

11. *Oh Shandy, dear Shandy, if only someone would give me your clock:* Tristram Shandy's father, 'one of the most regular men in everything he did . . . that ever lived', made it his invariable practice to wind the family clock on the first Sunday of each month, and then proceed forthwith to fulfil his marital obligations (Laurence Sterne, *Tristram Shandy*, Vol. I, Chapter 4). Mindless clockwork regularity is a defining feature of ordinary life as described through Marion in *Danton's Death*: 'Other people have Sundays and weekdays, they work six days and pray on the seventh, they have a spasm of emotion once a year on their birthday, a flicker of thought for their New Year's resolutions' (see p. 18). For Marion such a life was 'beyond comprehension' – but Leonce comprehends it all too well, and in his Utopia, out there in the imagined future beyond the end of the play, he will 'have all clocks in the kingdom destroyed, all calendars banned, then measure the hours and months by the flower-clock alone' (see p. 108).

12. *lazzaroni:* The term *lazzarone* (plural *lazzaroni*) was quite common in both English and German in the nineteenth century, to the extent that it even occurs in Büchner's school geography work: he noted in an exercise book that Naples had a population of 350,000, including '60,000 Laceroni'. The word bore very different meanings depending on outlook. To the clock-watching, productivity-minded functionalist the *lazzaroni* were beggars, loafers and parasites (a view clearly reflected in the *OED* definition of the word: 'One of the lowest class at Naples, who lounge about the streets, living by odd jobs, or by begging'); to the Arcadian idealist, on the other hand, they were the very image of how life should be savoured and enjoyed, how it should be *lived*, not merely spent. Büchner highlighted the contrast in the 'Promenade' scene of *Danton's Death*, when the two Citizens remonstrate with the beggar and offer him work – a proposition that to him is

absurd, since it would bring him 'A lovely coat but a worn-out body'. And anyway he needs no coat: 'The sun shines warm out here in the street, and life's so easy' (see pp. 31–2).

13. *It's Italy we'll go to:* In the Germany of this period there was an extraordinary fascination and yearning for Italy – not so much as a real, specific place, but as the perfect poetic contrast to what was so often perceived as the prosaic, cold, narrow-minded philistinism of home. Thomas Mann's *Death in Venice* is a famous but latter-day, more 'decadent' version of this contrasting of cultures: Mann's Gustav von Aschenbach blooms only to die in the passionate but pestilential air of Venice; but in the late eighteenth and early nineteenth centuries Italy held the promise not of melting dissolution, but of fullness, vitality, regeneration. Italy was Cockayne, it was Arcadia – which indeed constituted the epigraph *Auch ich in Arkadien! (Et in Arcadia ego* – 'I too was in Arcadia') that headed the most famous and influential text of the period, Goethe's *Italian Journey*, published in 1816–17. And the Arcadian dimension is clear in Leonce's speech: the 'ancient magic' of Virgil lay in conjuring up Arcadia, whose principal presiding spirit was the 'great god Pan'. The whole speech has been shown to be a collage of quotations and echoes from the Italian raptures of other writers (especially the poet August von Platen). The question is: how seriously do we take it? Traditionally the speech has been regarded as a mocking parody of the romanticization of Italy – just as the whole play has generally been seen as essentially dismissive and negative. A more contemporary view is that Büchner typically has it both ways: at one level the speech may seem to be a send-up of overworked enthusiasms – but at the same time it transmits a genuinely lyrical vision of magnificent potentialities.

14. *A garden:* The Piddle garden is doubtless in the same contrived, geometrical mode as the garden of Bum. A hidden stage direction may be gleaned from the words that Büchner has Lena say towards the end of II.1: 'Our dreams were very different, I suppose, as we read our books behind the walls of our garden amidst myrtle and oleander' (p. 94).

15.   *rosemary in my hair:* Rosemary is traditionally associated with both weddings and death. The reference heightens the poignant, profoundly non-comic sense of Lena as at once bride and corpse – and before Leonce marries her he first 'resurrects' her (cf. note 26).

16.   *Don Carlos:* The hero of Schiller's play of the same name (and of Verdi's opera on Schiller's model). But essentially this line is borrowed from Musset's *Fantasio* (II.1), where, in a parallel situation, the Governess assures the heroine: 'On m'avait dit que c'était un Amadis' ('They told me he was a true Amadis'; Amadis was the traditional epitome of faithfulness and nobility).

17.   *A wondrous voice . . . My strident memory:* In many ways, albeit in different terms, Leonce re-enacts the same essential crisis that Büchner figured in his Danton. This is certainly the case in respect of *memory*: both personae are haunted by a memory or awareness that threatens to destroy them. For Danton, only his own death could wipe out his memory (see p. 36); for Leonce – as this epigraph already suggests – his memory, and his attendant disconnectedness from the Now, will instantly disappear once Lena fills the icy vacuum of his being (cf. p. 86: 'I sit as though in a vacuum jar', etc.). Epigraphs are a curious feature in a play text, in that the theatre audience never encounters them. They thus amount to a kind of stage direction, offering the reader/actor/director a perspective onto ensuing events. And it is striking how very different a perspective is offered here from that implied in the *As You Like It* quotation at the head of Act I.

18.   *To me it's like a narrow hall of mirrors . . . blank wall:* Cf. the similarly grim image voiced through Camille in the climactic final gaol scene of *Danton's Death*: 'It's time we removed our masks: we'd think ourselves in a hall of mirrors – wherever we looked we'd see only the same ass's head, no more, no less: primeval, infinite, indestructible' (p. 68).

19.   *a dozen principalities . . . half a day:* Germany did not exist as such at this period; instead there was a plethora of separate states and statelets – a crucial factor in the extreme economic, social and political backwardness of the German

lands prior to unification under Bismarck in 1871. (The separate *Land* status of the old Hansa cities of Bremen and Hamburg within today's Germany is a last relic of this nineteenth-century particularism.)

20. *I have this ideal . . . in this spiritual body:* What seems to be envisioned in this speech of Leonce's is an infinitude of beauty that is wholly uncontaminated by *mind* with its 'secondary' processes of thought and reflection – Leonce himself (like Danton and Woyzeck) being gravely afflicted by the churnings of his own (male) mind. It is in just such terms, perhaps, that we are meant to understand the failure of love between Leonce and Rosetta – to whom, after all, he remarks: 'You're right, as always. What a clever girl you are, I do so appreciate your penetrating insights' (p. 84); and Leonce puts the corpse of their love to rest not in his heart, but in the brain-space of his skull.

21. *St Ottilia:* An eighth-century Alsace saint. When her father Adalric wanted to marry her off to a German duke, she fled; just as her pursuers were about to catch her, a rock face on the Schlossberg mountain (near Freiburg) opened to receive her and keep her safe. Lena's own fate/destiny/fortune proves, however, to be rather different.

22. *Ergo bibamus:* 'Let us therefore drink!' – a standard refrain in German student drinking-songs.

23. *the tower of Lebanon which looketh towards Damascus:* Quoted from Song of Songs 7:5.

24. *'Would not this . . . in a cry of players':* Hamlet, III.2.

25. *He was so old . . . How sad:* A classic instance of an implicit stage direction. Only when we have read this far can we begin to 'see' Leonce: not only his (Nordic) physical appearance, but also his characteristic demeanour and aura. This must retrospectively condition the reader's sense of Leonce in (say) Act I, Scene 1.

26. *Arise . . . and walk . . . :* Cf. Matthew 9:5; Mark 2:9; also Song of Songs 2:10. Büchner uses the same motif in *Lenz*, when Lenz attempts to raise the young child from the dead: see p. 156 and also p.271, note 27.

27. *yellow waistcoat and skyblue trousers:* This was famously the garb of Goethe's Werther, and sits comically on the person

of Valerio, who could scarcely be more un-Werther-like. Its comic inappropriateness is particularly marked here, since Werther killed himself, whereas his sartorial look-alike *prevents* the suicide of his master.

28. '*I know thee not, old man! I banish thee on pain of death*': Cf. *2 Henry* IV, V.3 (Henry to Falstaff).

29. ... *cylinders, pipes and windbags* ...: This whole passage is reminiscent of Büchner's letter to Minna Jaeglé of early March 1834: 'Everyone's face was the face of death, [...] and then, when the whole machinery began to grind away with jerking limbs and grating voice, and I heard the same old barrel-organ tune go tralala and saw the tiny prongs and cylinders bob and whirr [etc.]' (see p. 194).

30. *Pox, leave thy damnable faces and begin*: Cf. *Hamlet*, III.2.

WOYZECK

The first thing to be said about this most famous and influential of Büchner's plays is that, strictly speaking, it does not exist. Any supposedly 'complete' version – like the one presented here – is necessarily a makeshift, a patchwork assembled (or borrowed premade) by its particular editor, since Büchner left nothing but incomplete manuscripts when he died so unexpectedly in February 1837. (Although it is conceivable that Büchner wrote a final version that subsequently disappeared, it is almost certain that the surviving manuscripts represent all that he had managed to get done in the last few months before the Zurich typhus epidemic snuffed him out.)

These manuscripts are an editor's nightmare, for a whole variety of reasons:

1. They are not 'fair copies', but working drafts on poor-quality paper, often more scrawled than written, with words scratched out, over-written or added later; in consequence the writing is generally very difficult to make out, and sometimes impossible to decipher at all with any certainty, even for the most skilled

palaeographer. (This problem has been exacerbated by time and human interference, most notably that of the nineteenth-century editor Franzos, who applied chemicals to the paper, making the writing temporarily sharper – but then causing it to become even more faded than before. In addition, the treatment even bodily dislodged some of the ink marks and washed them confusingly into new positions.)

2. Büchner never bothered to number either his successive drafts, or the manuscript pages, or the individual scenes, so that the sequence and grouping of scenes is inherently problematic.

3. He included no title, and no list of characters, which between them might have offered a specific focus.

4. The extreme spareness of the writing and Büchner's avoid-ance of anything like a traditional dramaturgy mean that we have no ready-made 'grid' to help us locate and order the discrete elements.

5. Outside the manuscripts themselves, not a word of Büchner's concerning the play survives except for a couple of brief and unspecific allusions in his letters.

Despite all this, however, editorial scholarship has come a very long way since 1850, when Büchner's earliest editor, his brother Ludwig, simply omitted the *Woyzeck* fragments altogether on the grounds that they were 'thoroughly illegible'. The biggest single step forward is undoubtedly represented by Gerhard Schmid's comprehensive edition of 1981, which gives full-size facsimiles of the manuscripts (said to be clearer than the originals), together with Schmid's own page-by-page transcription, a list of alterna-tive readings given in previous scholarly editions, and a detailed commentary.

There are physically three distinct manuscripts, each consisting of a different kind of paper: a folio manuscript of twenty pages; a quarto manuscript of two pages (i.e. a single sheet); and a quarto manuscript of twenty-four pages. These three manuscripts contain what is generally (though not universally) agreed to be *four* separate scene sequences, now usually referred to (after Lehmann) as H1, H2, H3 and H4: the *folio pages* contain H1 and H2 (clearly written in that order, since H2 starts immediately after the end of H1, part-way down a page); the *single quarto sheet* contains H3;

the *quarto pages* contain H4. The four scene sequences are made up as follows:

H1 21 scenes: 2 fairground scenes; 1 two-sentence scene with 'Margreth' (= Marie); 18 scenes covering roughly the *second half* of the overall action as we now think of it (corresponding to scenes 12–29 in this edition).

H2 Nearly the same length as H1, but comprising only 9 scenes, covering roughly the *first half* of the overall action (corresponding to scenes 1–10 in this edition); the only overlap between H1 and H2 involves the fairground scenes).

H3 2 scenes only: 'The Professor's courtyard' and 'The Idiot. The Child. Woyzeck' (scenes 11 and 28 in this edition); neither scene has any equivalent in the other manuscripts.

H4 17 scenes, covering roughly the *first three-quarters* of the overall action (corresponding to scenes 1–20 in this edition); some of the scenes are new, but most are reworkings of scenes in H1 and H2, which Büchner duly crossed out in the earlier folio manuscript (strong evidence that H4 was written *after* H1 and H2).

Werner Lehmann labelled the H4 manuscript 'Provisional Final Draft'. While it is highly arguable whether H4 was quite that final, it is clear from even the most cursory glance at the Schmid facsimiles that H4 is far more orderly and considered than H1 and H2 with their scrawled writing and splatter of ink splotches, doodles and sketches. This, together with the fact that H4 both represents a revision of almost all the corresponding scenes in H1 and H2, and also introduces crucial new scenes, means that H4 necessarily constitutes the bulk of any composite 'complete' version, with the remainder made up of 'unrevised' scenes from H1, H2 and H3. This leaves the editor with a bundle of specific problems largely relating to the *make-up* or *position* of various scenes. These problems are highlighted in the Notes below – but in general it needs to be remembered that the solutions proposed are always essentially a makeshift compromise: if Büchner had completed his play, it would undoubtedly have been different – perhaps radically different – from what is offered here (or in any other composite 'complete' version). What is more, the biggest problem of all admits of no solution whatever, namely the fact that Büchner gives his play a subtly but distinctly different thrust and atmosphere in H4 – but a 'complete' version can be concocted only by borrowing scenes from the earlier, essentially superseded drafts. (It is for this reason that some of the more purist scholars in Germany refuse to attempt a composite version at all – a stance that is academically understandable, but practically not very helpful.)

In *Woyzeck*, as in *Danton's Death* and *Lenz*, Büchner's creative fire was fuelled, and perhaps initially sparked, by accounts that he had read of real-life events – in this instance various much-discussed murder cases, all *crimes passionnels* in which a man from the depths of society stabbed a woman to death. The least important of these is the case of the linen-weaver Johann Diess, who in 1830 murdered Christiane Reuter near Darmstadt. It is not certain how much Büchner knew about this case, though he does appear to have borrowed some details (the child; involvement of an army officer). Another case is that of the tobacco-worker Daniel Schmolling, who in 1817 murdered Henriette Lehne near Berlin; the details borrowed here mainly concern the circumstances surrounding the actual murder (visit to an inn; the murderer calling to collect his victim, taking her on a walk into the country, sitting her down, running off after the murder at the sound of people approaching, then returning later to search for the knife). By far the most important case, however, is that of the eponymous Johann Christian Woyzeck, an out-of-work, almost vagrant ex-wigmaker and ex-soldier who in 1821 killed Johanna Christiane Woost in Leipzig, and three years later, after much legal wrangling, was publicly decapitated before an audience of many thousands (Diess and Schmolling both ended up with prison sentences). Numerous major and minor incidents are traceable to this source, e.g. the woman's infidelity; involvement of a drum-major; two men having to share one bed; a fist-fight; the murderer finding his woman dancing with a rival; a row between the couple; acquisition of a dagger; repeated stabbing of the victim; involvement of a doctor, including physical examinations. The most essential element that Büchner borrowed, however, is that of

Woyzeck as visionary – or madman: the real Woyzeck saw visions, heard voices, thought the Freemasons were after him.

Apart from the nature of the crime that all three cases involved (stabbing of a woman by a man she was involved with), another crucial feature that all had in common was the question of whether the perpetrators were of sound mind, and therefore legally responsible for their actions. This problem was debated with particular vehemence in Woyzeck's case, both during and after the protracted period of trials, appeals and forensic psychological-medical examinations that ultimately brought him to the scaffold as someone who *was* after all deemed sane and accountable. And Büchner places this question at the very heart of his play – not in narrow legal terms, but in a much larger and more disturbing sense: *Are* people truly in control of their actions and therefore accountable for them? Or are they driven willy-nilly by inner compulsions and/or outer circumstance – by their elemental natures, by visions or illusions, by ambition or convention, by poverty and exploitation? Such questions scream at us with almost unbearable intensity from nearly every scene. And we should be wary here of the all too common view of Büchner's Woyzeck as a supreme victim, as someone essentially 'done unto' rather than 'doing'. The clearest victim of the play is in fact Marie, who is 'done for' in the most drastic sense before our eyes by Woyzeck himself. And why? The question of 'accountability' takes a devilish twist here: the Woyzeck of history was familiar as the prisoner in the dock upon whom justice was (supposedly) visited; Büchner's Woyzeck on the other hand is not the victim, but the would-be *agent* of supreme, not to say Apocalyptic justice: turning himself into jury, judge and executioner all at once, *he* holds *Marie* accountable for her wanton 'lechery', her 'sin so big and so fat', and presumes so far as to expunge her 'blackness' by extinguishing her life. The same question is implied here as in *Danton's Death* when Büchner had Danton challenge Robespierre (a man similarly bent on eradicating vice by eradicating lives): 'Are you heaven's policeman?'

This unhistorical dimension in the Woyzeck of the play goes much further still. The real Woyzeck was truly and absolutely at the bottom of the social pile, leading a life more deprived and marginal than most of us now could easily imagine: orphaned at the age of thirteen; trained in wig-making at a time when wigs were rapidly going out of fashion; able after his twelve years as a soldier to scratch only the barest living, without a home and often without even a sleeping-space; poorly educated, and apparently with little understanding or native intelligence. Büchner's Woyzeck is – relatively speaking – much better off, with a steady job, a steady wage and extra money from both Officer and Doctor, a barracks bed, a home and family of sorts with Marie. Far more importantly, Woyzeck may be one of the most graphically portrayed underdogs in world theatre – but he is nevertheless the most sensitive, most feeling, most intelligent, most *aware* individual in the play. In conception he is a true brother – however startling this might seem – to Leonce the unwilling prince and Danton the lapsed revolutionary. Whereas all the other figures in the play (with the partial exception of Marie and the Officer) are blithely, unreflectively at home within the cocoon of their particular role/persona/self-image, Woyzeck – like Danton and Leonce before him – is uncomfortably reflective and aware; he sees, hears, senses things that others are oblivious to. The paradox is typical: the strutting top-dogs of the play are blinkered robots, grim yet comic; the debased, deprived, exploited underdog is the most radiantly, subtly and movingly *human* of human beings – the perfect exemplar of what Büchner had propounded in his aesthetic credo in *Lenz* (see p.149).

Begun in Strasbourg in 1836 (probably in the last few weeks before Büchner left for Zurich), *Woyzeck* remained unperformed until 1913, but then rapidly established itself as one of the beacons of twentieth-century drama. No wonder, for even in composite, makeshift form, *Woyzeck* is an extraordinarily powerful piece of theatre. We tend to think that, whereas Büchner was lost on the poor benighted nineteenth century, we moderns have his measure. *Woyzeck* confounds such smugness. It constantly points beyond itself, from the very first scene in which sights and sounds are conjured up that are apparently unreal, yet disturb us as much as they disturb Woyzeck's foil, Andres. It takes us beyond the frontiers of the comfortably known, to a twilight realm where all conventional systems and their justifications seem questionable, where bafflement, perplexity, obscurity prevail, and become *our* essential experience too as we look in from outside. For Büchner makes the play seem to us as he makes Marie seem to the Drum-Major: 'Like trying to see down a well or a chimney'. As Woyzeck experiences the mushrooms, so we experience *Woyzeck*: the 'patterns' are clear to behold – but 'If only we knew how to read what they say.'

Notes

1. *CHARACTERS:* This list of characters has been put together for the sake of convenience: no list of characters appears in the manuscripts (nor any kind of title).

2. *Woyzeck:* In H1, the earliest draft, Woyzeck's first name was 'Louis', and this name was used to identify all his speeches except the first; he becomes 'Franz' only in H2.

3. *Andres:* The name carries the stress on the *second* syllable.

4. *Marie:* Different names were used in the earlier drafts: 'Margreth' in H1 and 'Louise' or 'Louisel' in H2. Like Julie in *Danton's Death*, Marie bears no resemblance to her historical analogue: Johanna Christiane Woost, the real Woyzeck's 'girlfriend' and victim, was a grossly uncouth and physically unattractive widow of forty-six. It is striking that Büchner forsakes all realist principles when creating his women figures, who are nearly all iconic rather than borrowed from life – and modelled mostly on either the *Vénus blanche* or the *Vénus noire*. Marie in *Woyzeck* is reminiscent in crucial respects of Marion in *Danton's Death*.

5. *Child:* According to Marie's remark in Scene 22 (p. 134), she and Woyzeck have been together for something less than two years, so that their child could not be older than about twelve months. But he appears from stage directions and the remarks of Marie and Woyzeck to be about three or four. Perhaps in a final version Büchner would have sorted out this inconsistency. (Historically, both Woyzeck and Schmolling had fathered children in earlier relationships, but not with the women that they murdered; Diess and his

victim had a child aged about four and a half at the time of the murder.) In any event, the part of the child, though non-speaking, is important in the economy of the play.

6. *The Officer:* In the original the character is a Captain (*Hauptmann*) – but 'Captain' in English has too many misleading connotations.

7. *The Professor:* In Büchner's manuscript of the relevant scene in H3 (Scene 11 in this version), the word 'Professor' (or its abbreviation) occurs only in the heading and the first third of the text; thereafter we encounter only the 'Doctor'. It is a matter of dispute whether Büchner envisaged two separate figures, or a single figure whose title he altered part-way through the scene. On balance, the latter seems more likely. In productions a single figure is certainly more convenient, but also more effective.

Scene 1 (H4:1)

'H4:1' indicates that the scene is taken from the H4 draft, and is the first scene in that draft; the provenance of all scenes will be given in this way, with additional comments where necessary. Following the trend-setting editions of Fritz Bergemann, most versions of *Woyzeck* over a period of several decades placed the shaving scene (Scene 6 in this edition) at the beginning. There is no basis whatsoever for this in the manuscripts, and Bergemann's high-handedness is particularly regrettable since it concerns the very first scene: a *Woyzeck* that begins with the authentic first scene has a fundamentally different aura and emphasis compared to a *Woyzeck* beginning (quite arbitrarily) with the shaving scene.

8. *Open countryside. The town in the distance:* The *place* is often explicitly stated, as here, but never the *time*. We can deduce it as being early March – but only if we take literally Woyzeck's statement in Scene 20 (p. 132) that he was born on 20 July, and that he is '30 years, 7 months and 12 days' old. Unfortunately this statement is itself problematic: see p. 262, note 38. All scene headings given alongside scene numbers are Büchner's own.

9. *... cutting canes in the undergrowth:* This is a challenging stage

direction. The common explanation that the two men are collecting material for basket-making is highly implausible: (1) Büchner's word '*Stock*' implies rigidity, not bendiness, and there are unsurprisingly no examples in Grimm (*Deutsches Wörterbuch*) or earlier dictionaries of the word being used in connection with basketwork. (2) Given Büchner's severe economy in the use of stage directions throughout the drafts, why ever would he bother to evoke something as random and irrelevant as basket-making? It is far more likely that Büchner is alluding to something much grimmer and more pertinent: the practice of corporal punishment, still standard in the German armies of the period. Thus one definition of *Stock* in Grimm is 'the stick of officers and NCOs as the visible symbol of their right to inflict corporal punishment'. Interestingly, Grimm also notes that the ornamental baton so characteristic of drum-majors is likewise known as a *Stock* – and constitutes 'a last harmless relic of the erstwhile practice [of beating]' ('erstwhile' because the relevant section of Grimm was published in 1914, when corporal punishment had long since been abolished in the military). Within the play itself the Doctor explicitly thrashes around with a stick (beginning of Scene 9); the Drum-Major can be presumed to carry his traditional baton when he first struts across the stage with his drummers beating the tattoo (Scene 2); it is easy to imagine the Officer wielding a big stick physically as well as metaphorically – as an officer he possesses one by definition. It is also worth noting that in the original (H2) draft of Scene 2, Büchner had Margreth (i.e. Marie) ask Woyzeck whether he has 'cut sticks [*Stecken*] for the Captain': *Stecken* commonly meant either a stick for walking – or a stick for beating (cf. Grimm). An army officer of the period would scarcely have needed an abundant supply of walking sticks.

10. *Yes, Andres . . . where the head rolls in the evenings:* The potential end of the play is prefigured in its opening line: the real Woyzeck's own head rolled in 1824. And this is no figure of speech: the prevailing method of execution involved the victim sitting upright in a chair, so that his head, once

severed by the executioner's horizontal sword stroke, went tumbling across the scaffold.

11. *the Freemasons:* Büchner took this detail from his sources. Freemasonry was extremely widespread in the eighteenth and early nineteenth centuries, being keenly practised on both right and left of the political spectrum. Its code of extreme secrecy frequently made it the natural focus of popular suspicion – as indeed it still does.

12. *A pair of hares . . . the green green grass:* Here as with almost all the snatches of song in his work, Büchner borrowed straight from the popular folk tradition – indeed in this case the song had not yet even appeared in printed form (it was first published in 1843). Büchner's own love of folksongs is particularly clear in one of his last letters to Minna Jaeglé; see p. 207.

13. *Flames . . . like mighty trumpets:* The historical Woyzeck claimed to have seen such visions. The play's vivid pattern of Biblical resonances begins at this point: the words echo Genesis 19:24–6: the destruction of Sodom and Gomorrah ('Then the Lord rained upon Sodom and upon Gomorrah brimstone and fire [etc.]'). But more particularly they echo the Apocalypse, e.g. Revelation 8:6ff.: 'And the seven angels which had the seven trumpets prepared themselves to sound. / And the first sounded, and there followed hail and fire, mingled with blood, and they were cast upon the earth [etc.]'.

14. *Don't look back:* This is probably a further echo of Genesis 19: it is when Lot's wife looks back at Sodom and Gomorrah in the midst of their destruction that she is turned into a pillar of salt (Genesis 19:26).

Scene 2 (H4:2)

15. *The tattoo marches by:* A tattoo (*Zapfenstreich*) was properly speaking not the bandsmen themselves, as Büchner has it here, but the actual signal on drum or bugle summoning all troops back to quarters in the evening.

16. *[Sings]:* The two verses that follow are taken from different songs (an ordinary folksong and a Hessian carters' song).

Büchner may conceivably have intended to choose just one for the final draft, but both appear in both versions of the scene (H2 and H4). Songs are crucially important throughout the play: they serve to add extra dimensions of emphasis, information and atmosphere; above all, they have a kind of transfigurative effect in helping to raise the drama from the merely contingent and personal to the realm of archetypal processes (the many Biblical references, echoes and allusions – not least Marie's name – have a complementary effect).

17. *and behold . . . like smoke from a furnace:* An almost verbatim quotation from Genesis 19:28.

Scene 3 (constructed from H2:3, H2:5 and H1:1)

Both this scene and the next are problematic. In H4 Büchner wrote down the scene heading – but then left one and a half pages of manuscript completely blank, and went straight into the scene with Marie and the earrings. We can only guess as to why he felt able to rewrite the preceding and succeeding scenes but not this one. The practical upshot, however, is that we have to improvise from the earlier drafts on a 'cut-and-paste' basis. H1 had separate scenes *inside* and *outside* the booth, and that is the pattern followed here to yield scenes 3 and 4.

18. (*MARIE*): Round brackets indicate that the word(s) in question were not present in the original. In this case, Büchner simply didn't indicate any speakers at all for the lines between the snatch of song and the Showman's speech. Note that brackets are *not* used where the different H1 and H2 names have been standardized to 'Franz' and 'Marie'.

19. Tears and joy: This type-face is used where Büchner's hand-writing is particularly obscure, and can be deciphered only on a 'best guess' basis. Different decipherers tend to offer different best guesses, and the most plausible of these is always adopted for this present edition.

20. *SHOWMAN:* The Showman exemplifies a problem that besets a translator all through the play: how to render non-

standard speech. The problem is most acute in the case of Woyzeck and Marie – and it remains essentially insoluble: any form of educated Standard English would clearly be wrong; but any *particular* form of demotic English would be no less wrong. In the case of Woyzeck and Marie I have tried to suggest a kind of 'universal demotic'. The problem presents rather differently in the case of the Showman. In the original he is a foreigner, indicated by garbled grammar and a sprinkling of French (Büchner even crosses out the German word *Liebling* in the manuscript and replaces it with the French *favori*.) This works very well in German, but there seems no ready analogue in English, hence the resort here to a brash busker-ese.

21. *Consider the creature . . . carries a sword:* A performing monkey is implied here in a mordant critique of prevailing civilization: are clothes, manners, the accoutrements of gentility perhaps nothing but a façade disguising sheer animality? Büchner had Camille express a similar possibility in the final desperate gaol scene of *Danton's Death*: 'It's time we removed our masks: we'd think ourselves in a hall of mirrors – wherever we looked we'd see only the same ass's head, no more, no less: primeval, infinite, indestructible' (see p. 68).

22. *Observe . . . giant strides:* Cf. the sardonic remark in the 'Promenade' scene in *Danton's Death*: 'Mankind is speeding with giant strides towards its noble destiny' (see p. 33).

23. *Just look at his tassles, and the woman's in trousers:* The *Woyzeck* fragments contain relatively few explicit stage directions. Directors and actors therefore have to scour the text for *implicit* stage directions and other pointers – such as this line here. This is in fact generally true of Büchner's theatre: even in *Danton's Death* and *Leonce and Lena* the look and feel of a scene are often most graphically conveyed through the dialogue, rather than through stage directions.

24. *her black hair . . . eyes so black:* See preceding note! This is one of many indicators within the dialogue of Marie's physical appearance. The 'eyes so black' may not be essential in a stage Marie, but black hair is practically a must, not only because the Sergeant's remark is otherwise nonsensical, but

because 'blackness' is a major symbolic leitmotif throughout the play in connection with Marie (as 'redness' also is).

Scene 4 (H1:2; but first three lines taken from H2:5)

25. *man, be natural:* The importance of nature (human and otherwise) and its imperative logic is posed even more forcefully in *Woyzeck* than in the rest of Büchner's work. The particular pattern of this present episode is repeated later in the play when Woyzeck likewise 'disgraces himself' by pissing in the street – driven to it, he claims, by his 'nature'. But the issue comes most sharply into focus in the person of Marie: Woyzeck destroys Marie to destroy her black sin – but *is* it sin, or is it an unbiddable natural process, like Woyzeck and the horse respectively 'disgracing' themselves – or like the voracious sexuality of Marion in *Danton's Death* ('It's simply my nature, can anyone escape it?'; see p. 18)?

Scene 5 (H4:4)

Scene 6 (H4:5)

26. *The Lord spake: Suffer the little children to come unto me:* Mark 10:14; see also Matthew 19:14; Luke 18:16. Woyzeck's sudden shift here from monosyllabic servility to articulate dominance comes at the exact mid-point of this superbly crafted scene.

Scene 7 (H4:6)

Scene 8 (H4:8)

27. *musculus constrictor vesicae:* The sphincter controlling the bladder.

Scene 9 (constructed from H4:9 and H2:7)

Another problematic scene. Büchner began to rewrite this scene in the H4 manuscript, but stopped at the point where the Doctor and the Officer insult each other in their leave-taking, and simply left three-quarters of a page blank. This blank space, together with the fact that he also drew no line through the corresponding H2 scene, clearly shows that he wasn't finished with his H4 revision. This present version uses the H4 rewrite as far as it goes, then tacks on the unrevised section of the earlier H2 scene.

28 Cossacks: The difficulties presented by Büchner's manuscripts are typified here. The relevant ink-squiggle has been commonly deciphered as *Kastrirte* ('eunuchs'); *Kürassire* ('cuirassiers') has also been proposed. Gerhard Schmid tentatively reads *Kosack* – certainly the most plausible suggestion.

Scene 10 (H4:7)

The positioning of this scene is particularly problematic. In H2 the equivalent scene was placed here, but in H4 Büchner repositions it *after* the (completely new) Marie–Drum-Major scene, and thus *before* the Woyzeck–Doctor and Officer–Doctor–Woyzeck scenes. This repositioning makes sense only on the supposition that Büchner intended to *remove* the Officer's baiting of Woyzeck in his reworking of the Officer–Doctor–Woyzeck scene, since it would make no sense for Woyzeck to react with great vehemence and surprise to cruel insinuations from the Officer *after* he had already caught Marie and the Drum-Major more or less in the act. But Büchner never completed his reworking of the scene – and once we put together a composite scene that includes the old H2 passage complete with the Officer's insinuations and Woyzeck's reactions, we are bound to return to the H2 scene order (though many editions ignore this logical imperative).

29. *No blisters on it:* Folklore has it that illicit kisses, lies, etc. leave a blister or other mark on the miscreant's lips (or tongue) by which his/her misdeeds can be recognized.

Scene 11 (H3:1)

Since H3 consists of only two discrete scenes, neither of which occurs in any form in the other manuscripts, they can only be arbitrarily inserted at whatever is deemed the most appropriate juncture. This first of the two scenes has been placed by different editors at all points of the play – early, middle and late.

30. *like David when he beheld Bathsheba:* Cf. 2 Samuel 11:2. Beyond the surface joke contrasting drying schoolgirl underwear with the luscious Bathsheba lurks an altogether serious allusion to the fatal goings-on between Marie and the Drum-Major. Bathsheba, who was 'very beautiful to look upon', was the wife of one of David's commanders, Uriah. She was unclothed when David beheld her from his palace-roof, but he didn't just look – he had her brought to his bed, where he made her pregnant. He then ordered that Uriah be committed to the hottest part of a battle, 'that he may be smitten and die' – which duly came about.

31. *ricinus:* A Latin term for animal parasites (ticks, lice, etc.).

Scene 12 (H4:10)

Scene 13 (H4:11)

32. he's got 'er the same as I had 'er once: If Büchner had included this line in a definitive edition, it might have fundamentally conditioned our understanding of Woyzeck. As it is, the line cannot be relied on. It reflects Lehmann's reading of the manuscript; the only words that Schmid can make out are 'he has her' and 'at the beginning', with indecipherable splodges in between.

Scene 14 (H4:12)

Scene 15 (H4:13)

Scene 16 (H1:8)

Some composite editions of the play omit this scene, but there is no good reason for doing so.

Scene 17 (H4:14)

Scene 18 (H4:15)

Scene 19 (H4:16)

33. *'Neither was guile found in his mouth':* This is a direct quotation from 1 Peter 2:22 (which in turn echoes Isaiah 53:9). It is Christ that Peter is referring to, and commentators have suggested that Büchner is hinting at a parallel here between Woyzeck and Christ, inasmuch as Woyzeck, too, is an

archetypal sufferer. The suggestion is plausible – but there is rather more to it. It is worth quoting not only verse 22, but also the verses before and after: 'For even hereunto were ye called: because Christ also suffered for us, leaving us an example, that ye should follow his steps: / Who did no sin, neither was guile found in his mouth. / Who, when he was reviled, reviled not again; when he suffered, he threatened not, but committed himself to him that judgeth righteously.' Woyzeck is indeed an archetypal sufferer – but it is certainly not the case that 'when he suffered, he threatened not, but committed himself to him that judgeth righteously'. Far from accepting his suffering, Woyzeck goes out and visits supreme suffering on Marie in a desperate and hubristic mimicry of divine justice. This touches on perhaps the profoundest issues that Büchner struggled with in his writing.

34. *'And the scribes . . . sin no more'*: Another direct quotation: John 8:3 and 8:11.

35. *'And stood . . . with the ointment'*: Quoted directly from Luke 7:38.

Scene 20 (H4:17)

36. *'May suffering . . . praise to God'*: See p. 267, note 7.

37. *Friedrich Johann Franz Woyzeck*: The real Woyzeck's given names were Johann Christian. We can only guess as to why Büchner preferred 'Friedrich Johann Franz' (after first using 'Louis' in H1). In the context of the note that follows, it is worth remarking that Büchner did in fact retain the name Christian, but transferred it from Woyzeck to his child (see Scene 28).

38. *30 years, 7 months and 12 days*: The real Woyzeck was forty-one when he committed the murder. It cannot be a coincidence that Büchner makes his birthday the Feast of the Annunciation (the day of Christ's conception), and makes him the same age as Christ is sometimes said to have been at his death; even the numbers of months and days are archetypally biblical. (One problem here is that the Feast of the Annunciation falls on 25 March, not 20 July. This is a curious mistake on Büchner's part – if it *was* a mistake.)

Scene 21 (H1:14)

39. *The sun shines bright at Candlemas,/ The corn it stands so high:*
There is another peculiar confusion of dates here: Candlemas
(the Feast of the Purification of the Virgin Mary) falls on 2
February, when the corn cannot possibly 'stand so high'. It
is not known whether Büchner borrowed this song from
some unknown source or created it himself.

40. *nobody left on earth, he:* In Büchner's German the child is gram-
matically neuter throughout. But 'he' rather than 'she' is
more appropriate in English here, as it sets up more resonances within the larger context of the play: see note 42.

41. *tiny golden insects stuck there as though by a butcher-bird on blackthorn:* The butcher-bird or red-backed shrike is a beautiful
but fiercely predatory songbird with the habit of lardering
its prey (mostly insects, but also small birds, rodents, lizards
etc.) by impaling it on the spikes of thorn bushes. The
German word is *Neuntöter*, literally 'nine-killer' – and the
names 'nyn murder' and 'nine murther' are similarly at-
tested in Elizabethan English (cf. *OED*: 'Shrike'); the bird
is sometimes still known as a 'murdering pie'.

42. *Once upon a time ... all on his own:* This 'anti-fairy-tale' is
justly famous: there is little to match it in German literature for bleak, laconic beauty. It is reminiscent of the
Marion monologue in *Danton's Death* in the sense that a
character suddenly pops up from nowhere, speaks a dramatically undramatic piece of narrative, then disappears
again without trace. The passage is wonderfully Büchnerian in
offering two contrary languages simultaneously: the *verbal*
language evokes an appalling vision of dashed hopes and
infinite isolation as the imagined child sits there sobbing for
all eternity, while the *stage* language shows a group of very
real children *not* disappointed or isolated, but gathered
around a granny in an iconic tableau of togetherness.

Commentators routinely remark that the Grandmother's
tale epitomizes the terrible loneliness of Woyzeck. At one level
this is clearly true. But it is equally true that an *actual* child,
namely Woyzeck's own son, is about to be thrown into
orphaned isolation – and by none other than Woyzeck himself.

Scene 22 (H1:15)

43. *(I'll catch me death):* The phrase is not Büchner's; it is added here for the sake of clarity (especially in stage performances).

44. *Moon's coming up as red as red/ Like a bloody knife:* The image suggests the Apocalypse: 'and lo, [. . .] the moon became as blood' (Revelation 6:12); 'The sun shall be turned into darkness, and the moon into blood' (Acts 2:20).

Scene 23 (H1:16)

Scene 24 (H1:17)

Scene 25 (H1:19)

45. *(Why so pale . . . in plaits today?):* The brackets here are Büchner's own. Commentators have suggested that he used them because he was undecided whether to keep the lines or not.

Scene 26 (H1:20)

Scene 27 (H1:18)

According to the H1 sequence of scenes, this scene *precedes* the two in which Woyzeck searches for the knife and throws it in the water – but it is more logical and more dramatically effective in the order given here.

46. *Come on, Marie:* In the original manuscript the child was called 'Magrethchen' – a diminutive of 'Margreth', the H1 name for Marie. One Margreth/Marie dies, but another takes her place.

Scene 28 (H3:2)

Whereas the other H3 scene ('The Professor's courtyard') could reasonably be placed almost anywhere, Woyzeck's wetness implies that this scene must come *after* Scene 26, and must therefore be one of the last three scenes. This raises the whole question of how the play should end, and there has been much argument about Büchner's precise intentions: Had he not yet decided? Did he mean Woyzeck to drown in Scene 27? Did he mean there to be an arrest/ trial/climactic decapitation? Such debates are essentially fruitless – and practically speaking unnecessary, since the last few scenes of H1 make a completely satisfying and effective ending, especially when this H3 scene is inserted too.

47. *He's fallen in the water, he's fallen in the water:* The first line of a popular children's counting-rhyme.

Scene 29 (H1:21)

LENZ

Büchner seems to have become interested in the 'Storm and Stress' playwright J.M.R. Lenz in early 1835, very soon after the completion of *Danton's Death* and his escape to Strasbourg. His new friend Gutzkow refers to 'your novella *Lenz*' in a letter of 12 May 1835, and mentions the project again in two later letters (in September 1835 and February 1836). In a letter to his parents from Strasbourg in October 1835 Büchner remarks that he has 'acquired all sorts of interesting material here about a friend of Goethe's, an unfortunate writer by the name of *Lenz*, who lived here [i.e. in Strasbourg] at the same time as Goethe and went half mad. I'm thinking of publishing an essay about him in the *Deutsche Revue*' (see p. 203). Given the circles he moved in in Strasbourg, it is no wonder that he became fascinated by Lenz's brief but dramatic sojourn with Pastor Oberlin in the depths of the Vosges in 1778: his friend August Stöber had published an article on Lenz; Stöber's father had written a biography of Oberlin; his fiancée's father, Pastor Johann Jakob Jaeglé, had delivered the funeral oration at Oberlin's burial in 1826; most important of all, Pastor Jaeglé gave him access to Oberlin's diaries with their plain, sober account of Lenz's arrival, rapid disintegration and ultimate removal under escort to Strasbourg.

Oberlin's description provided Büchner with the indispensable bones of his story. But out of this bare skeleton he creates an incomparably vivid and vibrant body of poetic narrative, the like of which Pastor Oberlin could never have imagined. Werner Lehmann's edition prints Oberlin's account and Büchner's

re-creation on facing pages (Lehmann, I.436ff.), and it is fascinating to compare the dry white bones and their reanimation by a
writer of genius. The opening pages are typical; Oberlin begins:
'He came here on the 20th of January 1778', and then in the
second sentence immediately recounts their first conversation.
Büchner borrows both details; but in between them he adds some
sixty lines of his own invention – and in the process creates one of
the most original, compelling and disturbing story-openings in
German literature. The same pattern continues throughout, to
yield a story of psychological disintegration – and much more
besides – that has never been surpassed in its sense of immediacy
and depth, its ability to move freely between the outer and inner
worlds, its ceaseless forging of a new narrative idiom. In the
judgement of Christa Wolf, one of Germany's foremost living
novelists, 'German prose begins with Büchner's *Lenz*'.

Lenz was not published in Büchner's lifetime, and there is no
surviving manuscript. Karl Gutzkow and Büchner's brother
Ludwig both published editions (in 1839 and 1850 respectively):
Gutzkow's was allegedly based on a 'clean copy' made by Minna
Jaeglé, and Ludwig Büchner's was probably derived in turn from
Gutzkow's (it was long thought to have been based on the Minna
Jaeglé copy, or perhaps even on the author's own original manuscript). Neither edition was complete, and neither is entirely
reliable; but there is nothing else to go on (though modern
editions do incorporate some minor details from Oberlin's
account, such as the name of the month in the opening sentence,
and the name – and hence sex – of the child that Lenz attempts
to raise from the dead). Even with these irremediable deficiencies,
however, *Lenz* stands as an unforgettably powerful narrative.

Notes

1. *the vicarage in Waldbach:* Properly speaking, 'Waldersbach'; the
    village is in the Steintal (Vallée de la Bruche) some
    twenty-five miles south-west of Strasbourg. The vicarage
    now houses the Musée Oberlin.
2. *Oberlin:* Johann Friedrich (Jean Frédéric) Oberlin (1740–
    1826) was the (Protestant) parish priest of Waldersbach for

no less than fifty-nine years, beginning in 1767. He became widely renowned and revered for the immense benign influence that he exerted on his community throughout a period of often drastic social change: he was instrumental in introducing or encouraging such things as nursery schooling; raising of the school-leaving age to sixteen; agricultural improvements; road-building; local loan schemes; development of weaving and other local craft industries. He was buried in the same graveyard at Fouday that figures in Büchner's story.

3. *a friend of Kaufmann's:* Christoph Kaufmann (1753–95) was a friend of Lenz and Lavater (cf. note 24), and was acquainted with Goethe and Herder. The term *Sturm und Drang* ('Storm and Stress') was first coined by him (in reference to a play by Klinger). It was Kaufmann who sent Lenz to stay with Oberlin.

4. *he sketched all manner of local costumes:* Russian and Livonian ones, as Oberlin reports (Lehmann, I.438).

5. *tokens:* Unfortunately it is not clear what Büchner meant by 'tokens' (*Lose* in the original).

6. *Are you a theologian? ... next Sunday:* The real Lenz had studied theology in Dorpat and Königsberg. He preached the sermon on his first Sunday in Waldersbach.

7. *Suffering be my sole reward, | Suffering be my praise to God:* Büchner used this second couplet again in *Woyzeck* (see p. 132). The two lines are attested in an obscure Pietist volume of 1735, but it is not known where Büchner himself came across them; the first couplet has not so far been traced at all, and may be Büchner's own creation.

8. *his head sank ... stood there over the mountains:* The image of death in life is one that Büchner repeatedly, obsessively re-creates: compare the descriptions of the dead lover, the dead earth, the dead moon delivered respectively through Marion, Julie, Lena (see pp. 18, 70, 98).

9. *The next morning ... but he felt quite calm:* What seems at first clearly to be meant as further evidence of unhinged behaviour is quite unexpectedly treated by both the narrator and Oberlin as perfectly normal, indeed the rock-solid

Oberlin promptly matches it from his own experience; and Lenz's philosophizing a few lines later (beginning at 'He continued:') is unmistakably Büchner's own. There is a powerful element of mysticism in all this: Büchner was certainly *not* essentially a materialist. As for the historical Oberlin, besides being a man of exceptional practicality (see note 2), he was also a dedicated mystic who had visions of his dead wife and the Virgin Mary, firmly believed that angels and devils were ever-present and readily encountered, and was sure that numerous illnesses were caused by evil spirits.

10. *to have a soul . . . of the moon:* Büchner embodies just such an elemental receptiveness and naturalness in the figure of Lena: '– you know what I'm like: I should really have been planted in a flowerpot. I need dew and night air as the flowers do' (p. 98). Women for Büchner are in general far less estranged from nature than men – and this applies as much to the *Vénus noire* figures as to the *Vénus blanche* ones.

11. *an indescribable harmony:* Cf. note 18.

12. *represented by a colour:* Büchner is certain to have read Daniel Ehrenfried Stöber's biography of Oberlin, *Vie de J.-F. Oberlin* (1831), in the course of which Stöber comments: 'Le rouge signifie la foi; le jaune, l'amour; le bleu, la science . . . Chacun des douze apôtres de notre Seigneur et Sauveur Jésus-Christ a sa couleur, qui le distingue particulièrement' ('Red signifies faith; yellow, love; blue, knowledge . . . Each of the twelve apostles of our Lord and Saviour Jesus Christ has his own particular colour'; D.E. Stöber was the father of Büchner's close friends August and Adolf Stöber).

13. *Stilling:* Johann Heinrich Jung, commonly known as Jung-Stilling (1740–1817), an autodidact who became – among other things – a doctor, academic and pietist author. He became famous through his autobiographical novel *Heinrich Stilling's Youth* (1777); he also published a kind of handbook to the Book of Revelations – hence the allusion to him here.

14. *the idealist period was beginning at the time:* Büchner uses considerable poetic licence here. There was in fact no 'idealist period' taking shape at the time (the late 1770s). What he is

anachronistically attacking through the medium of Lenz is the kind of idealizing he saw personified above all in Friedrich Schiller, whom he specifically dismisses in his letter of 28 July 1835 defending *Danton's Death*. But Schiller's classicizing work did not appear until well after Lenz's death in 1792. In the meantime his early work in the 1780s was programmatically and even stridently *anti*-idealistic; had Büchner but realized it, Schiller was in truth one of his closest kindred spirits. But leaving aside questions of anachronism and the rightness or wrongness of Büchner's image of Schiller, what he offers in this passage is a major statement of his artistic credo. What he saw and detested in the contemporary arts was essentially the same reductivism that he saw in philosophy and the new sciences, and above all in society. The common factor in all is their powerful tendency to reduce mankind and life to a set of mechanical processes and functions serving a need beyond themselves: the ridiculous puppets of the contemporary stage; the *homme machine* of Cartesian rationalism; the body as functional, purposive mechanism in the new sciences; the peasantry as work-machines and money-machines for the convenience of a parasitical ruling-class in everyday society. What Büchner seeks in the arts as in all other domains is modes of doing justice to the immensity of feeling, vitality, spirit, potential that resides in even the lowliest of human beings – and what he accordingly delivers in the ensuing couple of pages is one of the most intense and expressive artistic manifestos in German literature.

15. *Kaufmann was a keen supporter:* The historical Kaufmann was no such thing. Büchner invents this detail in order to cue Lenz's vehement reply.

16. *The Tutor and The Soldiers:* Lenz's two best-known plays, published in 1774 and 1776 respectively.

17. *the old German school:* This implies the great German tradition of painting in the fifteenth and sixteenth centuries: Dürer, Altdorfer, the Cranachs, Hans Baldung Grien, etc.

18. *an infinite beauty ... revealed afresh:* In this central respect of *beauty*, Büchner's aesthetic philosophy is essentially identical

to the scientific philosophy he will enunciate in his 'Trial Lecture', where he postulates 'a fundamental law informing the entire organic world ... a primordial law [*Urgesetz*], a law of beauty, which produces the highest and purest forms from the simplest outlines and patterns', and which produces in all its manifestations a 'necessary harmony' (see p. 184).

19. *the Apollo Belvedere:* The most famous representation of Apollo, long held in the Vatican's Belvedere. Found at Frascati in 1455, the statue was a Roman copy of a fourth-century BC Athenian original, and was regarded in the Renaissance as the classic image of perfect masculinity.

20. *Raphael's Madonnas:* Raphael (1483–1520) painted numerous Madonnas after he had come under the influence of Leonardo da Vinci in Florence. They are regarded as one of the supreme achievements of High Renaissance art.

21. *Christ and the disciples at Emmaus:* The picture is almost certainly the one by Carel van Savoy that is still to be seen in Darmstadt. There is even a specific reference to the painting in the diaries of Büchner's friend Alexis Muston, following a joint visit to the Darmstadt museum: 'Un Christ à Emmaus m'a également frappé, mais je ne me souviens pas de l'auteur' ('I was equally struck by a *Christ at Emmaus*, but I don't recall the artist').

22. *Then another one:* Büchner is probably referring to a painting by Nicolaes Maes, a pupil of Rembrandt's who for part of his career was particularly fond of painting women spinning, reading the Bible or preparing meals. A Maes painting that matches Büchner's description hangs in the museum at Gotha.

23. *letters from Lenz's father:* Kaufmann had met Lenz's father while in Russia the previous year (1777). Lenz's relationship with his father was continually and fundamentally strained; Büchner's own relationship with his father was also exceptionally difficult.

24. *Lavater:* Johann Kaspar Lavater (1741–1801). A protestant priest, but also a prolific writer who became a central figure in the cultural life of the period. He became famous and remarkably influential throughout Europe above all for his four-volume *Physiognomical Fragments* of 1775–8, which

argued that the individual's inner soul and spirit was physically imaged in their body, and especially in their face. (See also the 'Trial Lecture', p. 183, and p. 289, note 3.)

25. *It was profoundly dark . . . the Steintal:* What follows is one of the most remarkable passages in the work. As with the Marion episode in *Danton's Death*, a door is quite suddenly opened – and just as suddenly closed again – on a world apparently quite remote in atmosphere and setting from the remainder of the work. What makes it particularly fascinating is that just for once we are not seeing Lenz's *own* inner world: he suddenly functions as a kind of neutral lens on to a realm beyond. We enter and leave the hut with him, and see only what *he* fictively sees as an uninvolved spectator.

26. *the girl whose fate weighs so heavily upon me:* The reference can only be to Friederike Brion (1752–1813): in the summer of 1772 Lenz fell deeply in love with Friederike, one of the daughters of the vicar of Sesenheim (properly speaking 'Sessenheim', a village some 20 miles north-east of Strasbourg) – but nothing came of it. A year earlier Friederike had been the sweetheart of Lenz's friend Goethe, until he suddenly and famously abandoned her in August 1771. She never married.

27. *the corpse stayed cold:* Oberlin reports that the real Lenz did indeed attempt to raise a young child named Friederike from the dead (Lehmann, I.458). *Leonce and Lena* presents a very similar episode (see pp. 98–9) – except that Lena is only metaphorically a corpse and therefore *can* 'arise and walk'. In both these episodes Büchner displays his curiously obsessional, even morbid tendency to mingle death with love; indeed there is no love relationship in his work that is not figured in deathly terms, from the opening page of *Danton's Death* through to the final pages of the *Woyzeck* fragments.

28. *Pfeffel:* Gottlieb Konrad Pfeffel (1736–1809) was an Alsace poet, playwright and translator, as well as an educator and philanthropist. Oberlin's account tells how he had met Pfeffel on his journey, and how the latter was full of praise for the direct and benign impact that a country parson could have on his community (in this respect Oberlin himself was an outstanding model: see note 2).

29. *the Wandering Jew:* See p. 236, note 110.

30. *she loved another man too:* The 'other man' was Goethe (see note 26).

31. *it's just too boring:* Yet another recurrence of Büchner's central motif of *ennui;* cf. *Danton's Death* (p. 28), *Leonce and Lena* (p. 80).

32. *as if he were double . . . to save it:* It has to be emphasized that whilst *Lenz* offers the first description of schizophrenia in German literature, complete with a whole catalogue of clinical details (made possible, no doubt, by Büchner's medical training), we should none the less be wary of seeing the work as a kind of detached 'case study'. The figure of Lenz surely fascinated Büchner because he personified in extreme and heightened form many elements deeply familiar to Büchner himself. It is particularly revealing that most of the details of Lenz's inner world and his psychological disintegration were not recorded facts taken over from Oberlin's report, but were invented by Büchner himself. This present detail is a typical case in point. Cf. the splitting of the self that Marion describes in *Danton's Death*: 'I looked at my body, it seemed to me sometimes as though I were double, then melted again into one' (see p. 18).

33. *I couldn't bear people suffering I would save them, save them:* Cf. p. 232, note 83.

34. *[substantial passage missing]:* The surviving versions break off here before going straight into the final paragraph, but judging by the pattern in the rest of the text it is likely that Büchner wrote many more pages that were subsequently lost. Up to this point Büchner adapts practically all of Oberlin's account, and expands it in length by a factor of almost three; the missing passage corresponds to four full pages of Oberlin's narrative in the Lehmann edition (i.e. more than a third) – so that as many as eleven pages of Büchner's story might have disappeared.

35. *He sat in the carriage . . . for the rest of his days:* Lenz was conveyed to his friend Johann Georg Schlosser (the brother-in-law of Goethe). Schlosser and others looked after him until June the following year (1779), when he was taken

home to Riga by one of his brothers. He was found dead in
the street in Moscow in May 1792.

THE HESSIAN MESSENGER

The Hessian Messenger is generally acknowledged today as 'the
most significant revolutionary pamphlet in Germany prior to the
Communist Manifesto' (Thomas Michael Mayer). The nineteenth-
century historian Heinrich von Treitschke described it as a 'masterpiece of shameless demagogic eloquence'. In its own day it was
clearly perceived as a potentially serious threat by the authorities,
who variously described it as 'the most dangerous', 'the most
vicious', 'the most revolutionary' of the many seditious publications of the period, and who went to extraordinary lengths not
only to suppress it, but also to track down and if possible
eradicate every last link in the political network that had planned,
produced and disseminated it.

And there was indeed such a network: in stark contrast to all
Büchner's (later) poetic work, *The Hessian Messenger* was a collective
venture targeted at a particular audience for a particular purpose
within the context of a specific and painstakingly negotiated
political strategy. The most salient manifestation of this is the fact
that the text of *The Hessian Messenger* was the work of not one
hand but two. More specifically: Georg Büchner's original draft
was so drastically cut, reworked and added to by his fellow
conspirator Ludwig Weidig that the published version of July
1834, far from constituting a Büchner text with revisions by
Weidig, amounts in effect to a kind of palimpsest in which the
dominant overlay is Weidig's, and the underlay such portions
and remnants of Büchner's original as Weidig saw fit to retain –
and which, to Büchner's intense fury, did not include any of the
central core of his argument. (As for the heavily revised second
edition of November 1834, Büchner was not involved at all;
indeed, it was probably undertaken wholly or partly by yet

273

another member of the group, Leopold Eichelberg – whose reward was a thirteen-year gaol-sentence.)

Compared with the nobler ideals of the French Revolution, or even with the actual, existing realities of France, America or England, the political and socio-economic situation in the German lands was generally grim in the 1830s, and it was particularly grim in the Grand Duchy of Hesse. Politically speaking, the regime was in effect absolutist: although the monarchy had nominally become constitutional in 1820, the two-chamber parliamentary assembly was virtually powerless, and was anyway grossly unrepresentative, being drawn in the one case almost wholly from the nobility, and in the other from a tiny pool of high tax payers, all belonging necessarily to the upper echelons of the bourgeoisie. Moreover, the strongly reactionary and repressive impetus of the Metternich era throughout the German lands meant that the situation grew steadily worse, most notably in 1832, when the mass demonstration of revolutionary potential at the so-called 'Hambacher Fest' led the Frankfurt Bundestag to approve Austro-Prussian proposals that severely restricted the scope for opposition *within* the constituent parliaments of the Confederation, and criminalized extra-parliamentary opposition almost in its entirety by drastically curtailing the freedom of speech, association, assembly etc. – in the process inevitably strengthening the revolutionary underground. In socio-economic terms, too, the situation was ever more grievous for the great mass of the population, particularly in the physically separate and largest province of Upper Hesse – the target area of *The Hessian Messenger*: (1) Fully 80 per cent of the population lived on the land, with another 17 per cent in very small towns (300–5000 inhabitants; only the provincial capital, Giessen, numbered more than 5000). (2) The land itself was generally very poor, and rendered even less productive by continued use of the ancient three-field system. (3) The population grew rapidly throughout the period, thus straining slender resources even further. (4) Shortages were periodically exacerbated to the point of famine by Europe-wide crop crises. (5) Although serfdom as such had been abolished (in 1811), most peasants remained subject to the associated seigneurial dues, since they could not afford the land or money demanded for their redemption. (6) Double taxation was widespread, since the erstwhile lords of the province retained the right to levy taxes in addition to those imposed by the state government in Darmstadt. (7) Political and protectionist customs barriers imposed around the borders of the province increasingly inhibited the flow of goods (even to get to the rest of the Grand Duchy meant passing *four* state frontiers).

The result of all these factors was a relentless process of pauperization, graphically reflected in a much increased incidence of beggary, alcoholism, emigration – and serious social unrest, most notably the peasant uprising of September 1830 that is specifically referred to in *The Hessian Messenger* (cf. notes 14 and 16).

On 3 April 1833 an armed coup was mounted in Frankfurt, the capital of the German Confederation. With the active support of oppositional forces throughout southern Germany – including the key figure of Ludwig Weidig – a group of some fifty gun-toting insurgents, nearly all of them students from the comfortable middle classes, attempted to storm the police headquarters in the hope of triggering a popular revolution. The would-be coup was a fiasco: the attack itself was amateurish; the populus remained aloof; the authorities were comprehensively forewarned. But none the less it had important consequences: the authorities massively extended and strengthened their anti-oppositional measures; and the oppositional forces themselves were compelled radically to rethink their strategy. Contrived and arbitrary middle-class putsches were futile: the longed-for revolution could only be engineered if the colossal energies of the oppressed masses could somehow be activated and harnessed. For Georg Büchner – then a medical student in Strasbourg, and still in his teens – the episode only confirmed and sharpened his political insights: violence was the sole available means for change; but the *people* had to be 'ready to fight for their rights', and in the meantime it was hopelessly inept 'to play at toy soldiers with a tin gun and a wooden sword' (see p. 190, letter of 5 April 1833). The lesson was clear and decisive: 'I have *recently* come to realize that only the imperative needs of the great mass of the people can bring about change, and that all the beavering and bellowing of *individuals* is futile' (p. 191, letter of June 1833).

Given the wholesale criminalization of meetings, assemblies and the like, the only way to reach out to the masses was by means of clandestine pamphlets. These became more and more common during the 1830s, together with an ever more elaborate network of organizers, fundraisers, writers, couriers, printers, distributors – at the very centre of which was Ludwig Weidig, a schoolteacher in Butzbach (Upper Hesse), by then in his early forties and long since established as one of southern Germany's most tireless and influential revolutionary democrats. Büchner (who had meanwhile returned to continue his studies in Giessen) made contact with Weidig sometime in early 1834, while simultaneously setting up a revolutionary cell in Giessen (and another in Darmstadt), the 'Society of Human Rights', modelled on the revolutionary practice familiar to him from France. Insurrectionist propaganda was a central element in the programme of the new society, and Büchner duly elaborated and finalized a text which Weidig was supposed to get printed through his well-tried network. But Weidig's own politics were considerably less radical than Büchner's; furthermore, he had to accommodate the interests and wishes of a very broad spectrum of oppositional forces throughout Hesse and southern Germany – almost all of whom were again less radical than he himself was. His consequent drastic reworking of the text provoked 'extreme anger' in Büchner, who protested that the very heart of his argument had been cut out; but his ultimate acceptance of Weidig's rewrite, however grudging, is signalled by the fact that it was he (together with a comrade from the revolutionary cell in Giessen) who smuggled the final text from Weidig's home in Butzbach to the secret printer in Offenbach in early July 1834. On 31 July three close associates of Büchner's duly collected the printed pamphlets (probably some 300 in all), and made off, as planned, in three different directions.

Disaster struck at once. One of the three couriers, Carl Minnigerode, was arrested as he re-entered Giessen the following evening with 139 copies of *The Hessian Messenger* concealed in his boots, his coat-lining, etc., etc. The arrest was no fluke: typically for this period, one of the conspirators was a professional informer (indeed, the same man, Johann Konrad Kuhl, had also betrayed the Frankfurt putsch a year earlier). In the course of the ensuing months the activists involved in *The Hessian Messenger* were relentlessly identified and arrested, and then subjected to an appallingly punishing regime of solitary confinement and repeated interrogations that came to an end only in November–December 1838, when lengthy prison sentences were imposed on no fewer than thirty individuals. Though specifically betrayed by Kuhl at the very beginning, Büchner managed by a mixture of brazenness and good fortune to evade the clutches of the law. Weidig's fate was very different: arrested in April 1835, he was subjected to a particularly savage regime and committed suicide in his prison cell on 23 February 1837 (by a strange coincidence, just four days after Büchner's own death in Zurich).

Although evidence has emerged that *The Hessian Messenger* had considerably more impact on its (few) recipients than has traditionally been thought, the fact remains that it was scarcely less of a fiasco than the Frankfurt coup: not only did it fail in its objective of politicizing and mobilizing the peasantry of Upper Hesse (as it was bound to do in the given circumstances), but it also enabled the state authorities to close down an entire network of revolutionary activists. We cannot tell what Büchner would have done later (e.g. before/during/after the 1848 revolution) if he had remained alive; but we do know that in the two and a half years left to him after *The Hessian Messenger* he engaged in no remotely similar venture. Not because he no longer believed in revolution, but chiefly because he recognized that the conditions for a revolution did not yet exist.

So far as the text of *The Hessian Messenger* is concerned, no manuscripts of any kind have survived, so it is impossible to establish precisely or definitively which parts derive from Büchner and which from Weidig. Numerous scholars have advanced their different views – most notably in recent times Thomas Michael Mayer, currently the predominant Büchner expert, who has argued elaborately and very plausibly that the *first* half of the text is chiefly Büchner with additions by Weidig, whereas the *second* half is chiefly Weidig interspersed with remnants of Büchner (Mayer's suggested point of change is indicated in the Notes). But whatever the precise contribution of the separate authors may have been, *The Hessian Messenger* remains an often powerful and always fascinating example of political propaganda.

Notes

I am particularly indebted – both for the Introduction and for the Notes – to Gerhard Schaub and his finely detailed edition: Georg Büchner, Friedrich Ludwig Weidig, *Der Hessische Landbote. Texte. Materialien. Kommentar* (Munich, 1976).

1. *The Hessian Messenger:* The title was Weidig's. The term 'Messenger' (*Bote*) was particularly common in the titles of oppositional pamphlets in the early 1830s.
2. *First Message:* This clearly suggests that *The Hessian Messenger* as we know it was originally intended to be only the first in a series of such publications.
3. *Darmstadt, July 1834:* In reality the pamphlet was printed (secretly) in Offenbach. The heading was perhaps meant to mislead the state security services; it was perhaps also meant to give the pamphlet extra weight in the eyes of its potential readers, since Darmstadt, the state capital, was generally seen as the fount of all authority.
4. *Preface:* The entire 'Preface' was added by Weidig. It was almost certainly counter-productive (and was duly cut in the second edition of November 1834): it was condescending towards its potential readers, alarmingly conspiratorial in tone, and foolish in spelling out the advice contained in paragraph 4 (it was unsurprisingly considered a particular impertinence when Minnigerode tried to avail himself of this advice on his arrest).
5. *Peace to the peasants! War on the palaces!:* The slogan was borrowed from the French Revolution, where it had become a catchphrase: 'Paix aux chaumières [literally: cottages]! Guerre aux châteaux!' It was coined by Chamfort in 1792.
6. *gentry:* There is no really apt equivalent for the term in the original text: *die Vornehmen* – a term that chiefly connotes the aristocracy, while also implying the ruling class in general,

i.e. the class having high social status, money, privileges and power. The terminology was acutely problematic even when the pamphlet was written. According to Büchner's fellow activist August Becker (in the context of his judicial interrogation), Büchner originally wrote 'the rich' (*die Reichen*), but Weidig systematically altered this to the much narrower term *die Vornehmen* (in the second edition of November 1834 Weidig and/or Eichelberg went further still in order to avoid antagonizing the affluent, removing even the term *die Vornehmen* and instead substituting words referring solely to the princes and their minions). This redefining of the 'enemy' reflects the fundamental difference between the revolutionary perspectives of the two men: for Weidig, it was not merely conceivable but positively desirable that members of the affluent classes – not least the richer peasants – should join in the impending revolution; for the far more radical Georg Büchner, however, there was an unbridgeable gulf between the haves and the have-nots – and the revolution could only be achieved by the latter (cf. pp. 200–201, 204–5, letters to Gutzkow). This crucial polarization was to become ever more marked in the subsequent history of German left-wing politics right through into the twentieth century.

7. *Have dominion over every creeping thing that creepeth upon the earth:* Cf. Genesis 1:28,30. The entire text of *The Hessian Messenger* is permeated with biblical references. It has long been a commonplace of Büchner criticism that Weidig – a priest and Bible scholar as well as a teacher – superimposed the biblical quotations and echoes onto Büchner's original draft, but scholars are now generally agreed that this is unlikely: the allusions are too frequent, and too integral to the fabric of the text, to have been simply tacked on at the last minute. Büchner well understood the centrality of religion and the Bible to popular experience (cf. *Woyzeck!*) – and in consequence he regarded religion as an essential 'lever' that had to be worked on if the masses were to be politically mobilized (cf. p. 204–5, letter to Gutzkow).

8. *strangers devour his land in his presence:* Cf. Isaiah 1:7.

9. *Regales:* Regales (German *Regalien*) were dues automatically payable to the crown from the revenues of specific economic activities such as salt-works, mines, the mint, the postal service.

10. *6,363,363 gulden:* The arithmetic here is patently garbled: the figures add up to 6,363,436, and not 6,363,363 – let alone 6,363,364, as stated in the preamble to the table. The source of all the statistics has fairly recently been discovered (by Gerhard Schaub), and a comparison shows that Büchner's entry under 'Sundry sources' is also miscalculated, and should have read 64,098, not 64,198 – so that the correct grand total should in reality have been 6,363,336. Such slips are scarcely surprising, given the covert and hence extremely adverse circumstances in which the pamphlet was produced.

    It has long been maintained that Büchner was the first to use statistics in the service of political agitation, but in fact (as Schaub has demonstrated) he was continuing a practice already established by others.

11. *The people are their flock whom they herd, milk and flay:* This echoes Ezekiel 34:1ff., and Jeremiah 23:1ff.

12. *the clothes on their back are the skin of peasants:* Cf. Micah 3:2ff.

13. *the spoil of the poor is in their houses:* Cf. Isaiah 3:14.

14. *Vogelsberg ... Rokkenburg ...:* Many inhabitants of the Vogelsberg region were involved in the peasant uprising in Upper Hesse in September 1830. There was a particularly grim prison near the village of Rockenberg, not far from Friedberg.

15. *fire into the air once a year in the autumn:* Military exercises were traditionally carried out in September of each year.

16. *At Södel your brothers and sons were the murderers of their brothers and fathers:* The September 1830 uprising was finally suppressed at the village of Södel (near Rockenberg). Although in itself a bungled and relatively minor incident in which the army fired on innocent villagers who were mistakenly thought to be insurgents, killing at most two of them, the episode rapidly entered oppositional mythology as the 'Södel bloodbath'.

17. *See, he crawled into the world . . . as stiff and rigid as you:* Cf. The Wisdom of Solomon 7:1ff.

18. *a crown of thorns that you press upon your own head:* Cf. e.g. Matthew 27:27ff.

19. *the mark of the beast:* Cf. Revelation 16:2, 19:20ff.

20. *'this government is ordained of God':* Cf. Romans 13:1. According to Thomas Michael Mayer, it is from this point onwards that the text is almost exclusively Weidig's, with only occasional borrowings from Büchner's original draft (cf. p. 277).

21. *Father of Lies:* i.e. the devil; cf. John 8:44.

22. *their ways and doings:* Cf. e.g. Jeremiah 18:11; Ezekiel 20:43ff.

23. *their justice extortion:* Cf. Isaiah 5:7.

24. *They trample the land:* Cf. Habakkuk 3:12.

25. *and grind the faces of the poor:* Cf. Isaiah 3:15.

26. *'the Lord's Anointed':* Cf. e.g. 1 Samuel 24:6,10.

27. *A little while:* Cf. John 16:16–19.

28. *'Render unto Caesar the things which are Caesar's':* Cf. Matthew 22:21; Mark 12:17.

29. *For the Parliamentary Assembly: 16,000 gulden:* Given the nature of this line (which repeats the pattern used throughout the first half of the text), and the fact that the ensuing passage bears no relation to it, it is virtually certain that this is a marooned remnant of Büchner's original draft, retained by Weidig for no particular reason.

30. *'No one shall inherit privileges . . . the laws that they have passed':* Despite the impression given by the inverted commas, this is *not* a quotation, either directly or indirectly, from the Declaration of the Rights of Man and Citizen (1789/1791) – indeed it seriously misrepresents both the formal Declaration *and* the political realities of the day (by no means 'everyone' acquired the right to vote; it was not the King's 'sole' task to 'implement the laws', for he crucially retained the veto; furthermore, he remained for the time being legally inviolable and unanswerable – contrary to what is stated in the paragraph's second sentence). This whole passage has traditionally been ascribed to Büchner, but Thomas Michael Mayer is surely right to see it as being exclusively the work

of Weidig, who – in fundamental contrast to Büchner – hoped that the coming revolution would lead to a new, democratized monarchy, at once pan-German and truly constitutional.

31.   *exalted in their strength:* Cf. e.g. Psalms 21:13.

32.   *and their peoples rejoice:* Cf. e.g. Psalms 67:5.

33.   *serve the true God:* Cf. e.g. 1 Thessalonians 1:9.

34.   *and yet Grolmann ... rob you of two million gulden:* In 1830 a proposal was laid before the parliamentary assembly of Hesse which would have transferred the Grand Duke's private debts of two million gulden to the state, i.e. to the taxpayer. Though normally compliant, the assembly baulked at this particular measure, as is mentioned some dozen lines later. The reference to Grolmann may be a slip: Karl von Grolmann had been chief minister of Hesse, but he had died in 1829; but Büchner/Weidig might possibly have been referring to the dead minister's younger brother, Friedrich von Grolmann, who remained a conservative member of the assembly for many years.

35.   *The vultures in Vienna and Berlin ... face of the earth:* The dominant absolutist monarchies of Austria and Prussia were ruthlessly efficient in this period in identifying and stifling any signs of social or political unrest.

36.   *The Lord broke the rod:* Cf. Isaiah 9:4.

37.   *the worm within them dieth not:* Cf. Isaiah 66:24; Mark 9:44,46,48. The italics reflect the usage of Luther's Bible, where the Isaiah verse is printed in bold type for special emphasis.

38.   *and their feet are of clay:* Cf. Daniel 2:31ff.

39.   *God will give you strength:* Cf. e.g. Psalms 29:11.

40.   *turned from the error of your way:* Cf. James 5:20.

41.   *acknowledged the truth:* Cf. e.g. 2 Timothy 2:25.

42.   *but one God:* Cf. Exodus 20:3.

43.   *Most High:* Cf. e.g. Psalms 47:2.

44.   *united a people ... into a single body:* This echoes 1 Corinthians 12:12ff.

45.   *and hack it into four or even thirty pieces:* At the Congress of Vienna in 1815 it was agreed that the Confederation of

German States would consist of thirty-four principalities and four free cities.

46. *What God hath joined together let not man put asunder:* Cf. Matthew 19:6.

47. *turn a desert into a paradise:* Cf. Genesis and the story of God's creation of the world; but cf. also Isaiah 35:1f.

48. *travail and affliction:* Cf. Psalms 25:18.

49. *'messengers of Satan':* Cf. 2 Corinthians 12:7.

50. *'principalities and powers . . . in high places':* Cf. Ephesians 6:12.

51. *court of Baal:* Cf. e.g. Romans 11:4.

52. *Ha! So you govern . . . you are not of God:* These lines are a loose quotation from a poem by Gottfried August Bürger ('Der Bauer. An seinen durchlauchtigen Tyrannen', 1773).

53. *smitten Germany for her sins:* Cf. Leviticus 26:24.

54. *will heal her again:* Cf. Deuteronomy 32:39.

55. *just as the hunchback . . . no longer increases:* King Ludwig I of Bavaria (1786–1868) was not in reality afflicted with a hunchback (his only particularly striking physical feature was a very prominent nose). It is unclear whether Büchner/ Weidig knew this; but in any event they were following in a strong propaganda tradition – chiefly popularized by the pamphleteers of the French Revolution – of depicting royals and aristocrats as both physically and morally grotesque.

56. *Lift up your eyes:* Cf. e.g. Genesis 32:12.

57. *I say unto you:* Cf. e.g. Matthew 5:22.

58. *he that raises his sword . . . the sword of the people:* Cf. Matthew 26:52.

59. *When the Lord gives you a sign:* Cf. Isaiah 7:14.

60. *you have bowed to your labour in the thorn-fields of servitude:* Cf. Genesis 3:17ff.

61. *even unto the thousandth generation:* Cf. Exodus 34:7.

62. *with the water of life:* Cf. Revelation 22:17.

63. *be watchful . . . saying this prayer:* Cf. Matthew 26:41.

64. *Lord, destroy the rods of our oppressors:* Cf. Isaiah 9:4.

65. *let Thy kingdom come unto us:* Cf. Matthew 6:10.

ON CRANIAL NERVES

In early September 1836 the Philosophy Faculty of the new University of Zurich awarded Büchner a doctorate on the basis of his Strasbourg thesis *Mémoire sur le système nerveux du barbeau*, and this duly opened the way for him to move to Zurich and embark on an academic career as a *Privatdozent*. A formal prerequisite of such a post was the delivery of a 'Trial Lecture', and Büchner accordingly gave such a lecture on 5 November 1837 (the success of which may be gauged from the fact that the Rector of the university, the famous Lorenz Oken, promptly sent his own son to Büchner's ensuing course on 'The comparative anatomy of fish and amphibians').

The bulk of the lecture is devoted to detailed scientific argument (based largely on the much longer Strasbourg *Mémoire*). First, however, Büchner offers a kind of preface in which he briefly discusses the broader scientific-philosophical context of his argument, and stakes out his own position. It is this prefatory section that is translated here – one of the most revealing, challenging and controversial passages in all Büchner's work.

When Büchner speaks at the very beginning of his lecture of two conflicting approaches within the field of physiology and anatomy, one predominant in France and England, the other in Germany, he is reflecting a very real and fundamental divergence of views that affected the sciences as a whole during the critical half-century or so before the broad consensus emerged that we think of as 'modern science'. The challenge arose specifically in Germany in the closing years of the eighteenth century, and was essentially a revolt against the whole empirical-analytical thrust of scientific enquiry that had increasingly developed since Galilei, Bacon and Newton, and had become almost universal during the period of the Enlightenment. Goethe was a central figure in this revolt, which is graphically epitomized in a famous episode: the beginning of the friendship between Goethe and Schiller following a lengthy period of estrangement. One day in 1794 they happened to meet as both emerged in high dudgeon from a scientific meeting in Jena. Schiller voiced his disapproval of the fact that the natural world had been treated at the meeting in such an 'atomistic' way, and Goethe agreed in deeply characteristic terms: instead of nature being regarded as a plethora of separate and discrete bits and pieces, it should be recognized as 'vibrant and alive, carrying its wholeness through into all its parts'. This belief in *wholeness* is paramount: the prevailing empiricism seemed futile to Goethe and Schiller because it concentrated so heavily on the part, on the particularity of discrete data, that it lost all sense of the whole. They were by no means alone in this: the reaction against mechanistic, atomistic empiricism became extremely widespread throughout Germany, encouraged in particular by the Idealist philosopher Schelling, who from 1799 argued vehemently for a new *Naturphilosophie* – a new and *wholist* perception of the natural world.

Within a short time *Naturphilosophie* became the dominant mode of scientific enquiry at universities up and down the German lands. Its foremost academic proponent was none other than Lorenz Oken (1779–1855) – the man who ultimately became Rector of the new University of Zurich, and as such presided at Büchner's 'Trial Lecture' in 1837. Being profoundly anti-mechanistic, *Naturphilosophie* in all its various forms postulated some kind of all-informing or all-enveloping energy, force, vitality, spirit, divinity – and Oken was no exception: for him, light was God's consciousness; the air was His self-positing activity; the natural world was God manifesting Himself in ever more splendid metamorphoses from primitive slime right through to the magnificence of man. Such entirely speculative and untestable suppositions were at the heart of *Naturphilosophie*, and although in some respects they proved highly fruitful (Oken for instance was a founder of cell theory, and also – as Darwin himself acknowledged – propounded a form of evolutionism), they increasingly tended in their more extravagant and fantastical manifestations to attract odium and scorn, to the point that in 1840 the great chemist Justus von Liebig (already a professor at Giessen when Büchner was a student there) castigated *Naturphilosophie* as 'the pestilence, the Black Death, of the nineteenth century' (whose proponents, he once declared, should be 'thrown into gaol'). In essence, though, and at its best, *Naturphilosophie* was an attempt to *syncretize* the epoch's two antithetical attitudes of empiricism and idealism. In its fundamental wholist tenets it was unquestionably idealist, even metaphysical. But the *Naturphilosophen* used their idealist-metaphysical-mystical postulates as a *vantage point* from which to try to understand the real workings of the real natural world, to glimpse order within an otherwise unmanageable chaos of undifferentiated data. Throughout all his scientific-philosophical speculations, Goethe never strayed from detailed and painstaking observation and analysis of specimens; Oken published no fewer than thirteen volumes of 'straight' descriptive natural history. But their approach in their punctilious experimentation was always deductive and integrative, never inductive and atomistic: whereas the Baconian empiricist begins with the part (and in the view of the *Naturphilosophen* can never get beyond it), they begin with the whole – which indeed they believe to be always immanent in even the tiniest part.

Georg Büchner's 'Trial Lecture' – the detailed scientific argument as well as the prefatory section translated here – falls squarely within this *Naturphilosophie* tradition. His postulation of a 'primordial law', an *Urgesetz*, that brings forth the rich complexity of nature from a matrix of simple forms, is classic *Naturphilosophie*, echoing in particular Goethe's central belief in the *Urphänomen*, the primordial form from which all else derives. More importantly, the entire scientific argument of the 'Trial Lecture' (as also of the earlier and much longer *Mémoire*) is dedicated to substantiating a famous theory of *Naturphilosophie* – independently advanced by both Goethe and Oken – that the skull consists of metamorphosed vertebrae. This was a typical product of the belief that even the most complex structures of nature are derived from simple primordial forms. Oken took the argument to polemical extremes, and caused a sensation in his Inaugural Lecture as a Jena professor in 1807, when he roundly declared that 'The entire human being is but a vertebra'. Oken was mocked even then, and the almost universal disrepute that *Naturphilosophie* subsequently fell into is perfectly illustrated by the fact that, in his famous Croonian Lecture of 1858, Thomas Henry Huxley specifically chose to attack the vertebral theory of the skull, ridiculing the 'speculator' for his conjuror's ability to 'devise half a dozen very pretty vertebral theories, all equally true, in the course of a summer's day', and calling for support from 'Those who, like myself, are unable to see the propriety and advantage of introducing into science any ideal conception, which is other than the simplest possible generalized expression of observed facts.'

It is intriguing to wonder how Büchner's attitude might have changed had he lived to be forty, sixty, eighty – for it could scarcely have remained the same. But at twenty-three he presents a startling paradox: the man who seems to us in the late twentieth century to be a supreme modernist in his writing, and considerably ahead of his time in his politics, was decidedly *un*modern as a scientist-philosopher, not only giving his support to a doomed mode of thought and one of its central theories, but also attacking precisely that mode of functionalist empiricism that before long was to become a defining characteristic of modern science. But the paradox is perhaps more apparent than real: Büchner's scientific philosophy turns out on closer inspection to be fully at one with his philosophies of politics and aesthetics. A crucial pointer to this may be identified in his remarks (in the opening paragraph of the 'Trial Lecture') that what he terms the 'teleological' school 'knows the individual only as something that is meant to achieve a purpose beyond itself', and regards every living organism as merely a 'complex machine provided with functional devices enabling it to survive over a certain span of time'. Büchner abhorred the mechanistic, reductivist approach wherever he saw it: in philosophy (Descartes's *l'homme machine*; cf. Lehmann, II.179); in the arts (the 'clanking puppets' mocked through Camille in *Danton's Death*); in politics (the ruthlessly mechanistic 'rejuvenation' programme of Robespierre and Saint-Just); above all in the social reality of his time (the reduction of the masses to so many units of exploitation for the benefit of an idle, parasitical élite). All such attitudes/processes/systems ignore the essential vitality and value inherent in the individual – and this is precisely what Büchner opposes in the 'teleologists'. For him – and this is surely one of the most important programmatic declarations in all his work – 'Everything that exists, exists for its own sake.' But the 'teleologist' operates on the contrary principle: everything is merely a functional component, and is measured by the one criterion of 'fitness for purpose' – a purpose that is never intrinsic to the component, but always and necessarily *ex*trinsic to it. Thus eyes, tears, lips, skull, hands, etc. have no meaning or value in themselves; they are simply mechanical devices serving a purpose *beyond* themselves. This is a view that Büchner cannot accept – just as he could never accept the notion that individual human beings are merely cogs in a machine. As such his position is indeed 'philosophical', as he himself terms it – in fact it is distinctly idealist (most conspicuously perhaps in his assertion that the *Urgesetz* that gives form and shape to the whole of nature is a primordial law of 'beauty'). But this should not surprise us. After all, his politics were driven by idealism. So too, in a very real sense, was his poetic writing – where even the bleakest utterances are always essentially cries of despair at the fact that prevailing reality seemed so far removed from his cherished ideals.

The text of Büchner's 'Trial Lecture' derives from two separate sources: the first four-plus paragraphs were printed in Ludwig Büchner's edition of 1850, while the remainder of the text has survived in autograph form. It seems very likely that Ludwig Büchner took the now-missing first section of the manuscript for the purposes of his edition, and that this accounts for its disappearance (none of the various manuscripts used by Ludwig Büchner have survived; it is likely that all of them were stored together in the room in the Büchner house that was burnt out in a fire in 1851).

The 1850 edition shows omission dots after the opening phrase, 'Esteemed audience!' It has been suggested that Ludwig Büchner may have left out an entire page of the original manuscript, but it seems more likely that he simply omitted some of the formal greetings that are customary on such occasions.

Notes

1. *On Cranial Nerves:* The 'Trial Lecture' is traditionally known by this title, but it is not Büchner's (it was coined by Karl

Emil Franzos for his 1879 edition of Büchner's *Collected Works*).

2. *a teleological standpoint:* Büchner's use of the term 'teleological' is potentially misleading. The philosopher Christian Wolff had coined the word 'teleology' in the eighteenth century to define his metaphysical, theistic belief that, whilst living organisms were indeed 'machines' (as Descartes had argued), they were machines generated by God, and directed towards the fulfilment of His purposes, just as *all* phenomena in the world were in Wolff's view directed at the realization of His wise ends. But Büchner is imputing no metaphysic to what he calls the 'teleological' school. On the contrary, whereas their focus on the *purpose* of organs might seem to imply a progression into metaphysics (leading to the question of 'ultimate purposes' and a 'Final Cause'), the 'teleological' physiologists and anatomists confine themselves entirely to the materialist-mechanical realm: they are interested solely in the *functional, regulative* purpose of an organ and in its *efficiency*. It is in effect the *absence* of a metaphysical dimension that Büchner criticizes in the 'teleologists'. His own 'philosophical' position, by contrast, is altogether metaphysical; and as with *Naturphilosophie* in general, its metaphysic is essentially mystical.

3. *Lavater:* See p. 270, note 24. Lavater's central belief was that God and Christ were everywhere manifest in history and nature, and could be directly experienced both through the senses and through inner intuition. Büchner's approving mention of Lavater is particularly significant in that Lavater was a prime exponent of the 'intuition of the mystic' that is somewhat enigmatically referred to in the fourth paragraph.

4. *The teleological method ... an infinite circle:* It had been one of Schelling's most fundamental objections to empiricism that its practitioners moved in an 'eternal circle' by beginning with physical phenomena and the effects they displayed, deducing causes from these effects, then deducing effects from the causes thus deduced.

5. *a law of beauty:* Cf. *Lenz,* p. 149: 'The most beautiful images, the most resonant harmonies, coalesce, dissolve.

Only one thing abides: an infinite beauty that passes from form to form, eternally changed and revealed afresh.'

6. *which produces the highest and purest forms from the simplest outlines and patterns:* Cf. the final sentence of Büchner's *Mémoire sur le système nerveux du barbeau:* 'La nature est grande et riche, non parce qu'à chaque instant elle crée arbitrairement des organes nouveaux pour de nouvelles fonctions; mais parce qu'elle produit, d'après le plan le plus simple, les formes les plus élevées et les plus pures' ('Nature is rich and diverse, not because it constantly and arbitrarily creates new organs for new functions, but because from the simplest of designs it produces the purest and most sublime forms').

7. *the intuition of the mystic, and the dogmatism of the rationalist:* Büchner explicitly criticizes rationalist dogmatism in the ensuing sentence, but it is not clear whether he is implicitly criticizing mystical intuition too, or simply enumerating it as one of the two available 'well-springs of knowledge'. Commentators generally claim that he is indeed criticizing it, but there is no distinct basis for this. On the contrary, several details elsewhere in the opening paragraphs imply a strong element of the mystical in Büchner's own view of the natural world – in particular his sense (in paragraph one) of a (feminine) 'spirit' (*die Psyche*) seeming to 'dance behind the slenderest of veils', and his mention (in paragraph five) of metempsychosis, i.e. the belief that the foetus at some point becomes possessed of a spirit or soul. And of course the fundamental postulate of a 'primordial law' of 'beauty' is itself arguably both intuitional and mystical – as is the entire enterprise of *Naturphilosophie*.

8. *A priori philosophy:* The term appears to be meant here as a synonym for 'rationalist dogmatism'. The term implies a philosophy based on abstract notions, previous to actual experience, and quite remote from it.

9. *metempsychosis of the foetus during its life in the womb:* Cf. note 7.

10. *Oken's concept of representation in the taxonomy of the animal kingdom:* Oken maintained that God sought to represent Himself ever more perfectly in living beings, with man as the ulti-

mate, crowning organism. He also believed that man's various attributes were inherited from the lower creatures – memory from fish, seriousness from snails, caution from molluscs etc.

11. *tracing all forms back to the simplest primordial type:* This was one of the central aspirations of *Naturphilosophie*: see the introduction to these Notes (p. 286).

12. *'the skull is a spinal column':* Again, see the introduction to these Notes (p. 286).

13. *Several attempts have been made to answer this question:* Büchner's own attempt to provide an answer (particularly in his Strasbourg *Mémoire*) had a lasting impact. Johannes Müller (1801–58), one of the greatest and most influential physiologists of the nineteenth century, reviewed the *Mémoire* at length in very positive terms, albeit disagreeing with some of its conclusions; he even inserted references to it in his immensely influential *Handbook of Physiology*. (Müller, who began his career as an ardent devotee of *Naturphilosophie*, was a key figure in the decisive shift from 'philosophical' to empirical science – and his *Handbook* made a major contribution to this shift; Haeckel, Virchow, Du Bois-Reymond and Helmholtz were in due course all pupils of Müller's.) Although Büchner's speculative thesis subsequently fell, together with Oken's and Goethe's vertebral theory of the skull, his punctilious and innovative *descriptive* work ensured that his findings were quoted in textbooks right into the twentieth century (most recently in 1934 in a *Handbook on the Comparative Anatomy of Vertebrates*).

SELECTED LETTERS

Sad to say, Büchner's letters have fared even worse than his other writings. Of the seventy-plus that have survived at all, only thirteen exist in autograph form. The rest are secondhand; furthermore, the majority of these are not complete versions, but only excerpts specially chosen – and probably doctored – by Ludwig Büchner for the purposes of his 1850 edition of his brother's work (in which the letter extracts were explicitly intended to illuminate just one topic, namely 'the political movements of that period, and Büchner's part in them'). It is conceivable that the originals might one day come to light; but it seems probable that most or all of them were destroyed in the fire that damaged part of the Büchners' Darmstadt house in 1851.

Nevertheless, the surviving letters show a tremendous variety and richness, and convey a powerful sense of Büchner's constantly evolving concerns, opinions, attitudes and feelings.

Notes

1. (...) Both round-bracketed and square-bracketed omission marks are used in this selection of letters: (...) signifies a passage omitted by Ludwig Büchner in his original 1850 edition; [...] signifies a passage omitted for the purposes of this present edition.
2. *Ramorino:* Girolamo Ramorino, born in Genoa in 1792, executed in Turin in 1849 (for disobeying orders as a general in the Piedmont army). He joined the French army at an early age, and in 1830 volunteered for service in Poland's rebellion against Tsar Nicholas I, in due course acquiring the rank of general. Following the Russians' defeat of the Poles in September 1831, Ramorino, along with some six thousand other defeated rebels, fled Poland in the so-called Great Emigration – the majority seeking refuge in France. Poland's struggle for freedom was one of the great romantic-revolutionary causes in Europe in this period, not least because other governments – including Louis-Philippe's in France – revealed their true colours by refusing to help.
3. *generals Schneider and Langermann:* 'Schneider' was in fact a Pole named Sznajde; he and Langermann had both been generals with Ramorino in the failed rebellion.
4. *the National Guard:* The National Guard had been abolished

for political reasons by Charles X in 1827, but once he had been ousted in the 1830 revolution and replaced by Louis-Philippe, the new 'Citizen King' soon made the symbolic gesture of re-establishing the Guard.

5. *the Carmagnole:* see p. 237, note 124.

6. *le juste milieu:* Under Louis-Philippe the politics of *le juste milieu* rapidly became dominant, not least because of strong support from the King himself. Although ostensibly a policy of steering a sensible and reasonable 'middle course' between the extremes of left-wing republicanism and right-wing legitimism, the *juste milieu* rapidly proved to be little more than a cover for the political and economic ambitions of the conservative bourgeoisie.

7. *– and the comedy is done:* Although scarcely eighteen, Büchner already shows his characteristic tendency to inflate a splendid balloon of pathos – then prick it with sudden irony.

8. *It looks desperately like war:* The July Revolution in France in 1830 had triggered a wave of instability across the whole continent of Europe, and nationalist rebellions repeatedly looked as if they would suck in other countries and thus lead to full-scale war.

9. *the troubles in Holland:* In late August 1830 the Belgians rebelled against their Dutch overlords. Although initially defeated by William I, king of the Netherlands, the Belgians received outside support, most notably from the French, and armed conflict repeatedly flared up during 1831 and 1832 (the Belgians finally won their independence in 1839).

10. *the stories from Frankfurt:* These 'stories' related to the failed coup attempt in Frankfurt on 3 April 1833 (see p. 275). We can see by means of a small detail here how Ludwig Büchner's versions of the letters are by no means wholly reliable. The letter is dated '5 April'; but the coup only occurred on 3 April, and it is inconceivable that the news could have travelled to Darmstadt, been reprocessed into a letter, then travelled on to Strasbourg – all within forty-eight hours. Unless Georg Büchner accidentally misdated the original letter (not very likely), Ludwig Büchner must have made a mistake.

11. *its spies:* The authorities in this period maintained an elaborate and highly effective network of spies and informers. In due course Büchner and the others involved in *The Hessian Messenger* would themselves be betrayed – and by the selfsame man (Johann Konrad Kuhl) who had betrayed the Frankfurt coup a year earlier (see pp. 276–7).

12. *I consider revolutionary activity ... to be a futile undertaking in present circumstances:* Büchner may possibly have meant this at face value – but it is much more likely that he was telling his parents what they wanted to hear (a practice that is very marked in his letters home). Within a year, at any rate, he himself was deeply and dangerously involved in revolutionary activity.

13. *Were none of my friends involved in the affair:* Friends of Büchner's were indeed involved. A year later some of them would duly become members of either the Giessen or the Darmstadt section of Büchner's revolutionary Society of Human Rights.

14. *I have recently come to realize ... can bring about change:* This marks a critical development in Büchner's political thought – and it is precisely at this point that his stance as a protocommunist begins to take shape.

15. *I won't be getting myself involved ... revolutionary antics:* The reality was of course very different: although Büchner did indeed remain aloof from the political gesturing and 'antics' prevalent among his fellow-students in Giessen, he was soon busy establishing a new and genuinely radical revolutionary cell, and linking up with Weidig and his network for the purposes of mobilizing the Upper Hessian peasantry (see p. 276).

16. *I'm throwing myself into philosophy ... human concerns:* Büchner's attitude to philosophy was profoundly paradoxical. He detested rationalism, dismissing it in the 'Trial Lecture', and mocking it in *Leonce and Lena*; and yet he devoted immense efforts to mastering it, and hoped to teach it when he went to Zurich University (in the event he had to teach comparative anatomy – cf. note 35). The paradox goes much deeper: in his poetic works he is consistently, even obsessively, anti-

mind; yet he himself was supremely a man of the mind, an intellectual *par excellence* (though also a mystic, a sensualist and much else!).

17. *calling them du . . .:* As in French (*tu/vous*), there are different 'you'-forms in German (*du/Sie*) for familiar and formal use.

18. *Minna Jaeglé:* When Büchner went to Strasbourg in October 1831 to begin his medical studies, he took lodgings with the widowed pastor Johann Jakob Jaeglé. He and Jaeglé's daughter Minna (Louise Wilhelmine) were soon in love with each other; they became formally engaged later this same month (March 1834). Ironically, Büchner died just at the point when they could have expected to marry at last. Born in 1810, Minna was three years older than Büchner; she remained unmarried, and lived until 1880. A serious rift soon developed between Minna and the Büchner family after Georg's death, and it is largely because of this that a hostile image of her gained widespread credence in the nineteenth century. It now seems clear that this image was largely or even wholly unwarranted. As for the young Minna that Büchner loved, if there are any refracted images of her in his work, they are to be found in the likes of Lucile and Lena – certainly not in the likes of Marion or Marie.

19. *. . . as though in the grave . . . going to wake me:* Images of death, and of death and resurrection, clearly haunted Büchner throughout his life: they recur with extraordinary frequency through all the phases and modes of his writing, from his schooldays onwards.

   This and the following two letters show that Büchner suffered a grave collapse in early 1834 that temporarily destroyed his equilibrium both physically and mentally.

20. *by stagecoach, that is:* Büchner is referring to his intended journey to visit Minna in the coming Easter vacation (cf. final paragraph of following letter).

21. *oh, poor screaming musicians . . . in the flames:* This passage is strongly echoed in *Danton's Death*: see p. 69.

22. *as a model for Herr Callot-Hoffmann:* Büchner is referring here to E.T.A. Hoffmann, and more specifically to his first collection of stories entitled *Fantasy Pieces in the Manner of Callot*

(1814–15) – stories that focus repeatedly on deeply ambiguous figures who seem eccentric or even mad, yet in their very madness connect with a world of deeper truth that is closed to their more 'normal' fellow-humans. Like many other writers of the nineteenth century, both in Germany and abroad, Büchner was clearly much influenced by Hoffmann, and in particular by the constant ironic interplay in his work between the all too headily romantic and the all too soberly real.

23. *I'll leave in secret:* A further reference to Büchner's intended trip to Strasbourg to visit Minna. In the event he stayed in Strasbourg for about the first fortnight of April – a period of intense political turmoil throughout France that almost certainly further sharpened Büchner's own revolutionary resolve.

24. *I've been studying the history of the French Revolution:* What follows here is one of the most famous, most quoted passages in Büchner's entire oeuvre. It needs to be read with circumspection; in particular, it needs to be read in *context*. The letter as a whole is described in its final sentence as a 'charivari', and whilst not exactly a 'confused, discordant medley of sounds' (*OED*), it is certainly characterized by sudden complete switches of register/tone/mood, with the 'hideous fatalism' passage differing sharply from what precedes it, and also from what follows. The 'fatalism' passage is no calm and definitive statement of a considered position: it is the strongly rhetorical outburst of a 22-year-old still not fully recovered from a dangerous crisis of body and mind that has left him 'as though destroyed inside, not a single feeling stirs within me. I'm an automaton, my soul has been taken from me.' The larger context is crucial too: this apparent believer in a 'hideous fatalism of history' was in these very days and weeks tirelessly engaged in trying to *influence* history by preparing a revolutionary pamphlet and organizing militant revolutionary cells. And even after the abject failure of these ventures, when he frenetically pens *Danton's Death* with the threat of arrest and incarceration constantly hanging over him, he depicts history *not* as some-

thing determined by any 'hideous fatalism' or 'iron law', but as a process readily susceptible to manipulation by individuals – who are by no means projected as mere 'froth on the waves'.

25. *... that lies, murders, steals:* The passage recurs in modulated form in *Danton's Death* – where it again needs to be viewed with great circumspection (cf. p. 38).

26. *B. will have reassured you about my condition:* Probably Eugen Boeckel, a Strasbourg medical student and close friend of Büchner's.

27. *I was burning hot ... ecstasy of pain and longing:* There are strong echoes of this extraordinary passage in *Lenz:* see p. 147.

28. *... Minnigerode ... what's behind his arrest:* Carl Minnigerode was arrested on 1 August on his return to Giessen with a large number of copies of the newly printed *Hessian Messenger* hidden in his boots, coat-linings, etc., whereupon Büchner immediately scurried away to warn Weidig and the others in Butzbach, and the clandestine printer in Offenbach (cf. pp. 276f.). Büchner's professions of innocence and indignation are of course entirely feigned, no doubt partly in order to reassure his parents, and partly to deceive the authorities if the letter happened to be intercepted. His posture of injured innocence was extraordinarily effective vis-à-vis Konrad Georgi, the judicial quasi-commissar at Giessen University (English knows no real equivalent for Büchner's term *Universitätsrichter*: 'Proctor' is a lame approximation): Georgi had in fact received instructions to arrest Büchner, whom Kuhl, the police informer, had specifically betrayed, but Büchner had covered his tracks so thoroughly, and was so brazenly convincing in his show of indignation, that Georgi was successfully thrown off the scent.

29. *University Proctor:* See preceding note.

30. *I have letters from B.:* Almost certainly Eugen Boeckel (see note 26). Boeckel was a perfect alibi: Büchner met him in Frankfurt on 3 August while travelling to warn his associates of Minnigerode's arrest.

31. *Karl Gutzkow:* Karl Gutzkow (1811–78) was one of the leading oppositional critics and writers of the period in

Germany. A key member of the loose grouping known as 'Young Germany' (*Junges Deutschland*), he had just become literary editor of the new daily newspaper *Phönix*, which in consequence became for a while the best-known and most influential organ of intellectual opposition in the land. As Thomas Michael Mayer has pointed out, Büchner could not have chosen anyone better suited to helping him get his *Danton's Death* manuscript published.

32. *Herr Sauerländer:* Sauerländer was one of the few liberal publishers in Germany in this period (and among other things the publisher of *Phönix*). Büchner sent him a copy of *Danton's Death* on the same day that he wrote to Gutzkow. Prompted by Gutzkow, Sauerländer duly published the play later the same year (albeit in bowdlerized form).

33. *I had nothing to fear from the outcome of an investigation:* Needless to say, this was quite untrue. Having almost certainly been called in several times for questioning, Büchner knew very well that his arrest was imminent – and a 'Wanted' notice was duly circulated just a few weeks after his flight (cf. note 44).

34. *a Friedberg dungeon:* Hesse's political prisoners were normally incarcerated at Friedberg in Upper Hesse.

35. *the medical-philosophical sciences:* Medicine in this period was still not perceived as science in the sense in which we now understand the term, but as a branch of philosophy (indeed the very word 'science' was first used in its modern sense – by Whewell – as late as 1840). Typical of this state of affairs is the fact that Büchner could just as readily have taught philosophy when he went to the brand-new University of Zurich in 1836 (indeed he was keen to do so); in the event he lectured in comparative anatomy – itself a subject offered within the Faculty of Philosophy.

36. *A. Becker and Klemm:* August Becker and Gustav Clemm were both members of the Giessen section of Büchner's Society of Human Rights, and had both been centrally involved in *The Hessian Messenger*. On interrogation, Clemm rapidly caved in and confessed; his comprehensive betrayal of his associates gave the authorities vital and much-needed information, and led in particular to the arrest of Weidig.

37. *Rector Weidig:* The title 'Rector' refers to Weidig's post as schoolteacher at Butzbach.

38. *the Literary Supplement:* Büchner is referring to the literature section of *Phönix*, which Karl Gutzkow edited (see note 31).

39. *Phönix:* See note 31.

40. *I regard my drama ... must correspond exactly to its original:* Already at this stage, before *Danton's Death* had even been published, Büchner is preparing a defence against the wrath of his parents, more particularly his father: 'Don't blame me, blame history!'

41. *Sartorius:* Theodor Sartorius, a medical student, was arrested and in due course convicted for his part in the revolutionary activities in Upper Hesse.

42. *Pastor Flick:* Heinrich Christian Flick, parish priest in Petterweil, was a central figure in the network behind *The Hessian Messenger*, and was ultimately sentenced to eight years' imprisonment (like all the other convicted activists, however, he was released in 1839 under a general amnesty for political prisoners).

43. *Wilhelm Büchner:* Georg Büchner had two younger sisters and three younger brothers; Wilhelm Büchner (1816–92) was the oldest of the brothers. He was particularly close to Georg, and had been a fringe member of the Darmstadt section of the Society of Human Rights. He later became a very successful and wealthy chemicals manufacturer, and from 1848 onwards played an active role as a democrat member of numerous parliamentary assemblies (including, after 1871, the Reichstag).

44. *a requisition ... from Giessen:* A 'Wanted' notice had been officially gazetted in Frankfurt in late June; it was clearly also circulated to relevant police forces, including that of Strasbourg.

45. *I must say a few words about my drama:* *Danton's Death* had been published a fortnight earlier, in mid-July 1835. It seems likely from this letter that Büchner had already received signs of disapproval from his parents (as his letter of 5 May shows, he knew he could expect a hostile response). The letter is to a great extent a genuine and truthful statement

of Büchner's aesthetic position; but in his determination to
assuage his parents he also resorts where necessary to lies,
half-truths and specious rhetoric.

46. *the permission ... was gravely abused:* In a letter in early
March, Gutzkow had made it clear that the 'Veneria', the
'dirty bits', would have to be removed from Büchner's play.
He offered to visit Darmstadt to help Büchner make the
necessary revisions, but only a couple of days later Büchner
fled to France. Gutzkow then bowdlerized the text himself
(together with Eduard Duller, the overall editor of *Phönix*),
making altogether more than a hundred changes. Gutzkow's
interference was by no means gratuitous: official censorship
was extremely stringent at the time – indeed it is astonishing
that the censors let even the expurgated version of the play
through their net.

47. *The title is completely outrageous:* Duller had added a subtitle
of his own invention that grossly misrepresented the thrust
of the play: 'Dramatic Scenes from France's Reign of
Terror'.

48. *the proofreader ... never have uttered in my life:* Needless to say,
this is a bare-faced lie.

49. *... very little for Schiller:* Cf. pp. 268f., note 14.

50. *extremely unfavourable reviews ... stupid or immoral:* Büchner's
forecast was unerringly right: a long and vitriolic pseudony-
mous review appeared in late October castigating the play
for its 'filth', 'immorality', 'blasphemy', 'degeneracy', etc.
The review was almost certainly part of a fierce and con-
certed campaign then being waged in the press against the
'Young Germany' group in general, and Gutzkow in particular (in mid-November all Young German publications were
banned in Prussia, and at the end of November, Gutzkow
himself was thrown into gaol for several months for his 'immorality').

51. *I know nothing of any subversive goings-on:* Büchner clearly says
this only to reassure his parents. In truth he was very much
in the know (cf. p. 200, the letter to an unknown addressee).

52. *Deutsche Revue:* After quitting *Phönix* in August 1835 following major disagreements with Duller, Gutzkow planned to

start a new periodical entitled *Deutsche Revue* (on the model of France's *Revue des deux mondes*), but it never appeared because of the December 1835 blanket ban imposed throughout the German Confederation on all Young German publications.

53. *a topic in philosophy or natural history:* See note 35.

54. *the study of philosophy:* Büchner was probably already deeply immersed in his study of Descartes and Spinoza. He wrote extensive commentaries on the thought of both philosophers, and they were later meant to be the starting-point of his proposed lecture series at Zurich University (see p. 205, letter to Wilhelm Büchner).

55. *I don't by any means belong to Young Germany ... Gutzkow and Heine:* Büchner perhaps managed to reassure his parents by dissociating himself so clearly from the Young Germans, whose works had just been comprehensively banned. But they wouldn't have felt very reassured if they had realized that the reason for Georg's rejection of Young Germany was the fact that his own politics were far more radical – as he makes clear to Gutzkow himself in the letter that follows.

56. *... forgive me this small rebuke:* This curious passage shows Büchner in a most unusual light: nowhere else in the letters – or in any other part of his work – do we encounter any trace of the stuffy, censorious prudishness that is revealed here.

57. *I am busily getting a number of people to kill or marry each other on paper:* Büchner is clearly referring here to *Woyzeck* and *Leonce and Lena* respectively.

58. *a lecturer in philosophy:* In the event Büchner lectured at Zurich in comparative anatomy.

59. *Minnigerode is dead ... for three long years:* The rumour was untrue. Minnigerode was still held in gaol, but was released on health grounds in May 1837. He was forced to emigrate to America, and died there in 1894.

60. *I caught a cold ... But I'm better now:* This was almost certainly the initial stage of Büchner's typhus infection. Typhus became rampant in Zurich in the following weeks.

61. *in the casino:* Not a gambling casino, as in modern usage, but

a place where people gathered for drinks, music, dancing, etc.

62. *Leonce and Lena and two other plays*: This remark of Büchner's has provoked endless puzzlement and speculation. What were the 'two other plays'? One was presumably *Woyzeck*, but what was the other? And what on earth did Büchner mean by saying that the three plays would appear 'in a week at the outside'? This would imply that the plays were already in press, not to say fully printed – but there is no evidence of any kind that *Woyzeck*, in particular, was anywhere near completion at Büchner's death. As for the mysterious third play, Ludwig Büchner claimed years later that his brother was referring to a play called *Pietro Aretino*, supposedly already complete at the time of his death. A vigorous legend was subsequently fostered that Minna Jaeglé destroyed the supposed manuscript, along with other writings of her long-dead fiancé. But this now seems entirely fanciful – not least because there is no positive evidence that such a manuscript ever existed.

63. *I have no wish to die and am as healthy as ever:* Büchner was certainly already infected with typhus by this stage, and serious symptoms began to develop a few days later. He died on 19 February.

SELECT BIBLIOGRAPHY

Collected works

Sämtliche Werke und Briefe, ed. Werner R. Lehmann, 2 vols. (Hamburg, 1967/1971ff.; = 'Hamburger Ausgabe'). Originally billed as a four-volume *Historisch-kritische Ausgabe mit Kommentar*, but the project was abandoned after the first two volumes containing all the primary texts – one of the greatest misfortunes in the disaster-prone history of Büchner-editions. Cf. also Werner R. Lehmann, *Textkritische Noten. Prolegomena zur Hamburger Büchner-Ausgabe* (Hamburg, 1967).

Werke und Briefe (Munich, 1988ff.). Useful up-to-date edition with extensive critical apparatus by Karl Pörnbacher, Gerhard Schaub, Hans-Joachim Simm and Edda Ziegler.

Complete Works and Letters, ed. Walter Hinderer and Henry J. Schmidt (New York, 1986). Although not strictly a 'Complete Works', this edition includes translations of *all* Büchner's extant letters.

Individual works

Danton's Tod. Ein Drama, ed. Thomas Michael Mayer, in: *Georg Büchner: Dantons Tod. Die Trauerarbeit im Schönen*, ed. Peter von Becker (Frankfurt, 1980; = Mayer's 'Entwurf einer Studienausgabe'). Currently the best edition of the text.

'Dantons Tod' and 'Woyzeck', ed. Margaret Jacobs (Manchester, 1971ff.; = 3rd edn). German texts, English notes.

Leonce und Lena. Ein Lustspiel. Kritische Studienausgabe, ed. Thomas Michael Mayer, in: Georg Büchner, *Leonce und Lena*, ed. Burghard Dedner (Frankfurt, 1987). Currently the best edition of the text.

Lenz. Studienausgabe, ed. Hubert Gersch (Stuttgart, 1984; = Reclam 8210). See also companion vol.: *Georg Büchner. Lenz. Erläuterungen und Dokumente*, ed. Hubert Gersch (Stuttgart, 1987; = Reclam 8180).

Woyzeck. Faksimileausgabe der Handschriften, ed. Gerhard Schmid (Wiesbaden, 1981). Comprises 'Faksimile. Transkription. Kommentar. Lesartenverzeichnis'; currently the best edition of the *Woyzeck* fragments.

Woyzeck. Kritische Lese- und Arbeitsausgabe, ed. Lothar Bornscheuer (Stuttgart, 1972ff.; = Reclam 9374); see also companion vol.: *Georg Büchner. Woyzeck. Erläuterungen und Dokumente*, ed. Lothar Bornscheuer (Stuttgart, 1972ff.; = Reclam 8117).

Woyzeck, ed. Henri Poschmann (Frankfurt, 1985).

Woyzeck, ed. John Guthrie (Oxford, 1988). German text, English notes.

Georg Büchner, Friedrich Ludwig Weidig, *Der Hessische Landbote. Texte, Materialien, Kommentar*, ed. Gerhard Schaub (Munich, 1976).

Secondary literature (in English)

Benn, Maurice B., *The Drama of Revolt. A Critical Study of Georg Büchner* (Cambridge, 1976).

Grimm, Reinhold, *Love, Lust and Rebellion. New Approaches to Georg Büchner* (Madison, 1985).

Guthrie, John, *Lenz and Büchner. Studies in Dramatic Form* (Frankfurt, 1984).

Hilton, Julian, *Georg Büchner* (London, 1982).

James, Dorothy, *Georg Büchner's 'Dantons Tod': A Reappraisal* (London, 1982).

Lindenberger, Herbert, *Georg Büchner* (Carbondale, 1964).

Pascal, Roy, 'Büchner's *Lenz*: Style and Message', *Oxford German Studies* 9 (1978), pp. 68–83.

Reddick, John, *Georg Büchner: The Shattered Whole* (Oxford, 1994).

Richards, David G., *Georg Büchner and the Birth of the Modern Drama* (Albany, 1977).

Steiner, George, *The Death of Tragedy* (London, 1961; New York, 1963), pp. 270–81.

Stern, J.P., *Re-interpretations. Seven Studies in Nineteenth-Century German Literature* (London, 1964), pp. 78–155: 'A World of Suffering: Georg Büchner'.

—, *Idylls and Realities. Studies in Nineteenth-Century German Literature* (London, New York, 1971), pp. 33–48: 'Georg Büchner: Potsherds of Experience'.

Secondary literature (in German)

Arnold, Heinz Ludwig (ed.), *Georg Büchner I/II* (Munich 1979; 2nd edn 1982; = Special Number of periodical *Text + Kritik*); *Georg Büchner III* (Munich, 1981; likewise a Special Number of *Text + Kritik*). Important source-books.

Behrmann, Alfred, and Wohlleben, Joachim, *Büchner: Dantons Tod. Eine Dramenanalyse* (Stuttgart, 1980). Useful source-book.

Georg Büchner. Der Katalog (Basel, Frankfurt, 1987; = catalogue of September 1987 Büchner exhibition in Darmstadt). Useful source-book.

Georg Büchner Jahrbuch (Frankfurt, 1981–). Yearbook bringing together much current research.

Goltschnigg, Dietmar (ed.), *Materialien zur Rezeptions- und Wirkungsgeschichte Georg Büchners* (Kronberg, 1974). Useful source-book.

Hauschild, Jan-Christoph, *Georg Büchner. Studien und neue Quellen zu Leben, Werk und Wirkung* (Königstein, 1985). Important source-book.

Hinderer, Walter, *Büchner-Kommentar zum dichterischen Werk* (Munich, 1977). Important source-book.

Höllerer, Walter, *Zwischen Klassik und Moderne. Lachen und Weinen in der Dichtung einer Übergangszeit* (Stuttgart, 1958), pp. 100–42: 'Georg Büchner'.

Interpretationen. Georg Büchner (Stuttgart, 1990; = Reclam 8415). Contains essays on *Lenz* and each of the three plays.

Jancke, Gerhard, *Georg Büchner. Genese und Aktualität seines Werkes. Einführung in das Gesamtwerk* (Kronberg, 1975).

Knapp, Gerhard P., *Georg Büchner. Eine kritische Einführung in die Forschung* (Frankfurt, 1975). Useful overview.

—, *Georg Büchner* (Stuttgart, 1984; = revised 2nd edn).

Kobel, Erwin, *Georg Büchner. Das dichterische Werk* (Berlin, New York, 1974).

Krapp, Helmut, *Der Dialog bei Georg Büchner* (Darmstadt, 1958).

Martens, Wolfgang (ed.), *Georg Büchner* (Darmstadt, 1969; = 2nd edn). Useful compendium of essays by different critics.

Mayer, Hans, *Georg Büchner und seine Zeit* (Frankfurt, 1972; first published Wiesbaden, 1946/Berlin, 1947).

Meier, Albert, *Georg Büchner: 'Woyzeck'* (Munich, 1980).

Poschmann, Henri, *Georg Büchner. Dichtung der Revolution und Revolution der Dichtung* (Berlin, Weimar, 1983).

Sengle, Friedrich, *Biedermeierzeit. Deutsche Literatur im Spannungsfeld zwischen Restauration und Revolution 1815–1848*, vol. 3 (Stuttgart, 1980); pp. 265–331: 'Georg Büchner'.

Wittkowski, Wolfgang, *Georg Büchner. Persönlichkeit, Weltbild, Werk* (Heidelberg, 1978).

Visit Penguin on the Internet
and browse at your leisure

- preview sample extracts of our forthcoming books
- read about your favourite authors
- investigate over 10,000 titles
- enter one of our literary quizzes
- win some fantastic prizes in our competitions
- e-mail us with your comments and book reviews
- instantly order any Penguin book

and masses more!

'To be recommended without reservation ... a rich and rewarding on-line experience' – Internet Magazine

www.penguin.co.uk

READ MORE IN PENGUIN

In every corner of the world, on every subject under the sun, Penguin represents quality and variety – the very best in publishing today.

For complete information about books available from Penguin – including Puffins, Penguin Classics and Arkana – and how to order them, write to us at the appropriate address below. Please note that for copyright reasons the selection of books varies from country to country.

In the United Kingdom: Please write to *Dept. EP, Penguin Books Ltd, Bath Road, Harmondsworth, West Drayton, Middlesex UB7 ODA*

In the United States: Please write to *Consumer Sales, Penguin Putnam Inc., P.O. Box 999, Dept. 17109, Bergenfield, New Jersey 07621-0120.* VISA and MasterCard holders call 1-800-253-6476 to order Penguin titles

In Canada: Please write to *Penguin Books Canada Ltd, 10 Alcorn Avenue, Suite 300, Toronto, Ontario M4V 3B2*

In Australia: Please write to *Penguin Books Australia Ltd, P.O. Box 257, Ringwood, Victoria 3134*

In New Zealand: Please write to *Penguin Books (NZ) Ltd, Private Bag 102902, North Shore Mail Centre, Auckland 10*

In India: Please write to *Penguin Books India Pvt Ltd, 210 Chiranjiv Tower, 43 Nehru Place, New Delhi 110 019*

In the Netherlands: Please write to *Penguin Books Netherlands bv, Postbus 3507, NL-1001 AH Amsterdam*

In Germany: Please write to *Penguin Books Deutschland GmbH, Metzlerstrasse 26, 60594 Frankfurt am Main*

In Spain: Please write to *Penguin Books S. A., Bravo Murillo 19, 1° B, 28015 Madrid*

In Italy: Please write to *Penguin Italia s.r.l., Via Benedetto Croce 2, 20094 Corsico, Milano*

In France: Please write to *Penguin France, Le Carré Wilson, 62 rue Benjamin Baillaud, 31500 Toulouse*

In Japan: Please write to *Penguin Books Japan Ltd, Kaneko Building, 2-3-25 Koraku, Bunkyo-Ku, Tokyo 112*

In South Africa: Please write to *Penguin Books South Africa (Pty) Ltd, Private Bag X14, Parkview, 2122 Johannesburg*

READ MORE IN PENGUIN

A CHOICE OF CLASSICS

Jacob Burckhardt	**The Civilization of the Renaissance in Italy**
Carl von Clausewitz	**On War**
Meister Eckhart	**Selected Writings**
Friedrich Engels	**The Origins of the Family, Private Property and the State**
Wolfram von Eschenbach	**Parzival**
Goethe	**Elective Affinities**
	Faust Parts One and Two (in 2 volumes)
	Italian Journey
	The Sorrows of Young Werther
Jacob and Wilhelm Grimm	**Selected Tales**
E. T. A. Hoffmann	**Tales of Hoffmann**
Henrik Ibsen	**Brand**
	A Doll's House and Other Plays
	Ghosts and Other Plays
	Hedda Gabler and Other Plays
	The Master Builder and Other Plays
	Peer Gynt
Søren Kierkegaard	**Fear and Trembling**
	Papers and Journals
	The Sickness Unto Death
Georg Christoph Lichtenberg	**Aphorisms**
Karl Marx	**Capital** (in three volumes)
Friedrich Nietzsche	**The Birth of Tragedy**
	Beyond Good and Evil
	Ecce Homo
	Human, All Too Human
	Thus Spoke Zarathustra
Friedrich Schiller	**The Robbers/Wallenstein**
Arthur Schopenhauer	**Essays and Aphorisms**
Gottfried von Strassburg	**Tristan**
Adalbert Stifter	**Brigitta and Other Tales**
August Strindberg	**By the Open Sea**